FAMILY OR COUNTRY

STEVEN—His loyalty to country died at the hands of a brutal regime. Loyalty to his family meant his brother must die.

FRANK—Willing to sacrifice anyone to his violent political ideals, he had to be stopped before he destroyed the entire family.

CAROLINE—One brother knew her past. One brother wanted her future... if she lived long enough to have one.

ADELA—The man she loved was a powerful military officer with another identity he would kill to keep secret.

Other Avon Books by
Robert Houston

ARAFAT
CHOLO
MONDAY, TUESDAY, WEDNESDAY!

Avon Books are available at special quantity discounts for bulk purchases for sales promotions, premiums, fund raising or educational use. Special books, or book excerpts, can also be created to fit specific needs.

For details write or telephone the office of the Director of Special Markets, Avon Books, Dept. FP, 1790 Broadway, New York, New York 10019, 212-399-1357.

BLOOD TANGO

ROBERT HOUSTON

AVON
PUBLISHERS OF BARD, CAMELOT, DISCUS AND FLARE BOOKS

BLOOD TANGO is an original publication of Avon Books.
This work has never before appeared in book form.

AVON BOOKS
A division of
The Hearst Corporation
1790 Broadway
New York, New York 10019

Copyright © 1984 by Robert Houston
Published by arrangement with the author
Library of Congress Catalog Card Number: 83-91199
ISBN: 0-380-85506-2

All rights reserved, which includes the right to
reproduce this book or portions thereof in any form
whatsoever except as provided by the U. S. Copyright Law.
For information address International Creative Management,
40 West 57th Street, New York, New York 10019

First Avon Printing, January, 1984

AVON TRADEMARK REG. U. S. PAT. OFF. AND IN
OTHER COUNTRIES, MARCA REGISTRADA, HECHO EN
U. S. A.

Printed in the U. S. A.

WFH 10 9 8 7 6 5 4 3 2 1

This one is for Nancy

The author would like to acknowledge the muse of Bob Wyatt, the editing care of Judith Riven, and the help of all those kind Argentines and U.S. embassy staffers in Buenos Aires who, fortunately or unfortunately for them, it is impossible to name here.

"But I don't want to go among mad people," Alice remarked.

"Oh, you can't help that," said the Cat: "we're all mad here. I'm mad. You're mad."

"How do you know I'm mad?" said Alice.

"You must be," said the Cat, "or you wouldn't have come here."
—Lewis Carroll,
Alice's Adventures in Wonderland

"El tango es macho..."
—Café singer, Buenos Aires, 1982

Prologue

Even through the thick padding of the flight suit, Esteban was cold. He'd been cold since he got to Comodoro Rivadavia, hell, cold since he left Buenos Aires, just thinking about being here. The cargo door of the C-130 was still open, and past the crates of the American C rations stacked the length of the plane he could see thin snow beginning to slash by in the wind outside. Already the low, barren hills beyond the airfield were flat and gray, robbed of any features by the driving snow. How much less visibility would it take to keep this thing from taking off? he wondered. For any pilot but an Argentinian, there was probably already too little. Bloody gauchos, he thought with a twinge of pride that surprised him. He remembered a hand-lettered sign he'd seen in a bar in Buenos Aires just after the war had begun: "Argentina may not have Princes, but we sure as hell have gauchos." Oh, yes, God, yes.

But fewer gaucho pilots now than before. Some of the best ones were already underneath the icy water that he knew roiled and lashed against the cliffs just beyond these Patagonian hills. It was the same water he was about to fly over, heading toward a pair of half-frozen islands that, for all he truly knew, could be full of British troops by now. Troops waiting to blow this plane out of the air before it even touched that godforsaken land again. He resisted the urge to cross himself.

The plane's cargomaster, bundled like Charlie Brown in the American cartoon, came into sight outside, leaning into the wind and clutching loading papers that flapped like terrified birds in his hand. He walked carefully up the ramp to the plane, shook himself, took a quick look at the tied-down crates, and slipped his head out of the hood of his flight jacket. Esteban figured him to be about his own age, mid-thirties, but with the heavy, slumping Italian face of an overworked waiter in a cheap *confitería*. The man scowled, then pressed a black button by the cargo door. Something whirred, and the door began to close, rising up to meet the plane's fuselage like a whale's jaw. Esteban watched the bleak world outside vanish—first the row of camouflaged Mirage fighters at the end of the runway, then the hills, then the control tower and oil-field derricks, then the gray sky itself. He started when the door whumped shut. Jesus. They weren't even in the air yet, and already he was an old woman.

It was just that the dark came on so quickly, he told himself, just that the plane was so damn much like a tomb now. He shoved the image of a tomb away from him. That had been yesterday. That would be with him in the night and when he was alone, the rest of his life. But that was why he was here.

The cargomaster seemed to notice Esteban for the first time now. He reached into his pocket, pulled out two lumps of what looked like pink taffy, and held them out for him.

"Knead them first," he said. "Softens them."

"For what?"

The cargomaster, his heavy mustache tipped with frost, pointed toward his ears. "You'll want them. It's no 707, this thing." He sidled past the crates to the forward section of the plane, said something into the pilots' compartment, then came and sat beside Esteban on the webbed bench that ran the length of the fuselage. He began to knead his own lumps of wax. "You should fasten your seat belt. Up to you." He said it as if it were a dare. Esteban made no move for his belt and the cargomaster seemed to approve. "From Buenos Aires?" he asked.

"Buenos Aires," Esteban said. An engine wheezed

and kicked over, nearly as loud as if it were inside the plane with them. He hoped the others were even louder, so he wouldn't have to talk—or listen.

"You got the accent, a real *Porteño,*" the cargomaster said. He squeezed an earplug in and began to knead the other. "Reporter?"

Esteban shook his head.

"Government?"

Esteban shook his head again.

"Then what in the name of God you want to go to the Malvinas for?"

Another engine kicked over. Esteban raised his voice above it. "I've got a message for somebody."

"Hell, why didn't you just radio?"

"It's not that kind of message." He dug beneath his flight suit for his brandy flask. He and the cargomaster each had a slug, and Esteban went to work on his earplugs. "What's it like out there?"

The cargomaster shrugged. "Maybe we'll land, maybe we won't. Depends on whether the bastards have bombed the strip again before we get there—and whether our boys have had time to patch it."

"And if not?"

The cargomaster shrugged again. "It's a shithole, anyway. Better if we don't land. Who you going to see?"

The brandy hit bottom, and warmth splashed up from Esteban's stomach. Another engine kicked over. "Colonel Mondragon," he shouted over the noise. "You know him?"

The cargomaster's eyes darted to Esteban, then away. "No wonder you got permission to go. You a relative or something?"

"Or something."

"If we land, we might not be able to take off again, you know."

Now Esteban shrugged. The brandy was helping. He smiled. "It's all right. I know a woman in London. She'll put me up."

The cargomaster smiled back. "Don't let Mondragon hear that."

"Real patriot, is he?"

"Che, hombre! If he could, he'd have us doing suicide runs on Piccadilly." The last engine kicked over, and

the cargomaster plugged his other ear. Then he seemed to reconsider something. "But he's a good officer. And I'm a patriot, too. I don't talk against my officers."

And *you,* Esteban thought, are a cautious man—or a fearful one. He tried to shout an answer, but the cargomaster pointed to his ears and held his hands out in a palms-up "sorry" gesture. "Shame you didn't get here a day earlier," he yelled. "We just ferried Mondragon over from the mainland last night. You could have caught him here."

Esteban shoved an earplug in as the plane began to taxi. A day earlier. Yesterday. *Madre de Dios.* Again the sorrow and anger kicked their way into his mind. The feeling was this: you've had a dream the night before, and all the next day the vague sense of it hangs around the back of your mind, just at the edge of thought. When you really think about it, it disappears. You say, *It wasn't real,* and it wasn't. But the difference was this: you say this dream wasn't real, and that's a lie. It wasn't real; it had the jerky, flickering quality of an old silent movie—but it happened. And the trick now, before he bounced down onto the bomb-pocked landing strip of those frozen islands, was to relive it enough times to *make* it real, to dull the shock with repetition. He couldn't afford to make a fool out of himself in front of Mondragon, and he wouldn't.

BOOK ONE

Chapter One

Yesterday, then. His sister Adela *desperately* had to talk to him, she'd said when she called the night before, and had worked hard at sounding desperate. That had called for another brandy yesterday afternoon in Buenos Aires, as he waited to meet her. He hadn't bothered to pretend he was nipping that one. He could blame the brandy on the desperation, which hung in the wartime air nowadays like fog from the Río de la Plata—the River Plate, his English mother insisted on calling it—that swept by somewhere out of sight at the foot of the long hill to his right like a dun, moving sea.

Across the boulevard from the Café de la Paix, where he waited, a vast, improbable rubber tree spread beside the entrance to the cemetery of La Recoleta like an octopus in traction. Its centenarian limbs were held up by a mad cubist's arrangement of cables and posts among which children scrambled fiercely in the weak winter sun. Esteban (sorry, Mother: Steven) had watched them for nearly an hour—three brandys' worth of time—waiting for Adela to go in first. He had seen one generation of cardiganed clients here at the sidewalk tables of the café come, sip their afternoon coffees, and leave by now. But no Adela. She must have come earlier, must have been inside that damned mausoleum resort of Argentina's richest dead for half the day already, brooding. It would be like her. How many afternoons had she dragged him out of law school when she was in her "Brontë period," as his mother had called it, to sit him down on a prayer stool in that huge, garish family crypt of their grandfather's and spill her adolescent secrets to him? The only privacy in Buenos Aires, Stevie, she'd insisted, for people like us. And he had listened. As he'd listen today.

He dropped eight *palos* on the table for the waiter and stood, as he heard the squonk of martial music from the radio in the café behind him that announced another government communiqué about the war. A waiter near him stopped and stood at attention; most of the clients kept talking and drinking. The real news of the war for them—for "people like us," Esteban thought with a familiar bitterness—would come after tea on the evening news, when a new drop in the price of the peso was announced. That, at least, they could believe. He dodged an elegant Afghan walking an elegant man in jogging shorts, and stepped out into the squealing, honking war of taxis and buses that forever swirled around La Recoleta. *That* was the war that never stopped in this damned city.

The world had that peculiar clarity, that extra brightness of colors daytime booze brought. He'd been seeing the world more and more that way lately, since the government bastards in their tailored blue suits and school ties had closed his restaurant. Not that he was ever really drunk—he was at least a good enough Argentine to avoid that, so as not to be like those damned Indians who cluttered up the rest of the continent. It was just that he floated most of the time now: a Bloody Mary to shove off into the day with, martinis before lunch, a couple of brandies to soften the damp afternoons, an Old Smuggler or two before dinner, a couple of brandies more to soften the damp night. A nightcap. Or two, on a long night.

They'd killed the restaurant he'd owned because of the war, too. They'd wanted to for a long time, but it took the war to give them the final excuse. Why do you have only candles in here, Sr. Molina? they'd wanted to know. Don't you understand about lighting codes? What are you trying to hide? And this music, why is so damned much of it foreign? And your cook, that

Dutchman, does he have papers? He looks a little fay to us, too. Does he like boys; is he a *maricón?* Is that it? And your waitress, haven't we seen her at the stationhouse before—doesn't she pick up a few *palos* on the side after you close? A suspect place, this. Antipatriotic elements here, all these journalists and actors and foreigners and intellectuals. Stinks of immorality here. And you, isn't your mother English? Wasn't your father minister of justice in those corrupt days before our generals saved us? Didn't he let off criminals and terrorists until one of them blew him up, God give him rest, but he deserved it. And you, aren't you a lawyer? Aren't you one of the Molina family? Why do you want to run a decadent restaurant like this anyway—your grandfather's got half the money in Argentina, doesn't he? What's wrong with you? We know everything about you. About that woman of yours, Caroline—she lived in Paris, didn't she? Now there's a suspicious circumstance for you. Your sister's engaged to marry the vice commander of our heroic air force in the Malvinas. You should be down there beside him. After all, don't we remember you were the best middleweight boxer in university once? And now, a client comes into your "restaurant" here, a good Catholic citizen, and asks you to play his patriotic tape of "The Malvinas March," and you throw him out? No, no, señor Molina. No bribes this time. There's not enough money in South America to make us put up with your negativism now. *Viva la patria,* señor Molina! In the name of the United Argentine Armed Forces Command, Sr. Esteban Molina-Knifeton, we declare this establishment closed for Antipatriotic Activities in Time of War.

And privately, Sr. Molina, we advise you to walk easily. If it weren't for your grandfather and your sister's fiancé... well, people disappear, señor, people disappear, eh?

The next morning the door had been padlocked. They gave him an hour to get his things out of the apartment upstairs.

Should he have explained to them that he wasn't a lawyer anymore because he couldn't argue in courts where law was a joke? That he ran his restaurant because it was the only place in Buenos Aires where he could talk to people every day who actually *talked,* who had at least a portion of their minds left, and a few pieces of their integrity, who had the guts to ask forbidden questions in Time of War. That it was *because* his family had half the money in Argentina that he had to try to make a living? Crap. That last sounded specious even to himself. They would have told him that he was a thrity-four-year-old lapsed Argentine who dressed in English jackets, and who ranted about intellectual honesty but couldn't bring himself to leave the country he claimed to despise. At least his older brother, Francisco (sorry, Mother: Frank), had had the guts to move away to England. At least his younger sister, Adela, had had the decency to embrace her Argentine-ness and engage herself to a national hero.

But no, they wouldn't have told him that. He would have told himself that. That's why he hadn't explained anything to them.

And so what in hell did Adela have to be so desperate about? he asked himself as he passed beneath the huge rubber tree. The tree's limbs looked the same as when he and she had played in them as kids—a thousand goddamn years ago, and in another world. They'd been dressed up like store mannequins and hauled along on Sundays like the other kids of Buenos Aires's Best Families (or would-be Best Families) to spend their day with the dead. *Hey,* maybe he'd say to her today when he'd cured her desperation, let's go outside and have a drink and climb the rubber tree again. Let's let the war and your vice commander both piss off for one last afternoon.

And then he thought, as he passed between the two huge bronze gates, Fat bloody chance of that.

Inside its high walls, La Recoleta *was* a city. Esteban blinked to focus down the long main avenue, as crowded with house-sized mausoleums as an apartment block. A marble angel of death, scythe in midswing, glared at him from the roof of one of them, and a gaggle of blue-smocked groundskeepers watched him without much interest from beneath a magnolia. He adjusted his tie self-consciously and concentrated on walking a straight line along the stone-paved avenue. At intervals, lesser streets branched off, each as crowded with tombs as the avenue. On one corner, a neo-Greek marble tomb stood open with scaffolding around it, and its crypts empty. Sold, he knew. On its way down to make room for a newer, richer family's tomb. The bones burned and scattered in the Plata by now. He sped up, and to hell with walking a straight line.

He was in a familiar neighborhood. Down that street to the left was the smallish Duarte place. They kept their little sister Eva's body hidden beneath the others and not marked with her married name—Perón—to keep the crazies from finding her. And just past it, the statue of the drowned girl and her dog stood life-sized and bored, listening to the sentimental Italian verses her father had had inscribed in equal mourning for the both of them. And there ahead, a few meters beyond his own family's place, a bronze Firpo stood in his boxing robes, the Wild Bull of the Pampas with his hands taped and ready forever to take on Dempsey again— in any life. And all around, on roofs and in niches and over porticos, a host of blank-eyed neighbors watched Esteban approach, seeming to swirl and breathe in his brandy-fuzzed vision: crumbling marble generals, dictators, politicians, slaughterhouse tycoons, mere millionaires, granite honor guards—all of them cold as the winter sun, cold as the eyes of the groundskeepers that followed him down the avenue. And cold as the living hearts of the people who had built this place—"our kind of people"—who bought and sold each other's bones here, as if the living weren't enough for them to feed on.

And then he was in front of the massive bronze door with his own name on it, Molina, cast in flowery script among the angels and vines his grandfather had sent to Italy to have molded. "'Vanity,' saith the preacher, Grandpa," he said to make himself feel a little easier as he tried the huge padlock and found it was unlocked. Adela was home.

He put his shoulder against the door and shoved, wondering that someone as slight as Adela could manage it alone.

"Adela?" he said as the door swung open wide enough for him to see the empty, brocaded prayer stool on which he expected to find her waiting for him. His voice sounded hollow to him, as if he were in a bathroom. The air was cool and still inside. A single shaft of thin sunlight, with no heat to it, cut through the thick glass of a tall Gothic window and rested on the pink marble sarcophagus of his grandmother. He stepped into the room.

The marble of the columns and floor and stairway was Belgian, and all pink. But the walls and domed ceiling were lapis lazuli, a deep blue mosaic sky grouted with gold and spangled with stars of hammered gold above rainbow arches of pure silver. He'd been used to it once, and thought no more of it than if it had been wallpaper. But now, since he'd been away from it for years, it tightened his throat with something part anger, part awe.

"Adela?" Only the hollow silence answered him.

He started down the stairs to the second level, where his father was. Enough light bounced off the walls to show the way to the bottom, and then the darkness took over. Great God, was she waiting for him in this dark? "Adela?" he asked again. "Christ, *hermanita,* at least answer me." He stumbled against the cold hardness of a slab of marble, grabbed for balance, and felt a crystal flower vase slip away from his hand. Its shattering echoed and magnified itself like an explosion in a mineshaft. Esteban held on to the slab of marble, his breath short in the close air, terrified for a moment that the dark itself would smother him. He fumbled in his pocket for his lighter.

The yellow light sprang up against the walls. The lapis lazuli sky was almost black in this light, but the golden stars blazed. Just in front of him, the bronze plaque with his father's name caught the light and gave it back. Esteban took a step toward it and touched the sarcophagus. Twelve years now, twelve years since he had been in this place—the day they'd buried what was left of the old man after the terrorist bomb was through with him. Esteban was jerked back those twelve years, felt again the shock and then fear when the door to his bedroom slammed inward in the night from the force of the explosion, smelled again the dust and chemical smell in the hallway, heard his mother's and Adela's screams, stepped into what had been his father's bedroom and saw the jumble of things that had been his father and his father's bed. He turned away—quickly.

"God damn it, Adela," he shouted into the even more utter darkness of the level below, the level reserved for his generation. She wasn't here. She'd come and waited, and while he was swilling brandy, had slipped out of La Recoleta, had gone through the convent attached to it and out a side door. Damn her. Damn himself. He started up the stairs, furious.

But then another realization hit him. The door had been unlocked. Adela, the neat one, the responsible one, would never leave the door to this place unlocked if she weren't here. He whirled on the stairs, stumbled again, and the lighter flew out of his hand. He heard it clattering on the marble steps ahead of him, down toward the next level. He went onto his hands and knees, going down the stairs awkward as a dog, sweeping ahead of him for the lighter with his hand.

He found it near the bottom and flicked it once, twice, three times before it lit. He could have squeezed the goddamn thing into jelly. He was panicking, he knew. To calm himself, he concentrated on getting to his feet very slowly, very deliberately, sliding his hand up along the smooth marble wall to steady himself as he rose.

There were only two more steps before the last room, his and Adela's room. He held the lighter high, like a torch.

When he saw her, he caught the sound he was about to make in his throat just before it really became a sound. She lay easily on her marble slab, her wool skirt neatly tucked underneath her. One of her arms rested on her stomach; the other dangled off the edge of the slab, as if someone had tried to leave her hands folded but failed. Her eyes were open but not staring, as if they, too, had been deliberately arranged. They seemed to be watching something just beyond the lapis lazuli ceiling while her mind was busy someplace else, making wedding plans. Her black hair—the Molina hair, not his own reddish English hair—had been carefully smoothed out. He could hardly see the blue, even line around her neck.

He touched her arm. It was cold already, and rigid. Like a leg of beef, he thought with a shudder.

He backed away. The motion made the flame flicker, and the golden stars flashed. The look on Adela's perfect face was serious, purposeful. But not at all desperate now.

Florida Street was no longer a street. Pedestrians spent more than cars did, so traffic had been exiled to smaller, less exclusive streets. Now Calle Florida was a paving-stoned promenade, the world's longest promenade—if you believed the tourist brochures any more than you did the war news. Begin at one end of Florida by the huge oaks of Plaza San Martín at breakfast, stop for lunch in one of the teahouses or in a *confitería* on a side street, and you still wouldn't have shopped it dry by tea time. But by then it would be the hour for backtracking to Calle Lavalle, the nighttime promenade that intersected Florida back up near the Plaza San Martín. There you'd begin the circuit of the dinner restaurants and movie palaces and bars—till dawn, if you'd like, when you could start trying to find the far end of Florida again. Esteban had done that. More than once.

Caroline's studio was upstairs over a gallery on Florida, a gallery that sometimes showed a few of her paintings. Esteban suspected that Caroline had been sleeping with the gallery owner once, but he'd never asked and she'd never volunteered the information. The building was ornate and old, and from her bay window you could see the boutiques and jewelers and furriers and perfume shops stretching off like an elegant, expensive midway into the distance. Across the street, Harrod's window displays were underlined with signs that read, "Harrod's, the great Argentine department store, supports our heroic national cause." Esteban had delighted in the sign when it first went up. Tonight he saw it, detested it briefly, and forgot it. There was nothing funny in Argentina tonight.

The police had met him at La Recoleta, questioned him, questioned the groundskeepers, made photos. And they had taken Adela away. Then they had given him two hours in which to break the news to his grandfather and mother before they showed up to question them. Only common decency, they said—for a family like the Molinas. They'd given him a car and driver.

Halfway to his mother's he'd told the driver to turn around, to head for Calle Florida. He had to tell Caroline about it first, and he had to have a drink. If he could get through the story with Caroline, he could get through it with his mother.

But when he told Caroline about it, he felt as if he were telling her the plot of a B movie he'd just seen. She heard him out, holding his hand while he went through the story in a monotone. When he was done, he was as short of breath as if he'd run a mile. He needed the drink then.

"No," Caroline said. "Brandy I won't get you. But I'll make you some coffee."

"Caffeine's a drug, too," he said, forcing a smile. "Make me a double."

"Si, señor," she said seriously. "One *café doble,* at your pleasure."

His bags still sat in a heap in the corner, where he'd left them when he moved in after the bastards in the blue suits locked him out of his apartment. Part of the bed he could have, Caroline had said. But the closet was hers.

Somehow Caroline had always seemed to Esteban to be too neat for a painter. Her fingernails managed to be clean and filed and polished, her shoes were never paint-splattered, the loose bun of her dark hair never looked as if it had sketching pencils or dried paintbrushes hidden in it. He'd noticed that the other painters he knew seemed to lean toward bright, patterned clothing, and he'd decided it wasn't that they liked colors so much as that paint smears got hidden better in clothes like that. Caroline didn't need those clothes. Her white linen blouses and dark skirts and delicate cashmere sweaters were always spotless. And, God be praised, she never smelled of turpentine.

So he never thought of her as a real painter. Even though all during the time of the Dirty War against the guerrillas—throughout most of the seventies, in fact—she'd studied painting in Paris, she said. And she sold enough now to keep her going well enough: he'd seen her bright, round suns and primitive children and fishermen in more and more galleries the past year. But she never really seemed to care about it the way he thought a painter should. She always seemed just to be painting en route to somewhere, to be merely filling the time while she was waiting for something.

He knew he wanted it to be himself she'd been en route to, ever since she'd showed up in the restaurant one night with a quasi-famous Uruguayan actor. At times he thought it might be. But he'd never been sure. Like her closet, there was a part of her always off limits to him, never open to public inspection—no matter how often he shared her bed. Maybe, he thought, that was why he wanted her. When he told her that, she said he was perverse and that was why he'd never married: couldn't have what he wanted, didn't want what he could have.

He wanted her even more after that. He *was* perverse, he decided.

She returned now with two coffees, a double for himself, a single for her.

"Straight coffee?" he said.

"Made camphor out of all the whiskey in the house," she said. "Trick my mother taught me back in Tucumán." Through the skylight that she always complained gave her the wrong light, no stars showed. It would be raining soon, the sad Buenos Aires winter drizzle. That seemed proper to Esteban. Caroline sat beside him on the studio's one worn couch. "How are you, *guapo*? Can you talk about it any more, or do you want to wait?"

"The cops said they'd give me some time first before they talked to Mother. I'm supposed to tell her."

"How long?"

"Soon."

"Are you up to it? You're too calm."

"Somebody will have to be. Besides, it hasn't set in yet."

"Let it."

"Let that set in? Let Dachau set in. Let Auschwitz. Christ, Caroline."

"OK, get mad. Maybe that's good now."

"I've been mad for weeks. And I haven't been able to think for weeks."

"Then don't think."

"Could you quit being so *bloody* reasonable."

"No, I won't. If I can make you mad enough—the right kind of mad—you'll be human and let go."

He took a sip of the hot coffee and held it in his mouth until the pain turned to numbness. Caroline's bright paintings, all the pots and weavings the two of them had bought on summer Sundays at the flea market of San Telmo, were being swallowed by the evening gloom. He stood abruptly and flicked on a lamp. "Look, who did it? Why did they do it? And why the *way* it was done? *That's* why I've got to think. The cops sure as hell won't—not when everything's as 'sensitive' as it is now. Not when they've got so many damned ready-made explanations left over from 'disappearing' so many people. Pick an explanation, any explanation. Want me to hit you with a quick half dozen—all of them perfectly plausible for any standard political death?"

"No. I've heard them. And what makes you believe it was a political thing?"

"I don't—necessarily. But they will."

"OK. But when you do think, then what?"

"I don't know. *Do* something. I hope."

"That's Dick Tracy stuff, *guapo*. They've got you beat at it."

He flicked on another lamp, then another. The gloom scattered like cockroaches, but not completely. It hung on in corners and under tables and behind easels. He looked for more lamps. Caroline watched him from the couch. "Try my architect's lamp," she said. "On the drawing table."

He turned on her. "All right," he said, controlling his voice until he could hardly hear it himself. "You want me to be human? Reasonable, even? That means tearing my hair, doing some public weeping, then sitting on my hands, right? Believing in odds and hoping for the best, like everybody else in this poor, fucked-over country. Adela was my goddamn sister, Caroline."

"No, you won't do all that. I hope you won't do all that." She started to take a drink of her coffee, then put it down on an end table. She raised her eyes and met his. "You'll do whatever you have to, I suppose. No matter how stupid it is. *Because* you're human. I wouldn't be here with you if you weren't."

"Then why in hell did you...?"

"Because somebody has to point out to you how theoretically stupid it is to try to make sense out of anything right now." She held out her hand to him. "Sit down a minute." He sat beside her on the couch and she took his barely touched coffee cup from him, then leaned over and kissed him. He rested his head on her shoulder. He thought he might have cried, but he wasn't sure whether any tears really came or not. After a time, she pushed him gently away from her. "Go," she said. "See your mother before the police get there. I'll still be here."

"For what?"

"Theoretically, for whatever you need. But don't count on it." She smiled.

He stood. Light rain hissed across the skylight. *"Guapo?"* she said. "I'm sorry. Good luck."

Outside and around the corner his car and driver waited on the rain-slick street. He had to *do* something then, to think and, when he could, maybe to feel—good, vague purposes. They might even make the ordeal with his mother easier. But to do what, feel what, damn it?

Right now it didn't matter. He knew that there *would* be things to do, and that was enough. He rummaged around in himself for strength, strength he hadn't truly ever needed until now. Was it there?

It would be. It had to be.

His mother's eyes were too bright. They gave the lie to her organization, her collected dismissal of everything but the immediate, the necessary. It wouldn't do to cross her now, he knew; she'd fly to pieces like a whirring engine you'd dropped a wrench into.

"Well, of course it's grotesque," she said to the police investigator as she kept him standing, raincoat dripping, at the door of her long, many-bathroomed flat on Avenida Libertador. "It's more than that. It's macabre. It's hideous. But your telling me that doesn't get anything done, does it? There are arrangements to make. Why don't you just *go*, and let me deal with my family now. You do understand about privacy, don't you? At least you understand that, surely."

And then later, on the phone to his grandfather, insisting as always that he speak English with her:

"Yes, Carlos, they say she was killed—'murdered' is the word they won't say to me—and brought there during the night. But does it matter? It's because someone didn't want English blood in your damned hero's line, isn't it? No, no—don't contradict me. At least not now. Not until she's decently buried among her Argentines. What? Well, Great God, Carlos, if I'm not bitter, what do you think I'll be? Pulp, that's what I'd be—and will be as soon as it's all over. Let me have my blessèd anger, will you? What? Yes, there's something you can do. You can get one of your tin generals on the phone and get Steven onto an airplane for the Falkland Islands—in the morning at the latest. She has a fiancé to be told, and he mustn't hear of it secondhand or by telephone or such things. No, it's not impossible. *Nothing's* impossible in this wretched country if you're who you happen to be. I *insist* on decency now, Carlos. What? Carlos, how *can* I get in touch with Frank? There's a war on with England, or hadn't you noticed? Do you know what they said to me at the Intel office when I told them I wanted to telephone London? You might get one of your tin generals to arrange *that*, too. What? Oh, I know you're sorry. I know how you cared for her. I know you're suffering, Carlos, and I'm sorry for you. But I'm her mother, Carlos, no matter how you'd like to forget that. I'm sorrier for me, and I'm going to hang up now before I start screaming."

She put the phone down and stood with her hand on it, taking deep breaths and drawing herself up to her full height. She was finishing the scene properly, Esteban knew. He had seen it too many times—in fights with his father, in rages at himself or Frank or Adela. Her anger was operatic, orchestrated. He'd often wondered what kind of *real* rage she could be capable of if she weren't able to structure it and control it that way— the way she'd no doubt hit upon in her Gilbert and Sullivan days, before she'd gone on tour and met his father here and never returned home again. And he'd often wondered, too, if she hadn't seen Argentina all along as some sort of mammoth set for a Gilbert and Sullivan operetta that insisted on writing itself endlessly. It had amused her, angered her—but never involved her. Not until now.

"Good performance," he said.

"What performance?"

"I've known you all my life, Mother."

"What is it you drink, Steven? Brandy, is it?"

"Among other things."

"Get yourself some. And get me some. And then come sit down."

He poured them both one from the ceiling-high carved mahogany bar his father had sent himself home from Paris once, and sat beside her on the couch. The steel shutters were lowered against the rainy melee of taxis outside on Libertador, and a fire pretended cheer in the fireplace. His mother downed half a shot of the brandy, and coughed. Around her bright eyes, the skin was drawn tight, almost free of the wrinkles she spent so much time trying to hide. That had always been the only sign she'd been crying.

"Do you really think that was why it happened?" he asked her. "That business about bloodlines?"

"No, I don't. They adore British blood in their lines, war or not. I know why it happened."

"Then for the love of God, Mother, why—"

"Listen to me, Steven. I want you to do something for me. And I don't want you to ask why now. I don't ask much of you. But this I'm demanding, not asking."

He sipped his brandy and waited. Don't contradict, not now, he reminded himself.

"I was quite serious about your going to the Falklands. It's imperative that you go. We *must* be seen to do the absolutely proper thing. We *must* be seen to be still one of them. Do you understand? And then I want you to come back here as quickly as possible. I'll have something to tell you."

"Adela had something to tell me."

"I'm aware of that."

"You knew about it?"

"Some of it. Not all, I'm sure."

"Why not tell me now?"

"I don't want you down there knowing what I have to tell you. I want you talking to Jaime Mondragon and his kind with nothing but the pure light of innocence in your eyes. Is that clear?"

"No."

"And I want you to be very, very careful about everything you do, everyone you see, from the moment you leave here. Anything you say or do outside the expected will probably be reported."

"It usually is these days."

"This is different, Steven." She finished her brandy in another quick gulp. "My daughter is dead, and I'm grieving, but I'm not mad. I have two sons left, and I want to keep them. Mad, Steven, is the way your sister was killed. Mad is what's happened to those thousands of children here—those 'disappeareds.'" She shuddered. Esteban was afraid the brandy snifter would shatter in her hands, she was squeezing it so hard. He took it gently from her.

"And what about you?" he asked.

"There are provisions for times like these. If there are a hundred thousand Britons in Buenos Aires, half of them will have been to see me by tomorrow. God knows how many Argentine social climbers there are. I expect I'll see all of them."

"You could go to Grandfather's place on the river, in Tigre."

"I *want* them here, don't you see? I won't have to think till you get back. I'll tell you something, if you'll get me another one of those whatevers we're drinking." Steven rose. "Whoever did that to your sister was very considerate, very proper. They knew no one but you would find her. The newspapers won't know any more than we tell them—your grandfather will see to that, too. I'll be consoled by everyone for my poor child, my poor daughter who died so young of a bad heart—or whatever the doctors tell me to say she died of. No scandal, nothing to keep people away. Isn't that wonderfully considerate?"

She turned her face up to him with a bright, bitter smile. He held out the brandy to her. She slapped it out of his hand, turned her face away from him, and buried it in the couch. He sat beside her again and held her rigid shoulders. After a time, she raised a tear-streaked face from the couch. "Do this *right,* Steven. Come back to me. There's so miserably much more you have to do now."

When he left her, he knew there was nothing to think

about for now. He would do what she asked, come back, and then think. How did the line from *Lear* go? "A time to ask not what we think, but what we feel"? Something like that—or it should have been. Caroline wanted him to feel. All right, what *did* he feel? Pity for his mother. Pity for Adela. Revulsion. Some fear. And what was he mourning, if he was? He had loved Adela very much once. Lately—what had he really known about her? He would mourn the old Adela, then: he would hurt for what she had been and for what she might have been. And he would try to keep that hurt from turning into the thing that nearly every real emotion of his had turned into, almost since he could remember, surely since his father's death: anger, a kind of comforting, familiar mire of anger. That was true desperation. That was too easy.

So he had gone to Caroline's studio, had packed a clean shirt and a pair of jeans for the war, had awakened Caroline and kissed her and told her a lie about where he was going, and had flown out of the flatness of Buenos Aires just ahead of the small, cold winter sun that he watched rise from the eastern sea beyond the casinos and hotels of Mar del Plata, on his way to Comodoro Rivadavia, the last staging area before the Falklands (sorry, Adela: Malvinas).

He woke with a jerk. The cargomaster's arm was flung against his chest, holding him back against the wall of the fuselage. The plane had apparently dipped hard, fighting an air pocket.

"Told you to put on your seat belt," the cargomaster shouted, smiling. He loosened an earplug.

"Thanks." Esteban loosened one of his own plugs, then fumbled for the brandy flask. "Was I asleep?"

"Nodding," the cargomaster said. "First time I've seen anybody do even that much on this run."

Esteban took a pull on the flask and passed it. Outside, the sky looked as if you were seeing it through ground glass: a gray glow of fog utterly surrounded the plane. The wing tips flashed in and out of sight, and the plane bumped and rocked like a train on bad track.

"Where are we?"

"Coming in."

Esteban stood to get his circulation going. And there it was again, the bad taste of the dream that wouldn't go away, fuzzy as the fog outside the plane. Hell, he might still be dreaming for all he knew. He spread-eagled himself before one of the round windows. He wanted to see this thing, these islands that two countries were bellowing and slapping at each other about like a couple of dinosaurs.

They'd been flying just above the waves. But now, as they gained altitude for a landing, the islands lay raggedly before him in a clearing in the fog. They looked like moss when they first appeared in snatches through the belly fur of the clouds, a duller green on the sea green of the water surrounding them. Here and there on the heights, there were grayish patches he took to be ice. The coastline was nowhere smooth; the land seemed to send out tentacles into the water, so that he couldn't always be sure where the water left off and the land began. Not much to look at, he thought. Not bloody much to kill over.

He turned back to the cargomaster. "I told you," the cargomaster said. "A shithole."

"Will we land?"

The cargomaster shrugged. "We're going down, no? We'll see."

The plane bent its course into a long arc, doubling back to come in from the east. Esteban made out an airfield now, just to the west of town. Puerto Argentina, the town had to be—Port Stanley until the heroic act of national recovery. And then they were rushing over the peaked rooftops of the town itself. A few people waved from a long dock that jutted out into the bay and ended in a T, like a cross. "Seat belt, *now!*" the cargomaster yelled.

Esteban fumbled for a seat belt as he threw himself down onto the webbed bench. From the corner of his eye, he caught glimpses of the landing strip rushing up to meet them. Its edges were eaten away with bomb craters. On the strip itself he could see what had been craters, now patches of packed earth. Along it sat a row of small prop-driven fighter planes, some of them in ruins. He clicked the seat belt just as the plane hit, bounced, hit again. The cargomaster was thrown hard against him. The plane swerved and rattled, and the stack of C rations tilted crazily. Yet the pilot held on, jerking over the potholed land but staying on the runway until he was merely, mercifully, taxiing, until orange-suited ground support people were rushing out at them with their day-glow batons to guide them in, until Esteban's breathing remembered to start again and his gut decided to land, too.

"Shithole or not," the cargomaster said solemnly, watching the dinky control tower, blue-and-white Argentine flag flying from it, come into sight through the window, "we've waited a damn long time to be able to do this, brother. *Qué no?*"

"Qué no," Esteban said. Adela had given her grandmother's rings to the Cause for this, had seen them go to buy the missiles that made it possible for that flag to be there. And now he was seeing it, not she. He, who didn't give a good goddamn whose flag flew over these bleak chunks of rock and mud. *Mierda.*

He'd promised himself to try to keep the pointless anger from taking over. But it circled him, sniffing, waiting its chance to move in.

The Globe Hotel wasn't much: yellow brick, red roof, a story and a half high if you counted the loft, and a green picket fence. The view one way was the corner of a tin warehouse with the wharf beyond. From the rear, you looked up the concrete pavement of Port Stanley's main street, which rose past terraced lawns and evergreen shrubs to the top of the small hill the town was built on. The hotel was an inn in a Scottish village, draped now inside with photos of *el señor presidente* Galtieri, and Argentine flags. It looked as wrong as a Cockney in Gypsy beads. But it was what there was, and a fire burned in the lobby and his room had a kerosene heater and a decent bed. It was a damn sight better than what the troops he'd seen on the way in had: wet foxholes in the spongy ground, with blankets wrapped around their heads like in photos he'd seen of German troops in the retreat from Stalingrad. And these hadn't even begun the fight yet. *Dios, Dios.*

He had the bed. Jaime, *el coronel* Jaime Mondragon, vice commander of the FAA, Malvinas Sector, had the only chair. While Jaime studied the flower patterns on the worn linoleum, Esteban studied him in the orange light from the early, almost-Antarctic sunset outside. Jaime's face was clear as a plaster saint's. It was boyish still, an eagle scout's—or Hitler Youth's—sunburned face, blue eyed, with blond hair that curled in the dampness nearly into ringlets. It said, Trust me to do the correct thing, always. Esteban neither particularly liked nor disliked him. He seemed neither especially bright nor especially stupid to him; his conversation on the few occasions they'd talked alone in Buenos Aires neither put you to sleep nor excited you. He never said very clever things, but could appreciate them, or pretend to. What in *hell* had he and Adela talked about? Esteban often wondered. Or had she merely stared into those clear blue eyes and imagined they were talking?

He had listened to Esteban's story in a kind of stupor, the way a priest who was burdened with mortal sins might listen to the confession of a petty thief. He'd asked all the appropriate questions, looked properly shocked, muttered some things that sounded like anger, incredulity, or grief—but he wasn't there, he just wasn't there, and Esteban knew it. Esteban had even been prepared to comfort him if need be. But false comfort for a man who was only half listening to him was more than he could handle. He'd kept the story to the point, bloodless, like a military report.

When there was no more to tell, and Mondragon had exhausted his last painful sigh, he twirled his whiskey glass and said to Esteban, "You'll forgive me, Esteban."

"For what?"

"My head's not very clear these days. There's been too much dying. Adela's is far and away the most terrible, but..."

Esteban decided to accept the appeal and let the melodrama in it go. Maybe the poor bastard really had been through some of those things the television reports said he had. "I understand, Jaime."

Mondragon finished his whiskey. "I'm tired. God, I'm tired. Look, did anybody talk to Adela after you did?"

"Christ, I don't know. That's an odd question. Why?"

He hesitated. "I need to know—I want to know—everything about it. Isn't that natural?"

"Maybe. But why that?"

"The British did it. You know that, don't you?"

"I don't think I know that, no."

"They want to stop me. I'm hurting them too badly. They kill Adela, they leave her...where they left her, knowing you're planning to meet her there, of course, and I'm supposed to fall apart when I hear it. That's damned obvious, isn't it?"

Esteban forced a sigh. Do it *right,* his mother had asked. The pure light of innocence. "Mother thinks it's because we're half-British. It's obvious to her the rightists did it. The cops think it's obvious the leftists did it to damage the war effort. And how about the army and the navy? They're coming out of this war looking like a bunch of milkmaids. You people are heros. Isn't it obvious *they* have a grudge, too? Nothing's obvious in this damn country, Jaime."

"Keep your head. *I'm* not falling apart, no matter what the British want. You can't either."

"Didn't you hear me, Jaime?"

"The British did it, damn it," Jaime said. There was a warning in his voice. Did he need to believe that in order to hate the British as much as he wanted to—or had to? Esteban decided to let that go, too.

"The funeral's tomorrow," he said.

"What time?"

"Around one."

"I'll see you're there, but you'll probably be late. I can't go. You understand why."

"Have they landed yet?"

"I wish to hell I knew. There were commandos on the western island, but they didn't stay."

"Will they land?"

"Yes."

"Can you stop them?"

Jaime hesitated again. "For a while. For as long as we can." He got to his feet. His camouflage fatigues were perfectly tailored, perfectly pressed. Esteban remembered the men in blankets in the foxholes. "I'm on duty—Christ, I'm always on duty. I've got to go." Esteban watched his face work itself up to grief. But this, too, wasn't really grief. It was what Esteban had the unpleasant sense Jaime wanted too hard to pass for

26

grief. But why? Why did he have to pretend grief? Whether Esteban cared much for the man didn't matter: he'd never seen any kind of clue that Jaime, in his stiff-necked way, wasn't truly as in love with Adela as she was with him.

Jaime crossed the room and put his hand on Esteban's shoulder. It was a soap-opera gesture, Esteban thought. But he let the hand stay. "Keep your head," Jaime said again. "I'll grieve when there's time. You understand that, too, don't you?"

"I'll try."

"She was a saint, a martyr."

"If that makes it easier for you, Jaime."

"It was very correct of you to come here, Esteban. *Muy correcto.* I'll remember that."

He didn't wait for Esteban to let him out. When he was gone, Esteban eased himself down onto the bed and listened to the hiss of the kerosene stove. His anger was loose now, like a bull that wouldn't be stopped till it wore itself down. *Muy correcto! Mierda,* how he hated that phrase! Somehow telling Mondragon about Adela had begun to make her death real to him. As long as there had been somebody like Mondragon who thought of her as alive, as still a part of his life, her death wasn't final yet. Now it was. And Mondragon's reaction had been *muy correcto,* nothing more. Already he was concocting the convenient lie, the useful lie, to explain her death, the bastard!

Jesucristo! What a good Argentine he was, then. Whatever barbarity, whatever cruelty, whatever pretense—all of it was allowed, even praised, as long as the style was right, as long as it was *muy correcto,* as long as the conventions were observed and the taste was good. What had his mother said? Even the horror of Adela's death had been done "considerately." His stomach clenched. *Jesucristo!*

There was a knock at the door.

"Who is it?"

"Colonel Mondragon sends his regards, sir. He wants you to have this."

"To have what?"

"It's a bottle of brandy, sir. There'll be some supper along later."

"Leave it," Esteban said. And then as an afterthought, "Orderly?"

"Señor?"

"Thank the colonel for me. Tell him he's *muy correcto*."

Esteban savored his anger, an anger that was different now. It wasn't the tight anger that curled back on himself and poisoned him, like a scorpion's tail. He'd had enough of that. No, this anger had a warmth to it, a glow, that could heat things, move pistons—anger he could *use;* and he was grateful for it. Get mad, Caroline had said. *This* kind of mad.

He opened the door and picked up the bottle of brandy Jaime had sent to him. It was good brandy, and it ought to be a shame to waste it, he thought, as he poured it down the drain of the washbasin. But he watched it swirl away with a kind of relief now, a sense of freedom. He'd played his mother's scene. Whatever she hadn't wanted them to suspect him of, they didn't. And now she had something to tell him.

Chapter Two

The timing was wrong; the place was bad. His taxi squalled to a halt at a police barricade just at the corner of Government House. The taxi driver threw up his hands.

"No closer, señor. Sorry."

Esteban strained to see through the decals and tasseled Virgins that cluttered the view through the windshield. "What the hell is it?"

"Another patriotic manifestation in the plaza, I think, señor. And it looks like a wedding or a funeral or something in the cathedral."

"It's a funeral. And I'll walk." Esteban dropped a wad of pesos into the front seat. A cop waved his white-gloved hand frantically at the cab, and Esteban leapt out into the torrent of traffic just as the cabbie popped the clutch and slid into the stream. Wonderful, he thought as he dodged cars to the curb. Two blocks of chanting patriots to fight through to the funeral—which ought to be damn near over by now, anyway.

He sprinted as far as he could, until the crowd got too thick. Blue-white-blue Argentine flags, some of them faded to gray by recent overuse, hung limply in the damp air. An amplified voice from somewhere in the center of the crowd led chants and vivas, and somebody in an air force general's uniform stood looking silly, giving exaggerated thumbs-up signs to the crowd from the pink stone balcony of Government House. It was Perón's balcony, and as Esteban elbowed his way through the crowd, he couldn't help thinking how much better Evita must have looked on it than the stubby general, who could have been mistaken for Mussolini from this distance. Just before the next line of police barricades, the ones that kept the crowd away from the waiting limousines in front of the cathedral, a warty little man stuck a flyer in front of his face. Esteban saw that it was a copy of the United States Constitution.

"They don't even read their own constitution," the man shouted at him. "See what it says about resisting the tyranny of English kings? What happened to that, eh?"

Esteban brushed by him. On the police barricade, someone had tacked a poster of Alexander Haig in bed with Margaret Thatcher. Haig's tongue hung out as he mounted her dog fashion. Esteban vaulted the barricade and yelled at a cop, a sergeant, "Get rid of that goddamn thing!"

The cop grabbed Esteban and slammed him against the wall of San Martín's tomb, which was built into the cathedral. Esteban was sure he could hear the bones of poor San Martín rattle inside. Like his own teeth had when he hit the damp stone wall.

"What did you say, friend?" the cop said. Two more of them trotted up beside him, one of them unsnapping his white leather holster. Esteban shoved at the sergeant, and the other two pinned his arms to the wall. "I said get rid of that goddamn poster. It's a disgrace."

"To who? You a friend of la Thatcher's?"

"To my sister's funeral—that I'm trying to get to."

The cop backed up a step. "Molina?" he said.

"You got it," Esteban said.

The sergeant gave Esteban a stubborn, threatening look, then nodded to his two buddies. They let Esteban go, and the sergeant walked slowly over to the poster and ripped it off the barricade. He wadded it carefully into a ball and dropped it at Esteban's feet. "Ramón," he said to the cop who had unsnapped his holster. "Escort Sr. Molina inside."

Stone-faced, the cop wheeled and headed along the columned portico of the cathedral. Esteban followed him.

From behind, he heard the sergeant say in a flat voice, "Viva Perón, rich bastard."

That's right, Esteban thought as the cop stepped aside to let him go into the cathedral. To the sergeant he was a rich bastard that would be dealt with when the next revolution—or the next Perón—came along. And what the hell was he then to "our kind of people" who'd turned out for Adela's funeral? Where did he belong in this insane country? Did he belong anywhere?

The great, pealing organ and choir overwhelmed him when he stepped into the cathedral, heavy with dull gilt, incense, and candle smoke. From his pulpit, Archbishop Puglesi himself, robed and mitered like a character in a carnival float, glared down the avenue-sized aisle—straight at Esteban, he was certain. Missed your own sister's funeral, the old bastard was probably thinking. Bohemian. Freethinker. Not at all *correcto*.

But missed it he had. The place was packed, and from every pew, Guccied women and pin-striped men rose and stretched and edged into the aisles. Esteban recognized almost none of them, but he knew them all: the overly made-up women, their mouths set in practiced, permanent little sneers; the hard-faced men, their hair perfectly slicked back and their eyes cold as pesos. One or two of them seemed to recognize him as he began shoving his way against the stream of them like a salmon. They started to speak, but he ignored them. His mother would be near the front, with his grandfather. Caroline would be God knew where. He'd head for his mother first. If she had something to tell him about Adela's murder, she could damn well do it here in front of Adela.

He stepped up onto a pew to see ahead of him, and a woman in enough jewelry to buy Paraguay gasped and gave him an outraged look. He ignored her, too, ignored them all. Where the hell was his mother? He'd been to a bloody war and back to get to her, and now he couldn't make it a few hundred meters through patriotic chanters and overdressed parasites.

He spotted his grandfather first, surrounded by a sea of handshakers and shoulder clappers and sympathetic-noise makers. He scanned the area around them for his mother. He'd expected her there, but she was nowhere. He had a moment of panic. Had whoever killed Adela not stopped with just Adela? His mother had said she knew something about Adela's need to talk. Had she known too much?

No, thank God, no. He caught her out of the corner of his eye at first, moving steadily through the crowd toward the private chapel just off the nave. And she wasn't alone. He recognized one of the blue-suited men with her: he was the detective she'd sent away into the rain. His hand was on her arm, guiding her. Esteban tried to remember the plan of the cathedral. Yes, they could take her through the chapel and out that way. He glanced behind him; no chance, no chance at all of getting outside the cathedral in time to intercept them there. All right—it was time to apply geometry, then, the principle of straight lines and shortest distances. He climbed up onto the back of the pew, balanced himself, and stepped toward the back of the pew in front of him. By then the whole goddamned cathedral was watching him, but he concentrated on rhythm, on stride, on remembering how he used to walk for miles on railroad ties without missing a step.

He made it to the second pew from the front before one of his grandfather's *guapos*—his "pretty boys," which was the old man's term of endearment for his bone breakers and bodyguards—caught him. He recognized the man's askew Valentino face; he was an old standby of his grandfather's. "Touch me, Chuy," he said to him, "and I'll barbecue your balls."

But by then it was too late; his balance was gone and he was diving face first for the aisle. All Chuy had to do was hold out his arms and catch him and ease him gently onto the floor, flat on his back. Then to sit on him.

Esteban looked up at the circle of faces around him, like a patient on an operating table. The archbishop stared mercilessly down at him a moment, gave a violent sigh, and disappeared. His grandfather looked as if he were having trouble recognizing him, the way he would an unknown species of fish he'd run across on a beach.

"Are you in control of yourself now, Grandson?" he asked without rancor.

"Where the hell's Mother," Esteban demanded.

"We won't know that for a few days," his grandfather said. He made a little finger-flipping motion at Chuy. Chuy got off Esteban, helped him to his feet, and shook his hand fondly.

How long had it been since he'd seen his grandfather? Two years? Close to that, anyway. He was frailer than the last time he'd seen him; not thin, but frail. Now that Esteban was on his feet, he saw that he still had that way of looking at you with his head slightly lowered, like a bull about to charge, that he used to intimidate everybody who had to deal with him. As a child Esteban had had the impression that his grandfather deliberately squatted in front of him when he talked to him so that he could get the full effect of the head lowering. But even with his grandfather's generous padding still intact, Esteban had the sense that the old man's bones were withering away—that if you squeezed him too hard he'd crumple up like papier-mâché. It was something in the way he stood, something painful in his balance. Esteban had never been sure if he loved his grandfather or was afraid of him. At last, he supposed, he'd discovered you could feel both things at once.

His grandfather had come over from Spain in the chaotic times after the First War, with just enough money begged from solvent relatives to buy a hunk of sheep land in the green, cold Andrean foothills of Patagonia, a little *estancia*. By the depression, he'd expanded the *estancia* into enough other small-time businesses to be able to provide the capital to pick up other *estancias* from older families who went under. Then in the boom of the Second War, he had the capital accumulated to buy into shipping with a Greek shoemaker's son he'd known from his early days in Buenos Aires, a man named Onassis. After the war, he helped out a smart colonel named Perón with a few pesos at the right time, and so not only survived the years of *Perónismo,* but came out of them one of the dozen richest men in Argentina. Now it was real estate, furs, vast cattle *estancias* in the provinces, condo complexes in Miami and California—Esteban had only the foggiest notion of just what the hell his grandfather did own.

Frank had been the oldest grandson, the crown prince. When Frank deserted the family for England, the old man offered the succession to Esteban. Esteban turned him down, and they'd only stayed in the barest of contact since. Neither seemed to have minded.

"What's that supposed to mean, *abuelo*—that 'we won't know for a few days'?" Esteban said.

"Just that. I've asked the police to put us all under— oh, let's say protective custody—until they've got hold of the terrorists who did that thing to your sister. You, too, I'm afraid. And I think it's best if none of us knows where the other is, no? *Por si acaso*—just in case. Do you object?"

"Object? Of course I object. Christ, yes, I object." He turned to follow his mother. Chuy stepped in front of him, smiled sadly, and put an arm on his shoulder to turn him back around.

"Yes, you'd object," his grandfather said, more disappointed than angry. "You're a lawyer, aren't you? In any case, it's too late—it's out of my hands now. You'll have to talk to them about it." He nodded toward an uncomfortable-looking group of men in dark suits who huddled together around a column a few meters away. They might as well have worn tin badges, like cowboy sheriffs, Esteban thought.

"It was terrorists, then," Esteban said, annoyance feeding his sarcasm. "Terrorists killed Adela and left her for me to find like a bad joke. And now these"—he swept his hand toward the herd of cops—"public servants are going to protect us and dig out the few terrorists they somehow managed to overlook while they were busy throwing nuns out of helicopters. Are you comforted, *abuelo?*"

"No more than I was when the terrorists killed your father, Esteban," the old man said sharply. "Has your righteousness rotted your memory, too, Grandson?"

"No, Grandfather. If something's rotted, it's not that." Esteban felt a hand on his arm, but before he could turn to see who it was the hand was jerked roughly away. He sidestepped and ducked, adrenaline flashing. Then he heard a cry, and Caroline's voice calling, "Esteban!"

"It's OK, Chuy, it's OK," he said as he straightened up and gently unwound Chuy's massive fingers from

Caroline's arms. There was no embarrassment on Chuy's face. He'd done his job. "She's my...fiancée." Not the time to try to explain any other kind of relationship to his grandfather.

His grandfather peered up at Caroline through his eyebrows. Esteban had seen him appraise prize beef the same way. "Well," he said, his voice neutral. "I'd think I would have known that earlier."

"I'd think I would have, too," Caroline said, her voice echoing the neutrality.

The old man cut his eyes quickly to Esteban, then whipped them back to Caroline. He glowered a moment more, then smiled. In a moment more, he was wheezing a laugh. He made a stiff little bow, then offered his hand. "Carlos Molina," he said. Esteban admired him for that—no flowery *honored*s and *enchanted*s, just his name.

Caroline rose to the challenge. "Caroline La Fontaine."

"Ah. The furriers La Fontaine?"

"No. I'm from the provinces. From Tucumán."

"Tucumán? Radical country, isn't it? Guerrillas. Montoneros. No?"

Caroline left her eyes locked on his. "So I've heard. I was away during that time."

"Ah hah." Esteban knew his grandfather's mind. It was making notes: Check La Fontaines from Tucumán. Daughter Caroline. Background. Politics. Income. He'd probably know more about her when he was through than Esteban did. Damn it, why hadn't she waited a few minutes? As hard as he'd fought against the Molinas usurping his own life, now they'd go after Caroline's. "You knew my granddaughter, Adela, señorita La Fontaine?"

"Not well, I'm afraid."

"No, you wouldn't have. Esteban's family feeling isn't very exemplary, is it? Perhaps you can help us change that. On a better occasion"—he swept his eyes over the clustered mourners waiting their turn at him—"we'll get to know each other. Eh?" He gave her a little bow of dismissal, then turned to Esteban. "We'll all be going soon, Grandson. Perhaps you'll want to spend a few minutes with señorita La Fontaine now." He said it with a note of finality, a subject closed.

Chuy beamed and nodded them into a vacant pew as the mourners closed in again. Esteban checked the aisles. Clearer than before, but still cluttered with gaggles of chatting families. His mother could be halfway across town by now. There would be no sense in making a break for an exit, even if he thought he could make it. He noticed one of the cops by the pillar pointing him out to a buddy. His keepers, he thought. For how long— till they could find some "terrorist" to blame and satisfy his grandfather? Some "British agent" to satisfy Jaime Mondragon? Anybody—it didn't matter who—as long as somebody in power was satisfied. And what had his mother said? She knew *why* Adela was killed, but not who did it. What kind of help would that be after all? Christ, no matter how fine his anger was, he was no detective, no comic-book hero. It's just that they wouldn't even *try*, wouldn't even make a heading in their damned ledger for the truth....

"I talked to your mother," Caroline said offhandedly.

"When?" He tensed, then willed himself not to show it.

"Here, just before you made your grand entrance. Where did they take her?"

"I don't know. We're all going somewhere—into 'protective custody.' What did mother say?"

"She babbled."

"She doesn't babble."

"This time she did. The only time she had me alone, she kept talking about your going to her ski lodge in Bariloche, to get over things. I told her I didn't know anything about it, but she kept insisting. 'Tell him to get the key from Pepe in town; Pepe won't let anybody know he's there'—all sorts of things like that. Is there something I don't know, *guapo?*"

"No. But there may be something *I* know now."

"I thought that might be so."

Esteban checked the cops again. They still lounged uneasily, no doubt waiting for a signal from his grandfather. Chuy had gone back to watching over the old man, hovering close enough to throw himself in front of him if he ever needed to. The crowd around his grand-

36

father was smaller now, but there were still a few minutes left before he would be able to get away from them with any kind of grace. A few small minutes to think.

Bariloche. So far as he knew, even his mother hadn't been to that cold stone town in the Andes for years. What in hell could she possibly have been trying to tell him about Bariloche? And how long had it been since *he'd* been there? Two years, at least. Adela was the one who used the ski lodge now, she and Jaime Mondragon. They'd been skiers—he for the love of the sport, Adela for the love of the quiet of the mountains. Mondragon had promised her they'd go there for their honeymoon; she'd already had plans to go up alone and get things "set up" for them, whatever that meant.

To go up alone. This weekend. Sainted angels!

And she'd been planning to drive, she'd told him. To drive a thousand miles, a thousand slow miles over stretches of miserable road. What in the name of God would she want to drive that far in winter for? he'd asked her. Why not fly, like every other civilized person in Argentina did? She'd given him some flip excuse, something about wanting to be on her own for one last time, and he'd accepted it as the kind of blithering gesture people made before they got married.

But not now. If she'd wanted to drive, was there something she wanted to bring back with her? Something that it wouldn't do to have seen on a plane or a train?

But Adela?

Yet Adela was dead. He'd told himself he hadn't known Adela very well these last few years. Dear God, maybe he'd known infinitely less than he thought he had.

"Look," he said to Caroline. "I want you to leave now. Very naturally, just stand up, kiss me, and walk out as if you're on your way to buy a box of cat food or something."

"Bariloche?"

"Bariloche. I'm going to ask you to do something for me. It won't be anything you can't explain your way out of later if you have to."

"I'm not bad at that—like explaining how we're engaged?"

"I want you to rent a car, that's all. Get something ordinary, like a Falcon. Then meet me with it, someplace like—oh, a bar—the Forest Hills, on Maipú. Do you know that one?"

"I've seen it."

"What do you need? An hour?"

"If you're going to drive, what's wrong with *your* car?"

"It's too easy to trace."

"What's going on, Esteban?"

"I don't know what's going on. If I did, I wouldn't be going to Bariloche."

"Is it about Adela?"

"Yes."

She reached out and touched his hand lightly. "Let it go. She's dead, and whatever you're doing can't help that."

"No. It'll help *me*."

"But not me." She looked away from him.

"Do you really care that much?"

She hesitated, seemed to fix her eyes on the gilt saints of the altar. "I probably care that much."

"You've never said that before."

"Nothing was this serious before."

"I'll come back. We'll meet somewhere—Uruguay, if we have to."

"Sure." She shuddered, deliberately and a little exaggeratedly, as if she were throwing off a chill. "A Falcon?"

He reached over and took both her hands. "That'll do."

She pulled her hands away and, in a single motion, got to her feet and gave him a chaste kiss on the forehead. She walked away down the aisle without looking back.

He watched her until she disappeared into the bright wall of daylight beyond the huge open doors of the cathedral. He sat a moment listening to the noises of the building and the street, low voices echoing, something thumping and clattering in the distant organ loft as the organist got ready to leave, the faint loudspeaker from the world of Time of War outside in the plaza. He didn't want to get up. There was an easier kind of truth here in this building than the truth he was going to have to go outside and look for, he thought as a placid priest slipped into a confessional along the wall with an old woman. He envied the old woman her small sins.

When he turned back to the group surrounding his grandfather, he knew it was time. His grandfather was subtly letting Chuy blaze him a path through the few remaining sympathizers. The cops were hiking their pants and adjusting their coats, getting ready. Esteban caught his grandfather's eyes and smiled. The old man's face seemed to relax ever so slightly. And Esteban bolted.

Chuy managed to get a hand on him as he charged past the end of the pew, but Esteban wrenched free. One on one, Chuy could stop him. But he was a dozen years older. If Esteban could just gain running room, he knew he was safe.

He bulldozed a slight, old woman in a wig, who screamed and threw herself at her husband, a bundle of sticks even older and slighter than she was. The two of them went down in a heap. An overdressed little girl saw him coming and dove for the safety of a pew. He heard a man shout behind him, but he kept going, his feet loud as hooves on the marble floor. The wall of light was what he had to reach, the wall of light and the crowd.

And then the barricade-manning police sergeant and his two undercops were silhouetted in the light ahead of him, crouching, like goalies in a soccer match. He saw one of them reach for his holster. Esteban feinted, made as if he were going to avoid them and head around the last pew and up the other aisle toward the chapel his mother had left through. But he had to slow down to do it. And as he did, he caught a glimpse of Chuy not a dozen paces behind him and closing. The feint had cost him his lead.

As he skidded around the last pew he came face-to-face with a terrified black-gowned woman the size of a Mercedes. She screamed and threw her hands up in front of her face, and Esteban grabbed for her pearls. When the strand popped, most of them spewed like grapeshot. But not all. Esteban managed to hold on to a handful. And to fling them, just as Chuy rounded the pew behind him. Chuy's feet went out from under him like a cow's in a hailstorm.

The stunned cops were no obstacle after that. Esteban went for the one with his pistol drawn and spun him out of the way as neatly as a bowling pin.

Ahead of him, the crowd surged, vivaing. The blessed, hiding crowd.

Esteban was certain the cabbie thought he was mad, having him drive up and down the Costera Boulevard along the river for nearly an hour. But he let the cabbie's voice soothe him with its ramblings about the upcoming World Cup games and the rumors that the pope was going to come and settle the war, and he planned. Adela would have made it to Bariloche by tonight if she'd left on time. Already he was a day late for whatever it was she had meant to do there. If he left now, he'd need at least a day and a night's driving time to make it. He couldn't do it, not without stopping, not in the shape he'd let himself get into. So he'd make it sometime Sunday morning at the earliest. Would that be too late?

But damn it, too late for what?

It was early in the ski season, it was too cold for boating on the lakes, and with the war on, too, the place would be nearly deserted. What in hell could she want to find in a deserted ski lodge on the Chilean border in the Andes, of all places? Something important enough to be killed over?

And the most obvious fact sat before him like a rhinoceros, staring him down. Whoever had killed Adela to keep her from going to Bariloche must have known what she was going there to find. And would be there ahead of him.

The last long, sharp winter shadows of dusk cut across the narrow streets of the old San Nicolás section of the city center when the cab dropped him at the Forest Hills Bar and Whiskeria. He made the cabbie leave him a little north so he could come upon the place slowly. The Forest Hills was only a block off Florida, but he could have been in another world. The streets here were soot-stained, the sidewalks cracked. The restaurants were cheap chophouses and dim Chinese places, the shops empty and dusty, the people more polyestered than cashmered. From a record store to the south, on Lavalle, *Bolero* blared for a time, then gave way to the Beatles. It was the edge of the bleakest hour of the day, the empty time just before the teahouses and *confiterías* began to fill with people beginning the long, easy slide toward late dinners of *churrasco* steaks and thick sausages and spitted, crisped rolls of *matambre* beef and kid and good Mendoza wines—the worst time of the day, just before the best time.

But now was the best time for what Esteban needed. The Forest Hills was empty except for an old woman at a table, a dwarf at the bar, and Caroline. She didn't belong here; no one would know her. He'd chosen it for that. He stood outside the dingy window and watched her sip a whiskey, her slim hands locked around the glass as if it were heavy as cast iron. He regretted involving her in this even as much as he had.

He stepped back into a doorway as a squad car passed, a familiar dark-over-light-blue Falcon. The two patrolmen in it looked bored. If there was a bulletin out on him, they weren't looking for him here. At least he had that to be grateful for.

Inside the Forest Hills, he managed a smile as he slipped into the chair across from Caroline. She answered it warily.

"You're early," he said.

"You're late."

"Any trouble?"

"Nope. Not many tourists around these days. No lines at the Hertz people."

The waiter started for the table, but Esteban waved him away. "I can't stay here long," he said to Caroline, half in explanation, half in apology. "It's a long drive."

"I know. I'll take first shift." She lowered her eyes, then put her glass down nervously. But when she looked back up at him, what he saw in her eyes was defiance, not nervousness, as if she were daring him to say no. "I didn't want to go back to the studio so I stopped and bought us heavy coats. And changes of underwear, and toothbrushes. I hate it when people's teeth and underwear get dirty. It's all in the car. Whatever else we need we can get in Bariloche."

"No," he said.

The dare hung on in her eyes. "I've never been to Bariloche. They say it's like Switzerland."

"Give me the keys," he said.

"Rent your own car."

"I can't do that. They might check."

"And they won't check to find out if I've rented one when they figure things out?"

"They're stupid. I'll be out of town by then. And you'll be here to make excuses."

"Not me," she said. "I'm going to Bariloche."

"Damn it, why?"

"I'm your fiancée. You said so. Whither thou goest, *guapo*. I'll be thirty soon—I might not get another chance."

She'd closed him out, had shut the door on him. He knew that it would be like this from now on—parry and thrust—no matter what he said to her. So many of her motives were like her life before she'd met him: closed to the public. And that was the tacit condition she made. Without her ever having said it, he knew that if he pushed too hard she'd cut and run. Love me, love my locked doors.

He shoved away from the table, surrendering. "Where's the car?"

She stood. "Follow me." She took a few steps toward the door, then stopped. "Look," she said. "If you have to ask why I'm going with you, maybe I don't want to go after all."

The night hadn't brought Esteban his usual comfort as they drove out of Buenos Aires. The great shimmering and demanding signs along Nueve de Julio Boulevard, the hypnotic movie marquees, the lighted fountains, the spotlights on the obelisk—all the million lights that were his nighttime map of the city were blacked out. It's Time of War, the city's darkness had whispered at him. Time of fear and sadness. There's no relief allowed, by order of the United Argentine Armed Forces Command.

But he knew that was a lie, too. Buenos Aires was playing at war, as if the war were a World Cup soccer game. In the Malvinas, there was war. But in Buenos

Aires, there was only the pretense, the sentimentality of war. Old World War II movies clogged the television screen. Martial music crept up on you at bond rallies in restaurants, music and patriotic speakers whose clichés would make a goat puke. Journalists had never had to write about a war before, so the Sunday supplements were filled with softheaded articles about fighter pilots and spies and mothers of soldiers, articles written in a rhetoric that the writers must have raided half a century of old hyped-up war stories to find. Doleful commercials about sacrifice and fatherland assaulted you on radio and television, and no news commentator was free from the obligation somehow to work in a formula reference to the Sad Events in the Malvinas.

They were playing in the big leagues, in the finals, and at the same time trying to learn how to go about doing that. How to fight a war *correctamente*.

By the time Caroline had battled their way through the endless look-alike suburbs of Buenos Aires and into the haphazard shanties and factories of the province, Esteban was asleep. Caroline woke him to take the wheel just before dawn. They were far beyond any trace of the city, in the pampa by then. The moon was high and small and almost full. He could see only a single light in the distance, an *estancia* maybe, or a gaucho herdsman's campfire. A stream cut quietly across the road through a culvert just behind them; ostrich-plume stalks of pampas grass moved gently in the wind. There was nothing else to remind them they were in a place that men had ever inhabited: the lone and level grasslands stretched to a dim, moonlit horizon in every direction. Somewhere in the distance Esteban could make out the black, ghostly outline of a single line of poplars. The only other break in the flatness was an occasional undulation—not even really a hill—in the land, like a swell on a calm sea. Once Caroline was curled up in the backseat, falling asleep already, he paced ahead of the car a few yards to wake himself up fully. When he'd left the popping and creaking of the car's cooling engine behind, he had left behind all other sound but the chill rising and falling of the wind, too. He was the last man on earth—or the first. This is why he had never been able to leave Argentina, he told himself, *this*.

There was a ring around the moon. There might be snow before they reached the lodge. He prayed not. If there was snow in the mountains, there were no roads.

The pampa had given way to the dry moonscape of the Patagonian desert tableland as they began to rise up toward the Andes. It had been a land as endless as the pampa, it seemed, but the wind and scarce water had left behind shapes in some places as sharp and fantastic as coral reefs, or in other places soft and rounded as a woman. Almost nothing grew in the tans and browns of the earth and hills except purgatorial black rocks and thornbushes. It was late afternoon by the time they had left the tableland's dust and reached the cypresses and spruces and twisted, red-barked myrtles of the high country, the *cordillera* of the Andes. The roads were cracked and falling away into immense canyons in places as they climbed, and gigantic bushes roared madly around curves at them out of mists. But Esteban pushed the Falcon even harder, the higher they climbed. The snow was coming.

Low, thick clouds cut off the peaks of mountains, and the light was the color of concrete. They would be in the clouds soon, before they descended into Bariloche's long, green valley.

"And if it does snow?" Caroline asked, her eyes fixed on the belly of a cloud they were about to drive into.

"With luck, we can make it into Bariloche. But it's twenty kilometers of dirt road from there up to the cabin. Pepe usually plows it. If Pepe's sober. And if Pepe's plow's running. And if Pepe's wife doesn't have something better for him to do."

"Which means?"

"Guess."

"I don't want to."

The first fat flakes of snow spattered on the windshield just before they dropped down into the valley of Bariloche. Esteban gunned the Falcon as they hit the flat, more-or-less straight stretch of road before the town. His eyes ran over the forested mountains to the south, Cerro Otto, Cerro Cathedral. If it had begun snowing in the pass they just came through, it had already been snowing on those high ridges since midafternoon.

Ahead he could see a few lights already lit in Bariloche, even though dusk was more than an hour away. The great blue lake of Nahuel Haupi that Bariloche crouched beside, like a deer come to drink, echoed now the slate of the clouds. Like Switzerland, yes. What in Argentina wasn't like somewhere else, a Disneyland copy of everything the settlers had fled from? But did it have to copy the damned Alpine snowstorms, too? he thought angrily as the chalets and "casas de weekend" began to sprout along the edge of the highway.

He turned off the highway before they reached the center of the city. Pepe's house was in the old part of town, the part the Swiss and German settlers had built for themselves before the tourists came. The road turned from asphalt to cobble here, and the small windows and high stone walls that ran the length of the streets remembered people who understood cold and hard times.

"The Backside," Caroline said. "It's the French Backside, out of Lyon up toward Mont Blanc. My God, even the light is right!"

"It's imported," Esteban said, trying to recognize Pepe's door from among all the others that were hacked out of the stone walls. At last he took the chance and stopped at one house that looked more familiar than the others, something to do with a high, barred window. "Stay here," he told Caroline. "Try to look touristy if anything comes up."

Caroline put on a vapid, eager look as he slid out of the car. He blew her a kiss through the window. "Touristy," he said. "Not cretin."

"Is there a difference?" Caroline shouted after him.

He pounded the lion's-head door knocker so long, a scrawny woman from across the street came to her own door to investigate. He finally managed to get someone to open the shutter behind the small window in Pepe's door. He recognized Pepe's faded Catalan wife behind it, standing on tiptoes to see out. She didn't recognize him. He started to identify himself, but lost his chance. The shutter slammed. When it opened again, Pepe's face was behind it, whiskey blossoms glowing on his cheeks even in the weak light.

"Esteban? Esteban Molina?" he said tentatively.

"Qué tal, Pepe?"

The shutter slammed again. A rush of angry Catalan happened behind the door, first Pepe's voice, then his wife's. When the door opened, only Pepe was behind it. "She's worse than before," he said to Esteban, holding his arms wide for an embrace. "Some days she doesn't even recognize *me*."

Esteban let himself be swept into the comforting smell of Pepe's woodsmoke and red-wine embrace. When he was a child, he'd always thought of Pepe as the biggest man he'd ever known. Now, fully grown, he realized he hadn't been far wrong as Pepe's huge peasant arms crushed him.

"And la señorita Adela?" Pepe asked as he peered past Esteban toward the car. "She won't come into my house now?"

"That's not Adela," Esteban said. "Adela's not coming this weekend."

Pepe peered some more. Esteban turned and saw Caroline's hand rise up from the car window and wave. Pepe waved back. "Ah hah," he said. He looked back to Esteban, closed the door, winked, leered, and said, "Ah hah," again.

"Right," Esteban said.

"I think you're in a hurry?" Pepe said.

"In a hurry." Esteban tried to answer Pepe's leer. Pepe made no move to go dig the lodge's key out of the ancient rolltop desk that sat in the dim hallway, where Esteban knew he kept it. Instead, he reached for a bird-beaked wine *porrón* he'd apparently left on a side table when he came to answer the door. He shot a long arc of wine into his mouth as Esteban asked, mustering false casualness, "Anybody been around the lodge?"

Pepe wiped wine from his salt-and-pepper beard. "Who should have been around? Were you expecting somebody?"

"No." Esteban took the wine *porrón* Pepe offered him and arced himself a drink.

"I took a load of wood up Wednesday and aired the place out a little. My *compadre*, Raul, caretakes at the Giatina place just before the road turns off for yours. He lives there all year. You remember Raul? The *fachistas* cut his ear off in Catalonia."

"I remember Raul." The wine settled warmly into Esteban's stomach.

"I saw Raul last night. Raul would have told me if anybody had come along the road since Wednesday." He looked puzzled. "Why should anybody have come if you weren't expecting anybody, Sr. Esteban?"

"I don't know. That's why I asked."

Pepe looked even more puzzled. "Ah hah," he said.

Esteban took another arc of wine before he handed the *porrón* back. Not such a bad lawyer after all, he thought. "How are the roads?"

Pepe shook his head. "Closed. All closed onto the mountain since midday, señor. It's a hotel for you tonight, I'm afraid."

"Any plowing going on?"

"Not much. Nobody around to plow for."

"I want to get up there tonight, Pepe."

Pepe took a long pull at the *porrón,* watching Esteban with stricken eyes as he drank. "Oh, no, señor Esteban. A good warm hotel tonight, and first thing in the morning we'll get you plowed in."

"You won't plow for me now? There's time before dark."

Pepe raised his arm as if he were going to clap Esteban on the shoulder, then sighed and let it drop. "I can't. I lost it."

"Lost what?"

"The plow. In a game of *taba* with a gaucho." He flashed a smile that his stricken eyes gave the lie to. "But first thing—dawn—I'll borrow one and put it on the jeep." He crossed himself. "Before the blessed face of the Savior. First thing."

"Could I have the key?"

"Not tonight, señor. *Por favor,* not tonight."

"Look, Pepe. I'll go to a hotel," he lied. "If I find somebody there who knows where I can get the road plowed before dark, I'll do it. If not, first thing in the morning. All right?"

Pepe considered. His eyes eased. "Ah, hah," he said.

While he rummaged in his ancient desk for the key, asking questions about the family that Esteban answered with half lies, Esteban opened the shutter and watched the first snowflakes curl and dance past the bars of the window in the door.

"How good are you in snow?" Esteban asked Caroline as he made his cold fingers find the Falcon's ignition switch.

"Not much. I'm better at watching it."

"Then we're going to a hotel."

"Thank God."

"You're staying. I'm not."

"No?"

"No. I'm going to the lodge. I'll get as close as I can in the car, then walk the rest of the way."

"Pepe told you something."

"He didn't tell me anything. That's why I'm going."

Caroline thought it over. "If I'm stupid enough to have come up here with you without knowing any more about anything than I do, I suppose I should be stupid enough for that to make sense."

"Look. The only thing Pepe told me was that nobody has been up to the lodge yet. That means that we're here ahead of whoever it was—or whatever—Adela was coming up here to find. I want to stay ahead."

"Esteban—take Pepe with you."

"No. I wouldn't do that to him."

"When can he plow us in?"

"In the morning."

"Then wait. Please. I'll go with you then."

"If we can get in behind a plow in the morning, somebody else could, too." He turned to look at her. She didn't meet his eyes. Against the stone walls outside the window, her face was a marble profile.

"Is there *any*thing else about this you're not telling me, Esteban?"

"If there were, would I trust it to somebody dumb enough to come along with me on a trip like this one?"

She rested her hand on his thigh. Esteban was certain she hadn't heard him. She was locking doors again. "Will you send somebody for me in the morning?"

"As soon as Pepe has the road plowed, I'll send him back for you."

"And what if somebody makes it up to you before I do?"

"They won't—not until the roads are clear."

"If you make it, somebody else can."

He turned back onto the highway into the center of town. It was his time not to answer. If he did, he'd have to think, to admit the kinds of things to himself about what he was doing that might keep him from doing it. Things that would keep anybody who was sane from doing what he was doing—and sanity was a question he damn well didn't want to have to think about now, either.

The snow wasn't sticking to the stone plaza of Bariloche yet, but it would be soon. Already it was gathering in the angles of the peaked roofs of the dark buildings that surrounded the plaza—the Swiss clock tower, the medieval arches the road passed beneath, the cloistered and timbered movie set that was the center of town. He'd left Caroline in the varnished cedar *confitería* of the hotel Camino Real, a blank modern building as out of place in Bariloche as a spaceship in a sailing fleet. She'd been a statue, clutching a hot rum drink and giving him a smile that was trying hard to be brave.

He envied her. All along, he'd meant to contrive some way to leave her in town anyway until he knew what was waiting at the lodge. But still...he envied her.

He swung off the plaza by the clock tower. As he did, an image that had been following him ever since he left Pepe's caught up with him: Adela, no more than eight or nine, holding his father's hand beneath the clock tower, waiting to cross to the plaza and climb on the statue of the horseman. For some ridiculous, Proustian reason, that unimportant moment was the one that had stuck with him most vividly about Adela and his father and Bariloche. In the lodge, there would be other memories. But those would be blurred. There had been too many moments in the lodge; they all ran together somehow. Only Frank's image still lived in the lodge for him—Frank, who had been gone so long now that Esteban's memories of him in the lodge had had time to fix themselves, like figures in a photograph, and not be blurred by the recent past. Christ, had Frank even gotten word she was dead yet?

Knowing better, he checked the rearview mirror when he was past the clock tower to see if his father and Adela were still there. His anger congealed, packed itself like a snowball. He downshifted and swerved around a lone, battered Volkswagen with skis sticking up from its rack like antennae. The driver shook his fist at Esteban, Italian style. Esteban knew that if he stopped, he might kill the poor bastard.

The road was easy as far as the base of the mountain, but even at that, Esteban passed no other cars. You were where you were going by now—or you didn't try to go. Not with night coming. He kept the Falcon just at the edge of control: he would feel it slide on the new snow, would back off on the gas until the tires grabbed, then push it again. The forest was dark on either side of him, and already the cedars and myrtles were laced with snow, but the concrete sky still held enough light for him to see by if—when—he had to walk. But for how much longer would it last? Half an hour? Less? He eased the car out of a skid, then gunned it again.

He'd figured he could make it at least as far as the turnoff where the dirt road that led the mile or so up to the lodge left the main road to the Cerro Cathedral ski area. From there it was anybody's guess how far he'd get before he had to abandon the car—or it slid off into one of the tree-thick canyons the road skirted. He supposed he ought to take some kind of comfort in the fact that at least Pepe and Caroline would know where to look for him. Otherwise his body could lie in one of the canyons until the spring thaws came in October. He turned the heater up full and spread the down coat Caroline had bought him on the seat in front of it. Absorb that, you *cabrón,* he thought. All you can hold.

The dirt road curved sharply just after it left the main road, so that he was out of sight of the highway almost as soon as he was off it. The snow had gotten heavier as he climbed; if he'd had to stay on the highway for another two kilometers, he knew he'd have had to turn back. He switched on his headlights, which made the light in the forest seem even murkier. But the Falcon kept going, sliding, grabbing, sliding. His hopes rose. Every dozen meters he went was a dozen fewer he had to walk.

Until he hit the first truly sharp rise.

The Falcon lost traction almost as soon as it started to climb. Esteban jerked his foot off the gas—but too late. The road curved around a promontory and cut sharply upward to the right toward the canyon the lodge sat in. To the left, the land dropped away into a valley now invisible in the snow. Esteban remembered that once there had been a wooden barrier at the edge of the road. Now there was nothing, only white space with the dim outlines of the tops of a few trees visible below the level of the road. And the car was drifting backward, drifting as slowly and easily as a leaf on a pond toward the empty whiteness.

He gunned the engine again. The tires spun and the car began to plane on the snow, to drift faster and to turn itself sideways. Esteban hit the brakes. The car stopped, inched backward, then stopped again. But uneasily, grudgingly.

Esteban sat very still and cut the engine. The heater fan wound itself down last of all. An utter silence took its place, broken only by creaks and pops from the car that sounded loud as gunshots.

He knew he had to move. But if he were to try to get out of the driver's door, he'd step into only air and falling snow. As easily as he could, he set the emergency brake, then picked up the down coat and began to slide toward the passenger door. He got as far as the transmission hump before the car moved again.

He stopped, his loud breathing fogging the windows so that the outside world was disappearing shape by shape into a gray blur of crepuscular light. It was like being buried, he thought in a quick flash of panic, like opening his eyes and finding himself beside Adela. He made a sound, half grunt, half cry, and grabbed for the door handle. The door flung open, rebounded, and he slammed his open palm into it. He felt fiberboard crumple in the door panel from the impact, and a stab of pain. He shoved off from the transmission hump, clutching the coat to his chest, and dove for the snow.

He hit and rolled. He wanted to get as far from the car as possible, find as much clear air as he could.

He came to rest in the snow-clogged drainage ditch beside the road. Even before his vision cleared, he caught the slow shift of motion that was the car. It was moving away from him, evenly at first, then in little jerks as it hit rocks under the snow at the edge of the road. The only sound was the *whump* it made when its rear tire slipped over the edge of the road into the whiteness.

And then it caught, rocking and balancing as delicately as a tightrope walker on the edge of the cliff.

What would he have done to that balance, he thought, if he'd still been in the car? He lay until his breathing calmed, not thinking about the answer. When he got to his feet and started up the hill, he didn't look back at the car. If it were there in the morning, Pepe could get it free for him. But now the snow was coming into the black street oxfords he'd worn for Adela's funeral, now he had to make his shaking fingers find the buttons and zippers on the down coat, now he had to get to the lodge, to a fire, to his dead sister's appointment.

At first, when he saw the horse through the trees in the last of the ashy light, he told himself it had to be a guanaco or a wild llama. It was standing still as the saplings of the forest, an indistinct shape in the shed his father had built for his own horse when he had come here to ride in the summers. But as Esteban approached, it turned its head to watch him, probably as surprised as he was. They stood staring at each other a long moment. Then the horse, as if it wanted no part of anything that came as snow-covered and hulking out of the forest as Esteban, took a step backward into the darkness of the shed. Esteban came closer, wishing he'd taken the time to buy a flashlight in Bariloche. But as his eyes adjusted to the darkness of the shed, he saw that the horse was well fed and recently groomed, a big dappled mare—no horse a peasant would have, and God knew there would be no cause for a gaucho to have set himself up in these mountains. Could it belong to Raul, Pepe's one-eared friend? No—he wouldn't stable his horse a mile or more away from his house in a snowstorm.

On the wall hung a saddle, a plain military-style saddle. Esteban hefted it down and took it outside to check it for markings. There were none, not even a serial number or initials, as if it had deliberately been made untraceable.

The lodge was farther on yet, just over a ridge of rock. Esteban put the saddle back and pressed himself close to the warmth of the horse. It was clear—whoever had stabled the horse here could only be in one place: the lodge. So Adela had been expecting a someone, not a something. And whoever it was *had* gotten here first, after all, and had come in such a way that no one could possibly know he (or she) was here.

And would want to make sure that no one but Adela knew he had ever been here.

That meant one thing. Esteban had to find whoever was here before they found him. And had to make certain he was in control when they did meet. *Virgen purísima,* he wished to hell he had a gun, a knife, a set of gaucho's *boleadores* to throw—anything. Control—crap!

He left the warmth of the horse and headed for the ridge of rock between himself and the lodge. Even if for no other reason than that he'd freeze to death out here, he had to go on. And not by the road now, not by any way he could be easily spotted.

The smell of woodsmoke, the sharp, rich smell of burning spruce, reached him before he topped the ridge and saw the lighted windows of the lodge. Only the barest daylight remained in the woods now, and long, uneven rectangles of white Coleman lantern light splayed themselves out onto the snow from the lodge. It was a familiar place, a place that should have been comforting, with its peaked roof and broad porches and bark-slabbed walls that melted into the trees of the woods. But there was no comfort to it now. It was a strange house in a dark forest, a place out of all the grim tales used to frighten children with. He remembered those tales now, understood the fear again.

Only one chimney had smoke coming from it, the one in the living room. The other, the one that rose from the fireplace in the master bedroom, wasn't in use yet. He checked the windows that he knew gave from the kitchen and the guest bedroom. There was no light lit in either room. That left only the sleeping loft, where he and Adela and Frank had been exiled when they were kids. He couldn't see the loft's tiny window from this side of the house, but he dismissed the possibility that whoever was in the house could be up there—not in that cold, dark place, when there was a fire and a light in the living room.

He was grateful for one thing, he thought as he scrambled down through the loose stones of the ridge, his breath short in the thin air. He didn't have the car. If he had, he'd have sounded like a regiment of tanks approaching in this silence. Even as it was, he winced at every squeaking footstep on the new snow.

A set of french doors opened onto the porch on the side nearest him, doors whose draperies hadn't been shut against the night yet. At the porch, he went down on all fours; if he could keep near enough the wall, and low enough, he should be invisible, he figured, until he could scan the living room. And then what? he asked himself. Then what?

The living room was high, beamed, baronial—rough wood walls, a stone fireplace the size of a coal mine, heavy mahogany desks, overstuffed and tweedy couches, plenty of rattan. European and comfortable, built in his father's image of himself. And now, empty.

Or it seemed to be empty. A high-backed wing chair had been pulled out of its spot beside his father's old desk and sat facing the fireplace. There could be somebody sitting in it—there *had* to be somebody sitting in it. Asleep? Dozing? Even if not that, Esteban prayed, at least lulled. He would need seconds, no more.

He checked the crack between the french doors. It was clear: no bolt showing. And they swung inward, something that could save him another piece of a second. He edged backward, toward the woodbox.

When he picked up the length of kindling wood, he noticed his hand was bleeding. When had he cut it? Scrambling down the ridge? Rolling from the car? He was grateful for the numbness in his hands, wished it would spread to his mind, and he watched himself wrap his stiff fingers around the length of wood, just bigger than a billy stick.

He made certain his hand was on the doorknob and turning already before he sprang. Warm air slapped at him like foliage when he was inside the room. He was at the wing-back chair in less than half a dozen pounding strides, the kindling wood raised and ready. Don't strike, he told himself. Wait. Pin him if you can, see first.

But there was nothing to pin, nothing to strike at in the empty chair.

He whirled, his eyes leaping first toward the dark hallway, then along the tree limbs his father had had bent into banisters to lead to the loft. The end of the loft hung over the living room like a balcony, and light from the fire and Coleman climbed through its twisted railings and onto the ceiling like reflections from a shattered mirror.

Esteban stood paralyzed. Snow skittered toward him from the open french doors. He watched the figure materialize from the darkness of the loft as if it were a chunk of the night itself breaking off. "Dear God," he said under his breath, as he let the kindling wood dangle loosely beside him.

"I never could sleep anywhere but up there," Frank said to him in English, shoving the automatic pistol back into his belt. "Habit, I suppose. And you, little brother, are as damned noisy as ever you were."

Chapter Three

"It's rusty," Frank said as he struggled for a word in Spanish. "My own Spanish is rusty. Never was out of Argentina till I was nearly thirty, and I'm losing my Spanish. Balls."

"Say it in English," Esteban told him.

Frank kicked a log into place in the fireplace. In his riding boots, leaning against the mantelpiece with a drink in his hand, he looked to Esteban as if he should just be back from British colonial service in Injia, telling stories about tiger hunting. Esteban was trying to fit him into the shape of his memory of him. He was still as "imperially slim" as he had been—Adela, in adoration, had taken that phrase out of a poem to describe him. His features were as sharp, his hair as dark (though touched with gray at the temples; trust Frank to look distinguished as he got older, Esteban thought). He was still the "Argentine" in the family, ironically much more so than Esteban or Adela were, except for his pale blue eyes, as if some black Irish had crept into the bloodline.

But there were differences: a slight stoop to his shoulders, pores a little coarser in his face, some wrinkles where there had been none before. His familiar staccato laugh had slowed down now to the pace of someone pounding a nail with a hammer and sounded forced. And he seemed to laugh without smiling, which struck Esteban as somehow unnatural, unnerved him. But it was his eyes that had changed the most, in some way Esteban couldn't yet define. There had been a purity in them before, a distance, that had made people assume he was going to be a priest when he was younger. Now there was an edge, a hardness, a feeling that the distance had deepened so that you weren't sure he really was looking at *you*, but rather at some interpretation of you that came from *behind* the pale eyes.

Esteban tried to dismiss the uneasiness he felt with him. He put it down to the situation, to the fear that still hung around the corners of his mind from the trip up here.

"No, Spanish. I can't afford to slip out of it now," Frank said. He looked Esteban over, as if he were deciding something about him. "I suppose I've either got to explain to you or kill you, don't I, Stevie."

"Adela got both."

Frank turned away and gave the fire another kick, viciously this time. "God *damn* it. No, that's *not* it. If Adela had told somebody about my coming, then why am I here? Why are you here? Don't you know they'd have pounced on both of us? And Mother—why didn't they go for Mother, too? She knew I was coming."

"Did she know why?"

"Not specifically. Neither of them did. The message went by courier from Uruguay. We couldn't take the risk of letting too much out."

"Then it could have been the courier."

"Not a chance. He came right back to the British embassy in Montevideo. He'd never have done that if he'd talked to anybody he shouldn't have."

"None of that's much help, Paco."

Frank gave him a distant smile. "Nobody's called me that in years."

"OK. Frank, then."

"No. I like it." He moved away from the fireplace and sat on the couch beside Esteban, as if he needed to be close to him to be able to keep talking. "All right, here goes. See if *you* can make sense out of it. Just listen, let me finish before you say anything."

Esteban nodded.

"They dropped me just across the border in Chile, by

helicopter. The Chileans were only too glad to have a horse waiting for me, and a guide as far as the border. The more the Argentines—us, I suppose—are kept busy in the Falklands, the less they're going to be able to stir up trouble for Chile about the Beagle Islands. 'Chile in the Pacific, Argentina in the Atlantic,' all that rot. Which God knows you've heard enough about unless the beloved fatherland has changed more in the past few years than I think it has. From the border I was here in a day and a half. By yesterday. Just about the time of Adela's funeral, I imagine. We would have left here in the morning."

"For where?"

"I'm getting to that. Just *listen,* damn it. We were going to Comodoro Rivadavia. And then to the Falklands, or at least I was going to the Falklands. She was going back to Buenos Aires. Once she got me onto the base, I had these—" He pulled what looked like a set of military orders from his shirt pocket, and held them up long enough for Esteban to see Jaime Mondragon's signature at the bottom. "It was perfect: Jaime Mondragon's fiancée takes me to the base; Jaime Mondragon's signature gets me a flight to Port Stanley. When it was all over, I was supposed to vanish onto the islands and wait for the landing force. That simple."

"When what was all over, Paco?"

"The missiles. The bloody Exocets. I was supposed to blow them before they could be used against the landing force. Nothing to be done about the ones here on the mainland that the Mirages carry. God knows where they're stored, or even just how many there are. But I know just where they are on the Falklands, the land-based ones. Good people, the kelpers. Patriots."

"And after you blew them—what about Adela?"

"She would have been on a boat across the river to Montevideo before anyone figured any of it out. She and Mother."

"Before or after the wedding?"

"Don't be an ass, little brother. There wasn't going to be any wedding, of course. She was sent some information that made her change her mind—and that made her agree to meet me here. And that made her certain she couldn't stay in Argentina any longer, no matter whether she helped me or not. So it really didn't make any difference that she was going to help me. She wasn't really risking anything she hadn't already lost."

"What information? What the hell did you tell her?"

"I didn't tell her anything, personally. And don't ask for more than you want to know, Stevie. When the time comes that it doesn't matter anymore, I'll tell you."

"Fine. You simply arrange for Adela to find out something that fucks her whole life up—that might have gotten her killed, for all I know—and for what? Just to make her desperate enough to join in some cock-eyed scheme to blow up some damned French missiles for a comic opera war. That sounds like something that ought to be against the Geneva convention, Brother. And I'm what? Not to be trusted with information my little sister could handle?"

"No, it's got nothing to do with trust. I think I know who might have killed that little sister, that's all." Frank's voice was heavy with angry sarcasm. "When I know for certain, you can do whatever in hell you want with any kind of information you want. Until then, I just don't want you screwing up anything."

"Oh? I'd screw it up?"

"I don't know. I don't want to take the chance."

Esteban shoved up off the couch and went for another drink. He didn't want it. He only had to move, to get away from Frank's goddamn superiority, from this jumble of a story out of a bad World War II propaganda film. A story that was coming from his own brother, a story that his brother's presence here in this end-of-the-earth ski lodge made real. A story that his own presence made real. "Is that why you didn't come to me if you needed help?" he asked as he poured himself a dollop of Old Smuggler and filled the rest of the glass with seltzer. "I couldn't be trusted not to screw it up?"

"Think, Steven. What good would you have been? Did my information come to me wrong? Aren't you suspected of every kind of antifatherland activity in their book?"

"No. Your information didn't come to you wrong."

"Adela was beyond all suspicion. I had to involve Mother to get to Adela. And you were going to be told in time to get out of the country with them. I swear that."

"Thanks. Whether I wanted to leave the country or not."

"It had to be done. It *had* to. Do you know what one of those *maldito* Exocets can do to a ship? How many men it can take with it? If there's one single thing that it matters more to do than anything else in this war, it's to stop those things from getting off the ground."

Esteban sat beside Frank again, studying him, trying to see if there was any kind of bridge at all left between them. "Frank. Now *you* listen. I don't care who wins this war. Can you understand me?"

"Yes, you care."

"Christ."

"You care because we're both the old man's sons. Unless you're somebody I don't know at all anymore, you hate what's happened to this country as much as he did—and as I do. It's not likely, but if, just if, the bastards in the soldier and sailor suits who run things in Buenos Aires were to win this thing, or even make a 'heroic' showing, there'll be no stopping them. They've *got* to lose, so Argentina can win. *Comprende?*"

Frank was talking slowly, reasonably now, as he had when they were children and he'd explained something to Esteban like the rules of *pato* or cricket. Esteban had always trusted that reasonableness, that clarity—had found security in it. But now there was something— what?—a strident tone in Frank's voice that gave the lie to the reasonableness. Or maybe it didn't. Maybe they were just both tired and tight and afraid. Frank was his brother, for Christ's sake. What the hell was he doing judging him after twelve years of not seeing him?

"Why you, Paco?" he asked. "Why did they come to you for this?"

"They need an Argentine for it. I'm the right class, have the right connections. It's simple."

"That's not enough."

"All right. I know what I'm doing. I've been working with the British army—and the Americans. Call it making up for some of the damage Che Guevara did when *he* left Argentina. I've been training people, Central Americans."

"Great God."

"No, Stevie. Not what you're thinking. Not those ex-Somoza guardsmen. Not that bunch of butchers and swine."

"Then who?"

"People who still believe in something—and there are a few of them left. There's got to be something between Castro and Somoza, something decent."

"And they'll stay decent after they learn to blow things up?"

"They have to." He got to his feet abruptly. The violence of the move—the violence of his voice—surprised Esteban. Frank flung the remains of his drink into the fire. The fire hissed, and smoke puffed and snaked out into the room as Frank leaned back against the mantel and took a deep breath. "Look, Steve," he said, his pale eyes almost blanks in the Coleman light. "You're going to help me. You're going to get me onto that base at Comodoro Rivadavia."

"Why don't you go back, Paco? You've still got the horse. Go back."

"I'll go on without you. You know that."

"Then do, goddamn it."

"My chances of getting caught trying to slip onto the base—what are they?"

"Big."

"And if I do get caught? What happens to you and Mother?"

Esteban sat a moment, letting that sink in, trying not to believe it. "That's blackmail, Paco," he said quietly.

"No. It's fact. If I'm caught, I'll be dead and you and Mother will be implicated in spite of anything any of us can do. You might as well help me. That way we all at least have a chance."

"If you got forged orders for a flight to the Falklands, why not to get onto the base, too?"

"Why take the risk? Adela's I.D. could get her anywhere in the country—except the Falklands."

"I don't have Adela's I.D."

"You've been to see Mondragon once. Somebody in

power on that base knows you or will remember you. You can at least get past the gate."

"Not bloody likely."

"But possible. At least possible."

"Maybe. Barely maybe."

"You're a lawyer, little brother. You can do it. That's all I ask. Get me onto the base. I'll take it from there."

Estaban let his eyes wander back to the french doors he'd come in through. The snow was swirling heavily onto the porch now, drifting against the doors. Caroline would have had dinner by now, would be leafing through one of the hotel's magazines as she waited for the time to go up to bed. He remembered the envy he'd felt for her, knew in truth that he'd hoped he wouldn't find what Adela had been coming here to find. Then for a day, two days, he and Caroline could escape from the confusion and the Time of War—could have a piece of the honeymoon Adela would never have now. Could pretend that the world was not such a bad place, was in order again. Just for a little while.

But he had found what Adela had been coming for. The man whom, by all rights, he should love more than any other man he knew. But this was a man he wasn't sure he even knew anymore. Seeing him, listening to him was like going back to a house you'd lived in once, that was now lived in by somebody else. The same, but all changed.

And his own life was about to change in a way he'd never have considered in his wildest imagination. And there was not a goddamn thing he could do about it, except to try to survive it. Frank was right; he was trapped. Yet in an odd way he felt relieved. To survive was to act, to *do* something at last. And if there was something to fear in this, even that was better than the knot of anger and frustration in his gut.

But Caroline, knowing nothing—what about her? If he was involved, so was she. They'd surely come for her too. Sweet Jesus.

"There's somebody else," he told Frank. "If I get out of the country, she's got to be gotten out, too."

Frank visibly relaxed. "Anybody I know?"

"No."

"Adela's place is vacant. The plan was to take three people out."

"Your word—as my brother."

"My word. As your brother."

Esteban held his breath, let it out slowly. "We'll leave at daylight."

"You get up earlier these days than you used to, *chico*."

"Tell me one thing more, just out of curiosity. How the hell did you get Mondragon's signature on those papers?"

Frank dropped his eyes from Esteban's and turned to the fire again. "Adela got it for us," he said. He kicked another log and sparks shot up the chimney. "She sent us a copy of their wedding license, and we forged it."

The snow wore itself out, gave way to the moon just before dawn. Esteban knew; he was awake to see it. He'd fallen into an exhausted sleep watching the fire in the master bedroom—his father's old bedroom—make leaping shadows on the ceiling. But he woke shivering a few hours later, even under the thick Indian wool blankets he'd dug out of the closet. He was almost grateful for the cold, the exhaustion, the silence of the forest and the mountains that he could feel surrounding him like the fresh moonlight. It was no time, no place, for clear thinking. Fear was natural here; you almost didn't have to be afraid of it here, you could almost pretend that all you had to do was turn the page in the book of fairy tales and the fear would vanish.

Except that when he walked into the icy kitchen at dawn and found Frank pouring steaming water into a silver-inlaid gourd to make green-tea *maté*, the troll of fear hung on, dug its claws deeper.

"Sleep well?" Frank held the *maté* gourd out to him.

"Did *you?*" Esteban sucked the hot, bitter warmth of the *maté* up through the silver straw. He had a quick image of himself and Frank, teenagers, on horseback beside his father the day they'd bought the gourd and straw from the Indian who made it, far back in a blue-hazed valley of the *altiplano*.

"I've given up noticing," Frank said. He took the gourd and straw from Esteban and refilled it with water.

They'd keep passing it back and forth that way, gaucho fashion, until all the taste of the *maté* was gone, as they'd done on school mornings as kids. "God, I've missed *maté*. They sell something in London that's an approximation, but not a very good one. Look, there are some old heavy socks up in the loft and a pair of boots that probably belong to Mondragon. Wear them. I don't want your toes falling off."

"They didn't last night on the way up," Esteban said.

"You didn't have to dig a car out of the snow and get it down from the Andes last night."

"Pepe will be along with the plow—he says."

Frank scowled as he emptied the gourd again. "That ought to be good news. But it's not. Is he still a *borrachón?*"

"He still drinks, yes."

"Then he still talks too much. He can't know I've been here."

"He won't. I'll handle Pepe if I have to."

The straw made an ugly noise as Frank pulled at the dregs of the *maté*. He gave Esteban a sharp look that matched the noise. "I hope so, little brother. For all our sakes." His free hand trailed down and absently rested on the holster of the automatic pistol he'd been wearing last night—that Esteban wondered if he'd slept in.

Frank saw Esteban's eyes follow his hand down to the pistol, then their eyes met. "Don't even think about it, Frank," Esteban said. "Not Pepe. I'm warning you, my brother."

Outside, they led the dappled horse, its warm breath misting in the cold. The morning was orange, and an easy wind blew snow in powdery flurries from the spruces. Only the wind, their own crunching footsteps, and the gentle blowing noises the horse made to keep itself company as it picked its way through the snow broke a silence that seemed as vast as the white land that stretched out below them. There was snow as far into the crinkled distance as they could see—toward Chile to the west, Bolivia to the north, the Antarctic wilderness far to the south. Only the valley floor was spared; here and there among brown fields it still held on to some of its heavy green from the summer, and the lake shone a sharp, deepening blue as the sun climbed and the light turned from orange to pink to clear.

Half a mile—a slow half mile—from the lodge, Bariloche came into view. Esteban tried to make out Pepe's jeep among the tiny cars that crept along the road from town. He hoped Pepe had finished the *porrón* of wine last night—had finished a half dozen *porrónes*. And would sleep, sleep till nightfall.

He picked out the clock tower and behind it the hotel. Caroline would be getting up soon, waiting for him. He stopped imagining then.

"Christ Almighty, Stevie," Frank said as they rounded the curve and saw the Falcon.

"I never was much at parallel parking." The Falcon teetered in a gust of wind. Snow blew off it and vanished into the valley.

First they dug. The uncrusted snow swept easily away from the wheels of the car to the middle of the road. The snow was deep enough now that once the car was free and centered, they should be able to dig tracks at least far enough down the incline behind it for it to roll back to leveler, safer ground. And they had the horse. First to pull the car back onto the road, then to hold it steady as it eased back down the hill.

They lashed the car to a tree across the road in what both of them knew was probably a useless attempt to keep it more stable as Frank eased himself inside and let the parking brake out. But it held—for the moment it held—and Frank slipped back out of the car onto the snow laughing his slow, humorless laugh, red-faced and shaking.

The horse fought for footing on the frozen ground beneath the snow. It pawed, slipped, protested—but pulled. Its eyes were wide as Frank stood beside it with a knife ready to cut the line if the car went over the edge. Frank coaxed, while Esteban stood in front and kept a steady pressure on the reins, a pressure that made the horse try to jerk the bit out of its mouth, and slaver. The reins wanted to slip out of the gloves, stiff with age, that Esteban had found at the lodge. For a moment, he wrapped the reins around his hand. Then, with a shudder, he loosened them; if the car should go and Frank didn't cut the horse away quickly enough...

The car shifted a few inches closer to the edge then stopped again, as if it had hit a buried root or rock. Frank slapped the horse's flank and yelled in English, "Pull, you bastard!" The horse rolled its eyes, neighed— and reared.

The reins leapt out of Esteban's hands. But as the horse came down again and its weight heaved against the line to the car, the car moved, lurched forward. Not far, but enough. All four wheels sat firmly on the road!

And they heard the snowplow.

Frank slapped the horse again. This time it didn't rear, but threw itself forward as if it were trying to break loose from quicksand. And the car moved again, a meter, then two meters—and into the tracks they'd dug for it.

"That's it," Frank said. He jerked the door open, set the parking brake, and then rounded the car to slash the line that ran to the horse. The line snapped apart with a ping, and Esteban lunged for the reins. He and the horse fought each other, first toward the edge of the cliff, then toward the trees. By the time Frank slogged through the snow to them, he had his pistol out. Esteban heard the snowplow change gears as it started up the incline just around the curve—and then something else, another engine, another set of gears following the snowplow.

"Don't shoot him," Esteban shouted at Frank. "They'll hear it in goddamn Buenos Aires from here!"

Frank hesitated. The horse shook its head hard a last time and stood still. "Give him to me," Frank said, and jerked the reins out of Esteban's hands. He ran his eyes up and down the wall of trees along the hill back toward the lodge. There was a break in them a half dozen meters ahead—not a big one, but it was enough. "Get rid of Pepe," Frank yelled over his shoulder as he plunged forward with the horse. "Or I will."

Pepe's wide, pocked face showed nothing at all as his snow-flecked jeep rounded the curve and he spotted Esteban. And as the other jeep, the one with the two blue-overcoated, white-belted policemen in it, ground to a

67

stop behind Pepe, Esteban understood why. Esteban threw a quick look behind him. Frank was gone.

Pepe lumbered out of his jeep ahead of the two policemen, his face set in the same stricken expression it had had yesterday when Esteban had asked him about his "lost" snowplow blade. He got to Esteban only in time to whisper, "They came to my house. They made me take them," before the first cop was beside him.

The cop saluted. "Esteban Molina-Knifeton?" he said with all the sense of melodrama Esteban imagined Stanley had mustered when he greeted Livingston.

"That's a good guess," Esteban said. The other cop was taking his time getting to them. He stood and studied the tracks Esteban's Falcon had made for a moment, then kept coming. When he reached the spot where the horse had trampled the snow, he squatted, then let his eyes follow the flattened snow to the point where the horse had stopped struggling and individual hoofprints began. He stood again and began following the prints. He stopped, Esteban knew, when he saw that the tracks led off through the break in the trees.

"You're in danger, Sr. Molina," the first cop said. "You shouldn't be here." He was younger than Esteban and had a nose as pointed as a rat's.

"Am I charged with anything?"

The cop's nose twitched. Esteban imagined long whiskers. "You're in danger, señor. That's all. We were asked to find you."

"Fine. Now you've found me. *Muchas gracias*. There was a problem with the car, but that's dealt with now."

"Not that danger, señor. We have to ask you to come back to Bariloche with us."

The other cop broke in. He was older than the first and had the dark, heavy-lidded face of an Andean Indian. "How did you resolve the problem with your car, señor?"

"It was stuck. A man with a horse helped me."

"Did you know the man, señor?"

Esteban grabbed for the most likely lie. "Yes. His name is Raul."

"Raul who lives just at the bottom of the hill and has only one ear?"

"Yes."

"Raul has no horse, señor." The cop took another step toward the break in the trees. He unsnapped his white leather holster.

Frank must have crept through the woods while they were talking until he had ended up just beside the Indian-faced cop. When he fired, the range was almost point-blank. The bullet caught the cop in the neck, from the side, and slashed his spinal cord away so that his head flopped forward as if he'd just spotted a coin on the ground. He stood that way a moment, while the sound of the pistol echoed away into the valley. Then as he fell, Esteban dove for the ground. Another shot flashed from the woods, but the rat-faced cop had already flung himself behind the Falcon. Pepe hadn't moved; he stood still as a stump, wondering and thick-headed as mud.

"Get down, Pepe," Esteban yelled at him. Pepe looked at him as if he were trying to figure out who was yelling on such a fine morning, and Esteban crouched and sprang for him. As he did, the rat-faced cop, panicking, whirled and fired wildly at him. He missed, but Pepe glared at him, as if the cop had awakened him from a wine-happy sleep. He reeled when Esteban slammed into him, but kept his feet. Esteban rolled away from him.

As he scrambled back to his knees, he saw Pepe towering over the cop, who was frantically trying to get his pistol unjammed. Pepe watched the cop in curiosity a few seconds, said "Ah-hah" softly, then reached for him. He turned the cop away from him by the shoulders, put his huge knee into the cop's back, and jerked. When the man's back snapped, it sounded like a cork popping out of a wine bottle. Pepe turned him around again and held him by the throat until he stopped twitching. Then, as if he'd lost interest, he flung the man away over the edge of the cliff. Esteban listened for a moment until the crashing sounds in the trees below stopped.

Pepe turned to him and blinked. In the silence, Esteban heard only the whinnying of the horse and his own heavy breath.

"Frank!" he shouted. "Frank, goddamn you. It's over. Come out."

There was no answer.

"Frank," he shouted again. "If you hurt Pepe, you'll have to kill me, too, you bastard."

Esteban started when Frank stepped out of the bushes a dozen meters away, brushing snow off himself as if he'd only been for a piss. He glanced at the body of the cop he'd shot and turned away, his face a mask.

"Madre de Dios," Pepe said. His eyes were the size of onions.

"Hello, Pepe," Frank said, and stuck out his hand. It was trembling.

Raul would swear, Pepe said. Two Catalans in a place like this *had* to swear for each other—who else was there? Pepe would say he had plowed the cops up to the lodge, then had left them there. He and Raul had been drinking *maté* together when they heard a shot. By the time they got up to the lodge, everything was gone— jeep, the two very esteemed policemen, everything. (Chilean bandits, no doubt Chilean bandits: the mountains were infested with them.) They wanted to investigate, but how? There were tire tracks leading from the plowed road off to the cliff over the valley, but how could two poor stiff-jointed old Catalans go down into the valley in such snow? *Ay, carajo,* it would take climbers with ropes and pitons. And days, it could well take days to find out what was down there, no?

Frank chewed at the dry skin on his lip as he listened to Pepe. Pepe was eloquent, acting out his and Raul's testimony to the cops as if he were giving an impassioned speech for Catalan autonomy. What did he care— cops were *fachistas;* hadn't he been fighting *fachistas* all his life? There was good death and bad death. He knew good death when he saw it. When he was done and had waddled back to his jeep to begin the business of plowing away all the tracks and footprints that littered the road—and of shoving the Indian cop over the edge after his *compañero*—Frank said to Esteban, "That cockeyed story won't hold, you know. The cops will see right through it."

"It'll hold long enough for what you've got to do."

"It would almost be more merciful to shoot the poor son of a bitch."

"No, it won't be that bad. They won't believe him, but what can they do? What can they prove?"

"Do they have to?"

"Something like this, yes. So far as they'll know, it's a civilian thing."

Frank walked up the road a few steps behind Pepe who, gears clashing, was plowing the last of the hoofprints away. "I'll do the horse," he said to Esteban.

"Do what to the horse?"

"You want to leave him in the woods?"

"No. I want to give him to Pepe. I'd planned on that all along."

"Pepe!" Frank shouted. "You want my horse?"

Pepe stopped the jeep and considered. "How would I explain a horse, señor?"

Frank turned back to Esteban. "I don't like it either, little brother."

"Are you sure?"

"Yes, goddamn it, I'm sure." He turned angrily and strode away up the hill.

Esteban watched until he came out of the break in the woods. The horse walked beside him, calm now, nuzzling at his shoulder. Pepe stopped the jeep and looked away over the valley. Esteban got into the Falcon, turned the radio on, and tore a page out of the logbook the Hertz people had left.

"Dear Caroline," he wrote. "I'm sorry. Everything's a mess. Pepe will see that you get to the airport, but he can't answer any questions for you. I can't see you now, and I can't even promise you you'll be safe. Get back to Bs. As. as soon as you can, but don't go home. Check into a hotel, the Dorado on Tucumán, and use another name—use Menendez, so I can find you. Don't go out if you can help it, don't talk to anybody. I'll be there in three days at the latest. If I'm not, get out of the country however you can. Go to my mother's people in London if you have to—Knifetons, in Marcus Close. Mother should be there.

"This stinks, I know it does. But I want you to be afraid. You *have* to be afraid."

He put the pencil down. The radio shifted into an old tango, *"A Media Luz,"* and Esteban heard the lines in his head: "... and everything in half-light—as soft as velvet, the half-light of love." Fine. In half-light, you told people things like this, he thought. If you had to tell them things like this at all, you held their hands in half-light. How in hell did you tell them in this brittle winter sun, on a piece of smudged Hertz logbook paper, that through no fault of their own they had to throw away their lives and start over, a stranger in somebody else's country? How did you tell a woman you've been falling in love with that you've fucked up her life forever?

When he heard the shot, he waited until Pepe ground the gears of his jeep before he looked up. The jeep jerked forward and then stopped, straining against something. After a moment, it moved again, jerkily. The dappled form of the horse slid away from the plow and flopped over the edge of the cliff, legs flailing like pipes on a broken bagpipe.

"I'm sorry," Esteban wrote. "I love you." He got out of the car to give the note to Pepe. Frank waited for him in the road, lost in the distances behind his eyes, holstering his pistol.

Chapter Four

"Here's how it is," Frank said as they wound through the flat, tin-roofed nowhere of the outskirts of Comodoro Rivadavia. They'd left the day behind them somewhere in the black stones and thornbushes of the Patagonian desert. It was past three in the morning now; even the guards on the roadblocks outside town had given their I.D. only a sleepy look and waved them on into the smears of mist that hung in the air. The base would be different—Frank's nervous chatter told Esteban that they both knew that. "I tell them in England that of course we have *some* things here that aren't copies of somewhere else. I tell them about our national dog, for example, about how tough it is and how we bred it especially to hunt Argentine javelina, and how it doesn't exist anywhere else. Totally ours, I tell them. And then I tell them what we call it—*dogo*—and I say it slowly, *dog-o*, so they'll get it. Usually they don't."

"You really hate us, don't you, Paco." He'd been only half listening, trying to invent convincing lines for the guards at the air base.

"Us? Argentina? God, little brother. *I'm* Argentinian. What I hate is the goddamn pretense and cant and snobbery and mammoth inferiority complex and mania for being anything but Argentine. You remember Sarmiento? What was it, a hundred or so years ago, when he was busy sucking up to old Horace Mann and

Lincoln in the States and wanting to come home and be president of the country and writing his stuff about 'Civilization and Barbarity,' and telling the world what barbarity Argentina was capable of? He proved we were barbarians this way—he said he'd been up to Cordoba a while before, and in the whole second city of Argentina, he couldn't find one single man in a European frock coat. So there we bloody were: barbarians were barbarians because they didn't *look* like civilized people.

"So what did we do? We took him seriously. We built Buenos Aires to be a mongrel, part Leningrad, part Paris, part Rome, part Washington—a lovely, impressive mongrel, but a mongrel nonetheless. We put on frock coats with a vengeance, till we out-Bond Bond street now. We got busy being more European than the Europeans—or it's more American than the, etc., lately. We even exterminated the Indians the way the Americans did! And, God help us, Buenos Aires is the only city in the Spanish world that speaks Spanish with a goddamn Italian accent. And now we're even fighting a war that should have been fought by Europeans a century ago—and losing it, like good Italians would. They talk about us in England as if we were Nazis. We're not. We're not organized enough for that. Fascists maybe, but Mussolini fascists. Hitler wouldn't have us.

"But I'll tell you something else. We may have put the whole goddamn country into a frock coat. But we're still barbarians underneath it."

"Perón knew that."

"Perón! Perón knew it, but he was a tool and an idiot. No, little brother. Get past all the crap that your crowd pretends to, and you've got the real, untapped strength of Argentina."

"Barbarism?"

"Call it that. Call it pure force. Call it whatever's in a hurricane before it turns into a hurricane. But by God, it's *there,* waiting."

"All we need is a few decent people, eh? Like the ones you're teaching to blow up things in Central America?"

"No, Steve. We're capable of better than just decency."

"What the hell is *that* supposed to mean?"

"You'll know when the time comes. You should already, if you're my brother."

Esteban swerved to avoid a news-seller who was setting up his stand beneath a streetlight. Ahead was a sign pointing toward a broad, empty, mercury-lighted boulevard that ran along the sea cliffs, stark in the cold morning fog, a sign that said *"Fuerzas Aéreas Argentinas. Entrada estrictamente prohibida a todas personas ajenas."* Argentine Air Force. Entrance strictly forbidden to anybody who doesn't belong here. That's us, Esteban thought, his mouth tasting brassy. He swung onto the boulevard. "Paco?" he asked. *"Are* you Paco?"

"Now it's my turn," Frank said. "What's that supposed to mean?"

"A man shouldn't be afraid of his own brother, Paco. I think I am. Among other things. Tell me some jokes. Tell me what's on English television. Anything."

"What's on English television is that Argentina is a decadent, strutting country ruled by a bunch of warlords who are getting hell beat out of them in a war."

Esteban looked for any trace of humor or irony in Frank's face as they passed through the cold blue light of a streetlamp. There wasn't any. "Never mind," he said. He turned onto a side street and pulled over by a vacant lot. The air was heavy with the smell of the sea and oil refineries when he got out of the car. "Be grateful I got a car with a trunk," he said to Frank. "I'd hate like hell to get you into the base hanging on to the exhaust pipe."

As he arranged himself in the trunk, Frank unholstered his pistol and shoved it toward Esteban. "Take it," he said. "Use it if there's trouble at the gate. We can always back up and run."

Esteban started to shove the pistol back at him, but didn't. When he got behind the wheel again, he clicked the safety off and slid the pistol beneath the seat. He checked to see if he could reach it quickly. He could.

The guard shack sat at the end of the long boulevard, whose only purpose seemed to be to provide a grand entrance to the base. As he approached the shack's spotlights, Esteban sped up. If his business was to be urgent, he'd damn well better look urgent. He'd rehearsed the scene a dozen times while Frank slept on the way down from the mountains, covered details, answered hypothetical questions. None of which would do any good, but he had to pretend, to *feel* he was ready, even if he wasn't. He knew that ultimately he'd have to depend on one thing he'd learned in his lawyer's training above all others: bullying. He prayed to whatever he used to pray to that he hadn't forgotten it, and swallowed hard to try to get the brassy taste of fear out of his mouth.

As the air-police guard stepped out of the shack onto the roadway, Esteban deliberately waited a second too long and hit the brakes too hard, so that he squealed to a stop only a meter from the guard's upraised hand. The guard flinched, then scowled. His hand dropped to the trigger of the submachine gun that hung from his shoulder. Another guard stepped out of the shack behind him, slipping his own submachine gun off his shoulder and aiming it. Esteban rolled down the window and shouted, *"Apúrele!* Hurry up!" in as stern a voice as his dry throat could force out.

The guard, a kid with a face like a mean-spirited cocker spaniel's, scowled even harder. By the time he'd reached the window, Esteban had shoved two things toward him: his own I.D., and his father's old I.D. carnet that identified him as minister of justice of the Argentine Republic. Esteban had carried it since his father's death, partly out of sentiment, partly because it was just uncertainly impressive enough to get him out of traffic tickets. The kid's look changed from anger to puzzlement. "You know Colonel Jamie Mondragon?" Esteban demanded.

Puzzlement changed to worry. *"Sí, señor."*

"I'm his brother-in-law. I'm here to see him and it's urgent. Raise the gate."

"Pero, señor... Colonel Mondragon is on the Malvinas. Do you have flight orders?"

At least one question he'd anticipated, Esteban thought with small gratitude. "I'll arrange those with your operations officer. His name is Major Garay, no?"

"Sí. Major Garay."

"Fine. Now raise the gate."

The worry lines on the kid's face deepened. "With

your permission, señor, I'll have to call Major Garay. My orders are—"

"You'd wake Major Garay at this time of morning to tell him that the brother-in-law of the vice commander of the theater air forces wants to see him? You'd tell him that you suspect the vice commander's family of lying?"

The kid turned helplessly to the other air policeman, who was barely older than he was but had one more stripe on his overcoat. "Orders," the older one said with finality. He reached for the telephone.

Esteban laid his identification on the seat beside him, and left his hand there. It would take only a quick movement to reach the pistol. He calculated: the kid beside the car would have to go first; he couldn't take a chance on his being in the way when he aimed for the one in the booth. But they'd both have to be done quickly. The second one's gun was already unslung and ready....

Great God! What in hell was he *calculating?* Those were a couple of kids from the provinces, kids who were no more damned responsible for this miserable situation than he was—probably less so, since their yelling against it would have had even less effect than his. And he was *calculating* how to kill them? He raised his hand from the seat, gripped the steering wheel, and as quietly as possible put the car in reverse. He'd use the gun if he had to, but he'd run first if he could. He'd held on to that much honesty, at least.

The air policeman on the phone said a few sentences Esteban couldn't hear, then was silent while whoever was on the other end apparently checked something. In the silence, he shifted so that he could scrutinize Esteban. The muzzle of his submachine gun swung with him, so that it pointed directly at Esteban's head. Habit, Esteban prayed, just habit.

At length the man bent over the phone again, as if he could hear better by somehow getting closer to the desk. This time Esteban could make out what he was saying: *"Sí,"* three or four times, *"Sí."* But *sí* what, damn it? *Sí* arrest, *sí* shoot, *sí* let him pass? His hand gripped the steering wheel until he felt blood blisters start on the pinched parts of his fingers.

The man stepped out of the booth. "Get the jeep," he said to the other airman. Then, to Esteban, "You're lucky, señor. Colonel Mondragon is here tonight."

"Here?" Esteban said stupidly.

"On the base, señor."

"On the base?"

"Sí." The man looked at him oddly. "They come in for consultations, señor. Often. We'll escort you."

"No," Esteban said. His foot eased out on the clutch slightly. The spaniel-faced airman whipped out of the shadows in a Volkswagen jeep. Too late, Esteban thought, his mind leaping through possibilities. Back up, shift, turn around—no, the jeep had a running start on him. No good. But Jaime Mondragon *here?* What the hell would he say to him? I don't really want to see you, Jaime, it's just that my brother Frank is a British spy and is in my trunk waiting to go blow up your...

The air policeman slapped the roof of the Falcon and waved Esteban on. Esteban shakily dropped the gearshift into first. The Falcon lurched forward.

They wound through gray concrete-block buildings, empty and floodlit now, with stenciled signs on them: Commissary, Dispensary, Weapons Maintenance, Enlisted Men's Club, 4th Tactical Squadron Headquarters...Bachelor Officers' Quarters. *Mierda.* The jeep swung into a parking lot beside the BOQ. Esteban ran his eyes along the one-story block building to the single lighted room, which shone fuzzily through the mist. A shadow moved inside it, bending as if someone were dressing. He pictured Jaime Mondragon, in pants and undershirt and slippers, his correct face puffy with sleep and annoyance, sitting on the edge of his bed waiting for Esteban to give him the urgent message—while Esteban stammered out...what? His mind was as blank as was the face of the air policeman who leapt over the door of the jeep, gaucho-fashion, and motioned for him to follow him toward the building.

"Some papers," Esteban said to him in a whispered shout as he got out of the Falcon. "I've got to get some papers out of the trunk."

The kid nodded. Esteban made his way shakily through the patches of snow-turned-ice to the trunk, blessing the luck that had made him pull in with the rear of the car facing away from the floodlights of the BOQ.

"Don't get out," he whispered rapidly to the shape of Frank in the dark trunk. He leaned close and explained sketchily. He could hear Frank breathing in the chamber of the trunk.

Frank's voice came at him out of the dark, calm but tight. "Where are we?"

"BOQ. I'll leave the trunk lid cracked. Be gone when I get back."

"What'll you do?"

"I don't know—make up something for Mondragon about Adela's death and hope he's too sleepy to see it's bullshit until I'm off the base."

"Then?"

"You tell me. I'm supposed to get out of the country, right?"

"Go to Grandfather. Tell him whatever you have to to get to Mother. He won't let you go under, not family."

"And when I find Mother?"

"She knows the arrangements. You're on your own then, *hermano*."

Esteban hesitated. There should be so much more to be said than *this* after a dozen years. Should be, but was there? No matter. Whatever there might have been, it would go unsaid now—maybe forever. *"Cuídate*, Paco. Take care." He lowered the lid gently, driving away a brief terrible image of coffin lids.

He and the air policeman were met at the entrance to the BOQ by a yawning orderly, who showed them into a small dayroom. He checked his watch as he sat them down and offered Esteban coffee. "Be about ten minutes, señor," he said. "Colonel's expecting you, but he asked me to let him get himself together first." He winked. "Little *fiesta* last night. *Comprende?*"

Esteban forced a conspiratorial smile. "Old Jaime," he said. He picked up a copy of *Tal Cual* magazine with a picture of Margaret Thatcher dressed as Wonder Woman on the cover and pretended to read. The air policeman stretched and slumped in his chair. "Beats hell out of a cold guard shack," he said to the room. The orderly returned with coffee and sat, yawning some more and checking his watch every minute or so. Stories flashed through Esteban's mind: a jealous chauffeur who killed Adela because she'd been sleeping with him while Jaime was at war; his mother, who killed her in an insane patriotic rage because she was marrying an Argentine; Brazilian voodoo cults who— None of it was any good, all silly or absurd or simply stupid. What, then? What, damn it? Why would *he* be here with the message, and not the police?

Sometime during the ten minutes that were ten hours, a muffled cry came down one of the corridors outside. The orderly looked at his watch, yawned, and went back to waiting. "Nightmares," he mumbled. "They're full of them when they come back from out there...." He motioned vaguely southwest, toward the Falklands. The air policeman closed his eyes against the buzzing fluorescent lights and antiseptic walls.

When the orderly finally checked his watch a last time and stood to hold the door for Esteban, he looked relieved. He could go back to sleep, Esteban imagined. Sleep. God. He'd slept once, too, years ago. "Four seventeen, señor," the orderly said. "Corridor to your left, field-grade officers' suites."

Esteban remembered a story by Dostoyevsky, Turgenev—somebody—about a man who walked to his execution along a street that seemed to get longer, more nearly infinite, with every step he took. He understood the man as he walked past the closed doors of the corridor, past the snores and farts and moans of the sleeping majors and colonels and generals, his blank mind not able now to reach for anything beyond the imagined, correct face of Jaime Mondragon.

There was still only one lighted room: 417. The door was cracked, as if Jaime wanted to make sure Esteban made no noise by knocking. Nonetheless, he tapped lightly before he walked in.

The room was empty.

Another door led off it, this one ajar, too, with the sound of softly running water coming from behind it, as if a just-flushed toilet hadn't fully shut itself off. To win a war, Esteban thought. We want to win a war when we can't even get the goddamn plumbing to work. He stood waiting for what seemed five minutes before he walked across the militarily sparse room—a single bed, a dresser, a desk, a dark commercial carpet—to the other door. "Jaime?" he said. His voice sounded as loud as a landslide to him. "Jaime?" He pushed the door a few centimeters to see into the bathroom.

Jaime sat on the commode, his pants around his knees and his head thrown back against the wall behind the toilet tank. One arm hung against the toilet lever, holding it open. His tongue stuck the tiniest bit past his lips, and a red, raw line ran around his neck. Like the line around Adela's, only wider, rougher. His woven military belt lay across his lap where it had been dropped when it came from around his neck. The room smelled of fresh shit. Esteban held his breath, closed his eyes, then opened them again. Something rose in his throat, and he fought it down. He took a step forward and jiggled the toilet lever from beneath Jaime's arm. Jaime didn't move. Dear son-of-a-bitching God.

Esteban flicked out the light and backed out the door, shutting it quietly behind him. Jaime's brightly lit bedroom surrounded him like some kind of plastic bubble. It seemed close, airless, in spite of the open window. Esteban didn't think. He knew it had been Frank even without thinking—he knew Frank had waited outside the bright window until he'd seen the light go on in the bathroom and heard water running and then come in through the window. Thinking would mean he was trying to figure out *why* Frank had done it. Thinking would mean he was dealing with the fact that the blame would automatically fall on himself, not Frank. Instead of thinking, he was telling himself to sit down at the desk, to look at his watch, to stay as still as he could until enough time for a decent talk between putative brothers-in-law had passed, then to walk back down the corridor to the dayroom.

Sitting didn't work. He paced, abstractedly opened drawers, rifled through Jaime's papers—anything to make the time go. He even opened Jaime's briefcase— and hidden beneath pages of press releases that mentioned Jaime's name, found the stacks of hundred-dollar bills.

That Jaime should have dollars with him didn't strike Esteban as odd. Everybody in Argentina had dollars— a few tens for cabbies, boxes full of hundreds for *his* kind of people. In a country where the peso had lost half its value in three months, only fools didn't have dollars. But most people didn't carry stacks of them in briefcases in a war zone, ten-thousand-dollar stacks of them. What were you doing, Jaime? he asked the presence in the room. Getting ready to run? Planning on losing the war? But where was the money coming from? And then the clear answer came, even without thought, and Esteban shut the briefcase in a wave of revulsion. You were selling military supplies on the black market that should have been going to your own men, weren't you, Jaime, you prick. Esteban remembered the troops huddled in the freezing foxholes with blankets wrapped around their heads. What were they eating, cleaning their rifles with, staying warm with? What would they do when they aimed their rifles at a British marine and there was nothing in them?

His anger came back, like a welcome friend. He checked his watch, closed the window, turned out the light, pulled the door shut. "Ciao, Jaime," he said to the corridor, hoping to wake one of the other Jaimes who were probably asleep in their epaulets. Go to it, Frank, he thought. Blow their goddamn toys all the way to hell.

"Airman!" he said sharply to the sleeping kid in the dayroom. The kid jerked awake, fumbling awkwardly at the hood of his flight jacket. "Tell the orderly that Colonel Mondragon doesn't want to be disturbed until breakfast. Then meet me at my car."

The kid stumbled off, and Esteban made his way out into the cold, petroleum-smelling air, gulping it like water. When he got to the Falcon, he stood a moment, listening to a jet wind up somewhere on the base and letting the cold numb him. Then, after he made sure Frank had closed the trunk, he followed the kid's tire-squealing jeep through the barren, predawn base, his brief spurt of anger evaporating like the mist the sun would soon burn off. At the gate, he slowed only long enough to wave at the guard and get a go-ahead nod in return. He was glad he didn't have to try to use his voice. The bluster in it would crack like a raw egg now.

Down the wide boulevard, he pulled over onto the same side street where he'd stopped before to let Frank get into the trunk. He got out of the car to steady himself in the dark and solitude, clapping his hands against the cold. Back toward the base, a plane rose, heading past the cliffs and out to sea. Was it Frank's, he wondered? But did it matter? He was on his own now, as Frank had said. Wherever Frank was, his passing through Esteban's life had left it in as great a pile of rubble as that cache of missiles would soon be. Frank was invisible. But in a few hours, Esteban would be hunted as the man who'd killed the national hero. Christ, he wouldn't even have time to get into Buenos Aires before then.

"Shit," he said aloud.

The muffled knocking that answered him seemed first to come from the weedy vacant lot beside the car. He dropped down into a quick crouch and scanned the lot. Long shadows like teeth, cast by a picket fence, broke the light from a streetlamp on the corner. But enough light remained for him to see that the lot was flat and empty, with no place for anything larger than a rat to hide. Cautiously, he reached inside the car, under the seat, where he'd left the pistol.

It wasn't there.

The knocking came again, louder this time, and long enough for Esteban to locate it. It was coming from the trunk.

Still in a crouch, he moved back beside the rear wheel well. It couldn't be Frank—Frank had killed Jaime Mondragon and was on his way to the Falklands. But, damn it, it had to be Frank.

"Paco?" he said.

"Open the trunk," Paco's muffled voice answered.

"You son of a bitch," Esteban said as he fumbled the key into the lock and jerked the trunk lid open. Frank's slim body uncurled itself like a cat stretching. He held out his hand for Esteban to take. Esteban slapped it away. "What the hell are you doing here?"

"Saying good-bye, little brother."

"The missiles. What about the missiles?"

"No missiles. Sorry." Frank unzipped his jacket, pulled up his shirt, and undid a belt from around his waist, a belt with thin pouches in it like a money belt.

"Here." He held out the belt. "Plastic explosives. You do the missiles. I've done what I needed to so far."

Esteban took a step back from the belt. Frank shrugged, walked to the curb, and eased the belt down into a storm sewer.

"Mondragon," Esteban said. "All the time it was just Mondragon."

"Just Mondragon for now. The people in London won't think much of that, I imagine. They were counting on Exocets." He tucked his shirt in. As he did, the streetlamp glinted off the butt of the automatic pistol—the one Esteban had left beneath the car seat. It was stuck under Frank's belt now; the holster and gunbelt were gone. Frank saw Esteban staring at it. In a motion that seemed casual but wasn't, he slipped it out of the belt. "Steve, listen. I'm sorry—for all of this. But it *has* to be done... what I've done already—and the rest. There were plans, but they went wrong. Adela went wrong. The fact that Mondragon was here instead of on the Falklands went wrong. Adela was supposed to have plenty of time to get back to Buenos Aires and make it out of the country with Mother—and with you." He passed his hand wearily over one side of his face, as if he were trying to wipe the light from the streetlamp off it. *"Mira.* I didn't know if I'd make it back here from the Falklands or not after Mondragon was—dealt with. But I'm here, and there are other things I have to do now. You *are* on your own, little brother. The best thing I can tell you is what I already have. Get to Mother. Let Grandfather help you if you can—and if he will."

"Adela knew about Mondragon?"

"About what I had to do to Mondragon? No. She only knew about the missiles." He brought the pistol up, aimed it at Esteban. "Adela was too honest. If she'd known what I had to do to Mondragon, she wouldn't have gone along. And the filthy swine might not have had to kill her." He took a step backward, toward the darkness. "Don't try to come after me, Steve. Our sister's dead—God knows that's enough." He stepped backward again, gave Esteban a last, long look—a look without distances in it, a look in which Esteban almost recognized his brother—then turned and was gone. North, toward Buenos Aires.

Esteban watched him disappear into the fog and shadows between two gray, tin-roofed houses, Frank himself a shadow before he vanished. "God damn you, Paco," he said softly to the black space between the two houses. There were questions—dozens of questions, scores of them—that he ought to run after Frank and demand answers for, and to hell with the gun. But somehow it seemed right that Frank should be walking away into the Patagonian wilderness now. Jaime Mondragon had killed Adela; Frank had killed Jaime Mondragon and was gone again, like some sort of avenging angel. None of the *whys* really mattered right now. Frank wasn't Frank in this place; nothing had to make sense. In Buenos Aires, Frank could be his brother again; in the morning, the world might almost have to be logical again. But not here, not now.

Go home, Frank had told him. Go back to Mother. Christ, that things should ever be that simple again!

He closed the trunk of the Falcon. No, my brother, he thought. We're not done with each other yet, not bloody yet. Were there eleven million people in Buenos Aires? No matter. He knew he could find Frank better there than here, in so many ways. And he would. For the questions' sake. For Frank's sake. For his own sake. In this scummy Time of War, they were locked together now like brazed metal.

The car started sluggishly in the damp cold. They'd be coming after him soon, would expect him to be heading west to Chile. If there was anything in his favor, that was it. The only thing.

Chapter Five

An air hose he cut from an Esso station in the ragtag suburbs of Comodoro Rivadavia in the granite light of dawn served him as a siphon hose. He emptied the Falcon's gas tank, then poured less than a gallon back in. Enough, but just enough. The Falcon chugged to a stop in a wasteland of scrawny mesquite trees on the highway west toward Chile, and he used the battery to inch it off the road into the trees. It would look as if he'd tried to hide it. But they would find it. He'd panicked, they'd assume, and had left Comodoro for Chile on a nearly empty tank of gas. How long they'd look before they assumed anything else, he didn't know. With half luck, long enough for him to be moving already in the labyrinth of Buenos Aires.

But he'd need that half luck. The national hero was dead. They wouldn't wait.

The highway stretched flatly to the horizon to the west, and to the distant glow of Comodoro to the east, where already the air base would be at breakfast, where already Jaime Mondragon's room would be full of frightened, outraged officers. Someone in Buenos Aires would be being dragged out of his bed by now—a government minister, at least—with an urgent telephone call. Esteban checked the map he'd salvaged from the abandoned Falcon. He judged he was no more than a mile west of the last turnoff he'd passed. It was a dirt road, but it looked well kept and fairly well used. The map showed that it ran northeast, back toward the coast, and hit the Buenos Aires highway a few miles north of Comodoro. He set out at a jog. That was his road, his only way to avoid going back through Comodoro before he headed north.

He could hear the approaching whine of cattle trucks in the wind behind him for miles before they roared past him, flattening the roadside grass with their wake, and he ducked into the scrub to avoid them. His guess was that they would take the same side road he was headed for to avoid Comodoro, unless they were going into the city to unload at the docks. But it was that *unless* that kept him from flagging one of them down. Not yet. He couldn't take the chance that a driver would pull into town with news of a man who fit his description in the middle of nowhere at dawn heading not west, but north. No, he'd make it to the side road first, then flag one down.

At the end of the mile he'd figured on, he discovered that a mile is a hell of a lot longer if you're running than if you're in a car. It was good daylight already, and the turnoff was still not in sight. Now, any minute now, the trucks would be coming from the opposite direction, from Comodoro. And they'd be full of troops, not cattle. Where would he head then? Into that scrub waste that seemed to cover the entire world here? In his city shoes, with no food or water or sleeping bag, how long would he last? The day, at most. Not a night, surely.

A thinner whine blew to him in the wind from behind him, and he stopped to listen. His breathing was loud in the emptiness. It hadn't been this bloody labored after he'd jogged twice this distance when he'd been in training at the university. *Madre,* best varsity middleweight in the country or not, that had been a dozen years ago. He fought for his breath and listened to the whine grow louder, turn from wind to the clear sound of a car—not a truck—approaching. He stepped out into the road. He'd seen two men killed since he drove out of Buenos Aires, poor useless provincial cops who no doubt had a score of kids between them. Could he at least steal a car if he had to, leave some tax collector or cattle buyer stranded in this wilderness? Or worse?

He began waving the car to a stop even before it was more than a dark blot on the highway. That was his answer to himself.

By the time he saw that the blob was a jeep, not a car, it was too late to change his mind. He'd been seen, too. But it was no military jeep, this one. That much he could tell from the missing headlight and cracked windshield and the snowplow as it slowed for him— even before he saw the wide, pock marked face behind the cracked windshield. The potato-skin face that broke into a huge nervous grin as the jeep slid off the road onto the shoulder, spewing rocks like grapeshot.

"Que suerte, Sr. Esteban, que suerte," Pepe whooped as he fishtailed the jeep in reverse back toward Esteban. "What luck, what luck!"

He missed Esteban by inches. And before Esteban had a chance to clamber into the busted seat beside him, he'd shoved a wineskin at him. "I know it! I know you're going to ask me why I'm here," he said happily, as though he'd just deciphered a great secret. "True? Am I right, señor?"

"I'd thought of asking," Esteban said as he crawled over the door. "Vaguely."

"Ah hah," Pepe said, his air of triumph only a little fogged from the wine. "I knew." He jerked the jeep into forward and they lurched out onto the road. "Last night—no, in the afternoon. I'd just put your señorita on the airplane, no? And I went home, not even stopping for a glass of wine. And I began to consider. Pepe Ferran, I considered to myself, why do it? Why stay here and make up great lies for the police when they come? They'll believe you, no doubt, since a Catalan can convince a pope there's no devil if he wants. But what will they put you through before that? A *mierda,* a grand *mierda,* that's what.

"So I had a glass of wine and I said to my wife, 'We're going home, wife.' And she said to me, 'I *am* home.' So I had another glass of wine and I considered that I hadn't had a wife when I came from Catalonia, so that when I was back at home there I wouldn't miss having a wife much. That pleased me, I considered. And then

I discovered that I didn't have enough money to get to Catalonia with. So I considered again, and remembered that the police were coming because of you, Sr. Esteban. And that perhaps then you might advance me the price of an airplane ticket to Barcelona. Tourist class, of course. And as an obligation of honor—nothing more."

He swerved to miss what might have been an imaginary squirrel in the road, then went on. "But where *were* you? I wondered to myself, Sr. Esteban. You left Bariloche heading south. And where south? Surely not to Tierra del Fuego, to the Indians and the icebergs. That left only two places: Rawson, where there's nothing, and Comodoro Rivadavia, where the big military base is. And then I considered that if Sr. Frank had come into the country from Chile, there must be something military happening. So... I told my wife once more we were going home, and she didn't bother to answer me that time. And so..." He reached for the wineskin that Esteban still held. "What luck! I've found you already, no?"

"Yes," Esteban said, turning away to hide his growing smile. The cold wind whipped into the open jeep and flung the word away. Esteban buttoned his coat more tightly, and felt his smile slowly freezing. Who else was this cancer going to touch? Who else did he have the right to let it touch? "Pepe," he said. "Go home. For your own good, please, go home."

"I *am* going home," Pepe said.

"There's a man dead, Pepe, an important one. Frank's disappeared and they'll be hunting me to hell and back."

"Ah hah." He thought a moment. "What kind of man?"

"A colonel."

"Is that all? Thank God. I thought it might be serious!" He shoved the wineskin at Esteban again.

Esteban took it and shot a stream of the thick, dry wine at his mouth. Only half of it made it: the rest scattered all over his face and coat in the wind. He looked at Pepe, whose grin widened until it became a deep, rolling, raucous laugh. Esteban swiped at the wine on his face, then flung the empty wineskin up into the air, his own unexpected laugh answering Pepe's and flying off in pieces into the scrub wilderness that flashed by them. "Pepe," he said. "Next dirt road north you find, take it. And Pepe? Forget tourist class. First class, all the way—with your own damn stewardess if you want her."

The jeep was a marvel. Checkpoints? There were always beaches to hit or pastures to bounce through or rocky hillsides to barrel across to avoid them, while Pepe whooped Catalan insults and made pumping Catalan fists at the distant M.P.s. And as the day wore its way through noon and into evening, with tough *churrasco* steaks and more thick wine at trucker's cafés on the highway to break the drive, Esteban napped and felt his mind begin to clear, to function as it once had for the first time in weeks. He wanted to plug things in, flip switches, see light drive shadows out of the corners and holes that everything reasonable in his world had scuttled off into, to hear the pieces of what he'd thought was his life whir and click back into place. Frank said Mondragon had killed Adela. Fine. But how did Frank know that? Or did he really know it at all? Frank had dropped into his life from outer space, then slipped back out again. Did he have more reason to believe Frank than to doubt him? Angels of God, who knew?

Or his mother—had she known Adela was in serious danger? What would it take to make his mother place her own daughter in the kind of jeopardy she apparently had? He would have said before that nothing could have made her do that. But now...?

And assuming Mondragon had killed Adela—what could she have done to make him risk so much? Surely not just the business of his black-marketeering in war supplies. And how in hell had he managed to get to her to kill her, if he had? From everything Esteban knew, the war would have to have stopped dead for Mondragon to take time out from it.

And most of all, Frank. Frank had walked away from him toward the north. Not much really to go on if you were going to assume he was heading for Buenos Aires. From Comodoro Rivadavia, *everything* was north but penguins. Yet it was the only assumption he could make. Frank had said he had more to do in Argentina. If he walked away from the war zone, and if he wanted to screw up the war effort, then where was the next most logical place he would head? All the government and nearly half the population of Argentina were in or around Buenos Aires.

But, damn it, how could he be sure Frank's "more to do" had anything to do with the war at all? The people in London, whoever they were, had been expecting Exocets, Frank said. And Frank was double-crossing them. But for what? He hadn't even known Adela was dead when he came into the country. So he couldn't have been here just to go after Mondragon on Adela's account.

Nothing whirred and clicked. Things reasonable scuttled a little further back into their holes and corners.

Except Caroline. Before he looked for any mad answers to any equally mad questions, there was Caroline to find. This was the end of the second day since he'd seen her. He'd asked her to wait three days. She was the only secure thing, the only piece of his life that made sense now. He'd reach her—he *had* to reach her— by tomorrow night. And somehow to protect her from this surreal landslide of events that the phone call from Adela had started. A phone call that, like an ass, he'd decided was no more than some sort of delayed adolescent fit. God forgive him.

Soon they would leave the coast and head through the rich pampa of the province of Buenos Aires—if they made it that far. Already the air from the South Atlantic clawed less sharply at them around the cracked windshield. He imagined Caroline's room at the Dorado in Buenos Aires. It would be warm, with a good carpet and clean sheets, with a brandy from room service, with no wind, with the rustle of Caroline's crisp blouses instead of the hammering of the old jeep's engine. It would be a reasonable thing for a man to have a right to, for him to look forward to.

But not so. Not for him, not in Argentina, not in Time of War.

"We live in a country invented by Fellini, Pepe," he shouted through the wind. "Or maybe Lewis Carroll. Or how about Walt Disney?"

Pepe looked at him worriedly. After a time, understanding seemed to dawn and his face relaxed into pleasure. "Ah hah," he said. "Bambi, señor. No? I know that one." He winked.

"Sí," Esteban said. "Bambi."

Bahía Blanca was the rub. Bahía Blanca, White Bay, the neck of the funnel, the last city they'd have to slip past before they reached the relative safety of the maze of highways that grained the Province of Buenos Aires. The city that all roads crept through, unless you wanted to lose half a day by backtracking into the interior. The huge naval base of Bahía Blanca, and because of it, the security that would surely surround the town like a moat. The checkpoints they would pass on streets where there were no beaches to slip away onto, no pastures to rattle and bounce through. And the questions they'd have to answer, the identification they'd have to show.

As they approached the city in the deepening darkness, Esteban had watched the road signs as if they were stations of the cross. He'd studied the map until it had lost all sense and meaning for him, looking for the road around the city that wasn't there. And he'd tried to plan. But plan what? A full day had passed since the orderly would have discovered Mondragon's staring body. Enough time to have Esteban's description—and maybe Pepe's, too—telexed to every provincial commander in the country. If they were stopped, there'd be no bluffing, no explaining this time. There were only two things they *could* do: spot the checkpoints early enough to lose themselves in side streets before they got to them, or run them. The simplicity of the choice was almost a relief.

Almost. If they wandered half the night in the suburbs of Bahía Blanca, they lost time they didn't have. If they ran a checkpoint and survived, which wasn't likely even with the snowplow as a battering ram, they might as well have hired a blimp to announce they were in town. A choice that wasn't really a choice, then, options that Pepe's grunt told Esteban you didn't need a law degree to figure out, as they talked them over at a roadside bar just at the outskirts of the city.

"Could be worse, *patrón*," Pepe told him with grim cheer. He'd taken to calling Esteban *patrón*—boss—in the past hundred miles or so, as if, Esteban thought, he were practicing an old, half-forgotten peasant routine to get himself in shape for the mountains of Catalonia again. Or as if he were telling Esteban something about what he expected from him.

"Tell me," Esteban said. "Make it worse."

Pepe slid a copy of a late edition of *El Clarín* across the wine-sticky table. He'd filched the paper from the bartender and had been spelling out the headlines while Esteban planned. "You could be him. That your colonel?"

Esteban picked up the paper. "Vice Commander of Malvinas FAA Killed in Action," the headline said, in type even bigger than that which announced the exact dates the pope would come to settle (or bless, depending on which bishop was being quoted) the war. Jaime's face stared out at Esteban, serious and still saying *trust me, always*. Esteban imagined he would have approved of even this official lie; his own death was now *muy correcto,* a hero's death. The pope stood serenely below him, smiling. Esteban flipped the paper over.

"It could be worse," he said. He stood and began to button his coat. "It may be yet."

There was room for gratitude in lies sometimes, he thought. If the truth about Jaime's death had been printed, his own picture might well be in the place of the pope's under Jaime's. And the smiling bartender he was paying would be calling half the army down on him instead.

They hit the first checkpoint less than a mile from the bar. It was a small one, designed mainly to check cars that might be considering turning off onto a sandy road that led toward the beach—and probably by a roundabout way to the naval base. They avoided it easily by creeping through potholed roads in a neighborhood of cinder-block worker's houses. It cost them half an hour, but Esteban allowed himself a moment of small relief—no less welcome because he knew it was false. Pepe crossed himself and muttered in Catalan and rammed the jeep through somebody's backyard onto the main road again.

Onto the main road just in time for the second checkpoint. The checkpoint that was smarter than they were.

This one was spread across an avenue of low shop buildings whose fronts lined the street in an unbroken wall; a wall extended along half a dozen blocks by barricades that had been erected at all the side streets leading to the avenue. The jeep was funneled into the river of cars flowing into the checkpoint before they even knew the damned thing existed.

Pepe stared morosely at all the other cars that logjammed the avenue around them as they crept toward the barricade, as if somehow every other driver in Bahía Blanca was part of a *fachista* conspiracy to block any possible escape. A cab tried to cut them off and Pepe's mood lightened a little as he managed to gouge the cab's fender with the snowplow. But as they drew closer to the checkpoint, and the faces of the soldiers who manned it became real beneath their helmets, Pepe's own face sank into a tight, worried blankness. Esteban understood. Both their reasonable options were dead now. There was no room to run, no way to smash the barricade in this gridlocked nightmare.

All right, then, when reasonable options disappeared, there were still desperate ones. Adela learned that. Now he had to learn, too.

He wrenched open the jeep's warped glove compartment, then sorted among damp matchbooks and loose screws until his fingers closed over a greasy screwdriver. Pepe eased the jeep ahead another meter; Esteban ducked and crawled over the door, grateful for the panel truck ahead of them that hid him from the soldiers at the barricade. An astonished woman with a gaggle of bouncing children in the car behind craned to watch him as he struggled with the rusty screws that held the jeep's rear license plate on. He smiled at her and waved at the kids, making incomprehensible motions and mouthing nonsense words that he hoped she'd take as some harmless drunk's or lunatic's attempt to explain this thing he was doing. She nodded, and turned to pretend to explain to her children what the poor man was doing. Esteban gave up on the screw and pried at the license plate until it ripped loose.

Crouching, he made for the front of the car. As he passed Pepe, he handed the license plate to him. "Hold on to it," he said. The panel truck in front moved up another meter. "Close it up," he told Pepe. "Stay in line. Look normal." Pepe looked at him wonderingly and moved the jeep ahead. They were less than half a dozen cars away from the barricade now.

The screws on the front of the jeep were frozen solid with rust. Esteban pried one side of the plate loose, then began on the other before the screwdriver broke. He swore, flung the screwdriver into the gutter, and jerked at the plate. It bent, but held. He began to work it back and forth, feeling its sharp edges dig into his hands. Argentine steel, he thought as Pepe banged on the side of the jeep for him to move so he could follow the panel truck a carlength closer to the barricade. Why with all the things that we screw up in this country do we have to make decent damn steel?

The plate snapped just as the panel truck moved again. Esteban sprinted into the next line of traffic and held up his hand to stop a Renault that was crawling up beside the jeep. The Renault beeped and jerked to a stop at his kneecaps.

"Get out," he yelled at Pepe. "Cut the engine and push. Aim toward the curb."

He pounded on the window of the Renault. A bothered businessman lowered it just far enough to hear him. "Broken down," Esteban told him, trying to sound apologetic. "Let us get it to the curb."

The businessman looked exasperated, but nodded. Esteban checked the curb quickly for a space. A half dozen meters ahead a battered Peugeot was going through the customary shoving ceremony to make itself room to get out: forward and backward, forward and backward until all the other cars along the curb accordioned together out of its way. Esteban pointed. Pepe gave the jeep a mighty heave and cut the wheel hard. It missed the back bumper of the departing Peugeot by centimeters as it slid into the parking space and ground to a stop against the curb. Still wondering, Pepe patted it as if it had been a wise burro, then reached over the door and set the brake.

Esteban took the other license plate from him and buried both of them under a pile of wrapping paper in a trash can. "How many engines has this thing had?" he asked.

"Three. Maybe four," Pepe said.

"Ever changed the motor number on the registration papers?"

Pepe studied a moment. "No."

"God answers prayer. OK, ever steal a car?"

Pepe studied again. "Not recently."

"That'll do. Let's go."

"But *patrón*—the jeep."

"Pepe. They'll never trace it now. Understand?"

Light broke gently over Pepe's face. "Ah hah," He patted the jeep a last, fond time, hitched his pants, and turned to follow Esteban into the flow of window-shoppers—just in time to follow instead Esteban's gaze to the traffic cop who was bearing down on them from the corner. The cop's eyes were fixed on the empty space where the jeep's license plate had been. He snapped his fingers and pointed to Pepe in a "You—wait" gesture. Pepe stopped, took a step back, and looked for room to run. His fist clenched itself like a war club.

"Pepe, don't," Esteban said. He struggled with his own sense of being trapped, of being a bull in a chute. Running or fighting, Christ, either one would bring a half dozen of the submachine-gun-wielding troops from the checkpoint down on them. So much for options, desperate or not! But what else—where else? He froze, his mind mud.

And then the cop stopped. A man in the baggy slacks and pea coat of a dockworker had detached himself from the window-shoppers and stepped in front of him, as if he needed to ask directions. The cop tried to brush him aside with his white-cuffed hand. But the man didn't brush. The cop looked at him with annoyance, annoyance that turned to puzzlement when he looked down at the blade the man pushed into the coat that covered his sucked-in stomach. Shoppers seethed around them, but they stood locked against each other like bizarre lovers for a long moment, sending silent messages. Then the cop began to back up. He and the man in the pea coat moved like tango dancers toward a narrow alleyway between two shops. Just as they disappeared into the alleyway, the man's eyes left the cop's long enough to meet Esteban's. He flicked his head. "Move, get the hell out," the flick said, and Esteban nodded dumbly. The man's face was clear in the red light of a toy-store sign for the barest moment before it vanished with the rest of him into the alleyway. But Esteban would remember it, he knew: one half of it had melted. A stroke, a nerve severed in a knife fight—from the man's eyebrows to his mouth, the left side of his face slumped as if it were going to slide off his skull.

Esteban turned away as casually as he could. Pepe still stared at the empty mouth of the alleyway, as if it were a television set that had gone dead. He jumped when Esteban touched him, then crossed himself before he began to shuffle beside Esteban back along the avenue, away from the checkpoint. "You know him?" Esteban asked.

"Me?" Pepe said. "Know that one, *patrón?*"

"Salvation can be as ugly as anything else. What do you make of it?"

Pepe shrugged. "I don't make anything of anything that I can help not making anything of, señor Esteban. The man was as crazy as he was ugly? He hates police? He likes jeeps? God sent him? You should accept things like that, *patrón*. There's trouble in asking questions."

"Right," Esteban said. He glanced over his shoulder. Through the shoppers, he got a glimpse of the man with the melted face. He had come out of the alley and was moving along the street behind them. The cop was nowhere in sight. No, no questions. The man was his own answer: God may not have sent him, but somebody had. He knew who they were and what they were doing. But how long had he known? Had he followed them from Comodoro? Great Jesus, if he had, then who else could have been trailing them while they thought they were invisible, roaring across fields like boy-scout motocross racers?

Or had he been waiting for them here in Bahía Blanca all along? Hell, that was even more frightening. Somebody had known all along where they were headed— even before they did.

And who was Somebody? It might as well be God, sending them a guardian demon. Not the cops, not the military, those were out—even if they were having him followed, they'd never reveal themselves the way the man with the melted face had. Frank's people—whoever they were—were a possibility. But hadn't Frank betrayed whatever "people" he had? All right, who else? His grandfather was powerful, but not powerful enough to know where Esteban was heading even before he did himself. Or at least Esteban didn't think so; he really didn't know where power ended in Argentina now, not with the world flip-flopping around him. In any case, he figured that if his grandfather knew anything at all about what had happened to Mondragon, he'd want to keep himself as far away from the whole affair as possible.

So who was Somebody? Whoever it was made Esteban feel as small as he had in school when he realized that the priest who had descended on him in a cigarette-smoky toilet had been watching and waiting ever since he'd left the store with his pack of Jockey Clubs. He was *allowed* to think he was free, for some reason that was as far beyond him as the ways of God. He felt the old, frustrated anger coming back, and hated it. That was the past. That was no more, goddamnit, he told himself as he and Pepe turned off the avenue, beyond the first side-street barricade, and started up a dim street with low, modern apartment houses and half-grown spruces lining it.

Guardian demon or not, then, if the man with the melted face came around the corner behind them, he had to be stopped. Somehow. And whatever he had in mind. If they made it to Caroline, Esteban couldn't—wouldn't—have a guardian anything behind him.

At the first corner they came to, a small grocery store spilled light into the street over its sidewalk displays of waxy fruits and vegetables. Esteban pulled Pepe into it. "Have a banana," he said.

"I don't like bananas, *patrón*," Pepe said. His face was as long as the banana that Esteban thrust at him.

"Everybody likes bananas. How much time does it take to steal a car?"

Pepe took the banana. "Depends, señor. Once you find the car, not much."

"Don't be particular. Just get something inconspicuous. And don't damage it any more than you have to, all right? I hate car thieves."

"And you, señor?"

"Meet me back here—say, fifteen minutes? Is that enough time? I want to make a phone call."

"A phone call, *patrón?* No."

"No. But you should accept things like that, *verdad?*"

Pepe pondered, then frowned. He pocketed the banana without paying. They left the store together, and split up around the corner. But not before Esteban had seen the man with the melted face—half a block behind, moving as slowly and cautiously as a crayfish.

Esteban let Pepe get out of sight down the block, then stepped back into the shadows of a ramp to a parking garage beneath one of the apartment houses. He was afraid, yes. But not with the kind of fear that he had felt in the crypt before he'd found Adela, not the kind of trembling fear that had sent him scuttling in panic down those marble stairs after his dropped lighter. No, this was fear that was calmness, calculation, strength —the kind of fear that he'd felt before he stepped into the ring for a match in college. It was something he hadn't felt in years, had half forgotten. There was no time to analyze it, only to feel—and it felt good, felt alive.

He looked around for a weapon in the slight spill of light from a curtained window. On a ledge beside him was a geranium pot, empty now except for a cross-eyed cat that peered at him over the lip. He shooed the cat, who gave him a foul look and scuttled away into the shadows, then hefted the pot. It was heavy as a medicine ball, something to ram with, to buy a few seconds of surprise with. He crouched. From one of the apartments above came music that announced a rerun of "Gunsmoke." That had been his old man's favorite show. What would you think now, Papa? he wondered as the man with the melted face passed through the light of the grocery store and turned onto the blacked-out street. Your lawyer son in a dark corner in a nothing town, playing "Gunsmoke," discovering forgotten courage with a geranium pot on a parking ramp.

He let the man pass by before he came out of his crouch, the geranium pot held in front of him like a

100

shield. The man heard him and whirled before Esteban could speak. His hand went into the pocket of his pea coat and the switchblade clicked open before his eyes had a chance to recognize Esteban in the dimness.

Esteban rammed. The pot caught the knife and spun it away like a broken helicopter blade, then hit the man at chest height. The man staggered back soundlessly. Esteban rammed again. This time the man grabbed for the pot, and the three of them—man, pot, and Esteban—stumbled onto the dry lawn and went down, Esteban on top. The pot burst with a *whump*, and damp dirt cascaded over the man like compost. The man shoved blindly, and Esteban swung. He felt his fist connect with the dead side of the man's face, felt his knuckles rasp against the sandy dirt on it. The man was only an outline in the near darkness, but Esteban knew the dirt had to be in his eyes, his mouth—had to be blinding him for the few seconds he needed. He got to his knees and swung again, then again, then again. Against one side of the man's face, then the other, back and forth, his fists as heavy and empty of feeling as pistons. No Marquis of Queensbury in war, friend, he thought wildly as the man's hands quit trying to cover his face at last and flopped to the ground like fish when Esteban pulled them away. No referees, no split decisions. No pity.

He dragged the man off the lawn and into the bushes. All the day's thick wine and *churrasco* steaks rose in his throat, but he forced them back down. Only when he knelt beside the man and heard his even, steady breathing did he calm enough to take the quick, short breaths of cold air that he knew would bring his own heaving chest under control. The man was alive. *Gracias a Dios*.

Somebody shot at somebody on "Gunsmoke." Esteban stood and brushed the dirt from his coat, then raked the pieces of geranium pot from the lawn into the shadows. He took off his heavy coat and covered the man with it. He wouldn't need it now. No more jeep. And he owed this poor guardian demon—whoever he was—a favor. At least that. He turned away from him quickly.

In the light from the grocery store window, he checked his watch and saw that the whole thing had taken less than ten minutes. In one way, he knew he'd blown it.

He should have tried to hold the man first, tried to find out who he was, who'd sent him. But in another way, he didn't want to know. He thought he knew who he *could* trust. As for the rest—he was safer mistrusting them all equally. Paranoia? Maybe. But paranoia with probable cause, right, lawyer? In a country where everybody had gone crazy, the son of a bitch who was sane was in the most danger of all.

So maybe Pepe was the safest man in Argentina, he thought as a huge black Bentley eased to the curb and the power window hummed down and Pepe slapped a chauffeur's hat on his head. He rolled out of the driver's seat and, with a mock bow, opened the rear door for Esteban.

"Damn it, Pepe, I said to get something inconspicuous," Esteban said as he slid onto the plush leather seat.

"So?" Pepe's pleased smile wilted.

"This is inconspicuous?"

"Patrón," Pepe said as he eased himself behind the wheel and fumbled with the unfamiliar gears. "Whatever that word means, I don't know. But it's a fancy word, no? I thought you wanted a fancy car. You got one."

The Bentley hummed away from the curb. Esteban let his tension begin to drain away into the softness of the seat, the needed illusion of safety in it. "Right," he said to Pepe. "We got one."

"Did you kill him back there?"

"No."

"Good." Pepe said. "That's my job."

Esteban replayed the line in his head to listen for any traces of irony. There were none.

It was afternoon by the time the Bentley eased into the traffic of the far suburbs of Buenos Aires, a vast, run-down sprawl that had been shoved out of the city itself into the province. If Caroline was still waiting, she would have had to take the hotel room for a fourth day by now. Had she? Esteban wondered. He'd probably scared hell out of her with his note. Had she even checked into the hotel at all? Or had she vanished, as many a reasonable woman—or man—would have? He'd made her no promises, not of anything permanent. Christ, would *he* wait for himself under such blithering circumstances?

He made Pepe stop at a tiny store on a side street, where they shaved with a bottle of mineral water and a disposable razor; they owed Buenos Aires that much, though the smell of three days' bathless traveling would have to stay on the books. Pepe seemed close to tears when they walked away from the Bentley. But they needed the anonymity of a taxi now—needed any kind of anonymity they could get.

The driver of the battered provincial taxi they hailed—probably the only morose and silent cabby in Buenos Aires—circled the block unquestioningly before he stopped outside the Hotel Dorado. No one was waiting outside: that much Esteban could draw comfort from. But he hadn't really expected anyone there. You don't trap a bear by putting the trap on top of the bait. If they were waiting for him anywhere, they'd be inside.

"Wait with the taxi," he whispered to Pepe before he got out. "Give me ten minutes. I'll signal you." He pulled the last few half-million-peso notes from his wallet, less than enough to buy a decent television set now. "It's not enough to get you to Catalonia, but it's a start. Just in case." He pressed the notes into Pepe's hand. Pepe nodded.

"I'll wait," he said.

"There'll be more," Esteban said. "If I come back."

Pepe shrugged. "I didn't have a wife *or* money when I came from Catalonia. If I can go back without one, I can go back without the other." He gave Esteban a quick embrace.

The Dorado was as anonymous as the narrow street it was on, a street of stationers' shops, tailors, a couple of old, dark-paneled bars, a hole-in-the-wall Chinese restaurant. Esteban had chosen it for that. It wasn't the Plaza or the Sheraton, the kinds of hotels they'd look for him or Caroline in.

But it was comfortable, old-style comfortable. Red velvet, thick flowered carpets, brass bar, doormen in doormen's uniforms (not the silly footmen's suits of the Sheraton), elevators with elevator operators, not buttons. The television over the bar blared war news:

somehow the British had been heroically repelled but had landed, too. The pope was definitely coming. The bartender squirted seltzer, the desk clerk looked bored, a waiter peered up at the torch with a crossed sword and rifle beneath it that filled the screen every time another "official communication" was ready to come from the generals at the Pink House. No mention of Mondragon, Esteban thought as he checked the lobby and bar, which were both on the verge of emptiness except for a bored businessman or two and a woman who might have been a hooker. The official lie was being left alone. He was grateful.

"I think you have a señorita Menendez registered," he said to the bored desk clerk, who looked at Esteban's smudged suit and wrinkled tie and mentally held his nose.

The clerk, snotty and natty, checked the register. "No," he said.

Esteban's heart plummeted. "No?"

"No. There's a *señora* Menendez, but you specifically wanted a señorita Menendez, no?" He gave Esteban a look that was the pure essence of being *muy correcto*. In spite of his relief Esteban wanted to reach across the polished counter and rip the look off his face.

Instead, he controlled himself and said, "That'll do. What room?"

"Well, since you're not certain it's the *señora* you want, I'll have to ring her first, won't I?"

"Ring her." Esteban's control was going.

"Who shall I say..."

"Her gentleman friend."

The clerk hoisted an eyebrow slightly. "Oh?"

"Now. Ring her."

The clerk sighed and languidly reached for the phone. His accent was the singsong, Italianate affectation of a Uruguayan who was trying to sound like an old-line *porteño*. Better the Bolivian Indians who ripped up the parquet floors of the housing complexes the government built for them to use for firewood, Esteban thought. They were at least honest. Mad but honest. He let the thought take the edge off his irritation. Welcome back to Alice in Wonderland, to the Mad Hatter's endless tea party, he thought.

The desk clerk raised his other eyebrow as he talked into the phone. He surveyed Esteban, as if he were fitting him to a description that was coming from the person on the other end of the line. When he hung up, he looked offended. "Room 483," he snapped, and turned importantly back to a stack of bills beside an adding machine.

At the elevator, the "official communication" began to repeat itself on the television. It was number one hundred and something. How had the joke on the street gone? When they reached the last official communication, it would come in English, with a British accent. It hadn't been a bitter joke—there was almost a wistfulness about it. After the tea party had gone on long enough, you almost prayed for an Alice to come say it was nonsense and stop it all. With a stick, if she had one.

Except that this tea party was far from over. And there were heads that were off that could never be put back on again. And there would be more before it was over—maybe his own, maybe Caroline's or his mother's or Frank's.

The elevator doors opened. He glanced over his shoulder before he stepped in. Through the reflection-jumbled glass of the front of the hotel, he made out the taxi still waiting. Small hope, he thought. But hope.

The elevator rose with a shudder.

"You look like death warmed over," Caroline said. Her neatness doubled his own sense of grubbiness. She'd met him at the door looking tailored and collected, as if she'd just walked into the room from a day at the hairdresser's and dressmaker's. Only the haggard look in her eyes gave her away, the look of somebody who's been staring at walls too long. "Haven't been sleeping?" She pulled him to the center of the room, as if she wanted to examine him in better light.

"Too much sleep," he said. "No exercise."

She took his hands, the knuckles still raw from the fight with the man with the melted face, held them to her cheeks for a moment, then looked them over carefully. "Sandpaper knuckles," she said. "They'll give you away every time. I've been scared to death."

"But you waited."

She gave him his hands back and gestured toward her suitcase, packed and closed beside the door. "I was giving you till sundown. Maybe a little bit more."

"And then?"

"I took you at your word. Away."

"Where?"

She shrugged. "Uncrossed bridges, *guapo*. Never touch 'em."

"I don't believe that."

"OK. You said to go to your mother's family in London. I'd considered that."

"Did you have enough money for it?"

"We'll discuss that. Some things have happened."

"Yep. They have. Look, Pepe's downstairs with a taxi. How safe have you been here?"

"That's part of what I want to discuss. We shouldn't stay here."

Esteban looked jealously toward the bathroom with its gleaming shower. "What's happened?"

"Somebody knows I'm here."

"Somebody?"

"Not the government. The day I got here, a man came by. He gave me some money—two thousand dollars— and told me I should leave the country before anybody else was looking for me. He said they probably would be looking soon. And he wanted to know where you were."

"Who was he? How did he know to find you here?"

"I don't *know*. He just kept saying he was a friend of yours and mine and that he wanted to help. And he looked horrible—like the whole side of his face was about to slough off."

"Right," Esteban said. "We can't stay here. Did he come back again?"

"No. He was here the night I got here—two days ago."

Two days. Before Bahía Blanca. A lot of good it had done to leave the poor bastard under some bushes in Bahía Blanca, then, Esteban thought. The man had known where he and Pepe were heading all along— and he'd been in Bahía Blanca for some unfathomable reason, determined to see that they did make it here.

And when he woke up, he'd know right where to come. How much of a head start did they have on him? If he'd been unconscious all night, a decent one. But if he'd come around sooner than that—*Jesucristo,* he could be in the corridor right now, for all Esteban knew. But how, *how,* damn it, did he know where Caroline was? And why had he only warned her once, given her money, then left her alone? The man who had slit a traffic cop's throat in an alleyway in Bahía Blanca wasn't very likely a man who would ask a woman politely once to do something, then let it ride if she didn't.

And if a stranger like that knew where he was, who else did, too? And why was he being left alone right now?

Mother whore! An hour in Buenos Aires and already he was more confused than he'd been on that dark street in Comodoro Rivadavia. But movement, movement was all now. Confusion was stasis. Confusion was being found, being trapped.

He picked up Caroline's bag. "You could have left, then. And maybe you should have. But I'm glad you didn't."

Caroline opened the door for them. "There's a line in a poem, *guapo,* that goes something like this: 'Nobody has more terrible power than the one less in love.' If you didn't show up, I'd know which of us that was. Once upon a time, I was on the short end of that formula. I won't let it happen again." She leaned over and pecked him on the cheek as he passed her with the suitcase. "I'm glad you showed up, too."

"You'll have to tell me about that 'once upon a time,'" he said as he pressed the elevator button.

"No, I won't," she said. "You've got things to tell *me* about now. And we've got to figure out where we're going. I refuse to live in a taxi—even with you."

The morose taxi driver's meter had run out of numbers and started over again by the time he pulled away from the hotel. He'd greeted Caroline with a glum nod, asked no questions, and showed no surprise when Esteban told him just to cruise the Costanera Boulevard along the Plata. Nobody said much for a while, each uneasy in the presence of the others. Esteban was out of ideas, tired and empty as the wineskin he'd flung away just after Pepe had first picked him up. Go to another hotel? If Caroline had been found at one, she'd be found at another—in the same mysterious way as the first. Esteban was on the edge of becoming superstitious, a state he'd never been able to tolerate in anybody else before. Creative paranoia was one thing; superstition was another. But probable cause could damn nearly apply as well in the one as the other now. Whatever was pursuing them, watching them, teasing them, was beyond any human causality or power *he* could imagine.

So if not a hotel, then where? He'd lived a fairly public life before the war, in the good days of the restaurant. Any friend he could go to could be traced. And if they were friends, he wouldn't put them in that kind of jeopardy. So that was out, just as trying to contact his grandfather or his mother was—for now. Even if he knew where they were, since Mondragon's death they'd surely be watched as closely as cancer cells. As Frank damn well should have known.

So where? A tent in the wilderness? That, or leaving the country—which he wouldn't, couldn't, do until Frank was found, found before the goddamn *milicos* in their comic-opera uniforms got to him and "disappeared" him like the others.

Pepe had been silent while Esteban and Caroline carried on their sotto voce, desultory conversation about places to go, hoping that the cabby was as deaf as he was sullen. For all Esteban could tell, Pepe might have been asleep—until he broke one of the silences with a matter-of-fact, "I have a cousin."

"A cousin?" Esteban said blankly.

"Nobody knows he's my cousin. His name's not the same as mine. Even my wife didn't ever know him. He used to sell books once in some town up in Colombia, then he went back to Catalonia. That didn't work out, so he came here. I lent him some money to get settled and didn't tell my wife. He was a very wise Catalan, but I believe not a very smart one. He wound up marrying an Italian and owning a tenement, a *conventillo* in La Boca with all the other Italians." He paused, considering. His elephantine hands were crossed in his lap like a schoolboy's, and he looked shyly at Caroline. "It's not much of a place for a *dama,* but he owes me a favor." He paused again. "It's a thought."

"No," Esteban said. "It's not just a thought. It's brilliance. Caroline?"

"A *conventillo?* I suppose I lived in worse in Paris. Does it have a bath?"

"One," Pepe said.

"For everybody?"

"Sí, señorita. For everybody."

Caroline thought it over. "Ah hah," she said.

Esteban leaned over the front seat. "Driver? Turn around. La Boca."

La Boca had always been Italian, Esteban imagined—at least as far back as the time when the Italians began to flood the country with immigrants a hundred years ago. Most of them had moved on, had thought of La Boca as a ghetto, with its corrugated-iron houses and the smell of fish everywhere. They'd spread and gotten rich and turned Buenos Aires into this city with an Italian accent, this supposedly Spanish city that was sixty percent Italian now. But La Boca remained their only visible homeland, now that Italy was oceans and generations behind them. So the Italians who'd remained in La Boca, the true fishermen in this fishing village in the middle of a metropolis, were left alone and even treated with a kind of nostalgic reverence. Italian was still the language of the streets and the seafood restaurants, old women still dressed in their long black dresses and peasant shawls, concertina music still drifted along the sidewalks on summer nights, the old *conventillo* tenements with their open patios and balconies and cats and outdoor cookstoves and outdoor privies and jungles of hanging flowerpots still looked and smelled more like Naples than Argentina.

The cab wound along a street of bars and restaurants that was closer to a gulley than a street, looking for the house that Pepe vaguely remembered. Behind them at the end of the canal, the Plata was even grayer than usual in the dusk, and the bright yellow and blue and green and orange corrugated-tin houses—product of a wonderfully mad Italian artist's dream and project—

paled. On a wild guess by Pepe, they'd turned at the tiny triangular plaza of La Boca, one of the city's "free territories" that pretended to the notion that it was part of Buenos Aires only because it chose to be. (Pepe seemed to remember the bar on the corner.) Fishing boats, some in drydock, suckled up to the docks everywhere, already turning into silhouettes in the twilight, the *tinieblas* light between evening and night. An old paddle-wheel steamer that announced in peeling paint that it was from San Francisco, California—a casino that had never really gotten afloat before the bad economic times hit— listed along the promenade with a For Sale sign flapping and clattering from its railing in the wind. Picturesque, Esteban imagined it had been described in a hundred tourist brochures. Like no place else, anywhere. But tonight, more than anything, a good place to hide, he thought as he glanced behind him to see if they were being followed.

"Hah!" Pepe shouted suddenly, and slammed his fist down on the back of the driver's seat. The driver jerked the steering wheel, hit the brakes, and said something about Pepe's mother. Pepe ignored him. *"¡Aquí!* We're here!" He burst out of the taxi and through a narrow stone archway into the dark patio of a semiruined, once-elegant two-story house that stood starkly among the corrugated-iron houses on either side of it.

"We're here," Caroline said.

"I see," Esteban said. "Home."

"Home," Caroline said. Her voice got flatter.

Pepe burst back out of the stone arch as quickly as he'd burst in. He had a balding, fattish man wearing a baggy, double-breasted polyester suit in tow. The man was smiling in wonder and confusion and discomfort. An even more fattish woman with a mustache and a wart on her cheek and wearing a gaudily flowered housedress followed them at a couple of meters' distance and stood drying her hands on a dish towel in the archway, smiling grimly, as Pepe shoved the balding man's head into the taxi. "My cousin," he said proudly, as if he'd discovered some prehistoric animal. "Moribundo Lopez, of Catalonia."

The balding man stretched out a nervous hand. "At your service, señores," he tried, uncertainly.

Esteban took the hand warmly. "Thank God somebody is, señor."

Moribundo Lopez and his wife led them through a child- and cat-choked patio up a flight of wooden stairs, casting worried and suspicious looks back and forth while Pepe rattled in Catalan at them. Esteban caught enough to understand that he was Pepe's very good friend and that he and Caroline were fleeing something or another that had to do with Caroline's father and *fachistas,* and that Esteban had lots of money and would pay very well as long as the father and *fachistas* were kept in the dark. And *fachistas* were everywhere these days, no?

The room Esteban and Caroline wound up with had been, Moribundo told them, their son's room before he'd gone off to work in Miami. It was unheated, damp, unswept. Magazine photos of soccer players littered the walls, and light came only from one small window and a bare electric bulb. Esteban left Caroline to hang her things on the nails that served as a closet and went downstairs to wash in a jerry-rigged shower in a corner of the patio. The water was cold, but it was water, and when he came back to the room he felt marginally human again. Pepe, who was to sleep in the family's living room, had gone out to buy them both some clean clothes. The world was on its way to becoming tolerable.

Caroline was waiting for him on the bed, leafing through an old movie magazine that the son had left behind. "Horsehair," she said. "I've never known a bed to be stuffed with horsehair, I think."

"You're spoiled."

She ignored him and flipped the magazine closed. "Well, I'm ready."

"For what?" Esteban rested his hand on the teardrop curve of her bottom.

"Later for that," she said. "You've got things to tell me. Why are we here, what happened in Bariloche, where have you been for the past three days, did you kill Jaime Mondragon—that sort of thing."

"What in God's name do you know about Jaime Mondragon?" He pulled his hand away sharply, not angry but surprised.

"That he was killed in action. That you disappeared

and have come back as if you had a band of headhunters on your trail. That I don't believe Jaime was killed in action."

"Mind if I sit? I might need to." He eased himself down onto the hard bed, the movie magazine between them. The old coil springs squonked. Caroline's bright smile was fixed, but her hands began to make tight, small knots in the spaghetti belt of her skirt, knots like prayer beads. "No, I didn't kill Jaime Mondragon. Paco did."

She was silent. John Wayne stared up at them from the cover of the magazine. "Paco?" she said at length. "As in Francisco? As in your brother, Frank?"

"That's who was in the cabin in Bariloche. There are a couple of cops dead there, too."

"Paco again?" Her hands knotted more furiously, and her voice was so level it sounded unnatural.

"Paco again."

"And why was Paco in the cabin?"

"I don't know. He said he was here to blow up some missiles. But he didn't. I got him on the base at Comodoro, and he killed Mondragon instead."

"Any notion why?"

"He said Mondragon killed Adela."

Her eyes opened wider and found his. *"Did* he kill her?"

"I don't know. I have no idea whether or not to believe Frank. It doesn't sound very bloody possible. And how the hell would he know?"

"You're a clever family. He might know." He knew she'd intended cleverness herself, but it hadn't come out sounding that way. "Where is he now?"

"I don't know. Christ, how many questions am I going to answer 'I don't know'? I haven't seen him since Comodoro. I'm guessing he's here."

Caroline rose and went to the dusty window. It was fully dark outside now, and nothing was visible through the window except the cracked wall of another building. But she remained there, her back to him, staring out. "Well, *guapo,*" she said. "It doesn't look as if we have a great deal to do for a while. Why don't you begin all over and tell me everything that happened." Her voice now was as bright, as forced as her smile had been.

"Why?"

"I'm pretty involved, wouldn't you say? Shouldn't I know all of it?"

He told the story to her back. While she listened, she crossed her arms and hugged herself, as if she'd somehow fly apart if she didn't hold herself tightly. When he was done, she paused a long moment, then said, "And he never said who these 'people in London' were, what their organization was, anything?"

"Nothing."

"Yet you propose to find him here in Buenos Aires."

"Yes."

"How?"

"Ask people. Anybody I can think of from the restaurant who might have had contacts with groups like that. Then follow up what I can get. If anybody has those kinds of contacts, the people who used to come into the restaurant do."

"That could take a long time."

"It could, unless I get lucky."

"And while you're waiting to get lucky, we're going to keep on staying here without anybody noticing. And nobody you talk to is going to be a police informer. And your mother and grandfather are going to keep conveniently out of the way. And Frank is going to put off whatever he has in mind until you find him."

"Damn it to hell, *mujer*. Do you have a better idea?"

She turned to him. The light from the naked bulb hacked lines in her face, prophesies of the hardness that caught up with all *porteña* women of their class—his and hers—in middle age, in spite of who they were, in spite of the layers of imported makeup they might use. No, he thought. No, somehow I won't *let* that happen to you.

"Yes," she said.

"Yes, what?" He jerked his attention back.

"Yes, I have a better idea. Do you remember Enrique Bravo from the restaurant?"

"The editor?"

"Of *Posibilidades*."

"Sure I remember him. I met him through you, no?"

"I knew him in Paris."

"You never told me that."

"No, I didn't. Enrique Bravo was in touch with every exile group in Europe when he was there. If Frank's 'people' really do exist, Enrique Bravo will know them."

He was stung, jealous again of the vacuum of her past. "What about you? How many of those 'exile groups' did you know?"

She hesitated, looked for a moment as if she were about to get angry, then answered him quietly. "Not many. I was a painter, not a revolutionary. Remember?"

"No, I don't remember. I never knew you in Paris."

"I see," she said. She crossed to the door and slid the bolt, then turned back to him. She began unbuttoning her blouse. "Make love to me, Esteban. Please. Now."

"Pepe's showing up with the clothes," he said. "Any minute."

"I don't care."

"Who's proving what?"

"We both are," she said. She flung her blouse over the back of a chair and reached behind her to unsnap her brassiere.

Pepe's cousin reluctantly delivered the note to Enrique Bravo. Esteban didn't trust the telephones, and it would have been suicide for himself or Caroline or Pepe to show up in the offices of *Posibilidades*. *Posibilidades* always operated on the edge, risking with every issue a closing by the government for Unhealthy and Unpatriotic articles (and sometimes actually living with a month or two of being shut down). Since Jacobo Timerman's paper had been closed for good, if any place in Buenos Aires were watched, it was *Posibilidades*.

Nor did Esteban want to risk letting Bravo know where he was staying—for his sake and for Bravo's. He'd asked him to meet him in a place on the La Boca waterfront, a seafood bar called the Ultramar—a place where only locals were likely to show up. He had no way of being sure Bravo would even come. But Bravo did, weaving his tall, blue-jeaned body among the dusty fishing nets that hung from the ceiling until he found Esteban's table against the back wall.

"Your place was better," he said as he sat down in

a gaudy cane-bottom chair and signaled for a waiter. "I was sorry to hear about the closing."

"You should understand about closings," Esteban told him.

"Sí," Bravo said curtly. "And I'm probably chancing another one right now. What's the secrecy? Is it about your sister—whom I was sorry to hear about, too. Though I should add I was *not* sorry to hear about Jaime Mondragon."

"I was. But not for any of the reasons you probably think."

"I'll let that pass." A white-aproned waiter loomed over them. "Wine," Bravo said. "Something red, from Mendoza." He looked at the empty whiskey glass in front of Esteban. "You?"

Esteban shook his head. The waiter stood, pencil ready. "No eat?" he said in a heavy Italian accent.

"No eat," Bravo said.

The waiter threw up his hands and charged off toward the bar. "No eat!" he shouted toward the kitchen as he passed it.

"Well?" Bravo said. "The secrecy?"

"Caroline suggested we talk."

"How *is* Caroline?"

"She said she knew you in Paris."

"That she did."

"How well?"

Bravo shrugged. "We moved in the same circles sometimes."

"I'll let *that* pass. Did you get to London much?"

"When I needed to."

"You know I have a brother, I suppose."

"Esteban, everybody literate in Buenos Aires knows the Molina-Knifeton genealogy."

"That's evasive."

"All right, counselor. You have a brother in London. His name is Francisco. I've met him."

"What did he do in London?"

"Oh, something in importing, wasn't it?"

"No, it wasn't. That was for public consumption. Caroline thought you might have known that much."

"What's your brother done, Esteban?"

115

The waiter came back with a half-empty bottle of red wine, a bottle of seltzer, and a plate of bread.

"No bread," Bravo said.

"Bread," the waiter said. "No eat, no wine."

"Bread," Bravo said.

Esteban used the interruption. Bravo apparently wanted a trade-off, trust for trust. It was fair. He understood from Esteban that Caroline had told more about him than he probably wanted Esteban to know. He might need some security in return.

"My brother is back in Argentina," he told Bravo when their waiter had plunged again into the ballet of shouting, milling other waiters.

Bravo whistled softly. "Where?"

"Here, in Buenos Aires, I think. But I'm not sure. He was sent."

"Who sent him?"

"That's what I want you to tell me."

Bravo shook his head doubtfully. "It's been a while. I'm not in touch the way I used to be."

Esteban accepted the self-protecting, probable lie. "I'll take anything I can get. I want to find him. I *have* to find him."

"I'd imagine. Have you actually seen him? And when?"

"I saw him last four days ago. In Comodoro Rivadavia."

"The day Jaime Mondragon was 'killed in action.' *Bueno*. I understand."

"Do you? I don't."

Bravo sipped his wine, considering. "I only mean I understand that if, just if, your brother had anything to do with...well, anything...he's probably not in Argentina. Not if he's as sane as he was when I knew him in Paris."

"In Paris? Not London?"

"He came over a good bit. There were...consultations he had to make. And something about a woman, too, I believe, though I never knew for sure. In any case, if he's not in Argentina, he's no doubt back in London."

"No, he wouldn't be there. They wouldn't want to see him now."

Bravo finished his wine thoughtfully. "Mondragon wasn't the right agenda?"

"He wouldn't be in London. Leave it at that."

"All right. Then he's in Peru. And if he's not in Peru, the only man who knows where he is, is in Peru."

Esteban hoped the shock he felt didn't register on his face. "Peru!"

"Do you remember Hugo Santander?"

"The politician, yes. A little."

"The would-be politician. Heard of him lately?"

Esteban thought a moment. "No. There are lots of things we don't hear of here."

"Not *my* fault," Bravo said. "I'd publish 'em if I could. In the last days of Isabela Perón, when everything was going to hell even quicker than it is now, Santander looked into his muddy crystal ball and saw that he had to get out while the getting was still possible. He wasn't a radical, really, but he was just far enough left of center to be a danger to himself. That was when Velasco and his leftist generals were still running things in Peru, remember, and while they couldn't exactly welcome Hugo Santander with fireworks and *pisco* sours, they could at least turn their heads when he came into the country. And since Santander was closer to the Peruvian *Apristas* and their quaint brand of something like socialism than he was to anything else, the *Apristas* arranged for him to hide out."

"Why didn't he go to Europe, like the rest?"

"Not Hugo Santander. He was a real Latin American patriot, he said. He'd stay close to Argentina if he could and be the first to march back in when the generals fell. But he was smart enough to maintain touch with the European exiles—and self-exiles. One of those people he stayed in touch with was your brother. And there's where this gets fuzzy for me. Your brother never was precisely a socialist, though he hung around with them. And while he was working for Santander's organization—something called the Democratic Argentine Liberation Front, and how's that for a clichéd name—as a kind of coordinator among the various exile groups, he was also running off to do things for the British government. I never was quite clear on just what. I take it he was a kind of maverick, but everybody seemed to accept him because he was smart and tough and good at all those whatevers that he did. Ergo, if he screwed over the British, then it must have been on orders from—or at least at the suggestion of—Santander's group. And nothing like that could happen unless Santander himself gave the nod to it. So, either Francisco is with Santander, or Santander knows where he is. *N'est-ce pas?*"

"Reasonable—except for one thing. Peru's a big country. Where, precisely, *is* Santander?"

"That's as far as I can help you. Except to tell you that if anybody knows where he is, it would be Mario Garcia Tejada, the poet."

"Carajo. Is he still alive?"

"Almost stone deaf and nearly ninety, but he's the grand old man of the *Apristas.* He and Hugo Santander are old political allies. And both as dated as Marxism, if you want my opinion." He picked up a piece of bread and tapped it on the plate. "Hard as a rock," he said. "No eat. Have I been any help?"

"I wish you hadn't been."

"Do you know Peru?"

"I've been there."

"You should get to know it better. You *are* going, aren't you?"

"Do I have a choice?"

"I'm not in your shoes, Esteban. I think you were a hell of a lot better off running a restaurant. And let me tell you something. I had a great deal of respect for your brother, but he was one of the most secretive *pendejos* I ever knew. And there was something nobody *I* ever knew could get to or understand in him. I wouldn't bet a *palo* on what he's got in mind. I'm glad I'm *not* in your shoes." He got to his feet. "I take it the bill's on you?"

"On me. Enrique? How long have we known each other?"

"How long did you have your restaurant? Two years?"

"And you never even mentioned that you knew Paco—or any of this. Why not?"

"Che! I thought you knew it all, *hombre!"* He took a step away from the table, then paused. "We're so bloody provincial here. Sometimes I forget how damn

little we really do know about the world. You should live in Europe—or in a pinch, America, Esteban. For a while, at least."

"No thanks," Esteban said, fighting back a flash of anger at the cliché he'd put up with all his life. "Everybody in the country's too busy trying to be somebody else to know who in hell they are, anyway. Somebody's got to stay home." He rose and offered his hand. "I understand the risk you took today, Enrique."

Bravo shrugged. "I may need a risk from you someday. And be careful. You're in danger of becoming a patriot, you know, talking that way." He flashed a professional smile and ducked a fishnet, heading for the door.

Esteban watched him go, a sense of dread as gray and ponderous as the Plata itself rolling over him. Everything he found out made what he had to do even more impossible, an even greater burden. Peru! *Mierda.* Somehow, he'd have to get out of Argentina, then back into it. And while he was out of it, he had to locate a man somewhere in the jungles or the mountains or deserts of Peru, a man who might or might not even be willing to help him—if he could. He didn't expect to find Frank there; Bravo was wrong. Frank was still here in Argentina, probably in Buenos Aires. He was convinced of that. Frank was somewhere in this damp city, a time bomb ticking. And whatever else got blown to smithereens, he knew some things that surely would: himself, his mother, his grandfather, and Caroline.

Hunter and hunted: he was both. You were desperate, Adela, he thought. I understand what that means now. God forgive me for not helping you.

He looked at the check. The numbers made no sense to him. He scooped a wad of bills from his pocket and dropped them on the table. There was no time to bother with counting things now, like money or risks. He had a trip to make, a long one. And quickly.

"No," Caroline said. She was back at the window again, this time facing Esteban. "I don't like Peru. Peruvian women are mice. It might rub off on me. You go alone. You'll move more quickly alone, anyway."

"I want you out of Argentina," Esteban said. "What if I don't get back?"

"We've been through this before, remember? When you left Bariloche without me. You made it back."

"But you wanted to go to Bariloche with me then."

"That was different. I know you're able to look after yourself now—more or less. No." She swept her hand around at the soccer-player plastered room. "I just couldn't leave all this. Not for something like Peru."

"What's the real reason, Caroline?"

"That's not real?" She took his hand and held it a moment. "All right, the real reason is that if I leave now, I might never get back. This mess has to be cleaned up here first. I don't want to be an exile forever, Esteban. If I have to leave, I want to do it knowing I can come back—even if it's only someday. Read Dante. He knew about that."

"To hell with Dante. It's you I'm worried about."

"And your mother, and Frank?"

"If I could take them with me now, I would. You I *can* take."

"No. No you can't." She said it with such finality that Esteban almost could hear the tumblers turning, the locks clicking.

"Then what the hell will you do?"

"Pepe's here. I've got plenty to eat with the cousin's wife and her pasta downstairs. I may look like a hippo when you get back, but I'll be alive. Will you love me if I look like a hippo?"

"Never," Esteban said. He eased himself down onto the loud bed. The leaving had all been easier than he'd ever thought possible, at least the preparations for it—until now. Pepe's cousin had a passion for dollars. Caroline had two thousand of them that the man with the melted face had left her. For five hundred of those dollars, the cousin's wife's cousin was willing to risk the patrol boats on the Plata at night. Even running with lights out, they could be downriver to Montevideo, in Uruguay, in only four hours or so. And with part of the rest of those two thousand dollars, Esteban could be on an Aeroperu flight to Lima tomorrow morning. And in Lima, he could go to the Bank of America office and wire Miami for some of the money his grandfather had been stashing there for the family for years.

And if Caroline were with him, he might never have to come back. The thought had teased at him ever since he left the restaurant after his meeting with Enrique Bravo. What if he *couldn't* find this Hugo Santander, who could tell him where Frank was? What good could he do by coming back? He'd have taken his best shot. Why should he come back to Buenos Aires and commit suicide?

But Caroline *wasn't* going to be with him. And he was almost grateful to her for that. Because no matter how much he teased himself with the notion of staying in Lima, he knew that would only be another kind of suicide. He couldn't live with it, never mind how damned reasonable it was. That Caroline had closed the door on the possibility of running gave him, paradoxically, a kind of peace. The same kind of peace he imagined the Christians must have had when they saw the coliseum gates open and Nero's lions waiting, and knew that, yes, there was no chance of renunciation left now.

Son of a bitch, he thought. Lawyer turns martyr. Not likely. Not if he could help it.

His watch told him it was a few minutes past eleven. They would leave at 1:00 A.M. Less than two hours. He imagined the cold on the river, the searchlights of patrol boats. He shivered.

"You're cold," Caroline said.

"No," he said. Then, "Yes. Warm me."

She slipped down onto the bed beside him. With one hand, he pulled her to him. With the other, he folded the blankets back. He took off her shoes, and ran his hand slowly along her leg. She raised herself to let him slide her skirt up so that his hand could find the warmth he needed.

The lovemaking they slipped into was as slow, as easy, as measured as it had been sharp and quick and nearly brutal the night before. They moved like swimmers against one another, first Caroline on top, then him, swimming deeper and deeper into each other. And when they were done, he stayed inside her, listening. From the patio and the street came sounds of a concertina, of a child crying, of a cat battle, of a mother singing a lullaby in Italian, of dishes from a late supper clattering against one another, of a ship's lonely horn on the Plata. The sounds were a necklace, he thought, a necklace around himself and Caroline, binding them together, holding them up.

And then Pepe's knock on the door sliced through all other sounds. "It's time, *patrón*," he said. "It's time to go."

Chapter Six

Steel-cut Buenos Aires; frumpy, balconied Lima. It had been four, maybe five years since Esteban had seen it. BC, BR. Before Caroline, Before the Restaurant. Some legal thing had brought him here, something from another time and world. Now, the generals were out of power and the civilians had taken over again, in the endless game of musical thrones they played. The shantytowns full of jobless Indians from the Andes that had lined the road from the airport were gone, too, bulldozed away to keep from offending tourists, he supposed. But through the thin *garúa* fog that hung over the city all winter long, he could see that the dry Andean foothills which shouldered up to the city's edge were as scabbed with them as before. It was a sad city, still, off-white and gray, jumbled and disordered and crowded, but he liked it. It was wholly itself. It was as much itself as Buenos Aires was everywhere and nowhere.

He stopped first at the Bank of America: his grandfather's accountants might never miss the ten thousand dollars he withdrew. Then he followed the telephone directions of Mario Garcia Tejada's snippy, Mexican-accented wife to an address in San Isidro, the part of Lima where Esteban's own kind of people could be expected to live. Or would have a few years back. There were trees, a small park, cobbled streets, occasionally a tastefully hidden art gallery. Old, rambling mansions with ornate stone facades shared their space now with low-slung houses, and here and there a cocaine-money, social-climbing apartment house, complete with uniformed doorman, was pushing its way in. The cabby let him out beside what a sign said was the remains of a small pre-Inca temple mound, fenced to keep the Indians off, and pointed toward one of the old mansions.

As Esteban rang the bell and waited, he tried to remember what he knew about Mario Garcia Tejada. Hell, everybody knew something about him: he was a double whammy. You got a dose of him in your literature courses—a few heavy, slow poems about guanacos and llamas and waterfalls and the glory of the Latin American race (no Neruda, but not ghastly, either). And another dose of him in your history classes— or you had before the generals took over and rewrote the history books. Something about his being the intellectual spirit behind the *Apra* movement, the only really democratic movement in South America in its day, and having hidden out in embassies and gone into exile more times than most men had eaten breakfast. Esteban was nervous—not only because of what he might find out, but because he was meeting one of those people who weren't supposed to be really real outside your textbooks.

The entry hall where he waited didn't disappoint him. The hall was filled with photographs of Tejada with Hemingway, of Tejada with de Gaulle, with T. S. Eliot, with Eleanor Roosevelt, with Perón, with Richard Burton... with more men in uniforms and morning coats and berets than you could stock an American president's funeral with. But not many women. At least not in the later pictures, after Tejada had traded his broad-shouldered, slick-haired looks for the stolidness of a middle-aged politician/poet. And when the woman with the Mexican accent greeted Esteban with all the warmth of a dead tree, he understood why. She was steel, from the color of her hair to the color of her dress to the straightness of her backbone. Younger than Tejada by twenty years, Esteban guessed. The pictures with women had stopped about the time she came on the scene.

"I'm so glad you're not a *gringo*," she said as she led

him through a maze of hallways and sitting rooms to a study off a garden in back of the house. "They've descended on us like flies since they've discovered we can actually write. They scarcely thought we wore shoes down here before. Now they can't get enough of us—publishers, journalists, university sorts..." Her voice trailed off into offended boredom.

"Most people think Argentines are a species of *gringo*," Esteban said. "Most Argentines do, anyway." He smiled at the back of her head. She wasn't amused.

The little man with the huge hearing aid and the paunch who sat on a linen couch in the study was a long way from the man in the pictures with Hemingway. But he was still himself: he didn't greet Esteban, he received him. It was only when, after the small talk and the Mexican wife's leaving to see to coffee, Esteban mentioned Hugo Santander that Tejada dropped his public-man attitude and pulled himself forward on the couch so he could actually have a shot at hearing Esteban.

"You said Hugo Santander?"

"I want to find him!" Esteban shouted.

Tejada fumbled with his hearing aid. "Who are you?"

"I told you, señor Tejada. I'm a journalist."

"Then you should already know where he is. A good journalist would. Only Argentine intelligence wouldn't. They're not very intelligent." He smiled, pleased with himself.

"I give you my word. I only need to talk to him!"

"What?"

"I give you my word! I only need to talk to him!"

Police work on Tejada would be simple, he thought. No need for bugs. All you'd have to do is stand in the street and listen.

"Piffle," Tejada said. "Who sent you?"

Esteban took a chance. "Enrique Bravo, from *Posibilidades*."

"I know him. He's a good man. Who did you say you were?"

"Esteban Molina, señor. From Buenos Aires."

"I know that. About Buenos Aires. That accent's like a flag. I never cared for it. Sounds fay to me, *cazhe* for

125

calle and all that. Worse than Portuguese. You from *the* Molinas down there?"

"Probably."

"Father used to be minister of justice? Grandfather a plutocrat?"

"That's them."

"Can you prove it?"

Esteban dug the I.D. carnet with his father's picture on it out of his wallet, and handed it and his own passport to Tejada. Tejada studied the two a minute, then looked at Esteban again with calculating eyes.

"The resemblance is there," he said. "I knew your father, too. Had a great deal of respect for him. Anybody who could stand up to your grandfather the way he did deserves respect. What do you think of that war you people are having?"

"Right cause, wrong government," Esteban said.

"That's a good answer," Tejada said. "It doesn't say anything. All right. He's near Iquitos."

"Santander is?"

"Of course Santander. Write this name down. Nieves. Anselmo Nieves. He's a river pilot. You do know Iquitos is on the Amazon, don't you?"

"Sí, señor."

"Never can tell with Argentines. You know how you get rich in Latin America? Buying Argentines for what they're worth and selling them for what they think they're worth. Next thing, you'll be attacking New York. Anyway, this Nieves can take you down the river to Santander. His father was a jailbird and he's nasty as a javelina, but he's reliable."

"Where do I find him?"

"In the floating city. Ask. They'll know him."

"That's part of Iquitos?"

"The floating city? Of course it is. After a fashion." He fumbled open an onyx box on an end table beside him, and pulled out a business card. In a shaky hand, he initialed it and handed it to Esteban. "Give this to him. And I'll want something in return."

"Como quiere, señor. Whatever you want."

"Santander is supposed to keep in touch with us every week by radio. He hasn't been. This time it's been eight, nine days. Tell him I said he's getting old. He's forgetting things." He smiled. "And then you stop by here on your way back and let me know how he is. You people'll need him in Buenos Aires when you kick your generals out."

"You think he's all right?"

"Of course he is. We've got a man there with him. He'd let us know. The worst would be that Santander's run off with some native woman for a few days. And where's that girl with the coffee?"

Esteban offered to check on it. The last thing he needed now was to sit and drink coffee and listen to an old man ramble. But this wasn't any old man; he was the Grand Old Man of Peruvian Everything, the man who, with a word, could cut off Esteban's only access to Hugo Santander. So he put up with the Mexican wife's tirade against slow maids, her wheedling to get him to do an article on her days as a ballet dancer, her unhappiness with Lima in the winter—and when he got back to the study with the coffee, the Grand Old Man of Peruvian Everything was asleep.

It seemed to him they spent the whole morning over trees. Once the Fawcett Airlines plane had climbed out of the fog of Lima and crossed the terrible depths and peaks and hidden canyons of the Andes, the land flattened and turned green, as if they were flying over a lawn that covered the entire earth. Now and again, a slow river would snake through the green below them, with a canoe like a leaf on it, and once they flew over a seaplane at a totally inexplicable dock. Small clearings that might have been Indian villages—or only small clearings—showed up irregularly. It was like flying over the sea, Esteban thought: what went on beneath that green cover had to belie the innocence of it. He didn't want to think about it; he had his own jungle to hack through.

From the airport terminal that didn't bother with walls, to the plaza that was made useless by great flocks of shrilling jungle birds, Iquitos was unlikely. He'd been told there was a decent hotel, but he didn't bother with it. Instead he made his way along straight streets, past white, one-story shops filled with televisions and cosmetics and toasters smuggled from Brazil, through muddy marketplaces where dogs and vultures and Indians fought over the refuse heaps, toward the floating city. He'd slept decently in the Hotel Bolívar last night. If he had to doze on a riverboat tonight, he would.

He'd gotten a glimpse of the floating city as they circled to land. It was houseboats, all thatched, homemade houseboats. River people, Indians mainly, the stewardess told him. People who'd docked in Iquitos to work on the river-going plywood mills that set out from here, or at whatever they could earn a few *soles* doing. When times got too bad, they could take to the river again, drifting and fishing and, if necessary, clearing a little land here and there to plant a crop of *yucca* or corn before they drifted on. But for the most part they stayed here, lashed boat to boat like some kind of colonial animal, grafted onto Iquitos.

At the end of a long, muddy boulevard of sorts that led from the low heights of Iquitos proper to the river, he shoved his way through muddy, mostly naked children and pariah dogs onto the rickety wooden dock that anchored the floating city on one side. A hearty smell of rot hung over the place. The people on the houseboats watched him as warily as if he'd been a Martian. Nobody dressed as he was came into this world unless he was from the government, the enemy, he was sure.

"Anselmo Nieves?"

The answer he got most was a finger pointing farther on. Sometimes it would be accompanied by broken Spanish or a brief spate of some grunting language he'd never heard: Aquaruna, would it be? Yacu? It didn't matter; with each half-rotted plank that he crossed from houseboat to houseboat, he felt more and more trapped in a labyrinth of faces and sounds and smells that were their own kind of jungle. With each swell of the river beneath the planks, he felt more and more cut off from the solid world.

"Anselmo Nieves?"

"*Sí*," the man patching a fishing net on the railing of a tilting houseboat said. "*Soy yo*. I'm him."

Esteban held out his hand to the man. He felt foolish when the man kept tying his knots and only looked up at him with hard black eyes. He was at least mostly Indian, though not the stocky, broad-faced Indians who had been the Incas once. This man was sharp-featured, thin, dark—the build and face of people only a generation or two away from blowguns, curare, stone axes in the forest. He was fifty some-odd by standards of age Esteban understood, he judged, though the man may have been no more than thirty. There were faint, odd scars on his forehead that looked as if they may have been put there on purpose, and his hands were as scarred and as twisted as mangrove roots. "How can I serve you, señor?" the man asked flatly.

Esteban held out Mario Garcia Tejada's business card. The man didn't take it. "I don't read, señor."

"But you recognize the initials?"

The man glanced at the card. "Sí."

"I want to see Hugo Santander."

"Who, señor?"

"Dr. Tejada told me I should find you."

"I'm a river pilot, señor. Not a tour guide. Go to a hotel for that."

"Ten thousand *soles*, señor Nieves."

"That won't buy gas for my boat."

"Twenty-five."

"Argentine?" Nieves said.

"Yes."

"The last one of you gave me forty." Nieves looked down at his net again.

Esteban's breath quickened. "What last one? An Argentine?"

Nieves went on with the work on his net. "Same accent."

"All right. Forty thousand. When was he here?"

"A week, maybe. Nine days."

"What did he look like?"

"A little taller than you, a little older, a little skinnier. Black hair. I didn't like his eyes."

"What was his name?"

"I didn't ask."

"Did he have a business card like the one I showed you?"

"No. He had a letter. He said the signature on it was señor Santander's. It looked right."

So Frank had come here first, *before* he came into Argentina. Nine days ago? Eight? Either one would have given him the time he needed to get from here to Chile to the lodge in Bariloche. Was that where the double cross of the British came from? Had this Hugo Santander told him some new information, given him some last-minute change of instructions? But, Christ. What could a man hiding in this jungle know that Frank didn't? Santander must have persuaded Frank to change his plans, must have given him not new information, but a new idea.

A damn potent new idea. Frank didn't persuade easily.

"When can we leave?"

"In the morning. I have to get my boat ready."

"Ten thousand more *soles* if we can leave today."

"No, señor. It will be dark too soon. I told you, I have to get my boat ready. You don't think we're going on *this*, do you?" He indicated the city of other houseboats around them. "Go to the Hotel Turista. I'll come for you at seven."

It seemed to Esteban that the only totally unmoving thing in this floating world was Anselmo Nieves. He was in no mood to argue with that. Whatever there was to be afraid of in this place, in the jungle, Nieves was part of it. He felt that as surely as he felt the sweat trickle down his neck. Involuntarily, he took a step back before he said, "Seven, then, no later," in an attempt to make himself believe he was still in control of something. He turned away before Nieves had a chance not to answer him.

He might have felt the slightest motion on the boat before he felt the net, but the motion and the net came so nearly at once that he couldn't tell. Nieves hadn't jumped; he'd sprung. On instinct, Esteban flung his arms out from his sides to strike the net away before it had covered all his body, but he was too late. What he managed to do instead was to throw his balance off, so that Nieves jerked him down to the damp planks of the houseboat as easily as if he'd been a rotten branch. Then Nieves straddled him, his knees holding the net tight around Esteban. Esteban arched, trying to throw him off, but the rough cord of the net cut into his face, into his eyes. He lay still. Where he lay, there was no more than a meter between the railing and the cabin of the houseboat. There was no place even to roll away, if he'd wanted to try.

Nieves sat waiting, spiderlike, until he was satisfied Esteban had stopped struggling. Two other men from nearby houseboats had hopped the railing to stand over him. One of them held a hawkbill fishing knife loosely in his thin hand. "Señor," Nieves said. "There are no roads out of Iquitos. There is no airplane until tomorrow afternoon. The only way out of here between now and then is by the river, and the river is mine. Tonight I will make a telephone call to Lima. If it goes well, I will see you in the hotel at seven. If it doesn't go well, I may see you before then. Do you understand me? You have no place to go that I can't find you."

The fetid smell of garbage and feces rose to Esteban from the water between the houseboats. "I understand," he said.

"And one other thing. The last man, your *compatriota*, gave me one hundred thousand *soles* more when he came out from seeing Señor Santander. He told me Señor Santander wanted to see no one else until I heard from him. If I take the chance that I may be sent away for disobeying those orders, even with a telephone call to Lima, you will match those hundred thousand *soles*. Before we leave here tomorrow. Do you understand that, too?"

"Yes, goddamn it. Let me up."

"I don't like filthy language, señor. This is my home." Slowly, almost as if he hoped that Esteban would make a quick move, he slid off the net. Neither he nor the two men beside him made any attempt to help Esteban untangle himself. They watched him with the same blank curiosity with which their fathers might have watched a less-than-human member of another tribe struggle against a boa in a pit.

Esteban left the Gran Muralla *chifa*, Iquitos's version of the bad Chinese restaurants that Peru was doomed to, with the taste of moldy tea still in his mouth. The shrilling birds in the plaza were quieter now that it was dark, but in the streetlamps' glow the trees seethed with them like maggots, and a steady rain of their droppings whitened the cracked park benches and bandstand into the night. Beyond the streetlamps in one direction lay the jungle; in the other direction, the river. The air was a symphony of smells of things growing and dying, of flowers and decay, and was thick with coming rain. Esteban remembered the endless miles of green between here and the mountains, and the mountains themselves, which he'd seen from the plane this morning. Nieves was right. There was nowhere to go.

A gun would be useless. You couldn't kill anybody quietly in a hotel room with a gun. And the first thing the police would do then is contact the Argentine embassy. No, the first *official* thing—after they'd done whatever else they wanted with him.

In a hardware store that was just closing beside the hotel, he bought a machete and a whetstone. Back in his room at the Hotel Turista, a sixties-modern concrete box that was sinking back into the jungle already, he sat and watched the moths flutter at his window and sweated and sharpened the machete—and thought. If Santander didn't want to see anyone, that meant he and Frank had agreed on something nobody else knew about. Nobody in Santander's organization, nobody in London. So Santander was the only man besides Frank himself who could tell him where Frank might conceivably be. And Frank was the only man who could tell him why Mondragon had killed Adela—and could prove it. And Frank's life probably depended on his getting to him before he did...did whatever he and Hugo Santander had plotted out in this pulpy, dark place.

And living long enough to talk to Santander depended on a telephone call a *mestizo* Indian was trying to make, if the radios were by some chance working, to a semisenile old man who might or might not be at home even if he got through. *Madre puta.* He let himself think of the sounds of the tango singers he'd heard in the café, of Caroline's face in the candlelight as they sat at their table and talked late into the night with friends, then had gone upstairs to his apartment and wrapped themselves around each other till noon. He sharpened the machete, and waited.

He fell asleep sometime after the last noises had stopped on the street. When he woke at dawn, the machete had slipped out of his hand onto the sweaty, seaweed green tiles of the floor. He'd slept with the door unlocked. No one had come. When he went to splash tepid water on his face, he was shaking as if he had a fever.

Anselmo Nieves would tell him nothing more than that he'd talked to the señora of Dr. Tejada, and that the phone call had gone well. "Who do I listen to?" he said. "Dr. Tejada is Peruvian. Sr. Santander is Argentine, like you. I'm Peruvian."

They were on the Amazon by then, a few miles downstream where the Río Nanay washed into it. The Nanay was brown; the Amazon was green. So when the two met, for miles the Amazon was green on one side, brown on the other, like dyed silk. A few ponderous freight barges and passenger boats had set out with them. And the water buses were out, long wooden skiffs with thatched awnings that carried women and children from the Indian villages downstream into Iquitos to the morning market, and their husbands home from last night's taverns and whorehouses, Esteban guessed. It had rained during the night, and it was getting ready to rain again. Here and there fishermen threw light nets from canoes, arcing them out gracefully as a flamenco dancer's skirts, and when Anselmo Nieves flung the gristle from the hunk of roast pork he'd had for breakfast over the side, a school of *pirañas* tore it to bits almost as soon as it touched the surface of the water. The land had flattened since they left Iquitos— it was built on the only high ground for miles, apparently—and clearings broke the forest at fairly regular intervals, clearings around cane-and-thatch huts that sat in the middle of scraggly patches of corn or *yucca* and banana trees. Islands split the river constantly, islands that Esteban knew had to be as familiar to Nieves as the buildings on his own street in Buenos Aires were to him. If Santander had wanted to be safe, he'd found his place. No emperor's labyrinth could have hidden him better.

"Germans in here," Nieves said to him, almost as if he'd guessed what Esteban was thinking. "Some Russians, too. They have plantations. The government leaves them alone, they leave the government alone.

The government doesn't care much who they are; they're better than Indians." He spoke with the same blankness as he had on his houseboat yesterday: Esteban had no idea if the man hated or tolerated or liked him, or why. He couldn't shake the sense that Nieves and his people simply considered Esteban and other foreigners as something as inconsequential as the stones or bugs of the forest.

"And Argentines?"

"A few of them, too. Anybody that somebody else wants to kill, they come here."

"Does it work for them?"

Nieves shrugged. "Sometimes. Depends on how much trouble the other people want to take to kill them."

He sank back into his blankness. They'd been on the river more than an hour. It was another hour before he spoke again, and this time it was only to say, "In here," as he cut back on the motor and shoved the control stick sharply to the side. The boat dug into the water and headed for the riverbank, toward a patch of reeds that looked like hundreds of others they'd passed. But as if by some mirror trick, when they got a dozen meters away Esteban saw that the bank wasn't solid behind the reeds. They were at the mouth of a stream.

As the boat slipped through the reeds, Esteban asked, "How the hell did you recognize that?"

For the first time, Nieves smiled, a small, tight, triumphant smile. It was his only answer.

The stream was as big as a good-sized city street, though at one bend it widened to twice that and a few huts straggled away from it in the semblance of a village. But as they went farther upstream, it narrowed, so that in places they were lost in tunnels of arching trees that let light through only in slits or patches. Things splashed into the water away from them as they approached, and Esteban saw flashes of movement that he took to be monkeys or birds in the trees, though they always seemed to be gone before he could really see them.

At a small slough, Nieves cut the motor and drifted up to a rough dock. A path climbed from the dock to a little ramada that was like a Neanderthal bus stop.

After Nieves had silently tied the launch to the dock, Esteban crawled out and started up the path.

"No," Nieves said, and pointed to a canoe tied to the other side of the dock.

Now they paddled. The stream wound through trees whose roots walked out into the water, through vines like oriental bead curtains that hid the next stretch of cluttered water from them. A launch would never have made it.

After a quarter of an hour of paddling, they nosed into an even smaller slough than the one where they'd left the launch. There was another ramada here, and a path narrower than the last. This time they took it, dodging liana vines, swatting clouds of gnats, sweating. A thin, warm rain began. It was hardly noticeable here, hardly distinguishable from the sweat that already soaked Esteban's clothes. And the path was fairly well traveled and clear, so the going was not bad: Esteban had expected worse. The jungle, which looked so solid from above, wasn't. Plenty of light filtered through the trees, and there was little underbrush; it was more woods than jungle, not that different from parts of Palermo Park in Buenos Aires.

But yes, different, Esteban remembered. Thousands of unmapped miles different. He sped up to keep Nieves clearly in sight.

They stayed with the path for nearly half an hour. Once they passed a clearing with a couple of platform houses on stilts in it, and a small *yucca* planting around it. Naked, round-bellied children with orange stripes drawn on their faces watched them pass in silence from one of the platforms. At the edge of the field, a man and two women, all of them naked except for orange grass skirts, stopped hoeing. The man walked to a two-meter blowpipe leaning against a tree nearby and rested his hand on it, just in case. But Nieves plunged past, shouting something to the man in the grunting language Esteban had heard in the floating city. The man didn't answer, and as he dropped out of sight behind Esteban, Esteban saw him motioning furiously to the two women and the children to follow him into the forest, as if he were fleeing from something. Esteban

135

didn't like it; he silently damned Nieves for making him leave his new machete behind in Iquitos.

The path forked, and Nieves stopped. He listened a moment, then made a hooting sound, something like an old-fashioned steam whistle. He listened again. Nothing answered him. He frowned, hooted again, listened, and motioned for Esteban to follow him along the right-hand path. "We're almost there. Go quiet," he whispered.

The clearing at which the path ended was silent. Only the steady undertone of insects, the small hiss of rain, and the distant rustlings and creaking of the forest itself disturbed the dozen or so vultures who sat patiently around the yard and on the red-tiled roof of the house and thatch of the outbuildings. The place was— or had been—a small plantation. A low stone wall surrounded the wooden house, which had been painted sky blue years before, and three outbuildings. In back, Esteban could see an indentation in the forest that must have been a road or pack trail once, must have led to the dock where they'd left the launch. Back when whoever lived here *wanted* to be easy to reach.

Nieves hooted again, then motioned for Esteban to squat beside the wall. Then he made a circuit of the whole compound, keeping low beside the wall himself. When he got back, he squatted beside Esteban and said, "You, señor. Not me. You go up."

"Where are they, damn it?" Esteban answered.

"Anywhere. The señor said he didn't want to have company, no?"

"And those vultures?"

"A dead pig, señor. Maybe that." Nieves's black eyes gave away nothing.

"Sure." Esteban grunted. "Give me your machete."

Nieves wagged his finger in a *no* sign.

"Give it to me, damn it."

Nieves stared at him, and grew very still. Esteban had the odd sense that the man was shrinking back into the foliage, was becoming part of the vegetation of the forest itself.

"All right," Esteban said. "You'll wait for me, at least?"

Nieves seemed to relax. "Sí," he said curtly.

Esteban took a breath, then stood. He waited before he moved again, to give whoever might be in the house a look at him. Then he leapt over the wall. He came down running, zigzagging across the scraggly yard. The vultures in his path hesitated, then flapped a few meters out of his way. No more.

He vaulted onto the low porch, then flattened himself against the wall beside the door. "Señor Santander," he shouted. "I was sent here by Mario Garcia Tejada."

There was no answer from inside the house. Esteban inched to a window. He'd seen that the curtains were drawn, but he hoped for a crack in them large enough to give him at least a partial view.

They were pulled tightly. "Señor Santander!" he shouted again.

He made his way across the rough planks to the door again, and eased the screen open. The spring screeched and he froze, listening. Still nothing. He tried the door handle. It opened.

The stench was like a wind that shoved him back from the door. For a moment all his senses seemed to shut off, to try to protect themselves. He turned his head away and sucked in a lungful of the heavy jungle air, and held it. He wouldn't be long. He already knew what he was going to find.

One body was slumped on a flower-patterned couch. The other was sprawled through a doorway that led to a kitchen. Around each of them was a pool of something dry and black. Each glowed slightly in the dimness of the house, and insects scuttled away from them in the light from the doorway. But these weren't the men he was looking for! They couldn't be. They were huge, fat in a way a man of Santander's age shouldn't be. And, damn it, both of them were black!

He slammed the door behind him and stumbled out into the rain, biting hunks of air. The vultures watched him jealously as he trotted down the slick, reddish clay of the path to the gate. Nieves waited for him in the open, certain now that there was no one to be afraid of in the house.

Esteban fought to keep Nieves from seeing how shaken he was as he told him what he'd found. Nieves heard him out, keeping him fixed with his eyes. Did the bastard *never* blink?

"No, not black men, señor," he said when Esteban was done.

"Black men, goddamn it. I saw them."

"They're black now. I believe you. They swell up, they turn black, they burst open and everything spills out. After a week in the heat, señor, if the vultures and the animals can't get to them. I've seen it."

"A week—they've been in there a week?"

"At least, señor. I believe longer. Since the last time, *creo.*"

"Why didn't anybody know it? What about those people we passed?"

"They knew it."

"Then..."

"It's not their business, señor. You understand? It's trouble."

Esteban turned to look at the house again. One of the vultures, attracted by the scent, was on the porch now. "Yes. It's trouble." Over a week. "Since the last time" Nieves had been here. Esteban tried to picture it: Nieves waiting out here as he'd done this time, Frank inside the house, not being convinced by Santander to change his plans, but trying to convince Santander to *let* him change his plans. And Santander refusing, calling in from the kitchen the man *Apra* had left with him. And Frank taking the man from *Apra* first as he came through the door—had he used a silencer, a knife, a bayonet?—then turning to Santander, who watched from the couch, too horrified to move or call out again.

Then Frank walking calmly out and closing the door, telling Nieves not to disturb Santander. And had Nieves known all along what had gone on, or suspected it?

What... what in God's name had Frank so repulsed Santander with that Santander had to die for it?

"I'm going back in," he said to Nieves. "I'll need ten, fifteen minutes. No more. Will you wait?"

Nieves nodded. His expression didn't change.

Esteban ripped his shirttail into a rough bandana and wet it from the well beside the porch. Then he tied it over his nose and mouth, though he knew it wouldn't help much. At the porch, he kicked at the vulture, who moved away as far as the steps and settled again.

Inside, he tried not to look at the bodies when he pulled back the curtains, but they were there, were facts, like the couch and the yellowing, multiframed panorama of Lima on the whitewashed wall and the pictures of Saint Rosa of Lima and the Virgin of Luján beside it. He deliberately stared at the body he took to be Santander's on the couch until it stopped being more than merely a thing to him, then he walked to it. There wasn't enough left for him to decide how Frank had done it, and he didn't care. Those were Frank's details to live with, not his.

There was nothing around the body to give him a clue as to what they'd been talking about—no letters, no notebooks. He backed away from it and crossed to the other doorway in the room, the one that didn't lead to the kitchen. When he pushed it open, he found himself in a spare bedroom—two single beds, a shortwave radio, a desk, two armoires, a bookcase and a file cabinet, and a couple of straight-backed chairs.

The armoires gave him clothes, nothing more. The desk was surprisingly bare—writing paper, paper clips—not even any addresses. Yet a man like Santander needed to correspond, needed to be constantly in touch or he'd be forgotten.

The file cabinet was as much a puzzle as the desk. Or, no, it wasn't a puzzle, not if you drew the conclusion Esteban had to draw. There were letters, years of letters, in the file cabinet. But none from Buenos Aires— only from Europe or America. Frank had culled carefully: he couldn't afford to take everything with him, not with Anselmo Nieves waiting outside. So he only took what mattered now—and that was anything that could lead to him in Buenos Aires. Whatever happened after that he hadn't seemed to care about.

And that meant Esteban had to care, had to care more than ever now.

But what the hell good did that do him? That black, burst body in the other room had been his only link to Frank. What was left was Buenos Aires and hopelessness. If he even made it out of Peru now.

The noise that came from the other room startled

him at first, then, when he realized what it was, sickened him. He'd forgotten to shut the goddamn front door behind him.

On his way to the living room he picked up one of the straight-backed chairs. And as soon as he was in the room, he was yelling and swinging the chair at the black shape pulling at what had been the hand of Hugo Santander. The vulture flapped wildly, panicking, realizing it had no room to fly. Esteban caught its wing tip with the chair and spun it. It managed to rise a few feet from the floor, hopping more than flying, and when it came down, it was more disoriented than ever. It scuttled now, heading for Esteban. Esteban shoved the chair at it and it stopped. Then he took aim at its head, and missed, but came close enough. The bird knew for certain where its enemy was and understood that safety was in the opposite direction. It moved toward the front door, half hopping, half pushing itself along with its wings, like oars. Esteban let it go, almost envious that it was outside this room before he was.

He flung the chair aside and started after the vulture. And almost as if he owed the corpse a silent apology, he glanced at it a last time as he passed. The vulture had just begun, apparently, had only had time to move one of the bloated arms. But that had been enough. The small notepad that Santander had been holding in his lap was visible now, was still caught in a corner of Santander's pants pocket where it had been when Frank overlooked it beneath Santander's coat sleeve.

Esteban gingerly lifted it from Santander's lap and stepped to the light from the doorway. The first page was nothing but doodles, sharp, straight, angry lines, as if Santander had wanted to hide what was on the other pages. The second page was nothing, too: Santander had started his grocery list on it, then switched to more doodles. He'd only gotten as far as the first item, *papas*, potatoes. And then what? Frank had come in, the doodles had continued on the third page, a nervous man's way of talking to himself when he's being forced to listen.

And on the fourth page, there was a name. Or part

of a name. But that was enough. Esteban could fill in the rest of Caroline La F——.

He stepped out the door onto the porch and ripped the wet cloth from his face. Through the drizzle, Nieves seemed to be a long way off, as if he were seeing him through the wrong end of a telescope. Somebody had kicked Esteban in the stomach, and he couldn't get his breath. He raised the notebook and looked at the name again: Caroline La F., in an old, nervous man's handwriting. In that room with the stench of vicious, violent death, with the stench of the sure, final knowledge that the brother he'd almost worshiped once had turned into a man who could murder as casually as some men make love, he'd found Caroline's name. Connections made themselves like sparks leaping between wires, but they didn't matter now: Caroline and Paris and Paco, *of course;* Caroline's reaction when she heard Paco was back in the country, *of course;* Caroline's silence about her past, *of course;* Caroline's meeting him in the restaurant just after she got back from Europe, *of course;* Caroline's sending him to Enrique Bravo so that Bravo could tell him where to find Santander, though she knew where he was all along, *of course, of course, of course*...All you need is the one piece of the picture puzzle that makes it all come clear, and of course the picture was there all the time, the lines, the colors, everything.

But not everything, not everything at all. Her surprise when she heard that Paco was in the country was genuine, he'd swear to that. And Adela, what had Caroline's part in Adela's death been? If she were involved in this whole nightmare, and if Frank knew—or guessed—that Mondragon killed Adela, then why had Caroline not known, too? Or worse, why hadn't she been aware that Adela was in danger beforehand? That she *had* been aware and had kept it from Esteban was more than he could accept.

More than he could accept? Was he still not accepting things that didn't make sense? After coming from a country that had lost itself in a mad tea party, that settled its political squabbles by yelling, "Off with their heads"? After finding out that his mother and sister were involved in some spy-novel scheme to blow up missiles, for God's sake? After Adela? After Mondragon? After Frank? Why should he balk at being wrong one more time?

Because Caroline had been the one sure thing, the one decent, sane, reasonable thing he could count on. The colors in the picture of the world he'd had until a few weeks ago had all run, had all blurred shapes and faces and souls into something grotesque and unrecognizable. But not Caroline's face, not Caroline. If he accepted that she'd met him and loved him on *orders* as part of some Byzantine plot, that she'd tricked him, misled him, lied to him, kept him ignorant, made a fool out of him—if he accepted all of that this easily, then there was nothing left. He might as well stay here, go to the clearing they'd passed, and ask the man with the blowgun to take him in, to let him paint his face orange and hoe yucca with them and believe that the world was a rotten illusion, and only dreams were real. How easy, how tempting. And how wrong; what a bloody, goddamn lie!

The world was all he had. Argentina was all he had. Caroline was all he had. And his family... what of it he had left, he didn't know. But he had to find out—he had to slice through this damn twisted mystery somehow. To operate on the one thing left to him: pure, stupid blind faith. Faith that, if he'd been wrong—even wrong most of his life—he could find out where and why, and could put some of it right, could salvage something from it. Faith that, even if Caroline were involved in this goddamn horror, she *did* love him, and he loved her, and one way or another that love wouldn't get lost, get murdered, too.

He stepped down off the porch toward Nieves, who waited as impassively as a tethered horse. Faith was a hell of a big job, he thought as he stuffed Santander's notebook into his pocket. Faith that going back to Caroline would put something right, when the one person left who he was certain could tell him where to find his brother—find him and stop him however he could—was Caroline. Virgin fucking Mother! Now it was faith, was it, lawyer? And faith and irony didn't mix.

"Who knows where we are?" he asked Nieves.

"Nobody—except Dr. Tejada, in Lima."

"You'll have to tell him what we found. I know that. And if you tell him, he'll have to tell the police."

"Sí."

"I need a day, one day. I want to be out of the country before anybody finds out what's in that house. It's worth a hundred thousand more *soles* to me."

Nieves thought a moment, then nodded toward the house. "It's not going to make any difference to them in there."

"No."

"*Cómo no?* Then why not? Sure."

Sure. Why not, Esteban thought. One day, one more day. One day closer, Paco. Wait for me. I'm coming.

Outside the gleaming new Eastern Airlines office in the Hotel Bolívar, Lima's wrong-century grand hotel on the Plaza San Martín, an Indian, naked except for a ragged blanket thrown over his shoulders, rummaged through the trash while a grandmotherly lady in sensible shoes lectured him on his lack of moral values. Nobody interfered; after all, this was Lima. Esteban had seen the Indian when he'd checked into the Bolívar two days ago, begging *soles* and rummaging through other trash cans. The Bolívar was his territory, Esteban supposed. And no matter how little he made, the cop on the corner got part of it for making sure it stayed his territory. Pure symbiosis.

As he went into the airline office to reconfirm his flight back to Montevideo that afternoon, he dropped a hundred-*sol* coin into the Indian's hand. The Indian and the cop both needed it. And so did Esteban: charity went with faith and hope, and as long as he was operating on the last two, he might as well go for the magic number three. Nieves had left him as blankly as he'd met him, but after a night spent with the polished brass and softly glowing mahogany and quiet Peruvian courtesy of the Bolívar (he left the vapid modernity of the Sheraton to the American tourists, who probably deserved it), he could almost believe in the possibility of human warmth and reasonableness again.

Relieved, he found that the plane was indeed still scheduled and that, wonder of wonders, his seat was still confirmed. It left at one, three hours from now.

Time for a good early lunch of Peruvian *arroz con mariscos* and *anticuchos*, a last *pisco* sour, a last hot bath. He'd gotten through to Montevideo by phone yesterday when he came back from Iquitos. Pepe's wife's cousin would be waiting. And so would fear, and hiding.

But that would be tonight, and on the other side of a continent. Now it was intermission, and time could stop for a little while. He was determined not to think for these few hours: he knew what he had to do when he got to Buenos Aires—go to Pepe's cousin's, find Caroline. It was that simple. Beyond that, thinking was useless. A *pisco* sour was better.

The lady in sensible shoes was gone when he left the airline office, but the Indian was still there. He saw Esteban, smiled, and held out his hand.

"Otra vez? Again?" Esteban said, and reached for his pocket. Twice blessed was better than once, he supposed, if he was going to play by the rules.

The Indian didn't take the coin. He suddenly needed the hand to hold the blanket around him, since his other hand had a pistol in it. He opened the blanket enough so that only Esteban could see the pistol, a revolver, held close against his naked, dirt-streaked stomach. Esteban slowly put the coin back into his pocket. "All right," he said, darting his eyes to the cop on the corner. "You couldn't be stupid enough to try a robbery here. So what is it?"

"Vente," the Indian said. His hair was matted and uncut, and his eyes were veined with too many nights of grain alcohol and sleeping in doorways. "Come with me." He moved to Esteban's side.

"No," Esteban said. Bluff, he thought.

"Señor," the Indian said, his thin, rasping voice patient. "Look at me. What do I have to lose, señor. Eh?"

They stared at each other a moment. No bluff. "Where?" Esteban said.

"Not far. A few blocks." He said it almost apologetically, and stepped close to Esteban's side.

They left the Plaza San Martín and wound into a section of narrow streets, where small shops and *chifa* restaurants filled the lower floors of once-elegant office buildings, their carved facades now gray and crumbling in the city's smog. The Indian stayed at his elbow, weaving in and out of the sidewalk traffic beside him as if he were attached to him with an invisible string. In the middle of a block, the Indian touched his arm and nodded toward a door into a stairwell. There was nothing particularly sinister about it—only a door into a building that you might expect less-than-prosperous notaries and lawyers and dentists to have their offices in. Yet Esteban took a step back from it. He knew his fear didn't come from what you'd expect of the place, but from what you didn't.

The Indian nudged him and they made their way up a wooden staircase lit by dusty bulbs at landings, past doors that nobody seemed to be coming or going from. As he climbed, the feeling that he was in a tomb grew, and in spite of himself, his memory wouldn't let him alone—his memory of another tomb in Buenos Aires. Almost as if he'd been pitched back in time, the sense that he was suffocating, that all light would vanish around the next landing, that he was being forced to relive a nightmare, overwhelmed him. It was with something near gratitude that he saw that the door the Indian stopped him in front of was only an old-fashioned office door, and that light came from behind the window, on which was neatly painted, "Dr. Mario Garcia Tejada."

The Indian knocked.

"Quién?" a man's voice said from behind the door.

"Yo, señor," the Indian answered.

A bolt slid, and the door opened. Behind it was an office, cluttered with books and manuscripts and hung everywhere with tilting paintings and photographs and political posters yellow with age. The place was something from an old photograph itself, wainscotted and lit with dangling, shaded light fixtures, an office the original Panama Canal Treaty might have been signed in. Esteban glanced behind him before he stepped in. The Indian was gone.

Tejada's steel-haired, steel-spined wife sat at the overflowing desk. Besides the man who let Esteban in, there were two others in the room, all three of them barrel-chested Peruvians in cheap suits that fit the way suits always did on men who weren't designed to wear them. Esteban had dealt with men like them before, when his father was in the Ministry of Justice. Tough men, working men. The men you'd expect to be union enforcers or bodyguards for a party like *Apra*.

"My apologies, Sr. Molina," Tejada's wife said. Her Mexican accent grated on Esteban.

"If you knew where I was staying, you could have just phoned," Esteban said.

"I thought you might not want to talk to us now," she said. "After your trip to Iquitos. You promised my husband a report on Sr. Santander."

"There was nothing to report."

"No?"

"No."

"That he is dead doesn't seem to you worth telling us?"

Fuck Nieves, Esteban thought. For a quick moment, he wished he'd been Frank and could have left the son of a bitch in the river for the piranhas. "I'm a foreigner, señora. I didn't need... difficulties with the police here. You know I didn't kill him."

"Yes, I know that. But I think you might know who did."

"Where's your husband, señora? Shouldn't he be here?" Faint hope, Esteban thought. Tejada was in textbooks: men in textbooks could be reasoned with—false logic from somebody who was already grasping at straws.

"Dr. Tejada doesn't involve himself in details of the party anymore. His strength is limited. I handle the details."

"Such as myself."

She closed her eyes and nodded, an "if you will" gesture. Then, "No one here has any authority over you, señor. You realize that. The police will be informed, and you can make your case with them. But *Apra* has learned to conduct its own affairs, since we've had to for many years. Each new government that comes along seems to take special pleasure in persecuting us one way or another. Sr. Santander was under our protection. We want to know what you know before the police make that information unavailable. It could be very useful to us—and to people who might come to us as Sr. Santander did—in the future. Is that unreasonable?"

146

"No." He looked around at the three men. He'd told himself he might almost be able to believe in human reasonableness again, had he? Reasonable had nothing to do with it. Reasonable for him now had to be getting out that door in time to make an airplane to Montevideo—and keeping the Peruvian police from knowing anything until he did. Say anything, he thought. Buy a little time. Figure. "Nieves was paid to give me a day to get out of the country. He took the money."

"He's a poor man," Tejada's wife said. "I believe my husband also told you he was reliable. He proved that."

"Mira, señora. If I tell you everything I know and if the story satisfies you, will you see that I'm on my plane this afternoon? You say reasonable—that's reasonable."

"No. We can't afford trouble with the police, either. But I will make you a promise. We'll do whatever we can to see that you're represented well, and that we use whatever influence we have for you. Without us, well, as you say, señor, you're a foreigner, no? And one thing you should know. We've checked. The man Anselmo Nieves says he took to see Sr. Santander more than a week ago—the name he traveled under was Molina, too. I think you may indeed need us."

Esteban judged his distance. If he could ram the man nearest the door out of the way, he had a chance. If only the bloody door didn't open *in*... no—if only nothing. It was that or a Peruvian jail, and then an Argentine firing squad.

The man beside the door, forty-some-odd and built like a wrestler, caught Esteban's eye movement. He stepped closer to the door. It had to be now, Esteban knew, while the man was off-balance. He lunged.

The man tilted against the wall when Esteban rammed him with his shoulder—far enough out of the way for Esteban to get a hand on the doorknob. But damn it, the thing was locked! He fumbled at a knob above the handle, knowing that the time it cost him was too much, that it was futile now. As the lock clicked, arms grabbed him from both sides, jerked him backward into the room. He struggled, but he was as pinned as he had been in Nieves's net.

"Hold him. Quietly!" Tejada's wife hissed.

An arm went around Esteban's face, and a coat sleeve filled his mouth. He willed himself to relax, not to fight. Whatever strength he had, he'd need it for the Peruvian PIP, the state police, now.

"Quiet, I said," Tejada's wife ordered again. Above the coat sleeve, Esteban saw she was pointing at the door. There was a shadow on the other side of the glass, the shadow of a man who stood as if he were listening. In the silence, the shadow's arm rose and knocked softly.

"Quién?" Tejada's wife called. "Who is it?"

"Dr. Tejada?" The voice was slow, careful, like an old man's voice.

"He's not here." She motioned for the man that Esteban had shoved against the wall to lock the door. He nodded, and reached for the door—but not in time. The door slammed open against his hand and a man rolled through it. Not an old man—but Esteban understood why he'd thought so. With half his face frozen, the man had had to learn to speak all over again. His guardian demon had found him.

But this time, he had more than a knife. He swung an automatic pistol around at Tejada's wife and men, as if he were daring them, checking one by one to see if they wanted to challenge him. Esteban felt the arm around his mouth loosen, the man who was holding him step away from him.

"You are leaving today?" the man with the melted face said, the words coming out slowly, painfully. Involuntarily, Esteban looked away, as if he'd caught himself watching something very private.

"Yes. At one."

The man nodded. "I'll wait here. Go."

"Who the hell..."

"Go! *Lárgate!*" There was no love in what the man was doing. He pointed the pistol at Esteban. Esteban remembered the street in Bahía Blanca, the feel of the man's face as his fist had come down on it. No. No love. He understood the hate in the man's eyes. This had to be humiliating for him, whatever his reason for doing it.

He left the room without looking back. Tejada's wife was right—they did need to know what he knew about Santander's death. But what could he have told her without telling her about the rest, all the things they didn't need to know? And all the things he didn't know himself. Like who the man with the automatic pistol was, how he found him, again and again. And why. He was surprised at his lack of surprise. It was as if he'd come to expect the son of a bitch by now, like a recurring dream.

Had the man really come to see Caroline? Or did she know who he was all along—had they been working together? The closer he got to discovering something, the more it disappeared, like a Cheshire cat. And what was left? Only the smile, that damn taunting smile that kept his anger going. That kept *him* going.

On the stair landing, he heard the door to Tejada's office click softly shut. It was a room he wouldn't want to be in for the next couple of hours.

So this had been his intermission, he thought as he started downstairs. He slammed his palm against the banister. Time to get to the Bolívar for his bag and then to the airport. Just that.

Chapter Seven

He skirted La Boca's small plaza, where two shore patrolmen stood under a streetlamp idly tapping their nightsticks against their legs and looking with longing at the bar on the corner. Concertina music came from the bar, and slurred, homesick singing in Italian. If there was a war on, the people singing in the bar didn't know it tonight—or didn't care. Better for them, Esteban thought. The Uruguayan newspaper he'd dropped in the Plata as he got off the boat told what he knew the Argentine papers didn't. The British had started across the Malvinas toward Port Stanley. If they took their time, they'd be there in a week. And then it was over. Only we don't know it, he thought, because we're a people who believes in miracles and we're willing to listen to anybody who tells us we're about to have one— even the bastards in their tailored uniforms making their speeches on the balcony of the Pink House.

And did he believe in miracles himself now? He must. If the British would be in Port Stanley in a week, then whatever Frank had planned had to happen by then. A week. A week to find him, to stop him. No—a week at the most. There was no reason to believe Frank would wait the full week. He could be doing whatever it was now, could have already done it while Esteban was dodging patrol boats on the Plata.

And here was the trap: the fact that the man with

the melted face showed up again in Lima meant that he was being *allowed* to look for Frank, without question. And whoever was doing the allowing wanted Frank found, too. So if he did find Frank, what then? Would the allowing stop? Was he leading himself and Frank both more deeply into the trap?

No matter. Knowing that was a possibility couldn't make any difference in what he was doing—he couldn't let it. Frank had to be found. Period. What happened when he did—if he did—was something he'd have to deal with then, not before.

He stopped a moment outside the bar that the concertina music and singing came from. There were new posters in the window, put up beside the familiar patriotic ones that had been in every window in town for the past two months now. Some of the new ones were for the World Cup soccer games that began in Spain the following weekend; most were pictures of the pope in various poses, bordered by the blue-white-blue colors of the Argentine flag—not very subtle propaganda. Welcome, Your Holiness, they said. Everything is yours. Big weekend coming, Esteban thought. The British in Port Stanley, the national soccer team in Spain, the pope in Buenos Aires.

And Esteban Molina? He wished to hell he knew where *he'd* be.

He left the light and music of the bar reluctantly. Ahead of him was the almost-street that led to Pepe's cousin's *conventillo*. And to Caroline.

He was afraid. Of the varieties of fear he had sampled for the first time this past week, he knew that somehow this was the worst. What would he say to her? I found your name on a corpse in the Amazon jungle. I love you. Don't leave me because you've lied to me and might be involved in something monstrous. What would her face tell him? How much would he have to hurt her?

And with the fear, mixed with it in a terrible kind of witches' brew, was anger. He didn't have the vaguest real notion which of the two would be in control of him when he saw her. And were the two really that different after all?

The moon was small and distant, even though it was

full, and had an icy ring around it. It was too cold tonight for the people who would normally pack these streets, so his footsteps echoed clearly off the iron wall of houses around him. Irrationally, he expected someone at the *conventillo* to recognize them, to be at the damp archway to welcome him home. But the courtyard was empty. Only a skulking cat moved. He looked up at the long open gallery his and Caroline's room led from. The door was shut, and there was no window to tell him whether a light was on in it. He climbed the creaking, unsteady stairs, then moved along the gallery, his footsteps hollow on the planks.

At the door he knocked, waited, knocked again. He tried the door. It was unlocked, and behind it the room was in darkness. He carefully eased his way into the room, his arms making clumsy swimming motions ahead of him as he felt for the light cord. He found it, and when it broke off from the force of his jerk on it, he stood looking at it in surprise while the light swung crazily above his head. As long as he stared at that, he didn't have to look at the empty nails where Caroline's clothes had been hanging when he left.

He walked back out onto the gallery, leaned on his palms against the railing, and looked up. The moon was where he'd left it. It seemed farther away now, though he knew that wasn't true. He watched it until he was sure it was moving, as it should be, then dropped his eyes to the courtyard. Pepe stood there now, his face raised toward him, a silhouette against the long arch of light that spilled onto the moonlit paving stones from the street.

"When, Pepe?" he said.

"Four nights ago, *patrón*. Just after you left. She went during the night."

"I see."

"Do you want me to come up, *patrón*?"

"No. It's all right. Go back to bed."

Pepe didn't move. "Will you sleep?"

"I don't know. I'll try. Go to bed now."

There was a silence. *"Pues,* in the morning, then, *patrón."*

"In the morning."

He pushed off the railing and turned back to the room. The bare bulb still swayed, and the room rocked in cold, stark light.

BOOK TWO

Chapter Eight

Esteban took a chance. "Chuy?" he said to the voice that answered the phone at his grandfather's. If his grandfather had trusted anybody to keep his house in order while he was gone, it would be his chief *guapo*.

"Sí?" The voice was puzzled.

"Esteban. I need to talk to my grandfather."

There was a pause. "I don't think you should be calling here, Sr. Esteban."

"I know that, Chuy. Where's Grandfather?"

"He's not here. I thought you knew that."

"I do. But I need to talk to him. Can you arrange it?"

There was an even longer pause. "I don't know, señor. You give me a telephone number—no, you call back here. In one hour."

"One hour. *Gracias*." He hung up. Not long enough to trace—and if his grandfather's phone was bugged, it would be with the old man's knowledge and sufferance. There had been a time, before the war, when his grandfather could have had anything erased that was overheard, both from the tape and the operator's memory. Now, after Mondragon's death, who knew? All bets could be off. But it was time for faith again, stupid faith that it was his turn for something, anything, to go right. What else did he have left? Where else to go?

He'd wrestled with the idea of calling him most of

the night—or what was left of the night by the time he got to bed. Caroline's absence was like a death: it wasn't real yet, it hadn't had time to leave an empty space yet. In a way it was like Adela's death. As long as he was *doing* something about it, he didn't have to truly accept it. That was why his mother had needed the tide of visitors and the funeral arrangements for Adela. That was why he'd needed to go to Bariloche then; Caroline's leaving was why he had to call his grandfather this morning.

But the call wasn't only that, only a gesture to hide from grief. Frank had been his grandfather's great hope. The nearest thing to love he'd ever seen the old man show was for Frank. There'd been affection for himself and Adela, yes, but not the unqualified, obvious love he'd shown for Frank. Curiously (to himself), Esteban had never resented it. He'd given it to Frank as his due, as if Frank's place as firstborn, his dreamy distance had set him apart from ordinary people like himself. Adela hadn't taken it so well, he thought, but she was careful not to show it. At times he'd wondered if her embracing of everything Argentine with such passion—even her engagement to Mondragon—were a way of setting herself apart from Frank, of saying to her grandfather that *she* was the worthy one, since Frank had deserted them for England. But it hadn't worked— though in a sense she'd died for it—and their grandfather had still talked about nothing but Frank, even after he left for England.

And that was what was left for Esteban to count on, that passion for Frank in his grandfather. If it was stronger than patriotism, religion, greed—all the things his grandfather lived by—then he had an ally. If it wasn't, then he had an executioner.

He left the grocery store where he'd made the call and took a taxi across town to Retiro. Just in case they'd been able to begin to trace the call, he wanted to make sure the second one came from another part of town. Pepe and his cousin should be safe enough as long as Pepe stayed sober and hidden, unless there was a house-to-house search. Before he left to make the phone call, he'd given Pepe an envelope with two thousand dollars in it. Pepe had thanked him brusquely, had struck a pose and declared that he'd only go back to Catalonia when his debt was paid, i.e., when Esteban was either safe or dead. Esteban had promised to let him know, either way.

He made the second call from the Great Neck Farmacia and Perfumeria. Again, Chuy answered.

"Where are you, Sr. Esteban?"

Esteban told him.

"You stay there. I'm coming."

Esteban was buying his third bottle of perfume when his grandfather's silver Mercedes pulled up outside. He was sure he smelled like a Mexican whorehouse from all the perfumes he'd tried on, waiting. The odd look Chuy gave him when he slid into the Mercedes beside him told him he was right.

"I'm happy to see you safe, señor," Chuy told him. Esteban still couldn't get used to Chuy calling him señor. He'd been taught to think of him as a kind of retarded uncle when he was growing up.

"Did you think I wouldn't be?"

"We didn't know."

"How's Grandfather? And Mother?"

"Well."

"Just that?"

"Your mother wants to go home. She's not taking comfortably to ... where she is."

"And where's that?"

"Don't ask me, señor."

"All right, then will she get to go home?"

"I think so. Your grandfather isn't happy that she's not happy."

"He wouldn't be. She wouldn't let him be. Where are we going?"

"To your grandfather, señor."

So much for that, Esteban thought. Nor was it fair to ask Chuy for information. He couldn't give it, and there was no point in pushing him. They lapsed into the silence of the Mercedes, with its softly whooshing heater and quiet tangos from the rear-seat speakers. If Esteban's mother was well, that meant his grandfather had succeeded in protecting her so far. Thank God for that, at least. And she was going home, back to that long, empty, many-bathroomed apartment on Libertador, which they were driving onto now. His grandfather might have decided the worst was over, but Esteban doubted it. He knew his mother. It was more likely that his grandfather had simply washed his hands of her.

They headed west along Libertador, past buildings that were as familiar to Esteban as the back of his teeth: the naval mechanics school (he accepted as true the rumors of the "disappeareds" being taken there for "questioning" before they vanished), the faculty of medicine, the national police headquarters (he turned away), the sprawling parks and monuments of Palermo. He'd missed this city, he realized. In only just over a week, he'd missed it. Not the things that went on here, not his father's death, and Adela's, not the repression, the suffocating pressure to conform. No, he'd missed Buenos Aires in spite of those things. Was that a sign of real love—could you love a place like a person, in spite of the flaws? *Cristo y los ángeles,* what kind of exile would he make?

"There," Chuy said as they passed the Spanish Monument in Palermo. "The pope will speak from there." Already a wide platform was going up around the monument, covering three sides of it. The platform faced down the soccer-field-sized boulevard that led to the Plaza Colombia, with the mammoth statue of General San Martín rearing his horse in a battle charge at the legions of traffic that swept down on him. No traffic there when the pope spoke, Esteban knew. How many millions of people could jam their way onto the boulevard and into the open spaces of the park then? More than Esteban would want to be around to count, that was for damned sure.

"You going?" Esteban asked.

"If God wants," Chuy said.

If Grandfather wants, you mean, Esteban thought as they passed his mother's apartment and turned off toward the American embassy on Plaza Italia. It was the way to his grandfather's house. But his grandfather was in "protective custody" someplace, wasn't he?

"Chuy?" Esteban asked. "Grandfather never went away, did he?"

"Sí. He's at home, señor. Upstairs in your father's old apartment."

"But what about the protective custody idea?"

"Where better to be, señor, when everybody thinks you're someplace else?"

"And the police?"

Chuy smiled shyly, a smile as askew as his face. "With me around, you think we'd need police, *patito?*" He'd slipped, had used the nickname nobody had called Esteban since he went to *preparatorio* school. Esteban felt a rush of affection for him.

"Never, Chuy, never," he said. Chuy beamed.

Chuy had Esteban slide down out of sight as they approached the house, just in case. But Esteban knew where they were by the tops of the familiar facades they passed, the other grand houses of Palermo Chico that he'd memorized on his boring childhood Sundays after the ritual visit to the cemetery of La Recoleta. Some of them were embassies of medium-sized countries now—he'd tried to look up an old friend once and had gotten chased away from the house by a surly Ethiopian marine. A couple were museums. But his grandfather had hung on, had even bought the house behind him and demolished it for space to build a garden and swimming pool. The economies that had forced so many other families of Palermo Chico to look for more "sensible" houses hadn't ambushed his grandfather yet. He'd hold out to the last. He liked the style.

Esteban sat up as they swooped into the underground parking garage, where his grandfather had once pitched a barbecue for a thousand people. A quartet of cats scattered as Chuy opened the door for him and pressed the elevator button. His grandfather still collected them, Esteban saw, the way some people collected stamps. Possessions, the passion for possessions, even stray cats.

It was a passion that ruled the house. Christ, Esteban thought as he stepped off the elevator into the sitting room, there'd be no need to convert this place to a museum. It already was one. It had been at least five years since he'd been here. If there were a word to describe the change, it would be *more*.

This is the secret heart of the people who really rule

Argentina, he thought, as he waited for the doddering housekeeper, who moved like a mechanical toy and was the daughter of an official in the Czar's Imperial something, to go upstairs and announce Chuy and him. My people. The cluttered plunder of everywhere, like Buenos Aires itself. Ahead of him in the dining room, a table for eighteen under crystal chandeliers, flanked by great lucite bowls filled with thousands of souvenir matchbooks, no two the same. Cabinets full of oriental figurines, hundreds of them. A tapestry from France, paintings from Flanders, armor from England. Beyond the dining room, another sitting room, all done in white Miami modern, with a gigantic Hammond organ sharing center stage with a man-sized white plastic digital clock, lugged home, Esteban remembered, by a puffing Chuy from his grandfather's last Miami buying spree in '75. To the left he could only see a slice of the foyer, but he knew it wouldn't have changed much: still stuffed with ancient leather books, unread ("I only read books about money," his grandfather told him once), and ruled by deerhorns and mooseheads and mounted arquebuses and flintlock pistols and crossed battle-axes and swords, none of which his grandfather had the slightest notion how to use.

And the sitting room they were in, the centerpiece of the house: gold leaf on plaster columns, ceilings painted in garish, inept versions of the Sistine chapel, a Steinway grand, oriental rugs, more Oriental figurines, more Flemish paintings in gilt frames far larger than most of the paintings, portraits of his grandfather with generals and presidents, Victorian velvet furniture, marble tables, electronic cigarette lighters, onyx fruit, German cuckoo clocks...

Dear God.

"Señor?" The housekeeper, hands at her sides like a White Guard's at attention, bowed him toward the circular staircase. She gave him a grandmotherly pat as he passed, and mewed about how fine he was looking these days.

Past mirrored, padded dressing rooms with canopied beds—rooms from a Bogart movie—and up another flight of stairs was the apartment his grandfather had built for his father when he was in college. Frank had stayed there, too, in his turn, but the room hadn't changed. It was still fifties modern, spare and square and ugly. His grandfather, in an Oriental dressing gown, looked as out of place in it as a mandarin in a boutique.

"Well, Grandson?" he said, not getting up from his armchair. Chuy locked the door and stationed himself in front of it.

"I don't want to be here, Grandfather." Don't apologize, damn it.

"I suspected that. I also suspected that you *would* come. How was Peru?"

Their eyes met. Esteban glanced over his shoulder at Chuy, then looked back at his grandfather's sagging, glowering face. He *knew*. Goddamn it, he knew all the time! The man he'd ruled out from the first; the man who would go to hell before he got involved. *He* was the one who knew every step he'd taken. The family, the bloody Molina family *über alles!* Still, still!

"How, Grandfather? Damn it, how?"

"Sit down, Esteban. Would you like coffee?"

"No. I'd like a drink."

His grandfather nodded at Chuy. "Brandy?" he asked Esteban.

"That'll do."

"We haven't talked in some time. Actually, I don't know that we've ever talked much, have we?"

"Not much."

"Have you been jealous of Francisco? Is that why?"

"This may surprise you, but I don't think so."

"That does surprise me. I'd always thought that was the reason you'd kept away."

"*I* kept away?"

"Francisco would always come to me, ask me for things. I could, oh, influence him, the way he thought. You're more like your father—we never did get along well, even when he was a child. Did you know that?"

"Not that it went back that far."

"It did. I showed Francisco the way the world really works, how power operates, what money means. Firsthand. He seemed to understand it. And perhaps that's what my mistake was with him; perhaps that's why he went through that period of wanting to be a priest.

163

Perhaps that's why he's in Argentina now. He had the understanding, but not the temperament."

"How long have you known he was here, Grandfather?"

"I suspected it when I found out you'd been at Bariloche. I knew it for certain when Jaime Mondragon was killed. Pepe is a good friend to you, but he's not the most farsighted man. When he left his wife, she telephoned me, since she knew you'd been with him. He'd left a note behind, one you wrote to señorita La Fontaine. She threw it away in his jeep, apparently, and he took it into his house to destroy it. But something—wine, I imagine—interfered, and he didn't. I knew you'd been in Bariloche, then, and where to find señorita La Fontaine. When Mondragon was killed, I knew you'd gone to Bariloche to meet Frank."

Esteban took the brandy Chuy offered him. "Because you knew I couldn't have done it."

"You were undoubtedly a good lawyer, Esteban. Yes. They called me the morning Mondragon was found, so I knew how he'd really died. I never liked him, you know. Prissy, somehow—" He waved the thought away as unimportant. "But in any event, I knew you wouldn't have been capable of that. And that's a compliment."

"From you I'm not sure, Grandfather."

"I'm not sure *that's* a compliment."

Esteban raised his glass in a silent toast.

His grandfather chose to ignore it. "I'm not really certain why Francisco did kill Mondragon, though I've surmised it had something to do with Adela, since he died in roughly the same way she did. *Did* he kill Adela?"

"Paco thinks so."

"Did he say why?"

"No. Just that Adela knew something about Mondragon. I don't know what."

"And you, how did you know that Francisco was going to be in Bariloche?"

Esteban sipped his brandy. Had his grandfather known that it was Adela, and not himself, who was supposed to have gone to Bariloche to meet Frank that weekend? Did he know that his mother was involved? Esteban decided to take a chance, to use the only person who couldn't contradict him to shield his mother—if that were still possible. "Adela told me. She called me the night before she was killed. I was going to meet her to get the details."

"And you never got them. So you weren't involved with Francisco before? It was *Adela?*" His grandfather lowered his head and glared, challenging him to confirm something as absurd as that.

"Yes."

"Dios mío. I underestimated her."

"I think we all did."

"Do you want to hear the rest of this, or have I told you enough?"

"Not yet. Some of it's easy enough. When you knew where Caroline was going to be, you sent your man to her—the man with the dead face."

"I did. His name's Casares. I sent him down to the *estancia* in Río Negro a few years back to deal with a gaucho who was stirring things up. Socialist. The gaucho turned out to be better with his *facón* knife than Casares was with his switchblade. Severed some nerves. He's a good man."

"And once you knew that I was coming to meet Caroline in Buenos Aires, you knew we'd have to go through Bahía Blanca. So you sent him to meet us."

"Sí."

"Well. That's as far as I can take it. Why did you want me to reach Caroline? Why did you try to send her away in the first place? And Peru—how the hell did you know about Peru? And if you knew all these things, why in God's name did you let me go ahead with what I've done?"

"Do you resent me for that last part?"

"Yes, hell yes, I do."

"Then hear me out. I tried to send señorita La Fontaine away because this is a family affair. She's *not* family yet, no matter how much you may want to think of her that way. She becomes family the day the two of you go and ask God to make you a family. With a priest!" He banged the arm of the chair, and a little cloud of dust flew up from the padding. He pointed to the brandy bottle. Chuy nodded and poured him a snifter. He sipped it and went on, calmer but still glowering. "As it turns out, it's best she didn't leave. You'd probably never have gotten to Peru if she had, and somebody had to go find out what Santander knew. Somebody from the family, which means either you or myself, and you're a great damned deal more able to do it than I am. That's why I've let you go ahead all along—somebody had to locate your brother. Whatever he's in the country for, he's dangerous. To himself, to the family, and to the country."

"If you knew that, surely you've got people in the police who—"

"Didn't you hear me, Grandson? This is a *family* problem. No police, nobody outside the family."

Of course. Family, always the family—hadn't it been drummed into him enough by now? "Then why didn't you just come to me to begin with, if you knew where I was?"

"First, after you left the hotel, I *didn't* know where you were. Casares was supposed to stay with you, but you took care of that." There was pride, sneaking pride, in the old man's voice. "Second, you had to come to me— as you've done—before you'd trust me. *Verdad?*"

"*Verdad.* True."

"Now. You'll want to know how I came to send Casares to Peru." He was enjoying this, Esteban knew, enjoying showing his grandson that he wasn't yet an addle-headed old man. Esteban didn't begrudge it to him. Hell, he *was* admiring him, in spite of himself. "After I lost track of you, I knew sooner or later you'd have to go to Santander. I trusted your wits, which may surprise you. I knew that Francisco wasn't with you in Bahía Blanca, according to Casares, and the fact that you'd tear off with Pepe on that ridiculous trip to Buenos Aires told me that you and Francisco hadn't parted company according to any plan. And I knew Francisco hadn't come here just to kill Jaime Mondragon."

"How?"

"The same way I knew about Hugo Santander in Peru. Give me room, lawyer. I'll get to that. Where was I? Oh, Francisco. I knew that if Francisco were still in the country—and he was—that you'd try to find him. You're too much like your father to let something like that go. And to find him, you'd have to go to Santander. But by the time I got Casares up there, you'd already left Lima for Iquitos. So I told him to wait for you in Lima. If you didn't make it back to Lima, well...what you'd found out wouldn't be of any use to you—or me—would it?"

Esteban considered thanking him, but somehow that last statement had taken the edge off it. "That tells me everything but one. How did you know about Santander and Paco?"

"Because I've been supporting them for years."

"*Cómo?*"

"I've been supporting them for years. You heard me."

Esteban looked to Chuy and held his brandy glass up for a refill, then thought better of it. Now, of all times, was the time to stay sober. You needed to be sober to face the Cheshire cat's grin, to accept an invitation from the Mad Hatter. He accepted the invitation. "Yes, I heard you, Grandfather."

"They have to get money from somewhere, these outfits. I'm not the only one who's supporting one. I can give you a list that includes generals and admirals in the government, the damned hypocrites. Normally, it's a sophisticated sort of blackmail. Either they get the money from you through a bank in Switzerland, or they find their own ways. Why do you think we've been left alone since your father was murdered? I damn well knew your sister wasn't killed by terrorists, not if they wanted to keep their income."

"The convenient lie."

"No, *maldita sea,* the expected lie that didn't stir things up before they needed to be. Learn some things, Grandson, before you're too old for them to do you any good." His grandfather leaned forward in the chair and lowered his head even more, ready to charge.

"All right, the expected lie." Esteban let it go. He needed information now more than a fight.

His grandfather sat back. "Not that this bunch of Santander's was really a terrorist outfit. I could have lived with them if they'd taken over here—still can. I'd probably lose some land, and my taxes would go up, but I'd survive it. The important thing is that they kept the rest of the bastards off my back, the really dangerous ones. That, and the fact that your brother was part of them. He needed something like that after your father was killed, and he was doing less harm with Santander than he would have with most others." What would Paco think of that? Esteban wondered. A political remittance man. But maybe he *had* figured it out, maybe that was why he was working with the British, maybe that was why he'd come back to Argentina. Sometimes it was a hell of a lot less painful to bite the hand that fed you than to lick it.

His grandfather downed the last of his brandy. "And there I run out," he said. "Dead end. I know who Santander's people here are, and I've had them watched, but your brother hasn't been around. Now that the word's out that Santander's dead, I don't expect that he will be. How about you—any ideas? What's your brother after?"

Esteban shook his head. "I don't know. I wish I did."

"Then why did you come to me?"

"There's somebody who might know where to look for him, somebody who might not be as well hidden as Paco." He took a breath, held it, then let it out slowly. "I want you to help me find her. To use your contacts, wherever they are. Whoever they are—I don't care. Just as long as she's not hurt, and you can get her out of the country when this is done."

"She?"

"Caroline."

His grandfather sat back in his chair and motioned for another brandy. He gave Esteban a smile, the smile of a man turning over a perfect hand in a *monte* game before he reaches for the pot. "I have her," he said.

"You *have* her?"

"Your hearing's not improving, is it, Grandson? I have her. She's a guest in the summer house in Tigre. Has been for the past four days. I thought you might want her eventually."

"She came to you?" No, Esteban thought. No—all the connections that had come together while his grandfather had been talking, all the pieces of the torn photograph that had started to fall into place suddenly scattered again. There were too many pieces now.

"Of course not. I told you I'd had Santander's people watched. She showed up, and I brought her home. Couldn't get a thing out of her."

"Goddamn it, Grandfather..."

"And I'm not in the habit of torturing women. The jackasses in the uniforms do enough of that. I thought *you* might be able to talk to her. What's her connection with that bunch?"

"I don't know that, either." He didn't need to tell him about Caroline's name on Santander's notepad. The fact that she'd vanished while he was gone would explain his ignorance well enough.

"Then go find out. We'll find your brother."

"And when we find him, what then?"

"Get him out of the country. Get him some help. Maybe make a priest out of him."

"A priest!"

"God's dealt with worse. He's still my grandson—and your brother."

"I know." Suddenly the gap between himself and his grandfather opened wide as a continent, a continent of time and vision. His grandfather believed what he'd said, Esteban was certain of it. God could fix it. The old man could die with his soul at peace imagining Frank, a killer who surely would be hunted over half the world, repentant and safe on his knees in a cassock somewhere. In his grandfather's cluttered world, some things were truly that simple.

But how about himself? What did *he* have in mind for Frank? Out of the country, yes. Help, yes. But beyond that...? In a locked room somewhere for the rest of his life? *Madre,* was that any better than his grandfather's solution, after all?

"And Caroline, Grandfather? What about her?"

"You asked me to see that she's not hurt, and that she's gotten out of the country after this is over. I agree to that. But understand this: she'll go alone."

"What does that mean?"

"That I won't have her in this family. She's not suitable for you. Your father married an English operetta singer, and that was bad enough. But this woman's lived in Paris, has been mixed up with God knows what kind of political messes—and probably slept with God knows how many of the men who made those messes. I don't know her family and have got no way to predict what she might do in the future. Surely you're not blind to that, are you?"

Esteban kept his voice calm, controlled. The Cheshire cat's grin widened. "No, I'm not blind to that, Grandfather."

"I won't do something as pointless as cut you off— you've already done that pretty well yourself. I don't think it would faze you. It didn't bother your father when I tried it on him. But I'll tell you this. That woman is dangerous, and I'd rest easier before God if I turned her over to the bastards in the uniforms in any case. You're what's left of the family now, Esteban; Francisco's tainted—the bloodline goes through you or it dies forever. I've got to protect that—and you. And I will. Do you agree to that?"

Some things were truly that simple. Protect the family, protect the blood. It was beyond question, beyond doubt. It was the highest moral obligation his grandfather recognized. He believed him: either he agreed, or he didn't see Caroline again. He knew his grandfather would even sacrifice Frank for that, for the blood.

"I agree."

"We'll see if you do."

Esteban got to his feet. "Will Chuy take me to her?"

"No. I want Chuy here with me. Casares will."

"Casares? He's in Lima."

"He's here. He was on a flight out of Lima an hour after you were."

"That's good news," Esteban said. He walked to the door, which Chuy unlocked and held for him, and turned. "Mother's coming home?"

"There's no need to keep her away. Not since we know about Mondragon."

"Will you tell her about Frank?"

"No. He can do that himself, if he wants, when the time comes. She's free to go where she wants—here or England. It's not my concern now."

"Was it ever?"

"As long as your sister was alive and needed her, yes. I don't care for the English—especially not now. Esteban?"

"Sí, Grandfather?"

"I loved your father a great deal. I could have protected him, if he'd let me. I can protect you." Even though his grandfather's glowering look was intact, what was in his voice was the closest Esteban had ever heard him come to a plea.

"Thank you, Grandfather," he said. He wanted to hate him, but he couldn't. He thought he understood his father better in this moment than he ever had before.

Downstairs among the cats, the man with the melted face waited for him, rattling the Mercedes keys in his hand like dice.

The hour to Tigre was spent in near silence. Esteban knew that Casares would prefer to pull off behind a warehouse somewhere and get some of his own back. But like all of his grandfather's *guapos,* he was unquestioningly loyal. Even if that meant putting up with a man he'd more happily accept an order to kill than to take to Tigre. Esteban thanked him for Lima, apologized for Bahía Blanca, and Casares answered him with a cold civility in that careful, sad voice. What kind of life did he have? Esteban wondered. What kind of life would he *like* to have? He could pity the man. But more than that now, he knew that figuring out what went on in his head, what he might want that Esteban could offer him, was vital. Esteban had more of his grandfather in him, he discovered, than he'd thought.

Tigre was fading. The great Victorian summer houses that hid among the canals and creeks where the Luján joined the Plata were peeling, some of them, or had been bought on time-shares by the wrong kind of people, people who weren't rich. Most of the families who'd built the houses and those who'd gotten truly rich since had moved across the Plata to Uruguay. Tigre was too close to the city now, too close to the wrong kind of people, too close to vandals and terrorists. Only a few of the old families, like his own, held on to the houses, with their turrets and widow's walks and their kiosks built over the water, kiosks that often now listed like beached barges among the reeds.

His grandfather's house was as cluttered with gingerbread and porches as the living room in Palermo Chico was with furniture and figurines. But he'd held on to it for the same reason he stayed in Palermo Chico—the style, the old grand style he remembered from his boyhood in Spain. Even his speedboat that Casares brought around from the marina behind the baroque Grand Hotel de Tigre was the right style: hand-rubbed mahogany with polished brass fittings and leather seats, a veritable Dusenberg of boats.

They eased up to the dock of the summer house with the engine cut. As they'd approached the house, Casares had given three sharp blasts on the speedboat's deep horn, and by the time they'd gotten there, two men were on the dock to meet them, a gardener and another one of his grandfather's *guapos,* whom Esteban vaguely remembered having seen. Casares and the other *guapo* walked him as far as the porch, but let him go inside alone; they were *muy correcto,* even now.

Early afternoon winter sunlight lightly streaked the drawing room through the lace curtains of the tall windows as he stepped in. The house smelled of lilac balls, and the gleaming hardwood floors creaked softly under his feet. It was a house that echoed, a house where voices had always carried upstairs and into the bedrooms to comfort him when he lay fighting sleep on hot summer childhood nights, a house where secrets were impossible.

Caroline stood in a shaft of sunlight, half turned toward him as if she had been interrupted in posing for a portrait. Her hair was caught up in a bun, and in the watercolor light he thought there was something preRaphaelite about her, something from another time and place. His breathing was shallow, and his fingers felt brittle, as if, were he to try to hold on to something, it would slip out of his hands. He knew he loved her, but he hadn't realized how much until now, and he was afraid.

She smiled tentatively, took a step toward him, then checked herself. At length, after the silence had held so long he was afraid that in some Kafkaesque way they'd both been transformed into figures in a wax museum, Caroline said in a low, echoing voice, "Well? Is this it, *guapo?*"

"Is this what?" His own voice was dry as the stark sunlight.

"In the movies, you'd hit me. Or I'd break down. Or something."

"In the movies, yes."

There was another silence. Then she said, "Since you're not going to, why don't we sit down?"

With a courtesy so deliberate that he knew it would be comic anywhere or anytime else, he swept his hand toward the faded Victorian sofa that crouched beside the window. With equal formality, she arranged herself on it. He crossed the room and stood before her, then had a quick, self-conscious vision of himself as Inspector Poirot beginning to pace and question. Damn it, this was Caroline. He was in love with her. She looked the same, her voice was the same, the tightening in his loins when he thought of her beneath those neat clothes was the same. So what had changed, what invisible thing that hung in the air between them?

The definition of Caroline had changed, he thought. Just that. After all, who anybody really was didn't matter, did it? Just how you defined them in your life. Adela, Frank, his mother and grandfather, and now Caroline. And now Caroline.

"Shit," he said. He crossed the room and sat down hard in a spindly, high-backed chair, a gulf of hardwood fixed between himself and her.

"I thought I could find him," she said. He had to strain to catch her words. "I didn't want you to be hurt. I wanted you away while I tried to find him."

"That was considerate."

"If you're going to hit me, Esteban, do. But don't use sarcasm on me. Not you."

For a blind moment, he wanted to take her up on that, to rush across the room and slam her back against the wall and pound the whole story of her and Santander and Paco and who the hell knew what else out of her. But she looked so fragile against the brittle couch he knew he couldn't, wouldn't, no matter what happened. From her calmness, he judged, too, that she instinctively understood that was her best protection against his fear. "Sure," he said. "Civilized discourse, then. Why did you think you could find him?"

"You've talked to your grandfather. You know where his 'assistants' took me from."

"I do."

"I didn't lie to you, not totally. I *was* studying painting in Paris. But I couldn't help knowing those people. They were Argentine, and what was happening in Argentina was sickening. So I helped them. Not all of them; not the ones who would have murdered your father. And I never did enough to get myself in anybody's card file in the embassy—just sorted mail and stuffed envelopes and that kind of thing. There were pressures, Esteban. I think maybe you would have done what I did—no, I think you might have been ashamed of me for not doing more."

"What kind of pressures?"

"Pressures."

"Then what else did you 'do' for them, besides politically, I mean?"

"None of your damn business," she said, flushing. "Do you want me to go on, or not?"

He deserved her anger. Could he claim to be any different from the strutting, asshole generals he detested if he let their macho *mierda* take hold of him, too? How Argentine are you, Molina? My machismo, right or wrong? "Go on."

She composed herself. "They asked me to do one more thing for them. As I said, I wasn't in anybody's card file, so I wasn't being watched. They asked me to arrange for a boat to get three people out of the country, nothing more. Somebody was going to come into the country and blow up some missiles, and then I was going to be contacted. I swear to you I didn't know it was Paco until you told me he was here."

"And it was fine with you—it was a pleasant little thing to do, for somebody to come into the country during a war and blow up some missiles? No questions asked?"

"Would you *want* these generals to win? What would happen if they were heros? How much longer would we have to put up with them? Don't be a hypocrite, Esteban. You don't want that any more than I do."

"That was Paco's argument, too—at first."

"It was everybody's argument who worked with Hugo Santander."

"He's dead."

"Hugo Santander? Oh, God—when?"

"Just before Paco got here. He stopped in Peru first." Caroline's eyes began to glisten in the pale sunlight. She opened her mouth to say something, but he kept going, not wanting to give the tears a chance to gain body. He pulled Santander's notebook out of his coat pocket and sailed it across the room onto the couch beside her. "I found this on Santander. A grocery list and your name, and nothing else. I was going to ask you about your name. But I don't need to now, do I?"

She picked up the notebook and leafed through it abstractedly. "No," she said, and dabbed at her eyes with the sleeve of her blouse. "Not now."

"You knew Paco in Paris, didn't you?"

"I'd met him, yes."

He studied her a moment as she traced Santander's doodles with her finger. "It's all too neat, then. You knew Paco, you were working with the bunch he screwed over—my sister and mother were involved—and you don't know a damn thing except that you were supposed to meet a stranger and get him and two other people on a boat. I suppose you met *me* by accident, too. Just happened to walk in the café and, surprise of surprises, guess who ran it! You weren't watching me, keeping tabs, setting this whole thing with Paco up—using me to meet my mother and Adela so you could do what... negotiate? Get Adela to turn on Jaime Mondragon? What was in your goddamn reports? The time we made love under that goddamn beach umbrella at Mar del Plata? Or how about all the other times—did you keep a running tabulation for them: dates, places, how many times you came? Goddamn it to hell, *mujer,* you're just too son-of-a-bitching innocent!"

Her composure was gone. He was pounding her, each word as clean and light as his fists had been when he was pounding Casares on the lawn in Bahía Blanca. He knew it and he couldn't stop himself. He was liking it, and hating himself for liking it.

"Yes, no, yes, no, I don't know, I don't care—whatever you want me to say, Esteban. I knew you were going to be in your restaurant, and I wanted to meet you because your brother had said you were a decent man, that's all. I fell in love with you—and that's all.

I don't know who was talking to your mother and Adela, but I think I know what they told Adela, and if I'm right, she and your mother are decent, too. No matter what the motives were for involving Adela, she turned out to be a better patriot than any of us, if patriotism makes any difference anymore. And for the love of God, I wasn't reporting to anybody about anything, so leave me alone. Just... leave me alone." Her voice caught and she fought back a sob.

"What do you know about Adela? Damn it, what?"

"Your brother's people knew about Jaime Mondragon in Paris. I found out there. It *had* to be what they told her."

"What, for God's sake?"

"He was the Butcher."

"The *who?*"

"That's what they called him in France, the ones who remembered the Nazis who were like him. He was the one in charge of the 'disappeareds.' He posed as anything he could, talked to the mothers of those kids and told them he was there to help, that his own brother or sister or whoever had disappeared and he was going to help them get their kids out of the country. He was so damned oily, so filthily sincere—and then when the mothers broke down and told him where their kids were hiding, he went after them. And when he had them, his men tortured the locations of their friends out of them before they dumped them in ditches or in the Plata and started the whole thing again with their friends. *That's* why the whole Dirty War worked—because people trusted the bastard."

"And what the hell did Adela have to do with all that?"

Caroline made an impatient gesture with her hand. "She didn't have anything to do with it. Don't you see? She was trapped. When they told her about him, what could she do? She couldn't marry him and spend the rest of her life with him, knowing about him. And she couldn't just walk away from it. She *believed* in things, you've told me that yourself. She truly believed in Argentina and justice and... all those things we believe in when it's convenient for us. I suppose she tried as long as she could *not* to believe what all of us knew already about the *militares,* but when she knew for certain about Mondragon and the rest of them, she couldn't let it go the way most people could. That's what makes me ashamed, Esteban. I've just sat back and watched it all happen since I've been home from France. I've painted and been in love with you and said it would all keep getting better. Because I was afraid. But how long did it take Adela to make up her mind once she knew the truth? Five minutes, I'll bet—no longer."

"No, a little longer. Long enough to have last doubts and call me." He got up, and the spindly chair slammed back away from him into the wall. Yes, it made sense. They would have told his mother first—not everything, he believed her about that, but enough about Mondragon to convince her she couldn't let Adela marry him. And they would have told her that Frank was involved. And those two things would have been enough to convince her to go to Adela, to get Adela to listen long enough to be convinced herself. She had been as trapped as Adela once she knew the truth. She'd never have gone along with Adela's being put in the kind of danger Adela would have faced if she'd lived long enough to take Frank to the base at Comodoro Rivadavia. But that would have been the part they kept from her.

And all that explained why Frank knew Mondragon had killed Adela. "She would have had to tell Mondragon what she knew about him," Esteban said, as much to himself as to Caroline. "Her damned fair-mindedness wouldn't stop working, even then. She had to give him the chance to face her, to deny everything if he could. Right?" What had the cargomaster told him when he first flew to the Falklands to see Mondragon? They'd just ferried Mondragon over from the mainland the day before? "She called me, and I wasn't any help. Christ, I might have talked her out of it! But I put her off until the next day. So she went ahead and got in touch with Mondragon. And how much trouble would it have been for the vice commander to order a plane, a secret plane, from Comodoro Rivadavia to Buenos Aires? Then when he got there, she confronted him with what she knew— though she kept the part about Frank to herself, which was what killed Mondragon in his turn, the prick. Making sense?"

"Making sense," Caroline said, her finger still tracing Santander's doodles. Esteban walked to the window. Bare winter branches, brown cattails, sluggish green water—the whole scene mocked the distant sun.

"Mondragon knew her well enough to know she couldn't keep something like that secret forever, so he killed her. She must have told him she was going to meet me the next day, so he left her in the crypt for me. 'Considerate,' Mother called it. Shit. It was considerate, all right. But it was a warning, too. And I was too stupid to pick up on it. Thank God—the swine might have gotten away with it if I had."

"You wouldn't have gone ahead, anyway?"

"Hell, I don't know. If I'd realized what I was getting into, maybe not."

"Yes, you would have," Caroline said.

"Thanks." His sarcasm flopped. Damn it, why did he still need to hear things like that from her?

"And now everything depends on me, doesn't it? On whether you believe me. Frank's still out there."

"Yes."

"Whatever you may believe about the past, Esteban, believe this about the present: I want to find Frank, too. Now more than ever."

"Why more than ever? To prove something to me? What the hell would that change?"

"No. I mean now that I know what he's planning."

Esteban spun from the window. "You what!"

"Sit here beside me, just for a minute. I won't touch you. I promise."

He wanted to touch her so bad his throat was constricting like a Chinese finger puzzle. But not now, not yet, maybe not ever. The old cut velvet of the couch was dry as dead grass beneath his hand as he eased himself down beside her. She leaned over and held Santander's notebook so they could both see it. A faint perfume, changed by the scent of her own skin, met him as he bent close to her to look at the notebook. Was she as conscious of him as he was of her? He knitted his fingers together to keep from reaching for her.

"First of all," she said—her voice was under control now, but husky still—"why would Hugo Santander start making a grocery list in the *middle* of his conversation with Frank? Look—he started his doodling on the first page, then kept it up onto the second." He followed her finger as it traced Santander's slashes and swirls, which got tighter and tighter from the first page to the second, then broke up into sharp, angular lines after the single word, *papas,* he'd written in his shaky script. "And then here, at the end of *papa*...that's not an *s*, is it? It's just the *a* trailing off and turning into another doodle while he got *really* angry and started making those lines. So the word is *papa*, no? And would anybody buy a single potato?"

"Christ, Christ almighty to hell."

"Not *la papa*, Esteban. Not potato. *El papa.*"

No, not potato. Not the feminine form of the word. But the masculine, maybe the oldest pun in the language: *la papa*, potato. *El papa*, the pope.

The pope. The man who was arriving in Buenos Aires this afternoon. The man who would be in the middle of a crowd of more than a million people tomorrow.

The man whose name had been the reason Frank had killed Hugo Santander in the Peruvian jungle. And for what? There was only one thing, one proposal Frank could have made to Santander that would have been so monstrous that it made Santander's death absolutely necessary when he refused it: that the pope be killed, be assassinated. And that Frank be the one to do it.

Caroline's silence, the tight line of her mouth, told Esteban that she understood, too. "In the name of God, why?" he said. "The war's all but lost. The pope's not going to affect it one way or the other."

"No, he's not."

"Whatever's going on in Frank's mind—however bloody insane it might be—he's not stupid. He wouldn't have killed five people to get this far unless he had a reason for it. I know his mind."

"You used to."

"Is that all you can say?"

"What do you want me to say, Esteban? Do you want me to play guessing games about your brother's mind? Dear Lord, the only human being who can tell you what Frank's reasons are now is Frank."

"Is Frank, yes. Thanks." Things had whirred and clicked into place at last. And what did they show him?

The grin, the Cheshire cat's grin again, brighter and blanker than ever.

"None of Santander's people had heard from Frank—and now we know why," Caroline said. "There was one other place I was going to look, but your grandfather stopped that."

"Where?"

"In Mataderos, in the slaughterhouse district. There was a man there—I'd heard Frank mention him in France. At some kind of meeting. He was a mystic, a Gypsy, a revolutionary... something, maybe all of those. I don't remember. But I do remember that Frank said he was the only man left in Argentina he could really trust, and the other people at the meeting laughed. Frank got very angry."

"No, it wouldn't have been a good idea to laugh at Frank."

"The man's name was de Cadiz. I...I went to see him when I first got back from France."

"What for?"

"I took him something. I took him a message from your brother. I don't know what was in it—it was in some kind of code, I think."

"I see." Esteban got to his feet. Frank had manipulated them all—Adela, his mother, Santander, the British, his grandfather. Even Caroline had carried messages for him; before she'd ever come into his own life, she'd been his brother's goddamn errand girl! Frank was his brother and he loved him, he'd kept telling himself all along. That was how he'd defined Frank in his life—always in terms of who he had been. Caroline had said that he *used* to know Frank's mind. Did that mean he loved something that didn't exist any longer? He had thought when Adela died that he was mourning her for what she'd been when she was a girl, that since she'd grown up and fallen in with Mondragon and his kind, she was somebody he didn't know anymore. Then why not Frank? Adela had been the only truly honest one of the three of them, and she'd died for it—partially because of Frank. So why couldn't he see Frank as the only truly evil one of them?

Because nobody was wholly good or wholly evil, and maybe that's what he was learning at last. Frank had been his idol, and Adela the betrayer. Good God, if he saw the world that way, what the hell lack of difference might there eventually be between himself and Frank? Did he have to wholly love or wholly hate Frank? Or anybody? Frank had to be stopped, yes. And he told himself he was looking for him out of love, yes. Did that mean, then, he had to stop him out of hate?

No, the world wasn't that simple. *He* wasn't that simple. Hell, had it taken this long, and these events, for him to learn that? He felt something like relief wash over him, even now. Maybe he was lucky. Maybe some people never did learn those things. Had Frank? If he hadn't, maybe what there was left to feel for Frank was neither love nor hate, but pity.

Except that in less than twenty-four hours, Frank was going to try to kill the pope. Where the hell was there room for pity in that?

"If you went to Santander's people for help," Caroline said, "they'd kill Frank on sight. If you went to the police, they'd use this as an excuse to round up Lord knows how many hundreds of people, people who might not ever show up again."

"I know that. But I might have to—before it's too late."

"But not yet."

"No, not yet."

"That leaves your grandfather for you to go to—or yourself alone."

"Not my grandfather. If I go back to him, he'll have you on your way out of the country by dark."

Caroline didn't answer at first. She glanced at him, then turned away quickly, as if she were afraid he'd meet her eyes. "And you don't want that?"

No, Frank, no Grandfather—things weren't that simple. You make a decision, you *choose* to believe somebody, to define them a certain way. And then you take the chance that's always involved in that choice. Was that faith at work again, that great leap of faith priests were always ranting about? So be it. But here was the difference: it had nothing to do with God. Only people. And for this moment, only Caroline. "No," he said. "I want you to come with me. If you want to."

Caroline relaxed, as visibly as if someone had lowered a gun they'd had pointed at her. She still didn't meet his eyes, but said quickly and without hesitating, as if she wanted to get it out before he changed his mind, "I want to."

But he did hesitate. "I love you, you know."

She turned to him. "God only knows why."

"Right," he said. "Let Him figure it out. Let's go."

The gardener puttered among the stubby, cut-back rosebushes at the edge of the dead lawn when they came out onto the porch. He looked up briefly, then went back to his make-work. Casares and the other *guapo* waited in the kiosk, a gingerbread bandstand of a place, at the end of the dock over the water. Casares watched them approach, a cigarette burning absently between his fingers. The other man, who had been resting his head on his arms and watching the drab water pass, stood and made useless motions at straightening his tight suit. Esteban led Caroline to the beginning of the dock, then stopped.

"Just you," Casares said, and flipped his cigarette away. His voice sounded even more artificial when raised to cover the score of paces between himself and Esteban. "Not the woman."

"Both of us," Esteban said.

"Just you."

"We're going to the boat, Casares." Without taking his eyes off the kiosk, he slipped his wallet from his pocket and bent down. He counted out ten five-hundred dollar bills and laid them on the dock so Casares could see, then put a stone on top to hold them. "There's five thousand dollars here. You and your friend can divide it any way you want."

Casares glanced at the money, then back at Esteban. "Just you."

"I've got you, Casares. You have to take it. If you try to stop me, you'll have to kill me—I'll make sure of it. What would Grandfather do to you then? If I get into that boat with the woman, you'll never work for him again—I know that. But you'll be free, and you'll have five thousand dollars to start with. Do you know how many pesos five thousand dollars will buy now?" He was betting Casares didn't know. And that made it even better: dollars, limitless things, bought limitless freedom. He'd tried to figure out what it was that Casares might want that he could offer him. This was it, this had to be it. Freedom, an excuse to break the ties to his grandfather without deliberately betraying him, an act that Casares's code would never allow. And the security, no matter how false, to use that freedom. Casares was getting older. How much longer would he be as quick with his switchblade as he was now? How soon would he be sent to deal with another gaucho, one whose *facón* was quick enough this time to sever more than just nerves? Casares had to realize that, had to look at his melted face in the mirror in the mornings and think about it.

Casares stared. The other man watched him, waiting for his reaction.

"If you kill me, Casares, Grandfather will have you hunted to hell if he has to. You know I'm right, don't you? Both of you know that." He took a step out onto the dock. "We're coming now. The money stays. It'll be there when we're gone. Don't do anything stupid." He took another step.

The other *guapo* broke. He shoved Casares aside and started along the dock. This one wasn't a switchblade man: he slipped a revolver from a shoulder holster and brought it down like a cop on a firing range. He knew what he was doing, one arm propping up the other, himself moving slowly and steadily. The revolver was aimed at Esteban's shin, and stayed there. "Señor!" he shouted. "You'll fall first, then I have the woman. Pick up the money. Your grandfather, he doesn't care about the woman. But you do. Pick up the money and go back to the house."

He stopped a half dozen paces away. Over the man's shoulder, Esteban saw Casares begin to move. Esteban darted a look behind himself, then jerked his eyes back to the *guapo* again before he had a chance to rush him. The gardener was staying put, but what was happening on the dock had all his attention now. Would he step in if he had to, if they made a break for the woods? But *Jesus María*, what good would running do? Caroline's only chance was that he was between her and the bastard with the pistol. And even if they made the marshy, grown-over woods, how long could she outrun anybody with the heels she had on?

"That's it," Caroline said quietly behind him. "It's not worth it, Esteban."

"The hell it's not," he said. He reached back and took her hand. Casares was only a few steps behind the other man now. When he reached him, it would be no trouble for him to get around Esteban while his friend covered him with the pistol. To get around Esteban to Caroline. With his knife.

Esteban threw all his weight into slinging Caroline toward the cattails beside the dock, threw it so that the momentum he built kept him going toward the man with the pistol. He knew that the man would either be so surprised he wouldn't fire—or so surprised that he would. He prayed for the first and dove.

He saw the man stiffen and jerk the pistol up even before he hit him. But it was too late—he caught the man at midsection and the man folded over onto him like a tree that had been cut the wrong way. Esteban felt the rough boards of the dock rasp against his face, and kicked against a pylon, trying to shove himself free before the man had a chance to be the first to gain his balance. He prayed he'd taken the man's wind away, that he'd have a precious few seconds to get to Casares before Casares's switchblade could get to him.

But the man made no attempt to get his balance. And as Esteban shoved at him, he might have been shoving at a sack of sand. Only when his hand felt the thick wetness on the back of the man's coat did he let the man go, and catch his breath before he got to his feet. Casares stood over him, then leaned down and wiped his knife clean on the man's pant leg.

"You'll take me back to the marina," he said to Esteban.

"I'll take you," Esteban said.

"When the time comes, you'll tell your grandfather how it happened."

"You were protecting me, yes."

"I want him to know that."

"He will."

"I have a sister in Costa Rica. If you want, you can send more money there."

"I'll send it."

Casares nodded, a business finished. "Help the woman. Then help me. I want to put this one in the water. He'll never be found if he reaches the Plata." He squatted and began stripping identification from the body. Then, as if it were only an afterthought, he casually reached for the pistol the man had dropped on the dock. When he stood, it was with the astonishing quickness he'd shown when he'd turned on Esteban in Bahía Blanca, just before Esteban had rammed him with the geranium pot. The terrified gardener still stood at the edge of the yard, as rooted as the roses he'd been pruning. Casares shot him twice, rapidly, before the man had a chance even to raise his hand in protest. "Only you know now, you and the woman," Casares said.

"She'll remember it the way I do."

Casares nodded again, then squatted to finish stripping his friend's identification. "Two of them now. But help the woman first."

Caroline, mud staining her white blouse, struggled up from the cattails. She moved her arm as if she were making sure she could still use it. Esteban went to her. She was crying. Overhead, the sun was sliding into afternoon.

The pope should be landing soon.

Chapter Nine

Of all the thousands of things British in Buenos Aires, nothing was more anglophiliac than the Retiro railway station. Beneath its long, vaulted, and Victorian ceiling, dim coffee shops lurked among pink marble columns; the polished brass of the American Grille competed with its own heavy, dark wood to advertise empire; dingy skylights surrounded by neo-Gothic stonework seemed designed solely to turn the light gray. Like the day—which had turned damp and chilly and sunless—the place could have been transplanted intact from London.

Such ironies had exploded around Esteban like land mines on the way in from Tigre. (They'd left the Mercedes to Casares, who wasn't yet as desperate for anonymity as he and Caroline were.) Ironies like the sign on the wall of their anonymous second-class compartment that comforted them with the news that their train ticket included free life insurance; the posters on the gray warehouses that the yellow-and-black train crept past on its way into the station—posters of the pope that announced in Latin, TOTUS TUUS, Everything is Thine, beside posters of Argentine troops trying to prove with guns that the Malvinas weren't anybody's Thine but Argentina's; the Big Ben chimes striking three o'clock in the Plaza Britania in front of the station while the freshly painted sign beneath the clock tower tried to give them the lie with a new name, Argentine Air Force Plaza; Caroline beside him on the seat in a muddy blouse, a stranger he was in love with, the irony that mattered more than any.

For a moment in the echoing station he'd considered calling his grandfather. In a sense, the old man had a right to know about Frank. Frank was his grandson; what Frank did touched him, too. But as long as his grandfather didn't know he and Caroline were free and in the city, that was one more variable Esteban didn't have to deal with. If the time came that he *had* to call his grandfather, he'd do it. But until then, as long as there was any kind of chance at all that he could get to Frank alone, he'd take that chance. Knowing what Frank really had in mind (and there was still a possibility he was wrong about that) would wound his grandfather—and his mother, too, for that matter—much more than thinking Frank had simply disappeared.

That was going to be his job, the final irony. Frank had to become one of the "disappeareds." He had to find Frank, to save him from the horror of what he was planning, and to make him disappear from the face of the earth.

And to save another man, a good man who shouldn't disappear, a man who was hope to millions of people who, God only knew, needed hope. It was the only damned thing most of them had.

He grabbed a copy of *La Semana* from a newsstand. On the front of it was a picture of a frigate exploding, with a black-bordered insert of Jaime Mondragon standing in front of a Mirage. On the back was the pope. How much greater that irony was now than it had been in Bahía Blanca. Esteban swore under his breath, and dashed through the multitudes that crowded the traffic islands in front of the station, swarming onto minibuses on their way to camp out in streets and parks for a glimpse of this man of peace their war had brought them. "Fuck," Esteban said, and grabbed Caroline's hand for a final charge out onto Libertador for a taxi. They shoved a provincial sort in blousy *bombacha* pants out of the way and plunged into a cab ahead of him and his fat family. The cabby looked grateful.

"Mataderos," Esteban said to the cabby. "To the slaughterhouses."

As the taxi stormed out onto the boulevard, Esteban flipped through *La Semana* for the pope's schedule. Arrive tonight, go straight to the house of the papal nuncio on Alvear. No chance for Frank there: they'd have that narrow section of Alvear cordoned off tighter than a monk's lips. Then early in the morning, to the shrine of the Virgin at Luján. Frank might have a chance on that trip, but not his best one. The crowds would be smaller, and the pope would be indoors. Late morning, at eleven, the pope would be in Palermo, speaking from the huge reviewing stand Esteban had seen them throwing up around the Spanish Monument. A procession there, a procession back. But in the Popemobile, covered on three sides with bulletproof glass and escorted at full speed by half the cops in Buenos Aires. His security people had learned something since the Turk had gone for him in Rome.

The reviewing stand, then. The only time he'd really be in the open.

At eleven. It was after three now. Less than twenty hours.

"He'll go for him in Palermo," Esteban said to Caroline. It was the first time either of them had spoken since they'd left the train.

"It's a big park," Caroline said.

"What do you figure the odds are that he's in Mataderos?"

Caroline glanced out at the apartment houses whipping by outside the taxi, at the hundreds of thousands of rooms you could imagine a man hiding in. "Where else?" she said. "God, where else?"

In Flores, the working-class section of the city just before Mataderos, Caroline took over directing the cabby. Only a *porteño* could tell one section of the city from the other now: the European boutiques and luxury high-rises had given way to the miles of monolithic, look-alike apartment blocks, gray-streaked from pollution, and furniture stores and grocers and salesmen's hotels that the wrong kind of people lived in and bought in and stayed in. Orderly, clean, moderately prosperous, and dull. This Buenos Aires had always depressed

Esteban, but somehow gave him hope, too. It reminded him that Argentina was more than the small bunch of "his" kind of people who controlled it, that there was a tough skull beneath the painted, Fellini skin. Damnably thick sometimes, but tough.

And then from the *barrio de flores*—"the neighborhood of flowers"—to *Mataderos*—"the killing place"—the way was marked by the smell. It was a vague smell of rendering, the boiling down of parts of animals, a brown smell that mixed more and more with the scent of dung and hide and blood as you drove deeper into the section toward the slaughterhouses that sent the frozen carcasses of the great herds of cattle from the pampas to Europe, America, Russia.

Caroline tightened her window against the smell. "I hate it here," she said. "I've always wondered how the people who live this close stand it."

"They get used to it—don't notice it," Esteban said. Enough death, enough killing, when you realize that it's only the killing that keeps you alive, and you don't notice it. When had he started noticing? he wondered. After he'd walked out of his father's room the night of the bomb? And he'd learned to live with it, too, like the others. Until Adela, until Mondragon, until it had become as overwhelming as the smell that oozed into the taxi now.

Caroline leaned over the seat to the driver. "On the other side of the yards, by the offices."

The cab swung onto the avenue that paralleled the high white walls of the stockyards and slaughtering pens. The walls stretched out of sight, broken here and there by ramps and gates, and overtopped by the frames of vast, open sheds. Across from the walls, dun cold-storage warehouses four stories high loomed like old brick tenements, a worker framed occasionally by one of the huge doors like a man in a faded photograph. Some of the gates into the white walls of the stockyards were open, and inside them long Mercedes diesel cattle trucks idled in the mud, while muddy dogs with their tails tucked circled them fearfully.

The sight of his own name, Molina, lettered on a sign the size of a railway car that hung over a city of the open sheds shocked Esteban unexpectedly. Yes, he knew that it would be here. Yes, his grandfather had brought him and Frank here half a dozen times when they were children to show them what could be theirs one day, and to feed his own ego. But it had been years since then. The tie between himself and this place had drawn itself out into a thinner and thinner thread, until he thought it had snapped.

But it hadn't. Frank had brought him back here, had brought him home.

They drove the many blocks around the white walls until they reached the incongruous, perfectly trimmed lawns and the flags and pink, sprawling offices of the slaughterhouses, a place that looked not surprisingly like a British colonial office. "Here will do," Caroline said suddenly.

The cab swerved to the curb. Across the street from the office was a vacant lot and the remains of a *villa misera,* one of the shantytowns the government had bulldozed to make way for workers' apartments before the economy had collapsed. "Here?" Esteban said.

"For now," she said.

When the cab had turned the corner out of sight, Caroline started off at a quick walk behind it. Ahead lay only a two-story, gray concrete apartment block, surrounded by sidewalks and mud and broken bottles.

"He's in *there?*" Esteban said.

"That's the address. Or it was the last time I was here."

"It looks like workers' housing—for the slaughterhouses."

"Even Gypsies or seers or whatever have to eat. The man works. And we don't call them 'workers' in Argentina. They're the 'common people,' remember? You're starting to sound like a Cuban." She flashed him a smile, and he damned her again for making him still like her. "I didn't think you'd want to drive up in front in a cab. Did you?"

"Not particularly."

She gave him the smile again, and this time he understood that there was far more nervousness in it than humor.

"What's the man's other name, besides de Cadiz?" he said.

"Reynaldo. Like the fox. Perfect, no?"

"I can't wait."

They passed the second apartment house and stopped before the third. A leaf-choked concrete stairway led upstairs, a mangled tricycle half blocking it. Fronting it, a poster asked urgently for type A blood for our *chicos* in the Malvinas. A listless wind came up.

"It's not what I expected," he said.

"No. No Bogart. Those days are gone."

Esteban looked along the block ahead. There was nothing, no stores, no café. Just more bleak concrete and mud. "There's no place for you to wait."

"Reynaldo knows me. I should go, too." She shrugged. "It's up to you."

Tell me you trust me, he knew she was saying. "No, it's up to you," he said, and meant: I thought that was already decided.

Her nervous smile flickered, then went out. "Sure." She started up the stairs, then stopped. "What are you going to do when we're there?"

"Talk."

"And then? If that doesn't work?"

"I don't know."

"They'll have guns."

"They'll have guns. I don't think they'll use them. At least, Frank won't."

"Frank wouldn't have, or Frank won't?"

He hesitated. "Won't."

"Fine," she said, and started up the stairs again. This time she held on to the railing, tightly, to steady herself.

The *what ifs* began as he followed her. What if the thousand things that could happen besides the right one happened? If he didn't know Frank anymore, how much less did he know this man, Reynaldo? On a stupidity scale of one to a thousand, how far off the scale did walking into this situation without a gun rate? He could take Frank one on one, always had been able to. And if Frank wasn't willing to use his gun, he had a good chance against him. But he doubted that this Reynaldo was too mystic to use a gun. Christ, a Gypsy! He prayed Frank had enough reason left for him to get through to, at least long enough to catch him off guard. But a Gypsy—and a goddamn visionary to boot?

He gripped the railing, too. The cold aluminum stung him, and felt good.

The doorway had been painted once, but the cheap plywood had peeled and cracked away beneath the paint. The outline of numbers, 66, remained, even though the numbers themselves didn't. Caroline shot him a tight-lipped glance, then started to knock. He pulled her hand away, and eased her to the side of the door. "If anybody wants to know who it is, you answer," he whispered. He stood to the side of the door, too, shielding her, and knocked.

There was no answer. He put his ear against the door and listened. Nothing.

"It's my year for empty houses," he said, ashamed that he was relieved. And then he thought, Or for houses full of dead people. He knocked more loudly. "Paco?"

Not again. Not to be so close again, goddamn it. His relief flip-flopped, became rage. "Paco!" he shouted. "Paco, you bastard!"

A flabby woman's face beneath curlers like missile launchers popped out of a door down the open breezeway, then back in again. He stuck his thumb between his index and second fingers and shot her a fist. Caroline reached up and enclosed his fist and lowered it. "No help, *guapo*," she said. "Let's go."

He pulled his hand away roughly. "Not bloody yet," he said, and reached for his wallet. Nobody had bothered to add a dead bolt to the door—the sign of somebody who had nothing to steal—so that his American Express card slipped the lock easily. He flung the door open. Fuck it. If Paco was here, he'd heard him calling him. If he wanted to shoot him, let him. At least this damned comedy of empty rooms would stop.

The door bounced back and slammed against his palm; he stepped into a cold room, carpetless and furnished with a cheap plastic couch, white veneer end tables, and a couple of dinette chairs—only this time, no bodies, no vultures. But it was a cluttered room, too. Maps—the city, the country, the world, California, Palestine, England, God-knew-where—all over one wall; diagrams, cabalistic drawings of interlocking circles and trees of life, tarot figures, and political organization charts of everything from the IWW wheel to the succession of the Bourbons were connected with felt-tip lines and arrows from wall to wall over the rest of the room. And stuck haphazardly among them, velvet paintings of the Virgin of Luján, of the Last Supper, of Christ on the cross with his feet being licked by dogs; in other places, slick prints of Budapest, Dubrovnik, Salamanca, and a host of vaguely Byzantine/Turkish cities Esteban didn't recognize in his rapid, incredulous circuit of the room.

"This isn't a mind I'd want to live in," he said to Caroline when he'd done.

"It's a mind you'd have no choice about." She walked ahead into the single bedroom and bath. Esteban followed. He shoved open the bathroom door. Empty, except for half-squeezed toothpaste tubes and smashed roaches and fetid towels. When he turned back, Caroline was staring at the rumpled bed. Both sides of the sheets were turned down. "Two people," she said.

"There were. But not now."

"No." She looked up from the bed and turned to him. "And Palermo's a big park."

"He'd have to be there by now. He'd have to get into position tonight, before the crowds come."

"They've already started coming."

"Fewer than there'll be tomorrow."

"True," she said. "They'll have an easier time finding him now."

"They who?"

"The police."

"You want to call the police?"

"The police, the army, who else? Who do you choose, Esteban? Your brother or the pope?"

He studied her face. It looked tired, bland, serious. "I don't," he said. "I don't choose yet."

"You have to. *I* have to."

"It's after four. We can be in Palermo by five. How many places could he be if he wants a shot at the pope—how many hidden places?" Her face didn't change, didn't give him any hint whether she thought he was sane or mad. "I want till ten—I want a last chance." Desperation ran in the family, he thought. "I've come so goddamn far—you've come so goddamn far. If we call the cops by ten, tell them what we know, they can sweep

194

the place. And if they don't find him, they can always cancel the pope's speech. What's to lose? You said yourself that if we call the cops, they'll round up half the city."

She turned back to the wreck of a bed. "Then there's the other thing to think about."

"What thing?"

"We let him go through with it."

He crossed the room, turned her around, and held her by the shoulders. She kept her eyes on his chin. "Yes," he said. "There's that. And a million and a half people would tear him to pieces before he had a chance even to drop the rifle."

"But nobody would get rounded up because of us."

"Christ, if you think they'll be bad *before* the act, what would they be like afterward?"

"I know that. I wanted to be sure you did, that when you choose between your brother or the pope, you know it's not just that simple choice. I don't want it to hurt you."

"No. I know about simple choices. Simple solutions, maybe, but no simple choices. Agreed?"

"Till ten?"

"Till ten."

"You know it's impossible."

"Nothing's impossible until it's impossible." He looked around the bedroom, at the felt-tip lines and arrows that ran into it from the living room to more charts, and to a picture of Perón. Somebody had driven a hunting knife into his face. Just below it, a line led to the empty space where another picture had been pinned, and a dozen more arrows pointed sharply at the outline the picture had left. The wall behind it was full of slash marks. Esteban knew whose picture it had been.

Palermo's a big park, he thought. Last chance, my brother. Involuntarily, he began to chant the nearly forgotten words of the rosary somewhere in the back of his mind. "Be with us now and in the hour of our death," he heard as he stepped outside ahead of Caroline and noticed that he, too, had stopped smelling the odor of the slaughterhouse.

* * *

They were living off their capital. He was still the man who they thought had killed the national hero, and now he was chucking the only thing that had kept him safe so far: anonymity. He was going to plunge into the biggest concentration of cops assembled since the last coup. Faith and luck were depletable resources. The damnable thing was that you didn't know how close you were to depleting them until it was too late, until the ore car came up empty.

There was still faith left. He knew that because he was here, was stepping out of a taxi alongside the zoological gardens in Palermo. But as a blue-on-blue Falcon slowed, and the cop riding shotgun rolled his window down to get a better look at Esteban and the mud-splattered woman with him, Esteban doubted the luck.

The police car pulled over in the next block and waited for traffic to clear enough for him to make a U-turn. Esteban grabbed Caroline's hand and sprinted the broad Avenida de Heras toward the botanical gardens, cars squalling and honking, none slowing for them. They took a flagstone path, still running, for a dozen or so meters into the gardens, then stepped off it into a clump of bamboo. From there, they could still see the avenue, but for a few minutes at least, could be invisible.

The Falcon slowly cruised the avenue beside the park, lights flashing as it fought upstream against the one-way traffic. At the path it stopped, and the cop riding shotgun stepped out to get a better look along the path. After a moment, he got back in and the car cruised slowly on. Esteban let out his held breath.

"Some welcome," Caroline said. "What does it mean?"

"They didn't get a good enough look at us to know if I fit their description or not—assuming that's what they were after. It could have been you. You look like I've been beating the hell out of you."

"Maybe you should have been." She stepped back onto the path ahead of him. "I thought they were supposed to believe you'd headed for Chile."

"They were. For a while. But when I didn't show up at the border, even they are smart enough to have second thoughts."

They reached the avenue. Caroline nodded her head

in the direction in which the cop car had vanished. "Hope they don't have thirds."

"They won't," he said. He knew they'd had plenty of time to get a good look at him. But if he lied to Caroline, maybe he could believe it, too.

They were still a half dozen blocks from the Spanish Monument. But he wanted to slip into the crowds before he got there—to do that, and to let dusk catch them. Palermo wasn't only a big park, it was many parks, a labyrinth. In the dark, even if they had been or were going to be spotted, they had a chance to duck away. It was true about Buenos Aires that the trains still ran on time, that people still dressed for dinner, that the fountains still worked, that you could still walk in the parks at night. They could be just another couple, a little muddy from sneaking away from chaperons for a quick roll in the bushes, could take one more stab at finding what Buenos Aires did better than trains or parks or formal dinners: granting invisibility.

No, it did one thing even better than granting invisibility, he thought as they began the walk through the park. Surrealism.

The familiar wasn't familiar any longer. Since all of the signposts in his life had been wrenched out of place, he'd been able to take nothing for granted. He was seeing things he'd seen all of his life for the first time. Palermo was exotic, was Disneyland without meaning to be. Maybe it was because his senses were quickened, he thought, as he kept his eyes constantly in motion for the sight of two-tone blue Falcons bearing down on them along one of the mega-avenues, or for an elegant cop with his white leather trim and white linen cuffs. Or for a glimpse of something even more familiar: his brother's face in the crowds that had started to gather. But for whatever reason, in the growing dark, the huge planetarium to his right became a flying saucer, anchored by soaring walkways, ready to rise at any moment into the reddening city sky. And San Martín's rearing statue, big as a house, could easily leap down from its pedestal and thunder down the avenue, crying revolution again.

As they wandered, looking for Frank in dark stands of prehistoric-seeming trees and bushes that smelled of leaf mold and had been abandoned to prides of staring cats, time melted like a Dali watch. They stood on an imitation Venetian Bridge of Sighs in the Dutch gardens, watching families paddle across artificial lakes and race toy sailboats in lantern light, while the roar of traffic, the rumble of a train, the prolonged explosion of a 747 overhead played the wrong soundtrack. Giant clumps of aloe grew beside maples and elms; arbors of ruined bougainvillea led among nameless trees with roots like boulders. On the way to the Japanese gardens, they passed a club built like a Tudor mansion, where men and women toasted each other with champagne on a closed sun porch while winged lions on top of a skyscraper-tall Assyrian column glowered down on them. A naked, nubile statue of Youth lay ready to be deflowered not far from a black slave who broke his chains, a bronze socialist-realism version of Freedom. Busts of Gandhi and Garibaldi and George Washington smiled at them both. A pagoda in the Japanese garden glowed with plastic paper lanterns. Past it, among the dark trees of the German garden, people trained dogs on a miniature parade ground, dogs and people taking turns barking at one another.

They circled the Spanish Monument warily, ducking—when a cop looked in their direction—into the vendors and clumps of partiers who were camping out to be near the pope. Once they broke down in hysterical giggles when Esteban was sneakily trying to make sure a man sleeping in a tree wasn't Frank, and a vendor leapt out of the shadows to sell them a bouquet of papal flags.

The night deepened; the crowds thickened. Already stands of trees along the avenues leading to the Spanish Monument smelled of piss. There were no bathrooms.

"You'll have to wear a gas mask in here by tomorrow," Caroline said. "Can you imagine—a million and a half people with no place to piss? Worse than Mecca!"

But the giggles had vanished. It was almost ten. They'd left the nearby rooftops and balconies alone: there would be cops on all of those in any case. Caroline had her arms folded against the cold now as they shoved through the people who'd staked out their territory like jealous miners. Doorways, trees, bushes, parked cars, even sewers—they'd checked them all, anywhere within the radius a man with a high-powered rifle could get a shot from. Always gnawing at Esteban was the possibility that Frank could be wandering, too, that he would be hiding in mobility, and they'd pass meters from one another. But he kept on, shoved by the blind, stupid faith that hadn't deserted him—until now.

"Well, *guapo?*" Caroline said as she checked her watch at the base of the Spanish Monument. "We're five minutes over."

Already the police were setting up barricades and folding chairs for the dignitaries, shoving the ordinary people back, and the only traffic that approached the empty traffic circle around the base of the monument was the police cars and vans, ambulances and TV crews. Everybody in the proper chute, the proper pen, Esteban thought, like the stockyards. Floodlights lit the monument and the stage that surrounded it on three sides, all the scaffolding he'd seen going into place hidden now. A long ramp, covered in red with a white carpet running up its center, led to the spot where the pope would stand, center stage. The rest of the stage was hung in papal yellow, even canopied in it. From the minute the pope stepped from the Popemobile onto the ramp, he was a target.

"Yep. Overtime." From the safety of a gaggle of schoolkids who were announcing to everybody in hearing they'd been bused all the way in from Cordova, Esteban made one last survey of the avenues and park. He imagined cheers, chants, banners, horse guards. Then the shot, probably buried under the sound. Then the pope, his firm Slavic face surprised, maybe accepting...

No. Goddamn it, no. Esteban was no more religious than a tree stump, an apostate in that as in everything else. But no, just damn *no*. Frank wasn't worth it. He wasn't worth the pope, wasn't worth the chaos and death he'd cause. Nobody was worth that. Hell, how many people would be killed just in the stampede alone afterward? Then there'd come the roundups...

But he paused. That's your brother you're talking about, he told himself. That's your brother you're saying isn't worth it. That's the man you've barely survived these past couple of weeks because of. That's contradicting everything you've always been taught about family, and probably have secretly believed most of the time, no matter how much you deny it. And that's the fact you're going to have to live with the rest of your life: you, Esteban Molina-Knifeton, are about to be the man who called the whole state apparatus you hate down on your brother.

But he could give himself one more out, at least mentally. If they couldn't find Frank, they'd stop the pope's talk. Or they'd protect him somehow—God, they'd do something. And Frank would sink back into the nonpresence that he'd been. That he'd worked so hard to become.

Some out, he thought. Casuistry, a lawyer's trick. If he made the choice—and even now he wildly hoped somehow he wouldn't have to—he'd have to live with it, no matter what accident of consequences happened. He was choosing sanity over Frank, reason over family. It was a choice he'd half made for years. Now it was time for the other half.

He bit off as much of the cold night air as his lungs would hold. "Giving-up time," he said to Caroline.

"Esteban," she said. "If I tell you it's right, will that help?"

"No," he said. "It's easier for you."

She avoided his eyes, her face a book without a cover. "Then for God's sake, do *something*."

"Yes." One of the schoolkids brushed against him, and he pulled sharply back, as if touching might spread some contamination to the kid. "We have to find a telephone."

Caroline reached for his hand. He pulled back further. She let her own hand hang in the air a moment, then stepped out of the milling schoolkids and searched the buildings around the traffic circle. "There's nothing open here. You want to take a few more minutes—try again—while I look for a phone?"

"No," he said. "No more looking."

Again she reached toward him, and again he pulled back. "All right," she said. "There's an Esso station by your mother's building, isn't there?"

He looked behind him toward Libertador, the street

the pope would come along tomorrow. They hadn't bothered with it so far; it faced the back of the monument, hidden from the pope. "Hell, that's what?—seven, eight blocks away. Surely there's something closer." All along Libertador, great flapping banners hung from balconies in the yellow streetlight. TOTUS TUUS, they said. WELCOME, HOLY FATHER. BRING US PEACE. Esteban stood on tiptoe and let his eyes move along the wide avenue, looking for the lights of a *confitería*, a grocery, anything. But all he could see were banners and balconies and the people who stretched, he imagined, all the way to his mother's apartment. He strained to see if he could make out her balcony among the hundreds of others like it. He felt a sudden urge to go to her, to throw himself down beside her on one of her many couches and beg her to help him, to forgive him, to tell him he'd chosen correctly.

But he couldn't; and the thought that he'd been shoving away all through this worked its way through to him at last. He might never see her again. His throat tightened.

But yes, yes he would, he thought as another realization hit him. He'd see her tonight.

"Christ Jesus," he said.

"What do you see?"

"What I damn well should have seen all along."

"Frank? Do you see Frank?" Her voice was excited, and she gave a small jump to see above the heads of the crowd.

"No. I don't see Frank. But I know where he is."

"Then why in the name of the Holy Mother..." She stopped herself. "Your mother's."

"I told myself all along that with as many cops as there'd be, with that Popemobile he rides in enclosed on three sides, and as fast as he'd be going... but I forgot about the damned balcony. And I didn't know about the banners." The words were spilling out, tripping over themselves. "With a rifle and a scope, and something like a canvas banner to hide behind while you set up... the shot would come *after* he'd passed. A balcony low enough on the building to give you the low angle you'd need... *Jesucristo*, you could put two or three quick shots through the open back end of the damned thing.

201

If you were any good, one of them would hit, it would have to."

"But what about your mother?"

"She'd believe anything Frank told her. Hell, he could tell her he was bird-watching." He was already moving, edging through the schoolkids like a shark through guppies.

When they squeezed free, he broke into a run. Caroline stayed beside him, her heels clattering on the sidewalk like a machine gun. "Slow down!" she shouted.

"Keep up!"

A street vendor, his placard filled with patriotic ribbons and pope pictures and postcards of the Malvinas, turned toward the sound of their running—then ducked too late. His placard shoved him backward like a sail when Esteban hit it, and he went down in a heap into the gutter. *"Cabrón!"* he yelled after them. One of his co-vendors, a man twice Esteban's size, stepped out in their path half a block away. Esteban sidestepped, then rammed. This one didn't go down, but was stunned enough for them to slip by, still keeping stride. The vendor charged after them.

"Esteban! Stop!" Caroline shouted.

"No time," he shouted back. He was unstoppable, he was there! Faith and luck, they'd both held. He ran as he hadn't run since rugby days in the *preparatorio*. Catch me, you bastards, catch me now if you can! He was home—no more hiding, no more Cheshire cat, no more fear...

Caroline tripped and he saw the blue-on-blue Falcon heading him off almost in the same instant. The big vendor was yelling behind him, cheering the Falcon on, and as he turned he saw Caroline's shoe, and her heel, separated, rocking to rest on the sidewalk behind her. Her running was over. He stopped, his body urging him ahead, his mind a whirlwind of indecision. If he went back, he was lost. His only hope was to head for the trees of the German gardens beside the walk. He took a step toward them, then stopped again. If they couldn't get to him, she would do.

He was back beside her in three strides. He jerked her up by her shoulders. "Tell them anything," he said. "Tell them I was chasing you, I beat you, I tried to rape you, anything. Then get the hell away before the next round of cops comes. Go to Mother's. No, call Grandfather first. Take him with you. Tell him where I am. I love you." He slapped her. She fell backward and he kicked her. Make it look right, boxer, cowboy, hero murderer. Make it look right.

The vendor reached them. His face was murderous. Esteban managed to get a kick away against the placard, and patriotic stickpins scattered. Then he sprinted again—too late for the safety of the German gardens, where one of the cops from the Falcon had already cut him off. So he stayed on the sidewalk, picking up speed toward the other one. The cop pulled his pistol and aimed. For a frantic moment, Esteban considered throwing himself on the cop, taking the shot, then trying to keep going. But as the cop drew down without flinching, he knew he'd never make it: the cop would stop him from ten meters away.

He made sure he struggled so that both cops had to shove him into the Falcon. One of them used his nightstick. Just before he did, Esteban got a last glimpse through the back window. A man in jodhpurs from the German gardens, with a pair of *dogos* on leashes, was helping Caroline to her feet. The vendor had deserted her to look for his patriotic stickpins. Cops ran past them toward the Falcon, ignoring her. Go now, he yelled at her silently. Now!

The nightstick came down, a blur he never had a chance to feel.

The table was wet, and they kept dousing him with cold water. He was naked. A man, silver-haired and fatherly—like his own father would have looked now, perhaps—stood over him. He wore a uniform—tight fatigues and combat boots and no hat. The insignia on his lapels were air force. Esteban, when his mind settled into a single reality from the doze it had been floating in and out of, was surprised at that. The police rarely cooperated with the air force—or with anybody, for that matter—when they'd tagged a prisoner as theirs. The police, the air force, the army, the navy—each was its own separate government. A country of warlords, Frank had said. No wonder we can't fight a decent war.

Esteban tried to sit up, but couldn't. Only his head could move. The rest of him was strapped to the wet table.

The fatherly man leaned over him, studying him, as if he wanted to make certain he was fully conscious. The man had the fine features and clear eyes of a northern European—no heavy-jowled Italian peasant, no dark *mestizo* from the Andes. "Esteban Molina-Knifeton?" he asked matter-of-factly.

"Yes."

"I'm Brigadier General Felipe Kleist. My position is chief of criminal investigation for the Argentine Air Forces. That may give you some idea of the importance of the conversation we're about to have. Does it?"

"Yes."

"I have known your grandfather for many years. I knew your father. That you and I have to meet under these circumstances causes me considerable pain. But I was also a friend of Jaime Mondragon, so I mind the circumstances somewhat less. Do you understand?"

"No."

"No? You don't understand that you murdered Jaime Mondragon?"

"No, I don't understand that."

"Then who did?"

Esteban realized the absurdity of what he said next. But he had to say it, a token gesture to something he'd believed in once. "I'd like to talk to a lawyer."

Brigadier General Kleist's expression didn't change. "But Sr. Molina, you *are* a lawyer."

The tea party had started again. Esteban closed his eyes. "Have you ever read Franz Kafka, General?"

"Yes. He was decadent. He was a Jew. He has nothing to do with the Argentine reality."

"No. Of course not."

"Why were you in Palermo tonight, Sr. Molina?"

"I wanted to see the pope."

"Ah," Kleist said. "That surprises me. I wouldn't have thought you religious."

"I am."

"I don't believe you, señor. Frankly, I believe you detest religion. I believe your religion is libertinage, progressivism, promiscuity. I believe you have no re-

204

spect for authority, for the family. I believe that all those things which place the rest of the civilized world in the last stages of its decadence are the very things that appeal to you. Everything on your record supports those conclusions. You have nothing in common with the ideals of your fatherland. I am inclined to believe very little you say."

"You left out drug-crazed," Esteban said, and wished he hadn't.

Then his bones caught fire. He felt himself lunging against the straps without understanding why. A hand came from somewhere and crammed a cloth into his mouth just before his chin slammed forward against his chest, and he screamed. The fire kept up and spread from his bones to all of his body, until he was sure his limbs were shattering and falling away from him.

And then it stopped, just as quickly as it had begun. His head fell back against the wet table, and cold water doused him again. Only when his head struck it did he realize the table was metal. He felt as sore and exhausted as he might have after half a day's workout. The cloth was jerked from his mouth.

The clean-lined father face was leaning over him again. "Normally, we progress to this stage much later, Sr. Molina," it said. "But I believe there's urgency tonight. Why were you in Palermo?"

"To see the pope." He had almost no breath left, and the ache clung to his bones like a chill.

"Should we look for a bomb? You could save us a great deal of trouble—and yourself."

Christ, even he hadn't been thick enough to think Frank would try to plant a bomb. They'd surely check the ramp and speaker's stand with a jeweler's glass before tomorrow. "Look for a bomb," he said. He rolled his head away. For the first time, he noticed there were other men in the room. Two cops, and a man in an air force noncom's uniform. The noncom had the flat, *chato* face of an Indian. He stood beside an old-fashioned knife switch, from which wires ran toward the table Esteban was on. He kept his eyes fixed on Kleist, as if watching for a signal. Suddenly he reached up to the knife switch and pulled it. The fire struck Esteban again, now less a burning than pure pain, the essence of pain, as if the ache in his bones and muscles had dulled any refinements of it. The cloth went back into his mouth. Even though he was ready for it this time, the scream came from someplace he had no control over.

When the pain stopped and the cloth vanished from his mouth, Kleist said with a terrible courtesy, a brutal correctness, "No. You know a bomb would be too easy to find, don't you? You're lying, Sr. Molina. We know when you're lying. Please, don't." He leaned close. Even his nose hairs were perfectly clipped. "You know that President Galtieri will be beside the pope tomorrow, señor. You're half British. I can't find it in my heart to believe that even something like yourself would see any advantage in killing the Holy Father. You tried once to cripple the heroic act of national recovery in the Malvinas with your murder of Colonel Mondragon. I suspect you may have even murdered your own sister to distract him from his duties—which failed. If you think that assassinating President Galtieri will aid you, you're wrong. You can't alter destiny with the death of one man, lawyer. The only possible outcome of this is that whoever is working with you will be torn to pieces before even we can help him. You see that, don't you?"

"The war's lost, you ass." Thank God, he thought fuzzily, his mind sinking back into the lingering pain. Thank God you can't find it in your swine's heart to believe anyone would want to assassinate the pope. He tried to call up the itinerary tomorrow. The pope would be riding alone. President Galtieri, an imitation George C. Scott playing Patton as always, would already be there. He'd come by helicopter. No motorcade along Libertador. No reason to suspect anyone along Libertador. If his grandfather was right, if he'd been able to protect and take responsibility for his mother, they'd leave her alone. If Caroline and his grandfather had managed to get to his mother's, they'd be safe. His grandfather would get Caroline out of the country. And, greatest of ironies, he could get Frank out of the country. Frank would be safe.

Frank would be safe. His mother, Caroline, his grandfather—hell, even the Gypsy, maybe—all safe. And himself?

Christ, he hated martyrs.

Kleist reached down and slapped Esteban's testicles. Esteban closed his eyes again. "Well, Sr. Molina?" Kleist said. "Who, please. And where. The whys of all of it we'll deal with later, when there's leisure."

Esteban kept his eyes shut tightly, concentrated on the colors on the back of his eyelids.

Kleist's voice came from a distance now, measured and official. "It's Time of War, Sr. Molina. None of us can be allowed to forget that." Esteban felt a rough hand squeeze his mouth open, the way a dog's is forced open to give it medicine. The rag, wet with his own saliva now, jammed its way in, raped its way in. Then the pain jerked his body taut again, and kept going this time, kept going until mountains seemed to rise up on the edge of his vision, and grow, and he was receding among them as his own scream faded out into the darkness of the mountains.

When he felt the cold water again, he reached up to slap it away, and his arms moved. Moved freely, surprised as Lazarus's must have been, he thought, when they broke out of the winding sheet and found air again. Then there were hands helping him from the table, wrapping him in a blanket. He looked around the overlighted room, which seemed to breathe and pulsate around him, for the man with the father face, but there was no one besides the two policemen who now guided him through a door into a room, an office, with a couch in it. They laid him on the couch, then retreated to green desk chairs against the far wall. Esteban squinted to keep them in focus, but they kept receding from him, like the mountains. He closed his eyes, feeling the ache in his limbs, his chest, melt away into the warmth and softness of the couch. They were all waiting for something, he and these two mute cops. But he couldn't remember what. Probably for the father-faced man to come back. He relaxed and let the mountains close in around him again. The father-faced man would know what they were waiting for.

When he opened his eyes again, there was a figure hovering over him, only a bulky outline against gray morning light from a window. Esteban squinted, blinked, trying to give features to the outline. He made out an askew nose, slick, graying hair.

"Chuy?" he said. His mouth was full of straw.

"Sí, Sr. Esteban."

He closed his eyes again. The mountains started to come back, but he fought them away. He moved, and hurt. He tried to put the past hours back together, but everything was as jumbled and out of place as Assyrian columns and Tudor mansions in Palermo Park had been last night.

Last night. He opened his eyes. The morning light was still truly there in the window. "What time is it, Chuy?"

"A little after seven, señor."

"And today is Saturday?"

"Sí. Saturday."

"Where's Grandfather?"

"He's at home, waiting for you."

"At *home?* How long has he been there?"

"All night, señor. On the telephone—for you."

Esteban struggled up out of the blanket. He was as stiff as he'd been the morning after a boxing match. And his head felt as if he'd taken punches from Firpo for hours. "Do I have any clothes?"

Chuy stepped back and took a clean shirt from the back of a desk chair. He held it out for Esteban like a valet, a gorilla who'd become a valet. Esteban got to his feet shakily and let Chuy begin to dress him. At home—his grandfather had been at home all night. He hadn't been to Esteban's mother's apartment. Caroline was supposed to tell him about Frank, to take him with her. And, damn it, Caroline *had* reached him, or he wouldn't have known so quickly Esteban was here. The *militares* would have wanted more time to work on him before they called his grandfather—if they'd decided to call him at all. So why hadn't she told him the rest? And where was she now?

He looked around him as Chuy helped him into a pair of pants, his keys and wallet already in place in the pockets. The room probably had more bugs in it than a Patagonian outhouse. No questions, no mention of Caroline and Frank, however anxious he might be. "We're going to Grandfather's?"

"Sí," Chuy said, the long-drawn-out Buenos Aires *sí* that was almost a *sheeee* sound and was always accompanied by a cocked head and pursed lips, and that meant, *of course, how could it be otherwise...?*

"Does that mean I'm free?"

"No, I don't think so, señor. Not precisely."

Subject closed, Esteban thought. Chuy had gone as far as he wanted to.

When Esteban had dressed, Chuy rapped on the outer door of the office. It opened, and the two cops from the night before were standing there, still deaf mutes. One of them led the way, and the other guarded their rear along gray, institutional corridors for what seemed a half mile. They passed no one else, and every door seemed to have a padlock on it, as if all the secrets of Argentina were locked up here. Only when they stepped out into the cold, cloudless morning did Esteban recognize that they'd been in the vast, white military complex on Antarctica Argentina Street. It could have swallowed him like plankton, the way it had swallowed so many others. The Dirty War was over, but the machinery was still oiled. He shuddered.

The two cops abandoned them wordlessly at his grandfather's car—not the Mercedes that Casares was probably trying to sell in Brazil by now, but a long American Cadillac. As they eased away from the military complex onto the General Paz Beltway, a gray Falcon with its license plates covered bounced out of a fenced parking lot and fell in behind them. No, Esteban thought. Not free, not precisely. Chuy unhooked a telephone receiver from the dashboard and dialed, then handed the receiver to Esteban. "He'll want to talk to you," he said.

I'll bet, Esteban thought, I'll bloody well bet. He took the receiver.

Chapter Ten

"I'm sorry, Grandson," Esteban's grandfather said over the hiss of the radiotelephone. "There are too many damn governments in this country. Even I can't control them all. I would have had you out sooner."

"Are we being listened to, Grandfather?"

"No doubt. This is an open radio connection." He was silent for a moment, waiting for Esteban to go on. "We can talk when you get here. I wanted to make sure you were all right."

"I'm all right. But we need to talk *now*."

There was another staticky silence. "Give the phone to Chuy."

Chuy said sí a couple of times, then hung up. He checked the side of the road, then swerved off the beltway and stopped before a place named the American Bar Lido. He handed Esteban a telephone token. "Call him on the pay telephone." The gray Falcon with covered plates pulled in behind them.

In the bar, ecstatic crowds waved at the Popemobile as it roared up to the Church of the Virgin of Luján, six inches high on the television. Esteban edged his way down the long bar, keeping his eyes off the television. Luján was outside the city, the home of Argentina's miracle Virgin—whom Esteban hoped the pope was on good terms with. He'd need her. He prayed for a flat tire on the Popemobile, a thrown rod—anything to keep the pope out of the city longer.

As he reached the telephone, hidden in front of the toilet at the end of the bar, he checked the front door. A man in a blue suit and school tie—the uniform the clones of this bastard had worn when they closed down the restaurant—stepped inside it and rested against the end of the bar. Esteban turned his back and dialed.

"What in hell were you doing in Palermo last night with that woman?" his grandfather said with no hello when he answered.

"You're sure we can talk?" Esteban said.

"I've been keeping the bastard who listens to us in good suits for years. Isn't that right, Domingo?" There was a click on the line. Somebody had pulled a plug. "Now," his grandfather said.

Esteban checked his watch. "Listen, Grandfather. I want you to give me two hours, stop the pope—however you can. I'm sure you know who to call."

"Stop him from what?"

"From going to the Spanish Monument to talk. This is important: don't even let him leave the papal nuncio's. Do you understand me? He musn't even start for the monument."

The line went dead. Esteban banged on the telephone. Not now, damn it! Two-thirds of everybody who worked for Teléfonos Argentinos would be off today, sneaking out to see the pope. It was a miracle the phones worked at all—but just not *now*. The line sputtered and came back. "Are you telling me what I think you are?" his grandfather was saying. "That it's not the president he's after?" He apparently hadn't even noticed the dead line.

"Yes."

"Then I'll give you nothing, not a damn minute longer. Not if it's the Holy Father. Get off the line."

"No, Grandfather. Keep listening. I can stop it—I know where Paco is. I just need time to get to him."

"Where is he?"

Esteban considered it. What if he told his grandfather, asked him to send some of his men with him? But no, this was his now. Forget the fact that his mother and maybe Caroline would be in the way if any trouble

212

started between his grandfather's *guapos* and Frank and his Gypsy. He'd wanted Caroline to call his grandfather in on this when he thought there was no other way. But now there *was* another way. And after last night, after realizing that if there was going to be a martyr in all of this because of Frank, he was the one Frank was leaving behind to be crucified—after that, the last shot was going to be his own, nobody else's. For Adela, for the Time of War, for the Cheshire cat, for the whole bloody, pointless mess.

And Caroline, *was* she there at his mother's? He had only one reasonable thing he could assume: she'd understood before he did that calling his grandfather in was the next worse thing to calling the police or the army, a final act of desperation. And so she'd gone on alone, hoping... what? To stop Frank, yes. But how?

"No, Grandfather. You'll have to trust me this time."

"That's a damned switch. Since when should I begin to do that? Where's my man Casares? We had an agreement, remember?"

"Under duress. It doesn't hold."

"I don't think you understand, Esteban."

"Understand what?"

"You can't go anywhere on your own. You don't realize what the hell I had to promise to get you released to me."

"Then tell me."

"I had a goddamn cabinet minister out of bed at three A.M. I swore on everything I hold holy—and there are things, whether or not you believe it—I swore that I personally knew you didn't kill Jaime Mondragon, and that you had no intention of assassinating anybody. I came close to begging the pompous bastard—after I promised him a condominium in Miami—to let you prove it. I took personal responsibility for you. And I told him you'd give him the man they were looking for. They're out for blood, and they'll get it however they can. If they can save the president, they will. But they know he won't last past the end of this damned war, in any case. So they'd love to have a bona fide British-trained assassin to blame both Jaime Mondragon *and* the president on. They'll need all the scapegoats they can get. They'd much rather have Francisco than you—but remember, if they can't, you'll do."

"You mean they'd *let* Galtieri be assassinated?"

"Who, the air force? Galtieri's an army general. Think about it, lawyer. Think of the advantages. But only if they can legitimately show they've tried to stop it. And they still want to be paid for Jaime Mondragon. So don't press your luck."

"For the pity of God, Grandfather..."

"I never take stupid risks—at least not since the one I took when I decided to have children and grandchildren. I knew when you and that woman managed to get away from Casares—which raised my opinion of you, by the way—I knew that you were still going for your brother. And that you probably knew where to look. I was right, wasn't I?"

"Yes and no."

"Yes and no, hell, lawyer. You just told me you knew where he was."

"Yes, then."

His grandfather cleared his throat. "Then you've got to do that. You've got to give them Francisco."

Esteban listened to the hum and buzz of the wires, imagined his grandfather at the desk in his father's old apartment. What had the old man been thinking these past two weeks, surrounded by his dead son? What regrets, what trade-offs with himself had there been about the past? Esteban had thought only about the choices he had had to make. And now he knew his grandfather had made one, too. One as hard as his own had been.

"You could have let them have *me,* Grandfather."

"I damn well know I could have."

"Why didn't you?"

"That's just the kind of stupid question your father would have asked. Is that good enough for an answer?"

"Yes." Yes—but how many years too late?

"Then get back in the car with Chuy. You don't need to come here now. I told them I'd talk to you, and I have. Chuy will take you back to...wherever you were. Then you'll go from there."

Esteban looked over his shoulder along the crowded bar. An announcer on the TV was describing the pope's mass in the church at Luján, was calling it like a soccer game. The man in the blue suit and school tie sipped a glass of what looked like soda water, and watched. "I can't do that, Grandfather. I can't give them Paco."

"Damn it, then they'll take you. Don't you understand?"

What should he tell his grandfather? That if he took the bastards to Frank, he'd be taking them to his mother and Caroline, too? Even his grandfather couldn't buy or talk them out of that—assuming the idiot *militares* didn't decide to blast their way into his mother's apartment with missiles to begin with.

"And if they don't have either of us, Grandfather?"

"I made a bargain, Esteban. They'll come to me to collect."

God damn it to hell. Himself or Frank or his grandfather. There was a choice for you. Pick a card. Turn in your brother and save yourself, then try to live with that. Save your brother and go back to the steel table and the gentle courtesy of General Kleist—and after that, a firing squad. Or save both yourself and your brother, and hang your grandfather. No Arab, no Borges could have designed a prettier madness.

"You'll get one of us, Grandfather. But remember, two hours. And I'll contact you."

He hung up with his finger, but kept the receiver to his ear, as if he were still talking. The blue suit and school tie at the end of the counter still had its eyes fixed on the television. Esteban scanned the bar. There were only two doors—the entry and the toilet. He hung up the receiver quickly and stepped into the toilet. Could such an old trick really work? he wondered. No more Bogart, Caroline had said. With luck, the blue suit at the door wasn't a Bogart fan.

He locked the door. There was a single window, a small one above the toilet. It was the old-fashioned kind that had chicken wire laminated into it, and that had to be raised instead of cranked open. Wonderful. Ten to one it was painted shut years ago. He stepped up onto the toilet, flicked the lock, and shoved. Nothing. Frozen solid as a general's mind. And the chicken wire made breaking it useless. He stepped down from the toilet, his eyes darting frantically over the tiny room for something to pry with. Besides the things that were bolted down, he found only a wooden sign hung in front of the toilet, so that you could only see it after you were sitting down. "Ask for your LAVISEC toilet paper at the cashier." Oh, God, oh, Argentina, he thought, near tears.

Then, no, not everything wasn't bolted down. He lifted the heavy lid from the toilet tank, aimed, and rammed it upward against the frame of the window. The glass cracked—but there was more, the pop of ancient paint breaking loose. The window rose a few centimeters. Esteban jammed the tank lid into the opening and pried. The window moved again. He let the lid fall through to the outside, grabbed the window, yanked upward, and it slammed open to the top. As he scrambled out head first, he heard behind him the jiggle of the door handle, then pounding. But before there was time to hear more, he was out, was running across a vacant lot, his muscles freeing themselves with each step, the pain like spurs, the cold air in his lungs as exhilarating as pure oxygen, heading back for the last time into the Time of War, the pretty madness.

He hid behind a backyard rabbit warren, watched until both the Cadillac and the Falcon had circled the block a final time, then expropriated a cranky moped. When he was safely into another neighborhood, he found a taxi—a taxi that gave up a good six blocks from his mother's apartment. Nothing was moving. Pope fans had gotten as close as they could in their cars, then simply abandoned them in the streets. The sidewalks were clogged with people hurrying toward Libertador, knowing that by now they had no chance of finding a place near the Spanish Monument, and hoping to luck into a glimpse of the pope as he sped by on Libertador, to grab a piece of flying grace.

Even the side street leading onto Libertador was a solid sea of bodies for at least a block before the avenue itself. It was already worse than the chaos of a River Plate–Boca Junior soccer brawl. He shoved, sidled, begpardoned his way through the bodies toward the front of his mother's apartment building, hearing not the chants that were springing up everywhere, but the ticking of a clock, of the time bomb that Frank was. When he got his hand free, his watch told him it was nine o'clock. Nearly one of his two hours gone, and he had only reached the front door of the building.

He silently thanked Chuy for seeing that all his things made it into the fresh pants he'd brought, as he unlocked the door to the building. All he'd need was to have to buzz before he went up. Yet when he stepped out of the elevator, he knew that keys were useless now. What could he do, open the door to his mother's apartment and pretend the night latch wouldn't be on? Kick the door down, and pretend that nobody inside would shoot before they were properly introduced? All the way here, he'd tried without success to plan what he would do when he was *in* the apartment, not how he'd get in. He froze in front of the white door, looked at the blank walls of the elevator foyer for a solution, found none, dried his sweating hands against his trousers, and rang the buzzer.

He heard a slight rasp as someone opened the peephole in the door. Then another rasp as it closed. Then an hour passed, a month. He flattened himself against the wall, just in case.

A night latch slipped off. A dead bolt thunked, then another. The door handle turned.

His mother's face was drawn tight around her eyes, the old familiar sign, the only sign, that she'd been crying. She stepped back and looked him over the way she used to before he'd pass inspection on school mornings. "Praise God," she said in English. "All my sons."

Her eyes filmed with tears, and she held out her hands to him. He took them and let her lead him into the apartment. The expanse of the living room spread behind her—empty. "I thought I'd never see you again," she said. "When I heard they'd arrested you, I simply knew you'd be just as all those others have been—that you'd... Was it your grandfather who got you out? Was it Carlos?"

"Yes, Mother."

"Oh, I'll never loathe him again, then." She gave him a quick, hard hug, then stepped away from him and called over her shoulder. "Frank? It's all right. It's your brother! Isn't that wonderful?" She leaned close to Esteban. "He's been such a comfort to me, he and

Caroline. The other one, the one with the hair that looks as if it has mice in it, you know—I should be just as happy if he'd slither off somewhere...." She gave him another quick hug. "Thank you for helping to bring all my sons home. That's all that matters, isn't it?"

"Oh, yes," Frank said, stepping into the room from the hall and shoving his automatic pistol into his belt. "He's reliable, Mother. Tenacious. Bulldog tenacious, aren't you, little brother?"

Their mother turned and held out her hand for Frank. He took it, smiling, but his eyes on Esteban were as blank and unrevealing as camera lenses. Not just distant now, but blank. Imperially slim he was, still, but the healthy, tanned look he'd had in Bariloche was gone. His face was city pale now, and a little puffy. There even seemed to be more gray in his hair. Esteban imagined him in the tiny apartment in Mataderos these past weeks, yellowing like a plant out of sunlight, waiting, while he himself had chased and been chased over half the continent looking for him. He should be angry, or glad, or relieved—but he wasn't anything, and that surprised him. This was Frank standing before him, one hand in his mother's, the other held out for him to take, no more. The symbol that Frank had become for him wasn't Frank. The bloated bodies in Iquitos, the staring body of Jaime Mondragon, the dead policemen in Bariloche—what did they have to do with his brother, with the definition of his brother he'd held on to all these years?

Yet they had everything to do with his brother. Christ. Was it simplicity he was looking for again?

He took Frank's hand. "It's been a while, *hermano*," he said.

"That it has. Are you alone?"

"Just myself."

"Well. That's good news."

Their mother drew them close to her. "Is this all there is?" she said. "Just a handshake between you?" She was beaming.

"No, of course not," Frank said, and reached for Esteban to embrace him. Esteban stiffened, but Frank pulled him into a tight bear hug. "I warned you not to follow me," he whispered. "God damn you."

"Fuck off," Esteban whispered back. "Where's Caroline?"

"That's my business now."

Esteban broke away. "What the hell does that mean?"

His mother looked distressed. "What does what mean?"

"Where's Caroline, Mother?" Esteban demanded.

"Is that what you're upset about? I'll get her," she said, with a hint of mock jealousy in her look.

"No," Frank said. "Not yet."

"Yes, Mother. Now." Esteban locked his eyes onto Frank's.

There was a tense silence, then Frank said, "It's all right, Mother."

Puzzled, their mother dropped their hands and moved away into the hall. "What the hell did you tell her?" Esteban said when she'd gone.

"I told her that we're going to slip away into the crowds after the pope's speech—all of us. And that we're leaving the country. I don't want her to think differently." There was a warning in his voice.

"How much does she know about anything?"

"She knows I killed Mondragon, and she understands why. I told her I blew up some missiles, and she believes it."

"Nothing about the pope?"

"What do you think?"

"You're a prick, my brother. What's going to happen to her?"

"She won't be hurt."

"You're going to leave her behind?"

"She'll be taken care of. They won't hurt her."

"You're not counting on Grandfather for that, are you?"

"Yes."

"No, Frank. Just...no."

"You're here, aren't you? He did it for you."

"Great God—I didn't kill the *pope*."

"Neither will she."

"That's not the goddamn *point*...." The Cheshire cat leered, hissed, struck. Esteban walked past Frank to the glass door that led onto the patio. Through the slats of the steel security blinds, he watched the canvas ban-

219

ner flap against the railing—a perfect cover. "Why the pope, Frank? Why not the president?"

"You were never stupid, *hermano menor*. Surely you can see it."

"No. No, I can't see it."

He turned at the sound of footsteps on the parquet floor. Caroline came into the room from the hallway, his mother shooing her ahead of her as if she were shooing geese. And behind his mother, mostly hidden by her, was another figure, a man's, dark and no taller than she was. Esteban's eyes flickered to him, then dismissed him. Caroline. It was Caroline that he wanted to see, Caroline who mattered.

Her eyes darted to his, then to Frank's. Her blouse was clean now, and she had one of his mother's sweaters thrown over her shoulders. Her hands were folded in front of her as primly as a madrigal singer's. The whole effect of her—white blouse, hair in a bun, tweed skirt, sweater—was of propriety, a shy woman being introduced at tea. But her eyes never returned from Frank's, and when he motioned for her she went to his side. He put his arm around her waist.

Esteban made the two or three more steps to the couch and clung onto the arm as he sat down. He pulled up enough breath to say, "No, my brother. I was always stupid."

This was why Caroline hadn't told his grandfather where Frank was. This was why she'd come into the restaurant to meet him. This was why she never talked about her past. This was why she'd arranged for passage out of the country for Frank. This was why... why everything. And he'd believed her! An ass, a fool, an idiot babbling to himself about faith.

"I'm sorry, Esteban," Caroline said.

He nodded. He caught his mother's eye, and saw that she was as shocked as he was.

"Oh, dear Lord," she said. "I had no idea..."

"In Paris?" Esteban said, thinking, Of course, you twit, where else?

"In Paris," Frank said. "Sometimes in London."

"I didn't lie about the rest, Esteban," Caroline said. Her voice was hesitant, uneven. "I didn't know Frank was coming back—not until you told me. I never thought I'd see him again. I didn't plan it, any of it."

"You didn't think you'd see him again, so you took second best, right?"

"No, Esteban, *no*. I..."

"Mother?" Esteban forced his returning voice to sound as calm as he could. He had no notion if he'd succeeded or not. "Frank and I were talking something over. We could do with some tea, I think. Could you take Caroline into the kitchen and brew us up some? Please?" He hid behind the precise, deliberate English, the silly-sounding formality of it. It was a trick he'd learned as a boy: to change languages was to change personalities, to say things the other personality never could. God knew he needed that now.

His mother understood instantly and, her eyes beginning to flash in one of her orchestrated rages, held out her hand for Caroline imperiously, as if she'd just located a maliciously lost child on a museum trip. Caroline had become the enemy, the woman who was coming between her sons on their reunion. Esteban blessed his mother's English outrage, her fury.

Caroline's leaving helped. Not much, but enough for him to remember things. To remember that the pope was still coming, that he had much less than an hour now before he had to call his grandfather, that...

"Sorry, old man," Frank said, still using English. "I'd hoped to find her, of course. But I had no idea she'd just walk in on me like last night. Or about you and her."

Old man? Christ, he wanted to stuff *old man* down Frank's throat. "Sure," he said. He nodded toward the man who'd been in the hall behind his mother. All through the episode with Caroline he'd leaned against the wall at the entrance to the room, neither truly in it nor out of it. "What's that?" The less Frank thought he knew, the better.

"Reynaldo de Cadiz." Frank switched to Spanish. "My brother, Esteban," he said to Reynaldo.

De Cadiz nodded to Esteban, but didn't move away from the wall. His course black hair was long and unwashed, hair that mice might truly live in. He wore a red shirt of some cheap synthetic material ironed shiny, and the bloused *bombacha* pants of a gaucho, stuffed into high boots with silver coins sewn into them. Around his neck was a stained paisley bandanna—his concession, Esteban imagined, to Gypsyhood. Only his thin, fine features would have hinted at it otherwise.

"What's he for?" Esteban stuck to English.

Frank turned his blank eyes on Reynaldo. "Why are we here, *compadre?*"

Reynaldo's voice was a flute. He stood away from the wall, and as if reciting, said, "The phoenix rises from ashes. Christ rises from the tomb. Life comes from death."

"Fine," Esteban said. "I can pay twenty *palos* and get the same standard mystic crap from any fortuneteller. You're smarter than that, Frank. Is that why you're going to kill the pope?"

Frank laughed his staccato, unsmiling laugh. "Why are *you* here, brother mine?" He switched back to English.

He stopped himself from thinking of Caroline. "To keep you from killing the pope. Among other things."

"And how do you propose to do that? You don't have much time, you know."

"I don't know. I'm working on it."

"You think I'm going to do it because of what Reynaldo said? I'm mad as a March hare, no?"

"No, I don't. *This* is crazy, but you're not."

"I tried to explain it to you in the car on the way to Comodoro Rivadavia, Esteban. In one sense, what I'm doing *is* because of what Reynaldo says, though not in the naive way he may understand. What he believes in most of all is me. I met him in London. He's been back here waiting for me, for the right combination of time and events. The funny thing is that he plotted this time out astrologically before it happened, but I dismiss that. I'd never convince you I'm sane—saner than you, I think—otherwise."

"It would be tough."

"Then let me give you sanity. All over the world, the dead are propping up the dead. London, Washington, Moscow, Buenos Aires. Little wars here and there, threats, a revolution now and again that only changes such superficial matters as who owns what. But what's

222

the outcome, always? More people crammed into factories, into offices, into automobiles. A little more dying each time, a little more decadence, a little less hope. And what do we do about it? We write books. We make films. But nobody does anything, because we're terrified to. No, *they're* terrified to. Communist, capitalist—what nonsense. Underneath they all believe in the same thing. More death—more death of what's human in us."

"Which is?"

"I told you before. The force that's in the whirlwind before it becomes a whirlwind. The force that sweeps clean so that something new can grow. That's what survival is; that's what winter is for. We think we can make it always summer now. We think that we can renew ourselves without real death, without holocausts. There are no more barbarians left to invade the empire, Esteban, to wipe out the decadence. Not unless we create them, to let the force become the whirlwind."

"And you're going to do that. Here. In"—he looked at his watch—"in less than an hour. With one bullet."

"Yes. We can't simply lose this war, Esteban. We have to have a holocaust. There has to be something so unspeakable done here that everything collapses at once, that our own utter decadence is revealed to us beyond any doubt." He walked to the window and tugged the steel blinds up, then opened the glass doors onto the balcony. "Come here, *hermano menor*."

Esteban followed him out onto the balcony. They walked to the end of it so they could see past the banner. The morning was still clear, but less cold. All along Libertador, behind barricades that brass-helmeted horse guards patrolled, a seawall of people stretched toward the Spanish Monument. And at the monument itself, spreading like a lava flow, more people, an immense tide of people covering, it seemed to Esteban, the whole civilized earth. "There's the force," Frank said. "Perón's force, if he'd only carried it far enough. Let them lose a war, let the pope be destroyed in front of them, and they'll ignite a fire that can spread to every human being on earth. They won't understand it, but they don't have to."

"And it has to begin here."

"Only in Argentina. *Only* in Argentina. The force is

too buried in all the rest of the world. Only here is it still close enough to the surface to be reached. It was almost touched in Europe in the last war. But Hitler perverted it, let himself get caught up in the dream of mechanization. It survives here, without Hitler's perversions. It can begin from here again, purely."

Frank took Esteban's hand, as he had when he'd walked him to school years ago. His eyes weren't blank now; they glowed in their distances like bonfires. He led Esteban back inside.

"And what's your part in this, Paco?" Esteban asked him.

"After today, nothing. Reynaldo has some arrangements made for us. When the time comes, I'll be back if I'm needed."

Esteban took Frank's other hand. "The reasons are all there, Frank—the part about the death. But, dear God, the solutions are all wrong. Holocaust! It won't happen, my brother. It just won't happen. And even if it did, nothing would be left to start over with. Not this time. Don't you see that? *Nothing,* no people, nothing."

"Something will be. Enough. You can kill everything but life itself."

Esteban dropped Frank's hands. Reynaldo still leaned serenely against the wall. That was Frank's force, he thought. Frank's believing, mindless, deadly, chart-making force. So this was the end of the madness, of the tea party. To stop Frank, to end the party, he'd have to kill him. He was certain of that now: Frank believed too clearly, too totally, in what he was doing. There was no arguing with those eyes. And killing Frank would mean he'd have to kill the Gypsy, too. And what if he failed, assuming he *could* bring himself to kill Frank? If one were dead, the other would go through with the assassination. He checked his watch again. Twenty minutes until he had to call his grandfather, less than an hour before the pope passed by. God, God, God. If his grandfather made the call, even the cops could figure out the rest. Nobody—including his mother—would get out of this apartment except dead or in a police van. Think, he had to think. But Frank's eyes scorched him, Reynaldo's followed him like a painting's.

"I'll be back," he said. He tried to smile. It flopped.

"Philosophy always makes me have to piss." Anything, five minutes alone in a bathroom, to think.

As he passed by the kitchen, he saw his mother and Caroline, his mother fussing with tea things and Caroline seated at the table, watching his mother's motions as intently as if they were keys to salvation. Normalcy, he thought, the salvation in normalcy. Would any of them ever find it again? He paused, his stomach feeling a boot in it again. Caroline saw him and started up from the table. He began walking, too fast. As many goddamn bathrooms as his mother had, why could he never remember where one of them was?

Caroline caught him. He tried to pull away, but she held tightly. "You idiot," she said. "I could have stopped it—could have hit the rifle at the last minute if I had to. He wouldn't have killed me. Why did you have to show up?"

"What in hell are you talking about?"

"Oh! You *are* an idiot. I don't give a fig what you think. Frank and I were over years ago. I didn't tell you about him because you'd believe I had stayed with you because of him. All right, I did at first. But not afterward. Are you too thick to see that? Do you think I came here to start over with Frank again after, after... oh! *Mierda!*"

He tried to pull away again.

"Listen," she said. "Then believe what you want to. But I've been trying to figure out a way to get rid of that stupid rifle since I got here. I couldn't just throw it out a window into the street. It's too big to fit down the garbage chute—it wedges in. *You* figure out something."

The rifle—of course, the damned rifle! You didn't stop Frank, you stopped the rifle! He turned to her with such urgency she must have been afraid he was going to hit her, and she winced. "Where is it?"

"In the bedroom. That bedroom." She pointed toward the next door along the hall. *"His* bedroom—his alone."

It was there, all right, stretched out in the middle of the bed on a blanket like a baby. A military rifle, 6.5 or 7.5 millimeter, Esteban guessed. Polished, freshly blued, handled with love, no doubt, through the years Reynaldo had cradled it, waiting for his charts to tell him it was time. Esteban pulled the bolt back. A shell popped out. It was loaded, ready.

"Hiding it wouldn't help," Caroline said. "It's too big. They'd find it."

Esteban fumbled with the bolt until he found the catch, remembering what he could about his *preparatorio* military classes. He slid the bolt out and dropped it into his pocket. "That's it," he said. "It's dead. This is the only rifle they have?"

"I've looked," Caroline said. "I'm sure of it."

He sat down on the edge of the bed to compose himself before he went back into the living room, to let the blood stop pounding in his ears. Caroline sat beside him.

"How long were you...with Frank?" he asked her.

"Four years," she said. "I was only twenty-one when I met him."

"You loved him, then." It wasn't a question.

"Yes. I did."

"That was easy to do once."

"Yes, it was—once."

"You've only been with me two years."

"That's enough."

"For what?"

"To know I made a mistake the first time. I was with Frank. I never really believed Frank was with me."

"The power of the one less in love—that's where that came from?"

"That's where."

"And now?"

"For a while I thought it was the other way around, that I had that power. Now I'm not so sure, *guapo*. You've turned mean. You kicked the hell out of me last night." She smiled.

"Sorry."

"No, it worked. I got more sympathy than Jackie Kennedy."

He answered her smile and got to his feet. She followed him. "Well," he said. He waited for something else to say to come along. It didn't. His emotions were too jumbled, too beat to hell from half a dozen directions for any one of them to make sense.

"Well." They stood facing each other awkwardly, almost shyly. "What now?"

Whatever lightness had crept into the mood blew away like smoke. "We tell them their tea party's over."

"And then?"

"And then it's up to them. I don't know about our friend Nostradamus, but Frank seems pretty much in control. Mother's here—that should help. If he sees it's finished, I might be able to talk him down." And no, it's not finished, he thought. His grandfather was waiting—for a telephone call, and for one of his grandsons. "Keep Mother in the kitchen as long as you can. Stay with her."

Caroline nodded. "Kiss me?" she said.

"In my mother's house?" he said. "She'd never forgive us." He leaned over and brushed her lips. "There's more."

"You're generous," she said.

He stopped in the kitchen and dropped the bolt down the garbage chute. He listened until he heard it thud faintly against an empty box, two floors below in the basement. In the living room, his mother was serving tea, proper and furious. Reynaldo took his, still leaning against the wall, as if moving would disturb some delicate balance only he could feel.

"Mother..." Esteban began.

"I know. I'm going," she said. "This is hardly a social occasion." She moved off toward the kitchen, rattling the teapot much more than was necessary. "I lived with an Argentine man long enough to know how they feel about women and business. I think it's barbarous." Esteban knew she thought more than that: she figured she could find out more of what was really going on by pumping Caroline than by listening to her sons ramble.

No one spoke until she was gone.

From outside a chant began and swept its way along the avenue.

Juan Pablo Segundo
Te quiere todo el mundo...

John Paul the Second, all the world loves you. No, Esteban thought. Not all the world. "Paco. Let's sit down."

Frank glanced at his watch. "No time, little brother. Reynaldo? Go check the back door to the building. Make sure nobody's locked it. When you come back up, leave the elevator door open. Wedge it." Then, to Esteban, "I'm afraid you'll be coming with us, you know. For a while, at least. Whether or not either of us wants it."

Esteban watched the Gypsy go, grateful for chance's small kindnesses. "Paco," he said. "Sit down. It's over."

Frank looked at him, puzzled, those distant auroras still glowing behind his eyes. "All right," he said. "Then maybe we'd better sit. And you tell me what's over." Paco sat in one of his mother's white armchairs, one slim leg crossing gracefully over the other. God, Esteban thought. He's the only man I've ever known who can make the act of sitting down as precise as a dance step. He was afraid of what was coming, and yet still somehow he felt sorry for Paco.

Esteban sat on the couch across from him, the couch his mother had sat on the day after Adela was killed, the day this had all begun. He tried to think of some way to phrase it, wondering all the time if it were possible for Frank to use that automatic pistol from a sitting-down position. At last he blurted, "I took the bolt out of the rifle."

"Oh?" Frank's calm was glacial, unnerving. "Where is it, Stevie?"

"Gone, Paco. Where neither of us can get to it."

Frank stared at him, the puzzled look still in his eyes, as if he'd heard a noise somewhere he couldn't identify and was waiting for it to come again. At length he said, "I'd have put it down the garbage chute, I suppose. No chance of getting to it there in time."

Esteban returned the stare, and said nothing.

Frank's hand touched the pistol, a gesture as automatic as checking his fly might be. "I *want* to kill you, Esteban. I truly do."

"I don't think that surprises me."

"But what would surprise you is if I did, no? In our mother's living room, with Adela dead already."

"I don't know, Paco. I don't know you. I tried to tell you that in Comodoro." They'd been jerked backward in time. Frank was older, smarter, faster, and they were fighting over something, a book, a soccer ball, and Esteban knew that to challenge him was stupid, that he'd lose if Frank wanted to accept the challenge. But he'd begun, he had the ball or the book in his hands, and he couldn't let go. He could only wait for whatever mysterious process went on in Frank's mind to decide whether Frank would lunge for him or walk away. He hadn't known as a child what that process was, and his mouth had gone dry with fear of the waiting. He waited. He felt the dryness. No matter how much he told himself that they weren't children anymore, that everything had changed, he felt the dryness.

But then something happened to Frank that had never happened to him as a child, something utterly surprising. Something that Esteban had seen only once before, on the day of their father's funeral. He began to weep. And it was a weeping that was as involuntary as breathing, so involuntary that he wasn't sure that Frank even knew it was happening. His face didn't change expression; his mouth remained the same fixed line. Yet the tears slipped out of his eyes and hung on his cheeks like beads of sweat, as if they were ashamed of being there at all. It was the saddest weeping Esteban had ever seen.

"Oh, but I do know *you*, little brother," Frank said, his voice remaining steady. "I should have expected you'd do something like that. You asked me why I didn't come to you instead of Adela? You want to know why I left you in Comodoro? You know."

"And what now, Paco? Now that we both know I'm who I am?"

"The funniest part of all this is the way it's all reversed, Stevie. Adela with that damned English sense of honesty and fair play that got her killed. Me, the English one of us, understanding the strength of Argentina the way neither of you do. And you turning out to be like the old man—hell, like Grandfather—solid and stubborn and holding things together. Bloody Christ, where did *you* come from?"

It was a question Esteban had been asking himself too long to want to find the answer to right now. He kept blurting, kept throwing things out at Frank like cricket balls, half hoping to keep him off-balance, half realizing he didn't have the slightest notion what the hell else to do. "Grandfather knows you're here. I didn't tell him. I didn't have to."

"Ah, Grandfather. I thought I was done with Grandfather."

"He loved you, you ass."

"Love? He's what's wrong with Argentina, Brother. He's what's wrong with the world! Love?"

Esteban held on to his anger, clutched it like a sharp-toothed animal that was struggling to fight loose from him. "He's made a deal. When he got me away from them last night."

"From who? The *milicos* had you?" Frank said. "Mondragon's pals?"

So Caroline had been playing it close. His shaky confidence in her rose a notch more. "That's not important now. He promised them one of us, you or me, for Mondragon. If they don't get one of us, they'll go for him."

Frank's tears kept flowing, as if they were coming from the distances behind his eyes and not his eyes themselves, from some other Frank than the one who sat across from him and talked as if they were only commenting on a boring business proposal Esteban had made him.

"He promised them me, you mean. They already had you. Is that why you're really here, little brother? Where are they? Outside? You wouldn't have brought them up, of course, not with Mother here."

"That was Grandfather's deal, Paco. Not mine. What do you think?"

Frank blinked, and seemed to notice the tears for the first time. "I think... I think..." He reached up to wipe the tears away, and when he actually felt them with his hand, his face changed, seemed to twist itself into accord with them. His hand clamped into a fist and slammed down onto the arm of the chair. The teacup and saucer he'd left there bounced and slid toward the floor. As they hit and shattered, Frank said, his voice caught somewhere between a sob and a shout, "God *damn* it! I almost changed history! I almost made a difference. Don't you see that? Don't you have any fucking *vision?*"

The two doors opened almost simultaneously. The front one, with Reynaldo behind it, thudded against the wall just after Frank's fist hit the couch, just before the teacup and saucer shattered. The one into the hallway from the kitchen clicked and banged just afterward. Reynaldo, confused, spun into a crouch. He jerked the revolver from his belt and aimed it toward the sound from the hallway. Frank, half-blinded from the tears, raised a hand in front of his face as if he were trying to ward off a blow. Esteban was only inches off the couch when Reynaldo fired.

"No!" Frank bellowed at Reynaldo as the shot echoed in the room. Reynaldo held his crouch, his eyes darting from Frank to Esteban to their mother, whose surprised look clung unchanged to her face as she crumpled at the entrance to the hallway.

Esteban reached her first. As he knelt beside her, Frank tried to shove him aside and take his place. Esteban's anger broke, exploded. He clasped his hands into a double fist and swung sideways. He felt his knuckles sink into the softness of Frank's groin. Frank bellowed, clutched himself, and went to his knees. Esteban ignored him. There was blood beginning to puddle around his mother from a long rip in her dress.

He tore the dress open, aware that there were forms moving beside him but not seeing them. Only when he heard Caroline screaming his name did he allow the forms to take shape, realize that Caroline was clinging to the Gypsy's gun arm, wrapping herself around it and letting her full weight bring it down. Reynaldo shook her, a fox with a rabbit, but she held on.

Esteban vaulted backward in a rolling leap and grabbed for the Gypsy's legs. Reynaldo went down, Caroline on top of him. Esteban got a hand on the gun and wrenched it away.

But it was too late. Something cracked against his wrist with such a force that pain flashed all the way to his shoulder, and the gun spiraled away. Before the shock and pain let him reach for it, Frank was covering it with his body and pointing the automatic at him. This time, Esteban knew, he might use it.

He rolled back toward his mother. "Get back. Leave the woman alone," he heard Frank say to the Gypsy, his words clipped with pain and lost breath. But nevertheless, as Esteban tried to pull his mother's dress away with his aching wrist, failed, and knew it was broken,

Frank's hands took his place. Esteban let him take over, and the two of them knelt side by side as Frank gently rolled their mother over so that they could see the long gash just below her ribs. Blood was oozing out, but the sight of the gash against her pale skin—not the neat hole that Esteban had feared—was blessed.

"Shit," Frank said in English. "She's fainted. Help me." He pointed toward the couch. With his good hand, Esteban helped ease her onto the couch. Caroline snatched a pillow for her head, but when the Gypsy tried to move in to help, Frank elbowed him back. "Don't touch her," he hissed.

But then, as he straightened up, he handed the pistol back. Reynaldo took it with as pleased and grateful a look as if it were an offering of frankincense and myrrh. "Francisco—" he began.

"Cállate. Shut up," Frank said. "Get over by the door and keep that whore of a pistol in your belt. Don't take it out again until I tell you to." He turned back to their mother. "Put a cloth over that and call somebody," he told Esteban. "Do it quickly, before she loses too much blood."

"I'll do it," Caroline said.

"No," he said sharply. "Go to Reynaldo. We're leaving." He gestured with the pistol. Caroline didn't move.

"The hell you are," Esteban said.

"You're going to stop me with a broken wrist? And then who's left to take care of Mother? You always wanted to be the one who stayed at home, little brother. Now you can. While I do us a favor."

For a moment, while Frank had been crying, then in the few seconds they had been working together on their mother, Esteban had almost felt an unmuddied emotion. The pity he'd begun to feel turned real, and with it came something like affection, love, that went too deep for him to deny. Something from before, something residual, like a remembered taste or smell. But not now. Frank's arrogance was back, and with it the danger in him. His eyes had retreated into themselves again, had turned cold again, like dead suns.

"No favors, Frank."

"Oh, this one, yes. Grandfather promised the *milicos* one of us—" He turned briefly to Caroline. "That part you didn't know, did you, *amor?* You picked a family of us, didn't you? How was *that* for a Molina bargain?" Caroline's eyes touched Esteban's, but Frank reclaimed his attention before he could read whatever was in them. "He promised the *milicos* one of us. I'll tell you something. I want to kill you; no, I wanted to kill you. But that wouldn't do anybody any good, would it? Grandfather's dying would change something, and my dying would change something. But not yours. So it's not really your problem, is it? It's mine and Grandfather's."

"It's all mine, Frank. He made the damned bargain because of me. Leave him alone."

Frank walked backward to the door, his eyes holding Esteban's. "We keep saying good-bye, little brother, but you don't let it stick. This time, it has to. Take care of Mother. Tell her I'm sorry. Tell her...tell her I love her, if you give enough of a damn to."

"For God's sake, Paco. Leave Caroline. At least that. She doesn't want to go with you."

"Oh?"

"Ask her, damn it."

"Caroline?" Frank said.

Caroline walked to the door beside him. She met Esteban's eyes and shook her head almost imperceptibly, so nearly imperceptibly that Esteban wasn't sure he saw it.

"Don't, Caroline," Esteban said. "Whatever you're doing it for—whoever, Christ, whichever of us—don't."

"Shut up," Caroline said softly. "Shut up, *guapo*."

"You do owe me, little brother. Remember that, and it might make it easier. I have a right to salvage something." Frank touched Caroline's arm and she moved to the door ahead of him. She gave Esteban a last glance, then was gone. Frank stopped to whisper something to Reynaldo, then said to Esteban in English, "No brotherly love between you and our friend here, Stevie. Nothing for you to hide behind. Remember *that*, too." Reynaldo slipped his revolver from his belt, aimed it at Esteban, then Frank was gone, too.

Esteban dropped to his knees beside his mother. Reynaldo began to react, but checked himself. The elevator clanked and whirred just outside the apartment—down, then up again. Esteban's mother's breathing was even, and her bleeding seemed to have slowed. He brushed her hair away from her face as the elevator's whirring stopped and he heard the doors slide open. Reynaldo leaned through the apartment door and checked the hallway, then, with a little sucking noise between his teeth, disappeared. The door closed softly behind him.

Esteban checked his watch. Eight minutes.

He stuck his bad hand into his shirt to keep it from moving, from reminding him of the pain as much as possible. He rummaged in the first bathroom he came to until he found a gauze pad, smeared it with antibacterial jelly, and plastered it over his mother's wound as best he could with one hand. From outside, another cheer swept the avenue, then a new chant began, the pope's name repeated again and again, a soccer cheer, a mantra. He took the telephone receiver off the hook, laid it beside the telephone, and dialed with his good hand. Work, *cabrón,* he silently implored the thing. Work!

When he picked up the receiver again, it was ringing. He promised candles, Hail Marys, confessions.

No Chuy this time. His grandfather himself picked up.

"It's done, Grandfather. It's stopped."

"Swear it," his grandfather said.

"I swear it."

"Are you all right?"

"I am, but mother's not. Can you get somebody—an ambulance, a doctor—right away?" His grandfather had donated enough to own half a dozen hospitals if he wanted. There'd be no question if he called.

"I can. What happened?"

"I'll explain later. This is more important. I want you to leave, go anywhere, but leave the house. And do it now. Frank's on his way over there."

He waited for his grandfather to answer. He heard a hiss, a series of clicks, a hiss again.

"Grandfather?"

The hiss answered him.

"Grandfather, damn it!"

He pushed the button down and dialed again. A hiss, clicks, a hiss.

"God damn you!" he yelled at the telephone, and slammed the receiver against the telephone table. Had his grandfather's listener decided to pull the plug at last? Had Teléfonos Argentinos won again? Either, both—what mattered was how much his grandfather had heard before the line died. Esteban flicked the button down and began to dial again.

From behind him his mother's voice was weak but controlled. "Go there, Steven. Go quickly."

He cradled the receiver. His mother was propped up on one elbow, her other hand holding the gauze pad against her side. He went to the couch and knelt beside her again. Her face was the paleness of the couch, of her nearly white hair.

"Lie down, Mother. You're bleeding."

"Oh, bother. I know that. I took worse than this from a horse once. I'm more worried about the couch than I am me. Just get to your grandfather's before your brother does. Have you any notion at all what could happen if they meet in the state I'm sure they're both in?"

"I believe so."

"Do you? Do you know why I kept Frank out of the country all this time?"

"Why *you* kept him?"

"Your grandfather and I, though your grandfather wasn't aware I knew he was sending money to that . . . that gang of Frank's. Well, I was sending money, too. But not for the same reason your grandfather was. Frank *had* to be kept out of Argentina. The rest of them I didn't care twaddle about."

"But you wanted him back—you helped bring him back."

"What could I do? After I found out about that filth Adela was engaged to, what could I possibly do? I told her about him, and I told her where my information had come from. And then *she* wanted to help Frank come back into the country. Oh, and I did, too. He's my oldest son, my firstborn, Steven, and my prodigal. I thought perhaps it was time, that Frank was ready to come back. I believed what I was told about his working for the English and that he might do some good. At least I was right about that one thing."

Esteban didn't contradict her. Let her keep believing

235

that. Let her hang on to something of Frank intact.

"Then why had you kept him away?"

"To drive the Argentine out of him—and to keep him apart from your grandfather until he healed."

"Healed from what?"

"He blamed your grandfather for your father's death. He never told you that?"

"No. He never told me lots of things, I suppose."

"Your grandfather taught him too well, you know. When your father was killed, Frank couldn't just blame something as faceless as guerrillas or such. But he could blame your grandfather, couldn't he? He could say to himself, 'If Grandfather weren't who he is, this wouldn't have happened. If all Grandfather's kind of people weren't corrupt, this wouldn't have happened.' You wanted to straighten it all out by being a lawyer, like your father—for all that got him. Oh, but not Frank. Don't you see? He had too much of the Argentine madness in him, that no-middle-ground madness that's always too fixed on some other world that *might* be, to deal with the one that *is*. I hoped England would drive it out of him. And when he came back here working for the English, I thought it might have taken effect. Dear Lord, if he had to be a priest, at least he could have been an Anglican and given me grandchildren!"

Esteban smiled and gently helped her lie back on the couch. She didn't resist.

"But then he showed up here with that...person," she went on. "And now he's gone away to your grandfather's with him. The man shot his mother, and now they've gone away together. With your Caroline. And without you. And without me." Her eyebrows knitted. "And what's 'stopped,' Steven? You told your grandfather something was 'stopped.'" She winced and held out her hand for Esteban to help her to a sitting position. He started to protest but she cut him off. "No, no, don't tell me anything now. Just go to your grandfather's. If your grandfather has thwarted something Frank was involved in, then they're both dangers to each other, no matter what it all has to do with."

"And what about you?"

"Oh, dear Lord. Your grandfather will have a dozen ambulances here before you're out the door. Now *go*."

236

He sat next to her, his hand still in hers. She held on to it and studied his face, as if she were memorizing it. "Don't let him be hurt," she said, the skin around her eyes tightening. "You'll be all right, I know you will. But not your brother." She gripped his hand more firmly. "And Steven?" she said. "It has nothing to do with loving your brother more than you. You're a great deal older than Frank. You always have been. I'm asking you to do what I would have asked your father to do."

He eased his hand from hers, and stood. Frank and his grandfather were going to meet. He would never get to his grandfather's house before Frank did. And it had to be that way; all along it had had to be that way. Final gears slipped against one another, meshed, whirred, and the whole bloody edifice rose up and locked into place. Underneath everything that had happened these past weeks a theme had been beating—theme and variations and counter theme—had been building toward a hidden crescendo. The war, Caroline, Adela, Mondragon, Santander, the pope—those things had been only movements in a grotesque, heartbreaking tango that led up to this moment: his grandfather and Frank were going to meet. It had happened with the predictability and inevitability of Reynaldo the Gypsy's charts and horoscopes. It went far beyond a petty war in the South Atlantic, a scheme of politics. Argentina was his grandfather. For a dozen years Frank had brooded on that, plotting and preparing himself for his final confrontation, the final destruction of everything that was his grandfather in Argentina, and in himself.

And now that Esteban had smashed those plans of Frank's, had taken away the rationalizations that Frank had hidden behind and that had become so twisted that neither he nor Frank, nor anyone, had seen the truth behind them, there was nowhere else left for Frank to go. There was nothing left for him to hide behind. The meeting had to happen.

And Esteban had been the one who'd unwittingly arranged it. He'd never get to his grandfather's in time to stop it, no, but he had to be there. If Frank had written the tango, Esteban realized with a terrible certainty that *he* had conducted it—and would have to stay in the hall now until the last, shattering chord. Stay in the hall and, if necessary, discover and play the chord himself.

He flipped through the telephone directory hurriedly, hoping but only half expecting the name he was looking for to be there. A one-armed piano player needed help.

Moribundo Lopez was less afraid of bill collectors than Esteban thought he'd be. The name was there.

And Pepe was there. When he was done telling himself and anyone in hearing range how happy he was that Sr. Esteban, God be praised though he wasn't sure he believed in God, was safe and well, Esteban asked him if he knew how to get to his grandfather's house.

"How not?" Pepe said, Burgundy confidence blaring through the receiver. "Haven't I worked for the Molinas for twenty-five years—off and on?"

"I'm leaving my mother's apartment now. I'll be there before you. Try not to let anybody see you coming up to the house—anybody inside or outside. Come in through the underground parking garage. I'll leave the elevator unlocked. If I'm not there, go to Mataderos." He gave Pepe Reynaldo's address and told him how to find it. "Paco should be there, and another man. And Caroline. Don't go near them. I'll meet you at the main offices of the slaughterhouses—a big pink building. Do you know it?"

"I'll find it, *patrón*."

"Be certain. A big pink building. I'll be beside it, but out of sight."

"Didn't I find you in the deserts of Patagonia, señor?" Pepe said.

Esteban wasn't consoled. "Pepe? Whatever you do, don't take any serious chances. I need you, but not that bad."

"Chances, *patrón*? Only Spaniards take chances. A Catalan makes them."

When he hung up, Esteban tried his grandfather's number a last time. Hiss, clicks, hiss. Permanently dead, at least until the pope was done.

His mother was sitting erectly on the couch, working hard at looking brave. "I won't see you again here, will I?" she said.

238

"Not soon."

"I thought not."

"Where will you go? England?"

"Go? Why, nowhere. I live here now."

"You'd stay in Argentina? I thought..."

"I've had my children and raised them here. One of them is buried here, and another might be. My husband is buried here. Should I go home, like a returned colonial, and leave my dead behind me? I'm an expatriot in a nation of expatriots, child—a generation or so late, but that doesn't make much difference in the long run, does it? The Argentines will leave me in peace. It's the sons they crucify, not the mothers. Those are usually the rules, aren't they?"

"Usually."

"They're very correct here. They'll follow the rules." She seemed to notice Esteban's hand inside his shirt for the first time. "You're hurt."

"We're a good pair, then."

She managed a smile. "You'll let me know, won't you?"

"One way or another. I won't let you lose me. No such luck."

"We're in wretched shape for embracing. And you haven't much time. Perhaps you'd best..." Her voice caught. "Oh, I hate for my children to see me cry."

He touched her cheek. "Good-bye, Mother."

"Good-bye, my son."

At the door, he turned. "Frank asked me to tell you something. He said to tell you he loves you." Was it crueler to tell her that than to let her think Frank had walked away and left nothing at all? He didn't know. He'd never know.

"Dear Lord," she said.

He protected his arm as best he could as he shoved through the crowds. They had solidified since he'd come here, working people mainly, and people from the provinces, crammed together like soda straws in a rack. Vivas were breaking out, led by cheerleaders with bullhorns stationed strategically along the pope's route: *Viva the pope, Viva the church, Viva youth, Viva peace*. People resented his pushing through, pushed him back, and before he'd gone a dozen meters his arm throbbed so that he had to stop to drive the dizziness away. The day was still bright and cold, though in the sky, mare's tail clouds guided more rain in. There'd be little traffic in the rest of the city. As close as his grandfather's house was, Frank and the others would be there already. He took deep breaths against the waves of pain, and moved again.

Ten minutes, fifteen? How long did he wedge himself between bodies, a dull knife through thick butter? He couldn't raise his arm to look. He only knew that the vivas grew in frequency and intensity, that when he heard the sirens escorting the pope behind him on Libertador, he whispered, "You're welcome," beneath his breath as the human ocean around him was swept by a typhoon of screaming and movement, and that when he finally broke loose beyond the last few stragglers, a faint voice in the distance was begging with a heavy accent through a thousand loudspeakers for peace.

And another ten minutes for him to hail the only cab for miles. And another ten to get to his grandfather's house while the cabby explained why he was an atheist and that the pope could go fuck peace. Esteban pretended to listen, but his mind was at his grandfather's. Caroline had gone with Frank, and Esteban's reason told him she'd done it to protect all of them in some way. But, Christ, what good had his reason been to him lately? Yet after what had happened at his mother's, he had to trust her. He *had* to. Didn't he?

Love, faith, fear, instinct. Those were what was left for him to keep going with now. Just those. He was naked as the first roaring Patagonian Indian Magellan had found and thought to be a creature from a bad fairy tale. That was him, all right, Esteban Molina-Knifeton, Esq., of the Buenos Aires Molina-Knifetons, naked and hanging on to sanity by a thin thread of irony.

His grandfather's Cadillac looked small in the vast underground garage. There were no other cars, either there or on the street. And when the key he'd carried on his ring for years slipped into the elevator lock and turned, he felt no surprise. With Chuy around, what need to change locks?

But when he stepped out of the elevator, the first

thing wrong was that the ancient housekeeper didn't come padding up within seconds after the door opened. And the second thing was the silence. Before him the great, garish museum of a living room lay as quiet and cluttered as the tomb of a pharaoh. He walked through it to the foot of the stairs and listened. More silence, with only the faint rumble of traffic from outside to indicate life still existed anywhere. And as quietly as possible, as if his own footsteps would be a desecration of something, he climbed the long circular staircase. His pain dulled, driven back, he assumed, by the hard rush of blood he felt his heart sending through him. He knew how a jaguar felt, or a leopard, creeping along a branch in the darkness.

At the head of the stairs he listened again. Listened and heard the sound riding over the silence.

Music. An organ, one of his grandfather's half dozen organs. But from where?

He moved along the hallway on the balls of his feet, hearing every creak of a board beneath the carpet. The organ was too faint to be on this floor. Was there one in his father's old apartment? God, who could remember the organs his grandfather was always buying and shuffling around from room to room so that he could play his old tangos and sentimental Agustin Lara songs to his memories and a bored Chuy? But he felt his spirits rise. His grandfather was all right, was somewhere on the top three floors playing his goddamn organ! Miraculously, he'd beat Frank here—or Frank hadn't come at all. But he remembered what that meant. Caroline wasn't here either. If Frank had gone straight to the Gypsy's in Mataderos—or to God knew where—Caroline had gone with him.

Third floor and the music was closer. But not here, not yet. The fourth floor was where his father's old apartment was. He'd need a gun, he reminded himself as he took the stairs two at a time. A gun and his grandfather's car, and maybe even Chuy. Chuy could be trusted. Maybe it wasn't all hopeless. If they could get Frank out of the country, his grandfather might be able to stall. This goddamn government couldn't last long after the war. And new governments forgot things, started over....

The music wasn't coming from his father's old apartment, whose door stood open into the empty room. No, it was from the other room on the floor, the only other room. Adela's room.

His grandfather had had it built for her too late, after she was too old for it, the way he'd done most things too late. It had never been intended as a bedroom. It was her music room, he called it, her own private discotheque. The room had been finished just before Esteban's break with his grandfather, and he'd only seen it once, but that was enough. He remembered a plastic, electronic monstrosity, a monument to what his grandfather must have thought the seventies were. What in hell would his grandfather be doing in that room?

Chuy's feet told him. Chuy's huge feet, the heels of his shoes together like the ridge of a tent, as if Chuy had been standing at attention when he fell face downward into the room. And then beyond the expanse of Chuy's body, his grandfather.

Lights flashed and raced around a room-sized chrome arch above his grandfather's body, and strobes flashed in time to the bouncy, silly music from the organ. The rest of the room was littered with electric guitars, two-meter-tall white plastic speaker cabinets, a set of drums gleaming with stainless steel, a wall full of amplifiers and turntables and tape decks, glittering foil and dayglow posters of skinny adolescents with jeweled guitars, sweating and howling. And an organ, a mammoth electronic organ on a pedestal, its keys moving up and down to the tune of the silent computer that played it.

A wide swath of blood ran down the wall near his grandfather's body; it began just above a panel of switches and buttons that must have controlled the lights, the organ, the computer—and that must have sent signals to the servants quarters four floors below. His grandfather's hand had come to rest on the purple carpet at the end of the path of blood.

Between Chuy and his grandfather lay a sword. His grandfather's one addition to the room had apparently been the swords, a half dozen of them on racks among the rock posters, spillover from the armory of ancient, useless weapons in the foyer. Esteban saw the scene as it must have been: his grandfather and Frank coming in here to talk, leaving Chuy to watch the Gypsy and Caroline in his father's old apartment. His grandfather in a rage, deciding which of his grandsons he was going to sacrifice and snatching one of the swords from the wall. Frank knowing he could have knocked the sword away with his hand, but glad of the excuse at last, and firing the automatic. Chuy rushing in, and Frank meeting him. Another scene Esteban had to populate with his brother and dead men. He prayed to God that it would be the last.

He bent down beside his grandfather to make sure there was nothing he could do. And because his grandfather would have wanted it, he crossed himself. In death, his grandfather didn't glower anymore; in death, his grandfather's face was the serious, slightly pained face of any other old man after everything had let go for him. Esteban absently adjusted a fold of this old man's Japanese dressing gown and stood. He wanted the luxury of tears, as he'd wanted them after he'd found Adela. But tears would be just that, a luxury. He wondered who his grandfather had wept for, if he'd wept for anybody.

I'll weep for you, Grandfather, he said to himself. When there's time, I'll weep for you. I'll weep for all of us.

He cut off the flashing lights and the organ. The silence settled as quickly as a film breaks.

He knelt beside Chuy and slipped a revolver from Chuy's shoulder holster. The keys to the Cadillac were in his pocket. "Ciao, tough guy, *guapo*," he said as he got to his feet. In a sense, the sorrow he felt for Chuy was purer—because it was less mixed, less adulterated—than the sorrow he felt for his grandfather. But he knew it was that thicket of emotions that would make the mourning for his grandfather as real and as deep as it eventually would be, when the time came. How goddamn late he'd come to understand that the old man loved him, as best he knew how to love. One more lost might-have-been, he thought, and felt an immense sorrow for the old man's life—and for his own. My father, my sister, my grandfather. He savored the sorrow a moment, hated it, then let it begin the build to rage.

As he left the room, he turned to look into it a last time. His grandfather's body seemed very small, something discarded, an old man with an ancient sword lost in a jungle of ugly, misused technology.

Argentina, he said silently to the remnants of Frank in the room. Yes, Argentina, my brother.

He shut the door behind him. The orchestra was smaller now, but the music wasn't over yet. There was one more chord to play. His own.

He found the terrified, geriatric housekeeper trembling in a broom closet in the kitchen. He left her with instructions to call the police (they were at least competent at burials) but not to go upstairs. The police would be no problem. With the pope to look after, they wouldn't even arrive until he was already in Mataderos.

He was taking two chances. First, that Caroline hadn't let slip to Frank that she'd once taken him to the address in Mataderos. And second, that Frank and the Gypsy had planned on going back there. Both seemed probable to him, though God only knew what was really certain. If Caroline had told Frank they'd been to the Gypsy's apartment, she'd have cut off any chance of Esteban's tracing her. And Esteban had to keep assuming she wanted to be traced. As for the second probability, if Frank *had* succeeded in killing the pope, he wouldn't have tried to get out of Buenos Aires right away. The city would have been sealed tighter than a gaucho's wineskin. So he'd need a place to wait out the initial uproar.

The mare's tail clouds he'd seen earlier had swept their rain clouds in by now. A light drizzle misted the windshield, and the far sun had turned into a fuzzy gray glow behind the clouds. Winter again. Buenos Aires again. Esteban flicked on the radio. The pope had finished his talk, and the cheerleaders had taken over again, in competition with amplified guitars this time. At least this part of his timing had gone right, Esteban thought. In a quarter of an hour the streets would be murderous, a million and a half people trying to get home in the rain.

The throbbing had returned in his arm, but the Cadillac's automatic transmission saved him. He weaved the car in and out of the sparse traffic one-handed, wondering if he could aim a revolver with his left hand well enough to hit a target even from a meter or two away. With a small shock, he realized he almost felt good. He hurt, ached from the steel table last night and from Frank's blow this morning, but as the big car slalomed along avenues normally choked with traffic, he sank into an odd sense of freedom. He felt alone in a place that had always been so filled with other people, he'd forgotten what clear, unobstructed movement was like. He was going at his own speed, certain of where he was going, sure that he would do whatever had to be done when he got there. There was so much he didn't have to give a damn about anymore, so much he could never worry about anymore.

By the time he began the long circuit of the slaughterhouses and stockyards toward the Gypsy's apartment, the rain was steady. Almost no trucks idled in the mud today, and the block after block of cold-storage lockers all were shut. The pope again—everyone who could be there was at the Spanish Monument, and the rest were at home in front of their television sets. Occasionally Esteban got a glimpse of a few lonely head of cattle waiting out the rain beneath one of the huge open sheds. They were like survivors, he thought, the last inhabitants of a city after some great disaster. He felt a kinship with them, and shuddered.

He pulled in to the curb a block beyond the shut, pink administration building. As he drove past, he scanned the opposite side of the street in front of the Gypsy's apartment block. A few nondescript cars sat at random along the curb, all empty. The only thing he couldn't see into was a Volkswagen van, a blue one. It was parked almost directly in front of the Gypsy's stairwell.

He left the Cadillac and walked the block to the administration building, keeping himself partially hidden by the neat shrubs that lined the sidewalk here. At the building he drew a mental map of the stairwell and landing in front of the Gypsy's apartment. The door should be the second one from the landing. Number sixty-six.

And now? Should he wait, hope to catch a glimpse of movement inside the apartment? Fine. What if the glimpse never came? He'd have to wait until dark, until a light came on. And after last night with General Kleist, and with a busted wrist, what kind of shape would he be in by nightfall? Where the hell was Pepe? He should have had plenty of time to get to his grandfather's before him, since it had taken him so long to break through the crowds around his mother's apartment. If Pepe had, and had found nobody there, why wasn't he here, as he said he'd be? Had Pepe gone sour on him, too? Et tu, Pepe?

No, then. No waiting. This time he had surprise on his side. This time he was the one composing the music. He wouldn't give that up.

He stepped out of the shrubbery and wiped the rain away from his eyes. Wiped it away just in time to see the door to the Gypsy's apartment open a crack, then close again. He stepped quickly back into the shrubbery.

After a few seconds, the door opened again, this time fully. The first one out of it was Caroline.

She walked to the end of the breezeway by the landing and stopped, as if she were waiting for someone. At length the Gypsy followed her, carrying a cardboard box overflowing with books and papers—his bloody precious charts among them, Esteban judged. They were moving out. He'd been right. No waiting, not now.

Caroline led the way down the stairs, swinging something that seemed to be keys in her hand. At the van, she unlocked the back doors while the Gypsy leaned the box against the side of the truck. The doors swung open. And as they did, almost as if Esteban had willed it, Caroline turned toward the administration building.

He stepped out of the shrubs again and started toward her. He slipped Chuy's revolver out of his pocket with his shaky left hand. Caroline stood watching him approach across the wet cobbles of the street, transfixed, until he was halfway to her. Then she shook her head fiercely and motioned him away. He hesitated.

She motioned again, then mouthed something he couldn't make out.

Damn it, woman, he thought. It was so clear, a straight line from one place to another, from here to there. And now it was confused again.

Go back he wouldn't. But he compromised, and sprinted ahead to hide behind a battered Renault a couple of cars behind the van, out of the Gypsy's line of vision. The Gypsy hefted the heavy box and, fighting for balance, stepped into the back of the van with it. And then Caroline threw all her weight against the doors.

She looked around wildly for Esteban, but he was running toward her already. She met him and he jammed the pistol into his pocket and grabbed her hand. But where to? Not back toward the Cadillac: they'd be in the open too long. The Gypsy would be out of the van before they made it, out of the van and able to get a shot off.

"The stockyards," he said to Caroline. "Run."

This time he kept a tight grip on her hand and prayed to all the gods of the Argentine women's shoe-heel industry as they ran. He'd lost her once. He wouldn't do it again. Not this time, not this last chance.

They slipped sideways through the partially open gate of one of the truck entrances through the high, white wall. Esteban threw a quick glance over his shoulder. The driver's door to the blue van slammed open. He shoved Caroline behind the wall as the Gypsy dropped from the van to the ground and fired. The shot went wild, but Esteban slammed the heavy gate and looked frantically for a lock on it. There wasn't one.

Ahead of them waited only the hungry dogs with tucked tails, no big Mercedes trucks idling now. "There!" Caroline shouted, and pointed toward a bank of cattle chutes that angled downward from the far wall of the parking area. There was no other way to go; tall wooden fences surrounded the parking area on all other sides.

Mud and dung sucked at their feet like thick syrup in places as they stumbled and slid across the parking area. The dogs circled them, yapping and nipping. Esteban kept them back with handfuls of mud. The smell of the slaughterhouses was overwhelming here, no longer the general smell of boiling hooves and bones and fat that hung over the whole of Mataderos, but a clear smell of animals and blood and the tons of droppings that fear released. A warm smell if it had been in a barn on an *estancia;* a smell of death in this place of assembly-line killing.

Caroline clambered onto the chute ahead of him, then helped him up by his good hand. He had to stop for a moment when he was at the top of the chute beside her to fight a wave of dizziness from the pain in his wrist. But the sight of the gate to the street swinging slowly open pushed him back to his feet, and he and Caroline clattered down the slick wooden chute, their loud footsteps echoing through the nearly empty yards.

Ahead of them lay a wilderness maze of chutes, pens, fences, feedlots—and at the end of the maze, Esteban knew, the slaughtering machines. He'd seen them as a child, the old-fashioned ones that his grandfather insisted on using, and had been fascinated by them and afraid of them. He remembered metal bars clanking closed to restrain the cattle, then sharp steel spikes slammed down with a pneumatic spitting sound into skulls—a machine out of a nightmare, efficient and utterly impersonal. If he and Caroline could get beyond those, they'd come out onto the far side of the yards, into freedom.

"You can't keep going, *guapo*," Caroline said.

"What's the alternative?" he asked.

She glanced around her. "To keep going."

Hay and mud and dung. By the time they'd gone fifty meters, there was nothing else in the world. They ducked under railings and over them, slipped past chutes and around fences. The rain was heavier now, and steady as the traffic they heard building on the avenues somewhere outside the walls. Beneath covered stalls they stopped to wipe it away from their faces, then plunged into it again. How long they wandered, Esteban had no idea. The dizziness was winning. Each time he climbed or ducked beneath something, the pain seemed sharper than ever. He knew they were lost but not what to do about it. In the rain, everything lost its shape ten meters away. Keep going, that was all there was left. Keep going, and hope they found a gate before the Gypsy found them.

And then he saw his landmark. Even through the rain, the boxcar-sized sign hanging from the mammoth open shed was visible, the letters faint but unmistakable: Molina. His grandfather's name, his name, Frank's name. He pointed it out to Caroline.

"I never thought I'd be glad to see *that* name again," he said.

Once they were there, Esteban knew, they'd be home. Follow the shed, that's all they'd have to do. And if the gate were unlocked at the far end...

By the time they got there, he wasn't able to keep moving alone. Caroline had supported him the last dozen meters. Her hair was streaking her face like a thick veil, and she constantly had to swipe at it to see as she tried to keep Esteban from stumbling into the railings and posts he was aware he was missing by inches at every step. But they made it, stood at last under the cavernous tin roof and knew that at the end of it was safety.

"Rest," Caroline said. "Be a big spender. It's OK now."

"No," he said. You weren't safe until you were safe. You weren't out of the dream until you were awake, no matter how much you tried to tell yourself you were dreaming. He broke away from her and launched himself at a railing. He grabbed it and held on, then started dragging himself along it toward the slaughtering machines.

"You're going to have a heart attack," Caroline said as she pried his hands away from the railing and pulled his good arm around her shoulder. "You deserve a heart attack."

"Then don't wait," he said.

"After my investment in you? Move," she said.

He was aware of blacking out, of missing whole sections of the shed. But each time he came back to himself they were a little farther along, a little closer to the end of this Red Queen's blood-spattered labyrinth. And then they were in the last long chute, the one with no turnoffs, that led to the slaughtering machines. He saw them, gray metal frames like cages ranged across the entire end of the shed for what seemed a full city block.

And as he snapped his head to clear his vision, he saw, too, the Gypsy.

He was scuttling among the bars of the slaughtering machines toward them, still foxlike as he bobbed and weaved through and over the bars, somehow moving surefooted and quick through the mud. Esteban knew he'd make it to the end of their chute before they did, would be waiting for them at the slaughtering machines. He struggled to keep his vision clear. Behind them was the mud of the stockyards; if they turned back, he knew he'd never make it out again. To the sides along the chute were fences he knew he didn't have the strength to climb—and even if he did, the Gypsy could leap them before he and Caroline could even get to the tops of them. No. Ahead, straight ahead. He'd told himself in the Cadillac that was the only way he was going now. No more fences, no more mazes.

He shouted, made a sound that wasn't a word, and let that drag up the last grains of strength he knew he would be able to find. He flung himself away from Caroline, and tugged the pistol from his wet, clinging pocket. Caroline clutched at him. "Get down," she yelled. "Oh, God, get down."

She was just at his ear, but she was a thousand miles away. He stumbled away from her, lurching forward toward the slaughtering machines. The walls of the chute grew, and when the mud turned to concrete for the last score of meters before the machines, the surface stretched out before him wide and endless as the pampa. And the walls were surrounding him, like the mountains had done just before he passed out on General Kleist's steel table. But he'd make it. Oh, goddamn, he'd make it this time.

The Gypsy was in front of him now, crouching at the entrance to the slaughtering machine. Esteban tried to raise the pistol. But dear God, it was heavy. He swung himself forward, hoping the momentum would help him bring the pistol up. But the pistol was tied, was anchored with a special gravity at the end of his arm. The Gypsy watched him struggle with eyes as impassive as the eyes of Anselmo Nieves had been on the Amazon. It was as if those eyes that told him he was a thing, a creature with no more right to live than a stone, had followed him here, had been waiting for him. Frank's eyes, Nieves's eyes, the Gypsy's eyes.

Esteban stopped, no more than three meters away from the Gypsy. The Gypsy stood up. Behind him, Esteban heard Caroline scream as the Gypsy raised his pistol and aimed it with his dark fox's eyes. Esteban slipped to his knees, his legs no longer able to hold him. Get up, you bastard, he shouted at himself, get goddamn up!

He fell forward. His good arm caught him, and held, as the pistol skittered away along the wet concrete. The muzzle of the Gypsy's revolver followed him down.

And then the Gypsy's revolver disappeared—the revolver and the hand and arm that held it. Esteban had no notion how it happened, just that there'd been nothing else in his sight but those things, and now they weren't there anymore. His arm collapsed, then he was dragging himself, using his legs like levers, moving toward the place the Gypsy had been and toward his own pistol that lay barely beyond his reach.

He reached his pistol, and now he was at the bars of the slaughtering machine. He looked up as a wave of clarity, a moment of clear vision, washed over him. Caroline was kneeling beside him, sobbing and trying to help him get back to his feet. And the Gypsy and Pepe were locked against each other inside the restraining bars of the slaughtering machine.

The Gypsy was no scared provincial cop in Bariloche. Pepe was trying to get a tight enough hold on him to squeeze him as he'd done the cop, but the Gypsy was too tough, too lithe for that. He was jabbing at Pepe's kidney with his sharp fist, again and again, breaking Pepe's holds with a knee that kept slamming at Pepe's groin. Pepe howled, and at last shoved the Gypsy away from him. The Gypsy careened backward against the bars of the machine that held the steer's head in place. Pepe toppled toward him like a tower. When he hit him, his weight was a heavy side of beef that pinned the Gypsy against the bars. The Gypsy seemed stunned—stunned long enough for Pepe to twist him so that his head drove between the bars that came together to hold the steer's head.

Caroline managed to get Esteban to his knees.

Esteban's hand closed around a metal railing and he pulled himself upright. Pepe threw a frantic look over his shoulder.

"The button, *patrón*," he yelled. "The button!" He grasped something black that dangled on a spring above the Gypsy and pulled down on it.

Esteban stared stupidly at him for a long moment. Button, he said to himself. Button, button, button, button. The Gypsy's legs shot up and wrapped themselves around Pepe's. With the right leverage, Esteban knew the Gypsy could have Pepe on the ground in seconds. Button, damn it to hell, *button*.

And then he saw it, a red button the size of a checker piece in a gray steel box an arm's length in front of him. *PELIGRO*, a sign in red above it said. Danger. He let go of the railing he was holding on to and rocked forward. His balance slipped away from him and he slapped at the button as he tumbled toward Pepe.

His hand hit the box. The familiar pneumatic spitting noise shot through the shed. And as Esteban hit the concrete at Pepe's feet, he saw the Gypsy's legs twitch violently, then go limp.

Pepe's lovely, wine-sour breath enclosed the three of them—himself, Caroline, and Pepe. Esteban and Caroline sat side by side on the concrete, legs sprawled and Pepe hovered over them like a smelly angel. Caroline's sobs had turned to hiccups, and the world around Esteban was settling into a recognizable arrangement of things again. Even the roar of the traffic beyond the white wall was welcome in its familiarity.

"I lost myself, señor," Pepe was explaining. "No, the mother whore of a taxi driver lost us. I never lose myself. Then when I found your grandfather's elephant of a car, I knew you'd gotten here first. And when I saw that one"—he jerked his thumb toward the body of the Gypsy—"going through the gate into this place, I considered to myself that where he was going, yourself would be going. So I followed him. I always find you! No? Patagonia, Buenos Aires..."

"Paco," Esteban said. "Did you see Paco?"

"Where, *patrón?*"

"When you first saw the Gypsy. In here. Anywhere."

"No, disgracefully. Not since Bariloche."

Esteban held out his hand for Pepe to help him up. "Then we've got to get back to the apartment."

"How?" Caroline said. "Fly? You surely to God can't walk it."

The scraping sound on the concrete came in the seconds of silence during which he resisted the knowledge that she was right, insisted that she couldn't be right. Pepe jerked himself erect, started to move toward the sound, then stopped.

"You won't need to walk," Frank said as he picked up the pistol Esteban had dropped on the concrete. In his other hand he held the automatic that hadn't left him since Esteban had first seen him in the lodge at Bariloche. "I did it for you."

"For once, my brother," Esteban said. "For once you're too late. I got here ahead of you." He tried for a bravado he didn't feel.

Frank looked at the body of the Gypsy. "That, you mean? That would have had to happen anyway sooner or later." His eyes moved from the Gypsy to each of them in turn, then came to rest on Caroline. "Well, *amor*. You look like hell."

"I'm sorry, Paco," she said. "I truly am."

"Because you look like hell? No need to be sorry."

"You know better than that."

They held each other's eyes, then Frank looked away. "Yes, I know better than that." Frank's eyes kept moving, as if he were searching for something, trying to decide for certain where he was. They stopped on the huge sign that hung above them. "Family's together again, Brother," he said.

"Reunion," Esteban said. He was trying to make sense of Frank, of his being here. Surely when he discovered that the Gypsy and Caroline were gone, then saw the Cadillac, he understood what had happened—or enough of what had happened to know that he should have gone away. He didn't need the Gypsy. Caroline's absence told him she'd left with Esteban. So then what remained? Revenge? The image of their grandfather's body, of Mondragon's body sliced through Esteban's mind. Revenge. Yes. Frank was damn well capable of revenge.

But somehow, for a reason he couldn't put into words,

253

he didn't think Frank had come after them for that. There was something limp about him, about the way he stood, the way he held the automatic, the way he spoke. There was neither fire nor darkness in his eyes now. Just the distance, cool and hazy as the distances of the Andes the day the two of them had gone with their father to buy the silver *maté* gourds from the Indians, such a bloody long time ago. He studied Frank's face for a clue to what he wanted. In it, he saw some of Adela, some of his father, some of his mother, and some of himself. And behind it, perhaps, some of his grandfather. He saw Molina, maybe the most obscure clue he could have found.

"I visited Grandfather," Frank said.

"I know," Estaban said.

"It's all right about Father now. That's fixed." He said it as if he and Esteban had been in on something from the beginning, had been planning to make their father's death right all along.

"Yes, it's fixed."

"And Adela, of course. You know that's taken care of."

"I remember."

"How's Mother?"

"She'll be all right."

"Good. I'm pleased." The *me alegra*, I'm pleased, came out with the same meaningless flatness that *porteños* always gave it when they asked you how you were or how you'd slept. A formality.

"Bueno," Frank said, looking past them all. "That's all."

"That's all what?" Esteban said.

"I've done what I could. There's nothing else."

"Is that why you followed us?" Esteban asked. "To say that?"

"Oh, perhaps. To ask about Mother. Curiosity. Those things. I thought maybe that Caroline..." He looked at her, then away again, as if he were afraid that she'd see something he didn't want her to. "No, I didn't really think that. You were afraid not to come with me at Mother's, weren't you, *amor?*"

"Afraid of what would happen to all of us, Paco,"

Caroline said. She was crying softly. "You, me, Esteban."

"It would have been a hell of a life for you, anyway. I *am* sorry you had to see the part with Grandfather. There would have probably been more of that kind of thing eventually. You aren't cut out for it, I think."

"No," Caroline said.

"A matter of vision," he said. And then to Esteban, "Of how far into the distance you can see, Brother. *N'est-ce pas?*"

"No, Paco. Of what it is you see there, too."

Frank made a little motion of dismissal with his eyebrows. "Oh, well. That." He took a step toward them, then stopped. "Pope's leaving. War's over.... The radio says the British are in the suburbs of Port Stanley. That means we're no doubt negotiating a surrender, you know."

"Probably," Esteban said.

He took another step. The revolver was still aimed at them, but loosely, as if Frank had forgotten he had it. Then he stopped again, and his eyes traveled around him once more, moving up and down the rows of slaughtering machines that waited like mute soldiers. "So much mechanical death!" he said. "'In the destructive element immerse yourself,' Conrad said, didn't he? I don't think he had this in mind. But perhaps he should have." He swept his hand toward the machines, the white walls, in a gesture that would have been melodramatic had anyone but himself done it, or had the despair in his voice been less genuine. The gesture took in all of Buenos Aires.

Then without warning he put his free hand on the railing of the chute and vaulted into the next one.

Pepe started after him. "Señor Francisco, *por favor—*"

"Stay there," Frank ordered sharply, and tightened his grip on the pistol. Pepe pulled up.

Frank squeezed past the slaughtering machine. He walked toward the gate unhurriedly, a man with plenty of time. Every few steps he looked over his shoulder to make sure no one was following him. At the gate he shoved the latch up and swung the house-sized gate open. The thunder of the traffic rushed in as loud as a waterfall.

Esteban fought to his feet. "Paco," he shouted. "Paco, for the love of God!"

If he heard anything over the sound of the traffic, Frank gave no indication. He stepped to the curb and watched for a moment the eight lanes of cars racing in a savage rapids from one far stoplight to the other.

Esteban squeezed past the slaughtering machine as Frank had done, and tried to run. The world began to swirl around him again, but he kept his eyes fixed firmly on his brother. "Paco!" he shouted a last time. "Paco!"

Frank raised the pistol, aimed into the center of the traffic, and fired. The bullet vanished into the roar like a breath: nothing slowed, nothing stopped. He stepped off the curb. He kept firing until the first car hit him and spun him over the hood and out into the next lane of cars, like a man being sucked underwater by a tide.

Coda

There was a smell of rain in the warm breeze that slipped down from the Pyrenees. But the Catalonian August afternoon was still sunny, and the swaying shadows from the eucalyptus trees moved across the table in front of Esteban as gently as lullabies. He let his eyes wander from the letter and the plans for the new restaurant to Caroline, who dozed in a hammock across the yard from him. Strands of her hair rose and fell in the breeze. Beyond her in the little canyon that ran past the house, a peasant led a slow train of donkeys toward town for a saint's-day parade. There would be carnival rides and fireworks tonight, and tables heaped with food in the square, and good wine to taste from the vineyards at Villafranca de Panedés, across the valley. Esteban looked forward to it, something he'd almost forgotten he could do when he'd left Buenos Aires two months ago.

Pepe had found them the house, a great rambling country place where nothing worked, but which was being rented out by a cousin of his who had come into it in some obscure way during the revolution—from a *fachista* who didn't deserve it, he said. The town was Cervera, Pepe's town, and Pepe was the one who'd rounded up the work crew to turn the old wine cellar into a restaurant. There wouldn't be much business, probably a few tourists who wandered in off the Barcelona-Madrid highway to look at King Philip's ancient, abandoned university. But Esteban didn't mind. Cervera was a place where time went at a pace most of the rest of the world had forgotten. It was a place to heal, to start over from, to sort things out.

He got up from the table and went to kneel beside Caroline. She opened an eye and let her hand trail down his shoulder. "Time to get up?" she said.

"Not if you don't want to."

"I don't. What's up?"

"Pepe brought a letter from Mother," he said. "While you were sleeping."

"Bad news?"

"No. She's coming back to England for a visit. She says she wants to try leaving her dead behind her. See how it goes."

"That's a change. Will she come here?"

"For a little while. Not to stay."

Caroline thought a moment. "How do you feel about that?"

"That she's not going to stay? Good."

"No. About seeing her again. Is it too soon?"

He rocked the hammock, and Caroline closed her eyes again. "I've been thinking," he said. "I think I want a family."

"Haven't you had enough of those for a while?"

"There are two kinds of family, *mujer*. Those you inherit, and those you make. The first kind you always have to leave sooner or later."

"Not the way you did."

"No, not that way. But the second kind's what you start over with."

She opened her eye again. "You're a wise man, *guapo*. Or getting that way."

"Working at it."

"You'll have to marry me, you know. Remember, I'm almost thirty. My motives are impure." She smiled and touched his cheek.

"Thank God for impurity. Purity's for Argentina."

"Do you hate it?"

"Argentina? No. I love it, though God knows why."

"Amen," she said. "I'll want to go back one day, when things get better. That's fair warning."

258

"When things get better. Yes."
"Do you really think they ever will?"
"Someday."
"Faith again?"
"Call it that," he said. "It's what there is."
She opened her other eye and squinted against the bright sun. "Yep. It's what there is." She rolled over in the hammock and held out her arms. "Climb in."
"Sure there's room?" he said.
"Always, *guapo*. Always."

THE MOUNTAIN,
THE MANHUNT,
THE MYSTERY...

ARARAT

A NOVEL OF
GLOBAL ADVENTURE BY

ROBERT HOUSTON

This swift-paced suspense novel of international intrigue features an American reporter who joins an excursion to Mt. Ararat and instead finds himself detoured on a dangerous mission to the Soviet Union. There a global adventure of espionage, romance, danger and deception begins, stretching from Kurdistan to the Nicaraguan jungle.

Avon Paperback　　　　　　　　**80937-0/$3.50**

Available wherever paperbacks are sold or directly from the publisher. Include $1.00 per copy for postage and handling; allow 6-8 weeks for delivery. Avon Books, Dept BP, Box 767, Rte 2, Dresden, TN 38225.

Ararat 11-82

"Impressive...Complicated espionage."
The New Yorker

WAR TOYS
HAMPTON HOWARD

Set in Paris, WAR TOYS is the story of an ex-CIA agent who discovers that he has been set up as a disposable pawn by his own government—and decides to strike back with the very venom and calculated cunning that the CIA had taught him. This chillingly authentic espionage thriller takes the reader through a dazzling series of betrayals and counter betrayals, bitter vendettas and hairpin escapes.

"Gets off to a fast start...plenty of action."
The New York Times Book Review

"Awesome, total and satisfying...Howard grabs and holds our attention from the start."
Publishers Weekly

An Avon Paperback　　　　　　　**65557-8/$3.50**

Buy these books at your local bookstore or use this coupon for ordering:

Avon Books, Dept BP, Box 767, Rte 2, Dresden, TN 38225
Please send me the book(s) I have checked above. I am enclosing $_____
(please add $1.00 to cover postage and handling for each book ordered to a maximum of three dollars). *Send check or money order*—no cash or C.O.D.'s please. Prices and numbers are subject to change without notice. Please allow six to eight weeks for delivery.

Name _____

Address _____

City _____ State/Zip _____

Toys 1-84

"The finest thriller writer alive." *The Village Voice*

Elmore Leonard

STICK   67652-4/$3.50
Just out of the slammer, Stick is caught between drug dealers, high-flying financiers and lovely ladies. Will his scam make him a rich man or a memory?
"Jumps right off the page." *The New Yorker*

UNKNOWN MAN NO. 89   67041-0/$2.95
When a process server with the reputation for being able to find anyone is engaged to track down a missing criminal, he finds himself caught in a treacherous labyrinth of deception, betrayal and murder.
"Will keep you on the edge of your chair." *The New York Times*

52 PICK-UP   65490-3/$2.95
This chilling tale unfolds a ruthless game of sex and blackmail— in which the only way an angry man can win is murder.
"A tightly wound thriller with a smash-up climax."
The Village Voice

CAT CHASER   64642-0/$2.95
An ex-Marine intends to live life peacefully in Florida, but a sentimental journey leads him to Santo Domingo: a hotbed of intrigue, double-dealing and violence.
"CAT CHASER really moves." *New York Times Book Review*

SPLIT IMAGES   63107-5/$2.95
A Detroit homicide detective and his beautiful journalist lover track a rich playboy killer and his accomplice.
"Brilliant...Leonard is an impressive writer." *Washington Post*

CITY PRIMEVAL: HIGH NOON IN DETROIT   56952-3/$2.50
In pursuit of a murderer, Detroit cop Raymond Cruz finds himself face-to-face with a wily, psychotic killer.
"One can hardly turn the pages fast enough." *Miami Herald*

"Leonard can really write...He is astonishingly good."
John D. MacDonald

Buy these books at your local bookstore or use this coupon for ordering:

Avon Books, Dept BP, Box 767, Rte 2, Dresden, TN 38225
Please send me the book(s) I have checked above. I am enclosing $_____ (please add $1.00 to cover postage and handling for each book ordered to a maximum of three dollars). *Send check or money order*—no cash or C.O.D.'s please. Prices and numbers are subject to change without notice. Please allow six to eight weeks for delivery.

Name _____

Address _____

City _____ State/Zip _____

Leon 1-84